THE ESSENTIAL TALES OF CHEKHOV

Richard Ford is the author of five novels: *The Sportswriter*, *Independence Day* (winner of the Pulitzer Prize and the PEN/Faulkner Award in 1996). *A Piece of My Heart*, *The Ultimate Good Luck* and *Wildlife*; and two books of stories: *Rock Springs* and *Women with Men*. He is also the editor of *The Granta Book of the American Short Story* and *The Granta Book of the American Long Story*, both available from Granta Books.

THE
ESSENTIAL TALES
OF CHEKHOV

Edited and with an Introduction by

RICHARD FORD

Translated by Constance Garnett

Granta Books
London

Granta Publications, 2/3 Hanover Yard, London N1 8BE

First published in Great Britain by Granta Books 1999

3 5 7 9 10 8 6 4

Typeset in Fournier by M Rules
Printed and bound in Great Britain by Mackays of Chatham plc

Contents

Introduction

WHY WE LIKE CHEKHOV

Until I began the long and happy passage of reading all of Anton Chekhov's short stories for the purpose of selecting the twenty that follow, I had read very little of Chekhov. It seems a terrible thing for a story writer to admit, and doubly worse for one whose own stories have been so thoroughly influenced by Chekhov through my relations with other writers who had been influenced by him directly: Sherwood Anderson. Isaac Babel. Hemingway. Cheever. Welty. Carver.

As is true of many American readers who encountered Chekhov first in college, my experience with his stories was both abrupt and brief, and came too early. When I read him at age twenty, I had no idea of his prestige and importance or why I should be reading him— one of those gaps of ignorance for which a liberal education tries to be a bridge. But typical of my attentiveness then, I remember no one telling me anything more than that Chekhov was great, and that he was Russian.

And for all of their surface plainness, their apparent accessibility and clarity, Chekhov's stories—especially the greatest ones—still do not seem so easily penetrable by the unexceptional young. Rather, Chekhov seems to me a writer for adults, his work becoming useful and also beautiful by attracting attention to mature feelings, to complicated human responses and small issues of moral choice within large, overarching dilemmas, any part of which, were we to encounter them in our complex, headlong life with others, might evade even sophisticated notice. Chekhov's wish is to complicate and compromise our view of characters we might mistakenly suppose we could understand with only a glance. He almost always approaches us with a great deal of focussed seriousness which he means to make irreducible and accessible, and by this concentration to insist that we take life to heart. Such instruction, of course, is not always easy to comply with when one is young.

My own college experience was to read the great anthology standard, "The Lady with the Dog" (published in 1899 and included here), and basically to be baffled by it, although the story's fundamental directness and authority made me highly respectful of something I can only describe as a profound-feeling gray light emanating from the story's austere interior.

"The Lady with the Dog" concerns the chance amorous meeting of two people married to two other people. One lover is a bored, middle-aged businessman from Moscow, and the other an idle young bride in her twenties—both on marital furlough in the Black Sea Spa of Yalta. The two engage in a brief, fervid tryst that seems—at least to the story's principal character Dmitri Gurov, the Muscovite businessman—not very different from other trysts in his life. And after their short, breathless time together, their holiday predictably ends. The young wife, Anna Sergeyevna, departs for her home and husband in Petersburg, while Gurov, with no specific plans for Anna, travels back to his coolly intellectual wife and the tiresome business connections of Moscow.

But the effect of his affair and of Anna (the very lady with the dog—a Pomeranian) soon begin to infect and devil Gurov's daily life and torment him with desire, so that eventually he thinks up a lie, leaves home and travels to S—— where he reunites (more or less) with the pining Anna, whom he encounters between the acts of a play expressively titled *The Geisha*. In the weeks following this passionate lovers' meeting, Anna begins a routine of visiting Gurov in Moscow where, the omniscient narrator observes, they "loved each other like people very close and akin, like husband and wife, like tender friends; it seemed to them that fate itself had meant them for one another, and they could not understand why he had a wife and she a husband; and it was as though they were pair of birds of passage, caught and forced to live in different cages."

Their union, while hot-burning, soon seems to them destined to stay furtive and intermittent. And in their secret lovers' room in the Slaviansky Bazaar, Anna cries bitterly over the predicament, while Gurov troubles himself in a slightly imperious manner to console her. The story ends with the narrator concluding with something of a knowing poker face, that ". . . it seemed as though in a little while the solution would be found, and then a new and splendid life would begin; and it was clear to both of them that they had still a long, long road before them, and that the most complicated and difficult part of it was only just beginning."

What I didn't understand back in 1964, when I was twenty, was: what made this drab set of non-events a great short story—reputedly one of the greatest ever written. It was, I knew, a story about passion, and that passion was a capital subject; and that although Chekhov didn't describe any of it, sex took place, adulterous sex no less. I could also see that the effect of passion was calculated to be loss, loneliness and indeterminacy, and that the institution of marriage came in for a beating. Clearly these were important matters.

But it seemed to me at the story's end, when Gurov and Anna meet in the hotel, away from spousal eyes, that far too little happened, or at least too little that *I* could detect. They make love (albeit offstage); Anna weeps; Gurov fussily says "Don't cry, my darling . . . that's enough. . . . Let us talk now, let us think of some plan." And then the story is over, with Gurov and Anna wandering off to who knows where—probably, I thought, no place very exciting were we to accompany them. Which we don't.

Back in 1964, I didn't dare to say, "I don't like this," because in truth I didn't *not* like "The Lady with the Dog." I merely didn't sense what in it was *so* to be liked. In class, much was made of its opening paragraph, containing the famously brief, complex, yet direct setting out of significant information, issues and strategies of telling which the story would eventually develop. For this reason— economy—it was deemed good. The ending was also said to be admirable *because* it wasn't very dramatic and wasn't conclusive. But beyond that, if anybody said something more specific about how the story made itself excellent I don't remember it. Although I distinctly remember thinking the story was over my head, and that Gurov and Anna were adults (read: enigmatic, impenetrable) in a way I wasn't one, and what they did and said to each other must reveal heretofore unheard of truths about love and passion, only I wasn't a good enough reader or mature enough human to recognize these truths. I'm certain that I eventually advertised actually *liking* the story, though only because I thought I should. And not long afterward I began maintaining the position that Chekhov was a story writer of near mystical—and certainly mysterious—importance, one who seemed to tell rather ordinary stories but who was really unearthing the most subtle, and for that reason, unobvious and important truth.

(It is of course still a useful habit of inquiry to wonder, when the surface of reputedly great literature—and life—seem plain and equable, if something important might not be revealed upon closer notice; and also to realize that a story's ending may not always be the place to locate that something.)

In 1998, what I would say is good about "The Lady with the Dog" (and maybe you should stop here, read the story, then come back and compare notes) and indeed why I like it is primarily that it concentrates its narrative attentions *not* on the conventional hot spots—sex, deceit and what happens at the end—but rather, by its precision, pacing and decisions about what to tell, it directs our interest toward those flatter terrains of a love affair where we, being conventional souls, might overlook something important. "The Lady with the Dog" demonstrates by its scrupulous notice and detail that ordinary goings-on contain moments of significant moral choice—willed human acts judgeable as good or bad—and as such they have consequences in life which we need to pay heed to, whereas before reading the story we might've supposed they didn't. I'm referring specifically to Gurov's rather prosaic feelings of "torment" at home in Moscow, followed by his decision to visit Anna; his wife's reasonable dismissal of his suffering, the repetitiveness of trysts, the relative brevity of desire's satiation, and the necessity for self-deception to keep a small passion inflamed. These are matters the story wants us *not* to skip over, but to believe are important and that paying attention to them is good.

In a purely writerly way, I also find interest and take pleasure in Chekhov's choosing *these* characters and this seemingly unspectacular liaison upon which to stake a claim of significance and to treat with intelligence, amusement and some compassion. And superintending all there is Chekhov's surgical deployment of his probing narrator as inventor and mediator of Gurov's bland but still provocative interior life with women: "It seemed to him," the narrator says of the stolid Dmitri, "that he had been so schooled by bitter experience that he might call them [women, of course] what he liked, and yet he could not get on for two days together without 'the lower race.' In the society of men he was bored and not himself, with them he was cool and uncommunicative; but when he was in the company of women he felt free. . . ."

Finally, in "The Lady with the Dog," what seems good is

Chekhov the fastidious and amused ironist who finds the right exalted language to accompany staid Gurov and pliant Anna's most unexalted amours, and in so doing discloses their love's frothy mundaneness. High on a hill overlooking Yalta and the sea, the two lovers sit and moon off, while the narrator archly muses over the landscape.

> The leaves did not stir on the trees, grasshoppers chirruped, and the monotonous hollow sound of the sea rising up from below, spoke of peace, of the eternal sleep awaiting us. So it must have sounded when there was no Yalta, no Oreanda here; so it sounds now, and it will sound as indifferently and monotonously when we are all no more. And in this constancy, in this complete indifference to the life and death of each of us, there lies hid, perhaps, a pledge of our eternal salvation, of the unceasing movement of life upon earth, of unceasing progress towards perfection.

*   *   *

Over the years, "The Lady with the Dog" has come to stand high in my esteem as the story by whose subtleties I not only began to know how and why to like Chekhov, but also by its exemplary fullness I came to experience literature as F. R. Leavis portrays it in his famous essay on Lawrence, as the supreme means by which we "undergo a renewal of sensuous and emotional life, and learn a new awareness." Chekhov's representation of this minor-key love affair committed by respectable nonentities more than renewed, it helped give early form to my awareness of what the words "emotional life" might entail, but also conceal and importantly leave out.

Yet this one small masterpiece aside, what sort of awareness do we typically achieve when we read Chekhov's stories? (As though story writing were not a matter of beauty, felicity, restraint and implicitness but was an art harnessed only to Walter Benjamin's utilitarian injunction that "every real story . . . contains, openly and covertly something useful. . . ." and that "the storyteller is a man who has counsel for his readers.")

There is, of course, no *typical* Chekhov story, a fact that by itself should please us, and makes the pseudo-critical shorthand of "Chekhovian" essentially pointless. For if there are plenty of stories in which the surface of everyday life seems unremarkable and dramatically unyielding except that Chekhov makes it the object of intense narrative inquiry the result of which is, say, the exposure of unexpected emotional cowardice or painful moral indecision (the famous "Gooseberries" is such a story), there are also stories of unquestionably high, even fulminant surface drama that rattle the windows, alarm or enrage us, move us to tears, and then roar off to their appointed endings like freight trains. In "Enemies," a distraught young husband bursts into a physician's home late at night pleading that the doctor honor his oath by coming at once to the young man's expiring wife. (The doctor's own child has only moments before, and startlingly, breathed his last!) At pains, the doctor sets aside his private grief and complies. Yet when he arrives at the man's house, the wife, again startlingly, proves absent having gone off with another man. The story's title offers a sufficient hint of the furious night's outcome.

Likewise, if the standard Chekhov ending is thought to leave readers clutching at air for answers to the story's profound but ambiguous scruplings—answers the author may have been unwilling or found too intellectually reductive to provide—there is conversely the unqualifiedly *direct* Chekhov who routinely tells us exactly what he wishes us to know. In "The Kiss," another anthology regular, a young Cossack officer has his life turned topsy-turvy by the misplaced kiss of a mysterious woman he quickly become obsessed by. Later, alone, at the story's end, the young officer realizes bitterly that his own sensuous and emotional hopes will not be renewed because the mysterious woman will never be found nor the kiss repeated. "And the whole world, the whole of life," the narrator tells us, "seemed to Ryabovitch an unintelligible, aimless jest. . . . And turning his eyes from the water and looking at the sky, he remembered again how fate in the person of an unknown woman had by chance caressed him, he remembered his summer dreams and fancies, and his life struck him as extraordinarily meagre, poverty-stricken, and colourless. . . ."

And finally, if all of Chekhov's stories are thought to radiate importance and severity like the gray light that momentarily shines on poor, unkissed Ryabovitch, there is yet the burlesquing Chekhov of "A Blunder." There, the eager parents of an overly marriageable daughter eavesdrop through the wall as she is wooed by the district school teacher and minor poet, Shchupkin. The parents' plan is, at some compromising moment, to burst into the room like police, holding an ikon (the father, old Poplov, believes, "A blessing with an ikon is sacred and binding"). But just as the daughter's hand is finally, hungrily kissed by the unsuspecting Shchupkin, and the parents spring across the threshold burbling their would-be contractual blessings, Poplov discovers his wife (the too-eager Kleopatra) has brought with her not an ikon but an absurd portrait of an *author*—Lazhetchnikov—thereby scuttling the longed-for marriage. As the story's *envoi*, the narrator modestly informs us that in the catastrophe's excitement, "the writing master took advantage of the general confusion and slipped away."

Indeed, one regularly finds humor in Chekhov, often in surprising though never really mistakable moments. As in Shakespeare as in Faulkner as in Flannery O'Connor, the comic turn not only counterweighs and intensifies a serious story's gravity, it also humanizes our own fated intimacy with what's grave by permitting life's fullest, most actual context to be brought into view, even as it points us toward an approved method of acceptance: laughter. (Acceptance and life's dogged continuance being ever Chekhov's concerns.)

In the masterful long story "An Anonymous Story," a saga of revenge, moral deception, outrage, absurdity and flight, Chekhov almost at the story's opening movement sets out one of his signature—and in this case astoundingly acid—character summaries (partly of course calculated to delight us). And with it, he observes the nearly unplummable complexity and baseness of the human species, even as he strengthens our resilience to depravities in life we cannot control. So, it is Kukushkin, the classic Petersburger, civil councillor, cowardly cohort of the unscrupulous and reluctant husband Orlov, who becomes the special target of the author's venom:

He [Kukushkin] was a man with the manners of a lizard. He did not walk, but, as it were, crept along with tiny steps, squirming and sniggering, and when he laughed he showed his teeth. He was a clerk on special commissions . . . [and a] man of personal ambition, not only to the marrow of his bones, but more fundamentally—to the last drop of his blood; but even in his ambitions he was petty and did not rely on himself, but was building his career on the chance favour flung him by his superiors. For the sake of obtaining some foreign decoration, or for the sake of having his name mentioned in the newspapers as having been present at some special service in the company of other great personages, he was ready to submit to any kind of humiliation, to beg, to flatter, to promise.

In dismantling the wretched Kukushkin's impoverished character, it is as if Chekhov were subscribing to the ancient and comic maxim governing life's basic duality: if nothing's funny, nothing's really ever serious.

Far from his stories' ever sinking to typicality or being knowable by a scheme, Chekhov seems so committed to life's multifariousness that the stories provoke in us the sensation Ford Madox Ford must have had in mind when he observed that the general effect of fiction "must be the effect life has on mankind"—by which I've always thought he meant that it be persuasively important, profuse, irreducible in its ambiguities, full of diverse pleasures, and always on the brink of being unknowable except that our ordering intelligence ardently urges us toward clarity. In Chekhov, there are no potted or predictable attitudes about *anything*: women, children, dogs, cats, the clergy, teachers, peasants, the military, businessmen, government officials, marriage, all Russia itself. And if anything can be termed "typical" it is that he insists we keep our notice close to life's nuance, its intimate gestures and small moral annotations. "To be unloved and unhappy—how interesting that was," sixteen-year-old Nadya Zelenin in "After the Theatre" thinks after seeing a performance of *Eugene Onyegen*. "There is something beautiful, touching, and poetical about it when one loves and the other is indifferent."

The entirety of Chekhov's stories, in fact, often seem—but for their formal, sturdy existence in language—not even *artful* (although that would be wrong) but rather to be assiduous in mapping out degree by precise degree an accurate, ground-level constellation of ordinary existence—each story representing a subtly-distinguished movement in a single sustained gesture of life confirmed.

* * *

It is worth noticing now what precisely strikes us about Chekhov's subtlety—since surely the apprehension of great subtlety is what most of us emerge with after reading "Gooseberries" or "The Kiss," stories in which the surfaces of life seem routine and continuous while Chekhov goes about illuminating its benighted *other* terrains as a way of inventing what's new, sustaining or calamitous in human existence.

One exemplary subtlety is that what we readers finally learn about humankind—one of our new awarenesses—is often quite similar to what we might acknowledge about a person we know intimately. Indeed, our typical response to some signal moment of moral discovery in a Chekhov story—that whatever this character did is good, whatever that one thought is wrong—is almost always, consolingly enough, *recognition* rather than shock, as though we really knew in our hearts that people were like that, but until now hadn't needed to disclose it. Such is the case in "Peasants." There, a tubercular waiter Nikolay Tchikildyeev journeys home to his poor village perhaps to die, but also unfortunately to re-experience the grinding, battering, drunken poverty and debasement of his familial past. Tchikildyeev does indeed die, near the story's end, barely noticed by his preoccupied, disorderly kin. But before this can happen the narrator pronounces a sobering verdict we readers know to be true almost before we read it, although we might never have pronounced it for fear of what it might mean about us. (Chekhov, of course, means us to admit it, and makes that admission one of the story's shrewd ethical snares):

> Sasha and Motka and all the little girls in the hut huddled on the stove in the corner behind Nikolay's back, and from that refuge listened in silent terror, and the beating of their little hearts could be distinctly heard. Whenever there is someone in a family who has long been ill, and hopelessly ill, there come painful moments when all timidly, secretly, at the bottom of their hearts long for his death. . . .

Can we say, when we read this, that it's a complete surprise that life and long relation should culminate with such woeful news? But also can we say we have ever specifically *thought* that?

Or what of this disquisition on beauty from "The Beauties":

> I felt this beauty [the narrator declares of a young woman] rather strangely. It was not desire, nor ecstacy, nor enjoyment that Masha excited in me, but a painful though pleasant sadness. It was a sadness vague and undefined as a dream. For some reason I felt sorry for myself . . . even for the girl herself, and I had a feeling as though we all . . . had lost something important and essential to life which we should never find again.

Exquisite beauty's perturbing consequence in everyday life: Loss. Pain. Regret. A rather unpromising view. But who hasn't glimpsed it among beauty's brighter allures, only to force it brusquely out of sight?

Not that these stories overflow with pithy observation. Chekhov is *not* famously aphoristic, and seems mostly to prefer stressing the way life struggles unheroically toward normalcy rather than serving up moments in which it is exceptional or by canny observation caused to seem so. And as absolutely full of life's experience as the stories are, Chekhov also seems to proportion and blend the *amount* of complexity they contain, as though there were limits to the literary significance we can accommodate. His stories rarely resolve in highly dramatic, epiphanic endings. And by largely eschewing this strategy they seem to refer us back to their own often unsensational, interior details. There, we are to reconsider moments of overlooked decisiveness and issue and possibly see mankind more clearly. Consequently, we are not only moved that poor Nikolay the waiter goes home to die and *does* die rather undramatically (not at the end), but we are also affected as we re-view the story that Chekhov, master of fine human distinctions, has elected exactly these people, these unlikely peasants to elevate to the condition of human exemplars.

One can say with some assurance that in settling upon the short story as his chosen narrative form, Chekhov elected in essence not to represent *all* of life, not to make a big splash, but to fashion discrete parts of life and focus our attentions and sharpest sensibilities there as a form of indispensable moral instruction; to *not* attempt what Walter Benjamin says the novel *always* attempts: "to carry the incommensurable to extremes in the representation of human life." Chekhov made his stories precisely *commensurate* with life and with a view of it we can accept in an almost homely way. He almost never suggests that life isn't worth living, or makes us feel at a loss or even feel over-indebted to his genius. But rather he measures his genius alongside our own and according to what we can understand as an act of empathy whose message is that life is much as we know it to be in our efforts to accept and go on.

* * *

All this may just be a way of saying that the reason we like Chekhov so much, now at our century's end, is because his stories from the last century's end feel so modern to us, are so much of our own time and mind. His meticulous anatomies of complicated human impulse and response, his view of what's funny and poignant, his clear-eyed observance of life as lived—all somehow matches our experience. His stories could, we feel, be written today, appear in *The New Yorker*, and be read for their insight with avidity and delight—no alterations or footnotes to account for periodicity or foreign provenance. To us, such fresh aptness confirms not only the continuity and saving vitality of the literary impulse, but it also assures us that we ourselves are part of a continuum and are sustainable. How we feel today about a dying wife, our married lover, our unsuitable suitor, our loyalties to our forsaken family, about the overmastering way in which life is too dense with subjectivity and too poor in objectifiable truth—all this was exactly how Russians felt far away in time, and when just as now a story was judged to be a saving response. Chekhov makes us feel corroborated, indemnified inside our human frailty, even smally hopeful of our ability to cope, to order and find clarity.

With Chekhov, we share the frankness of life's inalienable thereness; we share the conviction of how much we would profit if more of human sensation could be elevated into clear, expressive language; we share a view that life (particularly life with others) is a surface beneath which we must strive to construct a convincing subtext in order that more can be clung to less desperately; and we share a hopeful intuition that more of ourselves—especially those parts we feel only *we* know about—can be made susceptible to clear, useful exposition.

This last, indeed, is the case with the sad, wounded, forsaken Pyotr Mihalitch Ivashin of "Neighbours," portrayed by Chekhov in full retreat from his botched effort to "rescue" his sister Zina from the arms of her pompous, married seducer Vlassitch. Here, near the story's end, is one of the great, full Chekhov moments, when as readers we recognize that although we may not have been exactly here before, we still recognize a situation and a set of emotions which *should* surrender a lesson—reveal some keener sense of how we actually *are* as humans, a sense for which conventional language and inquiry offer little help. Thus the need for literary notice.

Vlassitch walked by his right stirrup, and Zina by the left; both seemed to have forgotten that they had to go home. It was damp, and they had almost reached Koltovitch's copse. Pyotr Mihalitch felt that they were expecting something from him, though they hardly knew what it was, and he felt unbearably sorry for them. Now as they walked by the house with submissive faces, lost in thought, he had a deep conviction that they were unhappy, and could not be happy, and their love seemed to him a melancholy, irreparable mistake. Pity and the sense that he could do nothing to help them reduced him to that state of spiritual softening when he was ready to make any sacrifice to get rid of the painful feeling of sympathy.

Though shortly on and even more trenchantly, as Mihalitch enters the first bitter awareness that he has miscalculated love and passion and that such errors are to be the signature of his life, Chekhov's narrator notes:

He was heavy at heart. When he got out of the copse he rode at a walk and then stopped his horse near the pond. He wanted to sit and think without moving. The moon was rising and was reflected in a streak of red on the other side of the pond. There were low rumbles of thunder in the distance. Pyotr Mihalitch looked steadily at the water and imagined his sister's despair, her martyr-like pallor, the tearless eyes with which she would conceal her humiliation from others. He imaged her with child, imagined the death of their mother, her funeral, Zina's horror. . . . Terrible pictures of the future rose before him on the background of smooth, dark water, and among pale feminine figures he saw himself, a weak, cowardly man with a guilty face. . . . And thinking about his life, he came to the conclusion that he had never said or acted upon what he really thought, and other people had repaid him in the same way. And so the whole of life seemed to him as dark as this water in which the night sky was reflected and water-weeds grew in a tangle. And it seemed to him that nothing could ever set it right.

* * *

As readers of imaginative literature, we are always seeking clues, warnings: where in life to search more assiduously; what not to overlook; what's the origin of this sort of human calamity, that sort of joy and pleasure; how can we live nearer to the latter, further off from the former? And to such seekers as we are, Chekhov is guide, perhaps *the* guide.

To twentieth-century writers, of course, his presence has affected all of our assumptions about what's a fit subject for imaginative writing; about which moments in life are too crucial or precious to relegate to conventional language; about how stories should begin, and the variety of ways a writer may choose to end them; and importantly about how final life is, and therefore how tenacious must be our representations of it.

More than anything else, though, it is Chekhov's great sufficiency that moves us and makes us admire; our reader's awareness that story to story, degree by degree around the sphere of observable human existence, Chekhov's measure is perfect. Given the subjects, the characters, the actions he brings into play, we routinely feel that everything of importance is always there in Chekhov. And our imaginations are for that reason ignited to know exactly what that great sufficiency is a reply to; what is the underlying urgency such that almost any story of Chekhov's can cause us to feel, either joyfully or pitifully, confirmed in life? As adults, we usually like what makes us want to know more, and are flattered by an assertive authority which makes us trust and then provides good counsel. It is indeed as though Chekhov knew us.

Finally, the stories found here are never difficult but often demanding; always dense but never turgid; sometimes dour, but rarely hopeless. Yet occasionally, reading through the great body of Chekhov's stories (220 plus), I have experienced secret relief when a story, here or there, seemed somehow *lesser*, was possibly tossed off in a way that allows me to imagine this most humane of writers in a new light—as a man agreeably unburdened by some demonic masterpiece-only obsession, a man I could've known, as a writer indeed willing to take us unblinkingly into the musing consciousness of kittens(!) and offer us assurance us that nothing very important goes on there: "The kitten lay awake thinking. Of what? . . . The soul of another is darkness, and a cat's soul more than most. . . . Fate had destined him to be the terror of cellars, store-rooms and corn bins, and had it not been for education . . . we will not anticipate, however." ("Who Was to Blame")

And so, no more anticipation. Just read these wonderful stories for pleasure, first, and do not read them fast. The more you linger, the more you reread, the more you'll experience and feel addressed by this great genius who, surprisingly, in spite of distance and time, shared a world we know and saw as his great privilege the chance to redeem it with language.

Richard Ford
July 15, 1998

EDITOR'S NOTE

My criteria for selecting these stories have been tuned only to my reader's taste and instincts. I've made no attempt to propagate a theme or to "cover" Chekhov's period of great story productivity, from the early 1880s until 1902. Some devoted readers have supposed that Chekhov only really became "Chekhov" after he had lived on into the 1890s, when his stories seemed to become darker, graver. (He died of tuberculosis in 1904.) But to concentrate only on these rather late stories would represent Chekhov as more sober-sided, even more literary than he is, and therefore I have included some lighter-hearted, more whimsical and even melodramatic stories from the middle 1880s—all work I consider excellent. "A Blunder" and "Champagne" are such choices; also the wonderful animal story "Kashtanka" from 1887. In my view, Chekhov's graver stories, "Ward No. 6," "The Lady with the Dog," "Peasants," only gain in our esteem if we become aware of the breadth of experience, humor and temperament he cultivated and was heir to. And by this wider experience we can—to our enrichment—estimate the great arc of life he chose from, and from which his genius derived and flourished.

R. F.

A Blunder

Ilya Sergeitch Peplov and his wife Kleopatra Petrovna were standing at the door, listening greedily. On the other side in the little drawing-room a love scene was apparently taking place between two persons: their daughter Natashenka and a teacher of the district school, called Shchupkin.

"He's rising!" whispered Peplov, quivering with impatience and rubbing his hands. "Now, Kleopatra, mind; as soon as they begin talking of their feelings, take down the ikon from the wall and we'll go in and bless them. . . . We'll catch him. . . . A blessing with an ikon is sacred and binding. . . . He couldn't get out of it, if he brought it into court."

On the other side of the door this was the conversation:

"Don't go on like that!" said Shchupkin, striking a match against his checked trousers. "I never wrote you any letters!"

"I like that! As though I didn't know your writing!" giggled the girl with an affected shriek, continually peeping at herself in the glass. "I knew it at once! And what a queer man you are! You are a writing master, and you write like a spider! How can you teach writing if you write so badly yourself?"

"H'm! . . . That means nothing. The great thing in writing lessons is not the hand one writes, but keeping the boys in order. You hit one on the head with a ruler, make another kneel down. . . . Besides, there's nothing in handwriting! Nekrassov was an author, but his handwriting's a disgrace, there's a specimen of it in his collected works."

"You are not Nekrassov. . . ." (A sigh). "I should love to marry an author. He'd always be writing poems to me."

"I can write you a poem, too, if you like."

"What can you write about?"

"Love—passion—your eyes. You'll be crazy when you read it. It would draw a tear from a stone! And if I write you a real poem, will you let me kiss your hand?"

"That's nothing much! You can kiss it now if you like."

Shchupkin jumped up, and making sheepish eyes, bent over the fat little hand that smelt of egg soap.

"Take down the ikon," Peplov whispered in a fluster, pale with excitement, and buttoning his coat as he prodded his wife with his elbow. "Come along, now!"

And without a second's delay Peplov flung open the door.

"Children," he muttered, lifting up his arms and blinking tearfully, "the Lord bless you, my children. May you live—be fruitful—and multiply."

"And—and I bless you, too," the mamma brought out, crying with happiness. "May you be happy, my dear ones! Oh, you are taking from me my only treasure!" she said to Shchupkin. "Love my girl, be good to her. . . ."

Shchupkin's mouth fell open with amazement and alarm. The parents' attack was so bold and unexpected that he could not utter a single word.

"I'm in for it! I'm spliced!" he thought, going limp with horror. "It's all over with you now, my boy! There's no escape!"

And he bowed his head submissively, as though to say, "Take me, I'm vanquished."

"Ble—blessings on you," the papa went on, and he, too, shed tears. "Natashenka, my daughter, stand by his side. Kleopatra, give me the ikon."

But at this point the father suddenly left off weeping, and his face was contorted with anger.

"You ninny!" he said angrily to his wife. "You are an idiot! Is that the ikon?"

"Ach, saints alive!"

What had happened? The writing master raised himself and saw that he was saved; in her flutter the mamma had snatched from the wall the portrait of Lazhetchnikov, the author, in mistake for the ikon. Old Peplov and his wife stood disconcerted in the middle of the room, holding the portrait aloft, not knowing what to do or what to say. The writing master took advantage of the general confusion and slipped away.

1886

A Misfortune

Sofya Petrovna, the wife of Lubyantsev the notary, a handsome young woman of five-and-twenty, was walking slowly along a track that had been cleared in the wood, with Ilyin, a lawyer who was spending the summer in the neighbourhood. It was five o'clock in the evening. Feathery-white masses of cloud stood overhead; patches of bright blue sky peeped out between them. The clouds stood motionless, as though they had caught in the tops of the tall old pine-trees. It was still and sultry.

Farther on, the track was crossed by a low railway embankment on which a sentinel with a gun was for some reason pacing up and down. Just beyond the embankment there was a large white church with six domes and a rusty roof.

"I did not expect to meet you here," said Sofya Petrovna, looking at the ground and prodding at the last year's leaves with the tip of her parasol, "and now I am glad we have met. I want to speak to you seriously and once for all. I beg you, Ivan Mihalovitch, if you really love and respect me, please make an end of this pursuit of me! You follow me about like a shadow, you are continually looking at me not in a nice way, making love to me, writing me strange letters, and . . . and I don't know where it's all going to end! Why, what can come of it?"

Ilyin said nothing. Sofya Petrovna walked on a few steps and continued:

"And this complete transformation in you all came about in the course of two or three weeks, after five years' friendship. I don't know you, Ivan Mihalovitch!"

Sofya Petrovna stole a glance at her companion. Screwing up his eyes, he was looking intently at the fluffy clouds. His face looked angry, ill-humoured, and preoccupied, like that of a man in pain forced to listen to nonsense.

"I wonder you don't see it yourself," Madame Lubyantsev went on, shrugging her shoulders. "You ought to realize that it's not a very nice part you are playing. I am married; I love and respect my husband. . . . I have a daughter. . . . Can you think all that means nothing? Besides, as an old friend you know my attitude to family life and my views as to the sanctity of marriage."

Ilyin cleared his throat angrily and heaved a sigh.

"Sanctity of marriage . . ." he muttered. "Oh, Lord!"

"Yes, yes. . . . I love my husband, I respect him; and in any case I value the peace of my home. I would rather let myself be killed than be a cause of unhappiness to Andrey and his daughter. . . . And I beg you, Ivan Mihalovitch, for God's sake, leave me in peace! Let us be as good, true friends as we used to be, and give up these sighs and groans, which really don't suit you. It's settled and over! Not a word more about it. Let us talk of something else."

Sofya Petrovna again stole a glance at Ilyin's face. Ilyin was looking up; he was pale, and was angrily biting his quivering lips. She could not understand why he was angry and why he was indignant, but his pallor touched her.

"Don't be angry; let us be friends," she said affectionately. "Agreed? Here's my hand."

Ilyin took her plump little hand in both of his, squeezed it, and slowly raised it to his lips.

"I am not a schoolboy," he muttered. "I am not in the least tempted by friendship with the woman I love."

"Enough, enough! It's settled and done with. We have reached the seat; let us sit down."

Sofya Petrovna's soul was filled with a sweet sense of relief: the most difficult and delicate thing had been said, the painful question was settled and done with. Now she could breathe freely and look Ilyin straight in the face. She looked at him, and the egoistic feeling of the superiority of the woman over the man who loves her, agreeably flattered her. It pleased her to see this huge, strong man, with his manly, angry face and his big black beard—clever, cultivated, and, people said, talented—sit down obediently beside her and bow his head dejectedly. For two or three minutes they sat without speaking.

"Nothing is settled or done with," began Ilyin. "You repeat copybook maxims to me. 'I love and respect my husband . . . the sanctity of marriage. . . .' I know all that without your help, and I could tell you more, too. I tell you truthfully and honestly that I consider the way I am behaving as criminal and immoral. What more can one say than that? But what's the good of saying what everybody knows? Instead of feeding nightingales with paltry words, you had much better tell me what I am to do."

"I've told you already—go away."

"As you know perfectly well, I have gone away five times, and every time I turned back on the way. I can show you my through tickets—I've kept them all. I have not will enough to run away from you! I am struggling. I am struggling horribly; but what the devil am I good for if I have no backbone, if I am weak, cowardly! I can't struggle with Nature! Do you understand? I cannot! I run away from here, and she holds on to me and pulls me back. Contemptible, loathsome weakness!"

Ilyin flushed crimson, got up, and walked up and down by the seat.

"I feel as cross as a dog," he muttered, clenching his fists. "I hate and despise myself! My God! like some depraved schoolboy, I am making love to another man's wife, writing idiotic letters, degrading myself . . . ugh!"

Ilyin clutched at his head, grunted, and sat down.

"And then your insincerity!" he went on bitterly. "If you do dislike my disgusting behaviour, why have you come here? What drew you here? In my letters I only ask you for a direct, definite answer—yes or no; but instead of a direct answer, you contrive every day these 'chance' meetings with me and regale me with copy-book maxims!"

Madame Lubyantsev was frightened and flushed. She suddenly felt the awkwardness which a decent woman feels when she is accidentally discovered undressed.

"You seem to suspect I am playing with you," she muttered. "I have always given you a direct answer, and . . . only today I've begged you . . ."

"Ough! as though one begged in such cases! If you were to say straight out 'Get away,' I should have been gone long ago; but you've never said that. You've never once given me a direct answer. Strange indecision! Yes, indeed; either you are playing with me, or else . . ."

Ilyin leaned his head on his fists without finishing. Sofya Petrovna began going over in her own mind the way she had behaved from beginning to end. She remembered that not only in her actions, but even in her secret thoughts, she had always been opposed to Ilyin's love-making; but yet she felt there was a grain of truth in the lawyer's words. But not knowing exactly what the truth was, she could not find answers to make to Ilyin's complaint, however hard she thought. It was awkward to be silent, and, shrugging her shoulders, she said:

"So I am to blame, it appears."

"I don't blame you for your insincerity," sighed Ilyin. "I did not mean that when I spoke of it. . . . Your insincerity is natural and in the order of things. If people agreed together and suddenly became sincere, everything would go to the devil."

Sofya Petrovna was in no mood for philosophical reflections, but she was glad of a chance to change the conversation, and asked:

"But why?"

"Because only savage women and animals are sincere. Once civilization has introduced a demand for such comforts as, for instance, feminine virtue, sincerity is out of place. . . ."

Ilyin jabbed his stick angrily into the sand. Madame Lubyantsev listened to him and liked his conversation, though a great deal of it she did not understand. What gratified her most was that she, an ordinary woman, was talked to by a talented man on "intellectual" subjects; it afforded her great pleasure, too, to watch the working of his mobile, young face, which was still pale and angry. She failed to understand a great deal that he said, but what was clear to her in his words was the attractive boldness with which the modern man without hesitation or doubt decides great questions and draws conclusive deductions.

She suddenly realized that she was admiring him, and was alarmed.

"Forgive me, but I don't understand," she said hurriedly. "What makes you talk of insincerity? I repeat my request again: be my good, true friend; let me alone! I beg you most earnestly!"

"Very good; I'll try again," sighed Ilyin. "Glad to do my best. . . . Only I doubt whether anything will come of my efforts. Either I shall put a bullet through my brains or take to drink in an idiotic way. I shall come to a bad end! There's a limit to everything—to struggles with Nature, too. Tell me, how can one struggle against madness? If you drink wine, how are you to struggle against intoxication? What am I to do if your image has grown into my soul, and day and night stands persistently before my eyes, like that pine there at this moment? Come, tell me, what hard and difficult thing can I do to get free from this abominable, miserable condition, in which all my thoughts, desires, and dreams are no longer my own, but belong to some demon who has taken possession of me? I love you, love you so much that I am completely thrown out of gear; I've given up my work and all who are dear to me; I've forgotten my God! I've never been in love like this in my life."

Sofya Petrovna, who had not expected such a turn to their conversation, drew away from Ilyin and looked into his face in dismay. Tears came into his eyes, his lips were quivering, and there was an imploring, hungry expression in his face.

"I love you!" he muttered, bringing his eyes near her big, frightened eyes. "You are so beautiful! I am in agony now, but I swear I would sit here all my life, suffering and looking in your eyes. But . . . be silent, I implore you!"

Sofya Petrovna, feeling utterly disconcerted, tried to think as quickly as possible of something to say to stop him. "I'll go away," she decided, but before she had time to make a movement to get up, Ilyin was on his knees before her. . . . He was clasping her knees, gazing into her face and speaking passionately, hotly, eloquently. In her terror and confusion she did not hear his words; for some reason now, at this dangerous moment, while her knees were being agreeably squeezed and felt as though they were in a warm bath, she was trying, with a sort of angry spite, to interpret her own sensations. She was angry that instead of brimming over with protesting virtue, she was entirely overwhelmed with weakness, apathy, and emptiness, like a drunken man utterly reckless; only at the bottom of her soul a remote bit of herself was malignantly taunting her: "Why don't you go? Is this as it should be? Yes?"

Seeking for some explanation, she could not understand how it was she did not pull away the hand to which Ilyin was clinging like a leech, and why, like Ilyin, she hastily glanced to right and to left to see whether any one was looking. The clouds and the pines stood motionless, looking at them severely, like old ushers seeing mischief, but bribed not to tell the school authorities. The sentry stood like a post on the embankment and seemed to be looking at the seat.

"Let him look," thought Sofya Petrovna.

"But . . . but listen," she said at last, with despair in her voice. "What can come of this? What will be the end of this?"

"I don't know, I don't know," he whispered, waving off the disagreeable questions.

They heard the hoarse, discordant whistle of the train. This cold, irrelevant sound from the everyday world of prose made Sofya Petrovna rouse herself.

"I can't stay . . . it's time I was at home," she said, getting up quickly. "The train is coming in. . . . Andrey is coming by it! He will want his dinner."

Sofya Petrovna turned towards the embankment with a burning face. The engine slowly crawled by, then came the carriages. It was not the local train, as she had supposed, but a goods train. The trucks filed by against the background of the white church in a long string like the days of a man's life, and it seemed as though it would never end.

But at last the train passed, and the last carriage with the guard and a light in it had disappeared behind the trees. Sofya Petrovna turned round sharply, and without looking at Ilyin, walked rapidly back along the track. She had regained her self-possession. Crimson with shame, humiliated not by Ilyin—no, but by her own cowardice, by the shamelessness with which she, a chaste and high-principled woman, had allowed a man, not her husband, to hug her knees—she had only one thought now: to get home as quickly as possible to her villa, to her family. The lawyer could hardly keep pace with her. Turning from the clearing into a narrow path, she turned round and glanced at him so quickly that she saw nothing but the sand on his knees, and waved to him to drop behind.

Reaching home, Sofya Petrovna stood in the middle of her room for five minutes without moving, and looked first at the window and then at her writing-table.

"You low creature!" she said, upbraiding herself. "You low creature!"

To spite herself, she recalled in precise detail, keeping nothing back—she recalled that though all this time she had been opposed to Ilyin's lovemaking, something had impelled her to seek an interview with him; and what was more, when he was at her feet she had enjoyed it enormously. She recalled it all without sparing herself, and now, breathless with shame, she would have liked to slap herself in the face.

"Poor Andrey!" she said to herself, trying as she thought of her husband to put into her face as tender an expression as she could. "Varya, my poor little girl, doesn't know what a mother she has! Forgive me, my dear ones! I love you so much . . . so much!"

And anxious to prove to herself that she was still a good wife and mother, and that corruption had not yet touched that "sanctity of marriage" of which she had spoken to Ilyin, Sofya Petrovna ran to the kitchen and abused the cook for not having yet laid the table for Andrey Ilyitch. She tried to picture her husband's hungry and exhausted appearance, commiserated him aloud, and laid the table for him with her own hands, which she had never done before. Then she found her daughter Varya, picked her up in her arms and hugged her warmly; the child seemed to her cold and heavy, but she was unwilling to acknowledge this to herself, and she began explaining to the child how good, kind, and honourable her papa was.

But when Andrey Ilyitch arrived soon afterwards she hardly greeted him. The rush of false feeling had already passed off without proving anything to her, only irritating and exasperating her by its falsity. She was sitting by the window, feeling miserable and cross. It is only by being in trouble that people can understand how far from easy it is to be the master of one's feelings and thoughts. Sofya Petrovna said afterwards that there was a tangle within her which it was as difficult to unravel as to count a flock of sparrows rapidly flying by. From the fact that she was not overjoyed to see her husband, that she did not like his manner at dinner, she concluded all of a sudden that she was beginning to hate her husband.

Andrey Ilyitch, languid with hunger and exhaustion, fell upon the sausage while waiting for the soup to be brought in, and ate it greedily, munching noisily and moving his temples.

"My goodness!" thought Sofya Petrovna. "I love and respect him, but . . . why does he munch so repulsively?"

The disorder in her thoughts was no less than the disorder in her feelings. Like all persons inexperienced in combating unpleasant ideas, Madame Lubyantsev did her utmost not to think of her trouble, and the harder she tried the more vividly Ilyin, the sand on his knees, the fluffy clouds, the train, stood out in her imagination.

"And why did I go there this afternoon like a fool?" she thought, tormenting herself. "And am I really so weak that I cannot depend upon myself?"

Fear magnifies danger. By the time Andrey Ilyitch was finishing the last course, she had firmly made up her mind to tell her husband everything and to flee from danger!

"I've something serious to say to you, Andrey," she began after dinner while her husband was taking off his coat and boots to lie down for a nap.

"Well?"

"Let us leave this place!"

"H'm! . . . Where shall we go? It's too soon to go back to town."

"No; for a tour or something of that sort. . . ."

"For a tour . . ." repeated the notary, stretching. "I dream of that myself, but where are we to get the money, and to whom am I to leave the office?"

And thinking a little he added:

"Of course, you must be bored. Go by yourself if you like."

Sofya Petrovna agreed, but at once reflected that Ilyin would be delighted with the opportunity, and would go with her in the same train, in the same compartment. . . . She thought and looked at her husband, now satisfied but still languid. For some reason her eyes rested on his feet—miniature, almost feminine feet, clad in striped socks; there was a thread standing out at the tip of each sock.

Behind the blind a bumble-bee was beating itself against the window-pane and buzzing. Sofya Petrovna looked at the threads on the socks, listened to the bee, and pictured how she would set off. . . . *Vis-à-vis* Ilyin would sit, day and night, never taking his eyes off her, wrathful at his own weakness and pale with spiritual agony. He would call himself an immoral schoolboy, would abuse her, tear his hair, but when darkness came on and the passengers were asleep or got out at a station, he would seize the opportunity to kneel before her and embrace her knees as he had at the seat in the wood. . . .

She caught herself indulging in this day-dream.

"Listen. I won't go alone," she said. "You must come with me."

"Nonsense, Sofotchka!" sighed Lubyantsev. "One must be sensible and not want the impossible."

"You will come when you know all about it," thought Sofya Petrovna.

Making up her mind to go at all costs, she felt that she was out of danger. Little by little her ideas grew clearer; her spirits rose and she allowed herself to think about it all, feeling that however much she thought, however much she dreamed, she would go away. While her husband was asleep, the evening gradually came on. She sat in the drawing-room and played the piano. The greater liveliness out of doors, the sound of music, but above all the thought that she was a sensible person, that she had surmounted her difficulties, completely restored her spirits. Other women, her appeased conscience told her, would probably have been carried off their feet in her position, and would have lost their balance, while she had almost died of shame, had been miserable, and was now running out of the danger which perhaps did not exist! She was so touched by her own virtue and determination that she even looked at herself two or three times in the looking-glass.

When it got dark, visitors arrived. The men sat down in the dining-room to play cards; the ladies remained in the drawing-room and the verandah. The last to arrive was Ilyin. He was gloomy, morose, and looked ill. He sat down in the corner of the sofa and did not move the whole evening. Usually good-humoured and talkative, this time he remained silent, frowned, and rubbed his eyebrows. When he had to answer some question, he gave a forced smile with his upper lip only, and answered jerkily and irritably. Four or five times he made some jest, but his jests sounded harsh and cutting. It seemed to Sofya Petrovna that he was on the verge of hysterics. Only now, sitting at the piano, she recognized fully for the first time that this unhappy man was in deadly earnest, that his soul was sick, and that he could find no rest. For her sake he was wasting the best days of his youth and his career, spending the last of his money on a summer villa, abandoning his mother and sisters, and, worst of all, wearing himself out in an agonizing struggle with himself. From mere common humanity he ought to be treated seriously.

She recognized all this clearly till it made her heart ache, and if at that moment she had gone up to him and said to him, "No," there would have been a force in her voice hard to disobey. But she did not go up to him and did not speak—indeed, never thought of doing so. The pettiness and egoism of youth had never been more patent in her than that evening. She realized that Ilyin was unhappy, and that he was sitting on the sofa as though he were on hot coals; she felt sorry for him, but at the same time the presence of a man who loved her to distraction, filled her soul with triumph and a sense of her own power. She felt her youth, her beauty, and her unassailable virtue, and, since she had decided to go away, gave herself full licence for that evening. She flirted, laughed incessantly, sang with peculiar feeling and gusto. Everything delighted and amused her. She was amused at the memory of what had happened at the seat in the wood, of the sentinel who had looked on. She was amused by her guests, by Ilyin's cutting jests, by the pin in his cravat, which she had never noticed before. There was a red snake with diamond eyes on the pin; this snake struck her as so amusing that she could have kissed it on the spot.

Sofya Petrovna sang nervously, with defiant recklessness as though half intoxicated, and she chose sad, mournful songs which dealt with wasted hopes, the past, old age, as though in mockery of another's grief. " 'And old age comes nearer and nearer' . . ." she sang. And what was old age to her?

"It seems as though there is something going wrong with me," she thought from time to time through her laughter and singing.

The party broke up at twelve o'clock. Ilyin was the last to leave. Sofya Petrovna was still reckless enough to accompany him to the bottom step of the verandah. She wanted to tell him that she was going away with her husband, and to watch the effect this news would produce on him.

The moon was hidden behind the clouds, but it was light enough for Sofya Petrovna to see how the wind played with the skirts of his overcoat and with the awning of the verandah. She could see, too, how white Ilyin was, and how he twisted his upper lip in the effort to smile.

"Sonia, Sonitchka . . . my darling woman!" he muttered, preventing her from speaking. "My dear! my sweet!"

In a rush of tenderness, with tears in his voice, he showered caressing words upon her, that grew tenderer and tenderer, and even called her "thou," as though she were his wife or mistress. Quite unexpectedly he put one arm round her waist and with the other hand took hold of her elbow.

"My precious! my delight!" he whispered, kissing the nape of her neck; "be sincere; come to me at once!"

She slipped out of his arms and raised her head to give vent to her indignation and anger, but the indignation did not come off, and all her vaunted virtue and chastity was only sufficient to enable her to utter the phrase used by all ordinary women on such occasions:

"You must be mad."

"Come, let us go," Ilyin continued. "I felt just now, as well as at the seat in the wood, that you are as helpless as I am, Sonia. . . . You are in the same plight! You love me and are fruitlessly trying to appease your conscience. . . ."

Seeing that she was moving away, he caught her by her lace cuff and said rapidly:

"If not today, then tomorrow you will have to give in! Why, then, this waste of time? My precious, darling Sonia, the sentence is passed; why put off the execution? Why deceive yourself?"

Sofya Petrovna tore herself from him and darted in at the door. Returning to the drawing-room, she mechanically shut the piano, looked for a long time at the music-stand, and sat down. She could not stand up nor think. All that was left of her excitement and reck-lessness was a fearful weakness, apathy, and dreariness. Her conscience whispered to her that she had behaved badly, foolishly, that evening, like some madcap girl—that she had just been embraced on the verandah, and still had an uneasy feeling in her waist and her elbow. There was not a soul in the drawing-room; there was only one candle burning. Madame Lubyantsev sat on the round stool before the piano, motionless, as though expecting some-thing. And as though taking advantage of the darkness and her extreme lassitude, an oppressive, overpowering desire began to assail her. Like a boa-constrictor it gripped her limbs and her soul, and grew stronger every second, and no longer menaced her as it had done, but stood clear before her in all its nakedness.

She sat for half an hour without stirring, not restraining herself from thinking of Ilyin, then she got up languidly and dragged herself to her bedroom. Andrey Ilyitch was already in bed. She sat down by the open window and gave herself up to desire. There was no "tangle" now in her head; all her thoughts and feelings were bent with one accord upon a single aim. She tried to struggle against it, but instantly gave it up. . . . She understood now how strong and relent-less was the foe. Strength and fortitude were needed to combat him, and her birth, her education, and her life had given her nothing to fall back upon.

"Immoral wretch! Low creature!" she nagged at herself for her weakness. "So that's what you're like!"

Her outraged sense of propriety was moved to such indignation by this weakness that she lavished upon herself every term of abuse she knew, and told herself many offensive and humiliating truths. So, for instance, she told herself that she never had been moral, that she had not come to grief before simply because she had had no opportunity, that her inward conflict during that day had all been a farce. . . .

"And even if I have struggled," she thought, "what sort of struggle was it? Even the woman who sells herself struggles before she brings herself to it, and yet she sells herself. A fine struggle! Like milk, I've turned in a day! In one day!"

She convicted herself of being tempted, not by feeling, not by Ilyin personally, but by sensations which awaited her . . . an idle lady, having her fling in the summer holidays, like so many!

" 'Like an unfledged bird when the mother has been slain,' " sang a husky tenor outside the window.

"If I am to go, it's time," thought Sofya Petrovna. Her heart suddenly began beating violently.

"Andrey!" she almost shrieked. "Listen! we . . . we are going? Yes?"

"Yes, I've told you already: you go alone."

"But listen," she began. "If you don't go with me, you are in danger of losing me. I believe I am . . . in love already."

"With whom?" asked Andrey Ilyitch.

"It can't make any difference to you who it is!" cried Sofya Petrovna.

Andrey Ilyitch sat up with his feet out of bed and looked wonderingly at his wife's dark figure.

"It's a fancy!" he yawned.

He did not believe her, but yet he was frightened. After thinking a little and asking his wife several unimportant questions, he delivered himself of his opinions on the family, on infidelity . . . spoke listlessly for about ten minutes and got into bed again. His moralizing produced no effect. There are a great many opinions in the world, and a good half of them are held by people who have never been in trouble!

In spite of the late hour, summer visitors were still walking outside. Sofya Petrovna put on a light cape, stood a little, thought a little. . . . She still had resolution enough to say to her sleeping husband:

"Are you asleep? I am going for a walk. . . . Will you come with me?"

That was her last hope. Receiving no answer, she went out. . . . It was fresh and windy. She was conscious neither of the wind nor the darkness, but went on and on. . . . An overmastering force drove her on, and it seemed as though, if she had stopped, it would have pushed her in the back.

"Immoral creature!" she muttered mechanically. "Low wretch!"

She was breathless, hot with shame, did not feel her legs under her, but what drove her on was stronger than shame, reason, or fear.

1886

A Trifle from Life

A well-fed, red-cheeked young man called Nikolay Ilyitch Belyaev, of thirty-two, who was an owner of house property in Petersburg, and a devotee of the race-course, went one evening to see Olga Ivanovna Irnin, with whom he was living, or, to use his own expression, was dragging out a long, wearisome romance. And, indeed, the first interesting and enthusiastic pages of this romance had long been perused; now the pages dragged on, and still dragged on, without presenting anything new or of interest.

Not finding Olga Ivanovna at home, my hero lay down on the lounge chair and proceeded to wait for her in the drawing-room.

"Good-evening, Nikolay Ilyitch!" he heard a child's voice. "Mother will be here directly. She has gone with Sonia to the dress-maker's."

Olga Ivanovna's son, Alyosha—a boy of eight who looked graceful and very well cared for, who was dressed like a picture, in a black velvet jacket and long black stockings—was lying on the sofa in the same room. He was lying on a satin cushion and, evidently imitating an acrobat he had lately seen at the circus, stuck up in the air first one leg and then the other. When his elegant legs were exhausted, he brought his arms into play or jumped up impulsively and went on all fours, trying to stand with his legs in the air. All this he was doing with the utmost gravity, gasping and groaning painfully as though he regretted that God had given him such a restless body.

"Ah, good-evening, my boy," said Belyaev. "It's you! I did not notice you. Is your mother well?"

Alyosha, taking hold of the tip of his left toe with his right hand and falling into the most unnatural attitude, turned over, jumped up, and peeped at Belyaev from behind the big fluffy lampshade.

"What shall I say?" he said, shrugging his shoulders. "In reality mother's never well. You see, she is a woman, and women, Nikolay Ilyitch, have always something the matter with them."

Belyaev, having nothing better to do, began watching Alyosha's face. He had never before during the whole of his intimacy with Olga Ivanovna paid any attention to the boy, and had completely ignored his existence; the boy had been before his eyes, but he had not cared to think why he was there and what part he was playing.

In the twilight of the evening, Alyosha's face, with his white forehead and black, unblinking eyes, unexpectedly reminded Belyaev of Olga Ivanovna as she had been during the first pages of their romance. And he felt disposed to be friendly to the boy.

"Come here, insect," he said; "let me have a closer look at you."

The boy jumped off the sofa and skipped up to Belyaev.

"Well," began Nikolay Ilyitch, putting a hand on the boy's thin shoulder. "How are you getting on?"

"How shall I say! We used to get on a great deal better."

"Why?"

"It's very simple. Sonia and I used only to learn music and reading, and now they give us French poetry to learn. Have you been shaved lately?"

"Yes."

"Yes, I see you have. Your beard is shorter. Let me touch it. . . . Does that hurt?"

"No."

"Why is it that if you pull one hair it hurts, but if you pull a lot at once it doesn't hurt a bit? Ha, ha! And, you know, it's a pity you don't have whiskers. Here ought to be shaved . . . but here at the sides the hair ought to be left. . . ."

The boy nestled up to Belyaev and began playing with his watch-chain.

"When I go to the high-school," he said, "mother is going to buy me a watch. I shall ask her to buy me a watch-chain like this. . . . Wh—at a loc—ket! Father's got a locket like that, only yours has little bars on it and his has letters. . . . There's mother's portrait in the middle of his. Father has a different sort of chain now, not made with rings, but like ribbon. . . ."

"How do you know? Do you see your father?"

"I? M'm . . . no. . . . I . . ."

Alyosha blushed, and in great confusion, feeling caught in a lie, began zealously scratching the locket with his nail. . . . Belyaev looked steadily into his face and asked:

"Do you see your father?"

"N-no!"

"Come, speak frankly, on your honour. . . . I see from your face you are telling a fib. Once you've let a thing slip out it's no good wriggling about it. Tell me, do you see him? Come, as a friend."

Alyosha hesitated.

"You won't tell mother?" he said.

"As though I should!"

"On your honour?"

"On my honour."

"Do you swear?"

"Ah, you provoking boy! What do you take me for?"

Alyosha looked round him, then with wide-open eyes, whispered to him:

"Only, for goodness' sake, don't tell mother. . . . Don't tell any one at all, for it is a secret. I hope to goodness mother won't find out, or we should all catch it—Sonia, and I, and Pelagea. . . . Well, listen. . . . Sonia and I see father every Tuesday and Friday. When Pelagea takes us for a walk before dinner we go to the Apfel Restaurant, and there is father waiting for us. . . . He is always sitting in a room apart, where you know there's a marble table and an ash-tray in the shape of a goose without a back. . . ."

"What do you do there?"

"Nothing! First we say how-do-you-do, then we all sit round the table, and father treats us with coffee and pies. You know Sonia eats the meat-pies, but I can't endure meat-pies! I like the pies made of cabbage and eggs. We eat such a lot that we have to try hard to eat as much as we can at dinner, for fear mother should notice."

"What do you talk about?"

"With father? About anything. He kisses us, he hugs us, tells us all sorts of amusing jokes. Do you know, he says when we are grown up he is going to take us to live with him. Sonia does not want to go, but I agree. Of course, I should miss mother; but, then, I should write her letters! It's a queer idea, but we could come and visit her on holidays—couldn't we? Father says, too, that he will buy me a horse. He's an awfully kind man! I can't understand why mother does not ask him to come and live with us, and why she forbids us to see him. You know he loves mother very much. He is always asking us how she is and what she is doing. When she was ill he clutched his head like this, and . . . and kept running about. He always tells us to be obedient and respectful to her. Listen. Is it true that we are unfortunate?"

"H'm! . . . Why?"

"That's what father says. 'You are unhappy children,' he says. It's strange to hear him, really. 'You are unhappy,' he says, 'I am unhappy, and mother's unhappy. You must pray to God,' he says; 'for yourselves and for her.' "

Alyosha let his eyes rest on a stuffed bird and sank into thought.

"So . . ." growled Belyaev. "So that's how you are going on. You arrange meetings at restaurants. And mother does not know?"

"No-o. . . . How should she know? Pelagea would not tell her for anything, you know. The day before yesterday he gave us some pears. As sweet as jam! I ate two."

"H'm! . . . Well, and I say . . . Listen. Did father say anything about me?"

"About you? What shall I say?"

Alyosha looked searchingly into Belyaev's face and shrugged his shoulders.

"He didn't say anything particular."

"For instance, what did he say?"

"You won't be offended?"

"What next? Why, does he abuse me?"

"He doesn't abuse you, but you know he is angry with you. He says mother's unhappy owing to you . . . and that you have ruined mother. You know he is so queer! I explain to him that you are kind, that you never scold mother; but he only shakes his head."

"So he says I have ruined her?"

"Yes; you mustn't be offended, Nikolay Ilyitch."

Belyaev got up, stood still a moment, and walked up and down the drawing-room.

"That's strange and . . . ridiculous!" he muttered, shrugging his shoulders and smiling sarcastically. "He's entirely to blame, and I have ruined her, eh? An innocent lamb, I must say. So he told you I ruined your mother?"

"Yes, but . . . you said you would not be offended, you know."

"I am not offended, and . . . and it's not your business. Why, it's . . . why, it's positively ridiculous! I have been thrust into it like a chicken in the broth, and now it seems I'm to blame!"

A ring was heard. The boy sprang up from his place and ran out. A minute later a lady came into the room with a little girl; this was Olga Ivanovna, Alyosha's mother. Alyosha followed them in, skipping and jumping, humming aloud and waving his hands. Belyaev nodded, and went on walking up and down.

"Of course, whose fault is it if not mine?" he muttered with a snort. "He is right! He is an injured husband."

"What are you talking about?" asked Olga Ivanovna.

"What about? . . . Why, just listen to the tales your lawful spouse is spreading now! It appears that I am a scoundrel and a villain, that I have ruined you and the children. All of you are unhappy, and I am the only happy one! Wonderfully, wonderfully happy!"

"I don't understand, Nikolay. What's the matter?"

"Why, listen to this young gentleman!" said Belyaev, pointing to Alyosha.

Alyosha flushed crimson, then turned pale, and his whole face began working with terror.

"Nikolay Ilyitch," he said in a loud whisper. "Sh-sh!"

Olga Ivanovna looked in surprise at Alyosha, then at Belyaev, then at Alyosha again.

"Just ask him," Belyaev went on. "Your Pelagea, like a regular fool, takes them about to restaurants and arranges meetings with their papa. But that's not the point: the point is that their dear papa is a victim, while I'm a wretch who has broken up both your lives. . . ."

"Nikolay Ilyitch," moaned Alyosha. "Why, you promised on your word of honour!"

"Oh, get away!" said Belyaev, waving him off. "This is more important than any word of honour. It's the hypocrisy revolts me, the lying! . . ."

"I don't understand it," said Olga Ivanovna, and tears glistened in her eyes. "Tell me, Alyosha," she turned to her son. "Do you see your father?"

Alyosha did not hear her; he was looking with horror at Belyaev.

"It's impossible," said his mother; "I will go and question Pelagea."

Olga Ivanovna went out.

"I say, you promised on your word of honour!" said Alyosha, trembling all over.

Belyaev dismissed him with a wave of his hand, and went on walking up and down. He was absorbed in his grievance and was oblivious of the boy's presence, as he always had been. He, a grown-up, serious person, had no thought to spare for boys. And Alyosha sat down in the corner and told Sonia with horror how he had been deceived. He was trembling, stammering, and crying. It was the first time in his life that he had been brought into such coarse contact with lying; till then he had not known that there are in the world, besides sweet pears, pies, and expensive watches, a great many things for which the language of children has no expression.

1886

Difficult People

Yevgraf Ivanovitch Shiryaev, a small farmer, whose father, a parish priest, now deceased, had received a gift of three hundred acres of land from Madame Kuvshinnikov, a general's widow, was standing in a corner before a copper washing-stand, washing his hands. As usual, his face looked anxious and ill-humoured, and his beard was uncombed.

"What weather!" he said. "It's not weather, but a curse laid upon us. It's raining again!"

He grumbled on, while his family sat waiting at table for him to have finished washing his hands before beginning dinner. Fedosya Semyonovna, his wife, his son Pyotr, a student, his eldest daughter Varvara, and three small boys, had been sitting waiting a long time. The boys—Kolka, Vanka, and Arhipka—grubby, snub-nosed little fellows with chubby faces and tousled hair that wanted cutting, moved their chairs impatiently, while their elders sat without stirring, and apparently did not care whether they ate their dinner or waited. . . .

As though trying their patience, Shiryaev deliberately dried his hands, deliberately said his prayer, and sat down to the table without hurrying himself. Cabbage-soup was served immediately. The sound of carpenter's axes (Shiryaev was having a new barn built) and the laughter of Fomka, their labourer, teasing the turkey, floated in from the courtyard.

Big, sparse drops of rain pattered on the window.

Pyotr, a round-shouldered student in spectacles, kept exchanging glances with his mother as he ate his dinner. Several times he laid down his spoon and cleared his throat, meaning to begin to speak, but after an intent look at his father he fell to eating again. At last, when the porridge had been served, he cleared his throat resolutely and said:

"I ought to go tonight by the evening train. I ought to have gone before; I have missed a fortnight as it is. The lectures begin on the first of September."

"Well, go," Shiryaev assented; "why are you lingering here? Pack up and go, and good luck to you."

A minute passed in silence.

"He must have money for the journey, Yevgraf Ivanovitch," the mother observed in a low voice.

"Money? To be sure, you can't go without money. Take it at once, since you need it. You could have had it long ago!"

The student heaved a faint sigh and looked with relief at his mother. Deliberately Shiryaev took a pocket-book out of his coat-pocket and put on his spectacles.

"How much do you want?" he asked.

"The fare to Moscow is eleven roubles forty-two kopecks. . . ."

"Ah, money, money!" sighed the father. (He always sighed when he saw money, even when he was receiving it.) "Here are twelve roubles for you. You will have change out of that which will be of use to you on the journey."

"Thank you."

After waiting a little, the student said:

"I did not get lessons quite at first last year. I don't know how it will be this year; most likely it will take me a little time to find work. I ought to ask you for fifteen roubles for my lodging and dinner."

Shiryaev thought a little and heaved a sigh.

"You will have to make ten do," he said. "Here, take it."

The student thanked him. He ought to have asked him for something more, for clothes, for lecture fees, for books, but after an intent look at his father he decided not to pester him further.

The mother, lacking in diplomacy and prudence, like all mothers, could not restrain herself, and said:

"You ought to give him another six roubles, Yevgraf Ivanovitch, for a pair of boots. Why, just see, how can he go to Moscow in such wrecks?"

"Let him take my old ones; they are still quite good."

"He must have trousers, anyway; he is a disgrace to look at."

And immediately after that a storm-signal showed itself, at the sight of which all the family trembled.

Shiryaev's short, fat neck turned suddenly red as a beetroot. The colour mounted slowly to his ears, from his ears to his temples, and by degrees suffused his whole face. Yevgraf Ivanovitch shifted in his chair and unbuttoned his shirt-collar to save himself from choking. He was evidently struggling with the feeling that was mastering him. A death-like silence followed. The children held their breath. Fedosya Semyonovna, as though she did not grasp what was happening to her husband, went on:

"He is not a little boy now, you know; he is ashamed to go about without clothes."

Shiryaev suddenly jumped up, and with all his might flung down his fat pocket-book in the middle of the table, so that a hunk of bread flew off a plate. A revolting expression of anger, resentment, avarice—all mixed together—flamed on his face.

"Take everything!" he shouted in an unnatural voice; "plunder me! Take it all! Strangle me!"

He jumped up from the table, clutched at his head, and ran staggering about the room.

"Strip me to the last thread!" he shouted in a shrill voice. "Squeeze out the last drop! Rob me! Wring my neck!"

The student flushed and dropped his eyes. He could not go on eating. Fedosya Semyonovna, who had not after twenty-five years grown used to her husband's difficult character, shrank into herself and muttered something in self-defence. An expression of amazement and dull terror came into her wasted and birdlike face, which at all times looked dull and scared. The little boys and the elder daughter Varvara, a girl in her teens, with a pale ugly face, laid down their spoons and sat mute.

Shiryaev, growing more and more ferocious, uttering words each more terrible than the one before, dashed up to the table and began shaking the notes out of his pocket-book.

"Take them!" he muttered, shaking all over. "You've eaten and drunk your fill, so here's money for you too! I need nothing! Order yourself new boots and uniforms!"

The student turned pale and got up.

"Listen, papa," he began, gasping for breath. "I . . . I beg you to end this, for . . ."

"Hold your tongue!" the father shouted at him, and so loudly that the spectacles fell off his nose; "hold your tongue!"

"I used . . . I used to be able to put up with such scenes, but . . . but now I have got out of the way of it. Do you understand? I have got out of the way of it!"

"Hold your tongue!" cried the father, and he stamped with his feet.

"You must listen to what I say! I shall say what I like, and you hold your tongue. At your age I was earning my living, while you . . . Do you know what you cost me, you scoundrel? I'll turn you out! Wastrel!"

"Yevgraf Ivanovitch," muttered Fedosya Semyonovna, moving her fingers nervously; "you know he . . . you know Petya . . . !"

"Hold your tongue!" Shiryaev shouted out to her, and tears actually came into his eyes from anger. "It is you who have spoilt them—you! It's all your fault! He has no respect for us, does not say his prayers, and earns nothing! I am only one against the ten of you! I'll turn you out of the house!"

The daughter Varvara gazed fixedly at her mother with her mouth open, moved her vacant-looking eyes to the window, turned pale, and, uttering a loud shriek, fell back in her chair. The father, with a curse and a wave of the hand, ran out into the yard.

This was how domestic scenes usually ended at the Shiryaevs'. But on this occasion, unfortunately, Pyotr the student was carried away by overmastering anger. He was just as hasty and ill-tempered as his father and his grandfather the priest, who used to beat his parishioners about the head with a stick. Pale and clenching his fists, he went up to his mother and shouted in the very highest tenor note his voice could reach:

"These reproaches are loathsome! sickening to me! I want nothing from you! Nothing! I would rather die of hunger than eat another mouthful at your expense! Take your nasty money back! take it!"

The mother huddled against the wall and waved her hands, as though it were not her son, but some phantom before her.

"What have I done?" she wailed. "What?"

Like his father, the boy waved his hands and ran into the yard. Shiryaev's house stood alone on a ravine which ran like a furrow for four miles along the steppe. Its sides were overgrown with oak saplings and alders, and a stream ran at the bottom. On one side the house looked towards the ravine, on the other towards the open country, there were no fences nor hurdles. Instead there were farm-buildings of all sorts close to one another, shutting in a small space in front of the house which was regarded as the yard, and in which hens, ducks, and pigs ran about.

Going out of the house, the student walked along the muddy road towards the open country. The air was full of a penetrating autumn dampness. The road was muddy, puddles gleamed here and there, and in the yellow fields autumn itself seemed looking out from the grass, dismal, decaying, dark. On the right-hand side of the road was a vegetable-garden cleared of its crops and gloomy-looking, with here and there sunflowers standing up in it with hanging heads already black.

Pyotr thought it would not be a bad thing to walk to Moscow on foot; to walk just as he was, with holes in his boots, without a cap, and without a farthing of money. When he had gone eighty miles his father, frightened and aghast, would overtake him, would begin begging him to turn back or take the money, but he would not even look at him, but would go on and on. . . . Bare forests would be followed by desolate fields, fields by forests again; soon the earth would be white with the first snow, and the streams would be coated with ice. . . . Somewhere near Kursk or near Serpuhovo, exhausted and dying of hunger, he would sink down and die. His corpse would be found, and there would be a paragraph in all the papers saying that a student called Shiryaev had died of hunger. . . .

A white dog with a muddy tail who was wandering about the vegetable-garden looking for something gazed at him and sauntered after him. . . .

He walked along the road and thought of death, of the grief of his family, of the moral sufferings of his father, and then pictured all sorts of adventures on the road, each more marvellous than the one before—picturesque places, terrible nights, chance encounters. He imagined a string of pilgrims, a hut in the forest with one little window shining in the darkness; he stands before the window, begs for a night's lodging. . . . They let him in, and suddenly he sees that they are robbers. Or, better still, he is taken into a big manor-house, where, learning who he is, they give him food and drink, play to him on the piano, listen to his complaints, and the daughter of the house, a beauty, falls in love with him.

Absorbed in his bitterness and such thoughts, young Shiryaev walked on and on. Far, far ahead he saw the inn, a dark patch against the grey background of cloud. Beyond the inn, on the very horizon, he could see a little hillock; this was the railway-station. That hillock reminded him of the connection existing between the place where he was now standing and Moscow, where street-lamps were burning and carriages were rattling in the streets, where lectures were being given. And he almost wept with depression and impatience. The solemn landscape, with its order and beauty, the deathlike stillness all around, revolted him and moved him to despair and hatred!

"Look out!" He heard behind him a loud voice.

An old lady of his acquaintance, a landowner of the neighbour-hood, drove past him in a light, elegant landau. He bowed to her, and smiled all over his face. And at once he caught himself in that smile, which was so out of keeping with his gloomy mood. Where did it come from if his whole heart was full of vexation and misery? And he thought nature itself had given man this capacity for lying, that even in difficult moments of spiritual strain he might be able to hide the secrets of his nest as the fox and the wild duck do. Every family has its joys and its horrors, but however great they may be, it's hard for an outsider's eye to see them; they are a secret. The father of the old lady who had just driven by, for instance, had for some offence lain for half his lifetime under the ban of the wrath of Tsar Nicolas I.; her husband had been a gambler; of her four sons, not one had turned out well. One could imagine how many terrible scenes there must have been in her life, how many tears must have been shed. And yet the old lady seemed happy and satisfied, and she had answered his smile by smil-ing too. The student thought of his comrades, who did not like talking about their families; he thought of his mother, who almost always lied when she had to speak of her husband and children. . . .

Pyotr walked about the roads far from home till dusk, abandoning himself to dreary thoughts. When it began to drizzle with rain he turned homewards. As he walked back he made up his mind at all costs to talk to his father, to explain to him, once and for all, that it was dreadful and oppressive to live with him.

He found perfect stillness in the house. His sister Varvara was lying behind a screen with a headache, moaning faintly. His mother, with a look of amazement and guilt upon her face, was sitting beside her on a box, mending Arhipka's trousers. Yevgraf Ivanovitch was pacing from one window to another, scowling at the weather. From his walk, from the way he cleared his throat, and even from the back of his head, it was evident he felt himself to blame.

"I suppose you have changed your mind about going today?" he asked.

The student felt sorry for him, but immediately suppressing that feeling, he said:

"Listen . . . I must speak to you seriously . . . yes, seriously. I have always respected you, and . . . and have never brought myself to speak to you in such a tone, but your behaviour . . . your last action . . ."

The father looked out of the window and did not speak. The student, as though considering his words, rubbed his forehead and went on in great excitement:

"Not a dinner or tea passes without your making an uproar. Your bread sticks in our throat . . . nothing is more bitter, more humiliating, than bread that sticks in one's throat. . . . Though you are my father, no one, neither God nor nature, has given you the right to insult and humiliate us so horribly, to vent your ill-humour on the weak. You have worn my mother out and made a slave of her, my sister is hopelessly crushed, while I . . ."

"It's not your business to teach me," said his father.

"Yes, it is my business! You can quarrel with me as much as you like, but leave my mother in peace! I will not allow you to torment my mother!" the student went on, with flashing eyes. "You are spoilt because no one has yet dared to oppose you. They tremble and are mute towards you, but now that is over! Coarse, ill-bred man! You are coarse . . . do you understand? You are coarse, ill-humoured, unfeeling. And the peasants can't endure you!"

The student had by now lost his thread, and was not so much speaking as firing off detached words. Yevgraf Ivanovitch listened in silence, as though stunned; but suddenly his neck turned crimson, the colour crept up his face, and he made a movement.

"Hold your tongue!" he shouted.

"That's right!" the son persisted; "you don't like to hear the truth! Excellent! Very good! begin shouting! Excellent!"

"Hold your tongue, I tell you!" roared Yevgraf Ivanovitch.

Fedosya Semyonovna appeared in the doorway, very pale, with an astonished face; she tried to say something, but she could not, and could only move her fingers.

"It's all your fault!" Shiryaev shouted at her. "You have brought him up like this!"

"I don't want to go on living in this house!" shouted the student, crying, and looking angrily at his mother. "I don't want to live with you!"

Varvara uttered a shriek behind the screen and broke into loud sobs. With a wave of his hand, Shiryaev ran out of the house.

The student went to his own room and quietly lay down. He lay till midnight without moving or opening his eyes. He felt neither anger nor shame, but a vague ache in his soul. He neither blamed his father nor pitied his mother, nor was he tormented by stings of conscience; he realized that every one in the house was feeling the same ache, and God only knew which was most to blame, which was suffering most. . . .

At midnight he woke the labourer, and told him to have the horse ready at five o'clock in the morning for him to drive to the station; he undressed and got into bed, but could not get to sleep. He heard how his father, still awake, paced slowly from window to window, sighing, till early morning. No one was asleep; they spoke rarely, and only in whispers. Twice his mother came to him behind the screen. Always with the same look of vacant wonder, she slowly made the cross over him, shaking nervously.

At five o'clock in the morning he said good-bye to them all affectionately, and even shed tears. As he passed his father's room, he glanced in at the door. Yevgraf Ivanovitch, who had not taken off his clothes or gone to bed, was standing by the window, drumming on the panes.

"Good-bye; I am going," said his son.

"Good-bye . . . the money is on the round table . . ." his father answered, without turning around.

A cold, hateful rain was falling as the labourer drove him to the station. The sunflowers were drooping their heads still lower, and the grass seemed darker than ever.

1886

Hush!

Ivan Yegoritch Krasnyhin, a fourth-rate journalist, returns home late at night, grave and careworn, with a peculiar air of concentration. He looks like a man expecting a police-raid or contemplating suicide. Pacing about his rooms he halts abruptly, ruffles up his hair, and says in the tone in which Laertes announces his intention of avenging his sister:

"Shattered, soul-weary, a sick load of misery on the heart . . . and then to sit down and write. And this is called life! How is it nobody has described the agonizing discord in the soul of a writer who has to amuse the crowd when his heart is heavy or to shed tears at the word of command when his heart is light? I must be playful, coldly unconcerned, witty, but what if I am weighed down with misery, what if I am ill, or my child is dying or my wife in anguish!"

He says this, brandishing his fists and rolling his eyes. . . . Then he goes into the bedroom and wakes his wife.

"Nadya," he says, "I am sitting down to write. . . . Please don't let anyone interrupt me. I can't write with children crying or cooks snoring. . . . See, too, that there's tea and . . . steak or something. . . . You know that I can't write without tea. . . . Tea is the one thing that gives me the energy for my work."

Returning to his room he takes off his coat, waistcoat, and boots. He does this very slowly; then, assuming an expression of injured innocence, he sits down to his table.

There is nothing casual, nothing ordinary on his writing-table, down to the veriest trifle everything bears the stamp of a stern, deliberately planned programme. Little busts and photographs of distinguished writers, heaps of rough manuscripts, a volume of Byelinsky with a page turned down, part of a skull by way of an ashtray, a sheet of newspaper folded carelessly, but so that a passage is uppermost, boldly marked in blue pencil with the word "disgraceful." There are a dozen sharply-pointed pencils and several penholders fitted with new nibs, put in readiness that no accidental breaking of a pen may for a single second interrupt the flight of his creative fancy.

Ivan Yegoritch throws himself back in his chair, and closing his eyes concentrates himself on his subject. He hears his wife shuffling about in her slippers and splitting shavings to heat the samovar. She is hardly awake, that is apparent from the way the knife and the lid of the samovar keep dropping from her hands. Soon the hissing of the samovar and the spluttering of the frying meat reaches him. His wife is still splitting shavings and rattling with the doors and blowers of the stove.

All at once Ivan Yegoritch starts, opens frightened eyes, and begins to sniff the air.

"Heavens! the stove is smoking!" he groans, grimacing with a face of agony. "Smoking! That insufferable woman makes a point of trying to poison me! How, in God's Name, am I to write in such surroundings, kindly tell me that?"

He rushes into the kitchen and breaks into a theatrical wail. When a little later, his wife, stepping cautiously on tiptoe, brings him in a glass of tea, he is sitting in an easy chair as before with his eyes closed, absorbed in his article. He does not stir, drums lightly on his forehead with two fingers, and pretends he is not aware of his wife's presence. . . . His face wears an expression of injured innocence.

Like a girl who has been presented with a costly fan, he spends a long time coquetting, grimacing, and posing to himself before he writes the title. . . . He presses his temples, he wriggles, and draws his legs up under his chair as though he were in pain, or half closes his eyes languidly like a cat on the sofa. At last, not without hesitation, he stretches out his hand towards the inkstand, and with an expression as though he were signing a death-warrant, writes the title. . . .

"Mammy, give me some water!" he hears his son's voice.

"Hush!" says his mother. "Daddy's writing! Hush!"

Daddy writes very, very quickly, without corrections or pauses, he has scarcely time to turn over the pages. The busts and portraits of celebrated authors look at his swiftly racing pen and, keeping stock still, seem to be thinking: "Oh my, how you are going it!"

"Sh!" squeaks the pen.

"Sh!" whisper the authors, when his knee jolts the table and they are set trembling.

All at once Krasnyhin draws himself up, lays down his pen and listens. . . . He hears an even monotonous whispering. . . . It is Foma Nikolaevitch, the lodger in the next room, saying his prayers.

"I say!" cries Krasnyhin. "Couldn't you, please, say your prayers more quietly? You prevent me from writing!"

"Very sorry. . . ." Foma Nikolaevitch answers timidly.

"Sh!"

After covering five pages, Krasnyhin stretches and looks at his watch.

"Goodness, three o'clock already," he moans. "Other people are asleep while I . . . I alone must work!"

Shattered and exhausted he goes, with his head on one side, to the bedroom to wake his wife, and says in a languid voice:

"Nadya, get me some more tea! I . . . feel weak."

He writes till four o'clock and would readily have written till six if his subject had not been exhausted. Coquetting and posing to himself and the inanimate objects about him, far from any indiscreet, critical eye, tyrannizing and domineering over the little anthill that fate has put in his power are the honey and the salt of his existence. And how different is this despot here at home from the humble, meek, dull-witted little man we are accustomed to see in the editor's offices!

"I am so exhausted that I am afraid I shan't sleep . . ." he says as he gets into bed. "Our work, this cursed, ungrateful, hard labour, exhausts the soul even more than the body. . . . I had better take some bromide. . . . God knows, if it were not for my family I'd throw up the work. . . . To write to order! It is awful."

He sleeps till twelve or one o'clock in the day, sleeps a sound, healthy sleep. . . . Ah! how he would sleep, what dreams he would have, how he would spread himself if he were to become a well-known writer, an editor, or even a sub-editor!

"He has been writing all night," whispers his wife with a scared expression on her face. "Sh!"

No one dares to speak or move or make a sound. His sleep is something sacred, and the culprit who offends against it will pay dearly for his fault.

"Hush!" floats over the flat. "Hush!"

1886

Champagne

In the year in which my story begins I had a job at a little station on one of our southwestern railways. Whether I had a gay or a dull life at the station you can judge from the fact that for fifteen miles round there was not one human habitation, not one woman, not one decent tavern; and in those days I was young, strong, hot-headed, giddy, and foolish. The only distraction I could possibly find was in the windows of the passenger trains, and in the vile vodka which the Jews drugged with thorn-apple. Sometimes there would be a glimpse of a woman's head at a carriage window, and one would stand like a statue without breathing and stare at it until the train turned into an almost invisible speck; or one would drink all one could of the loathsome vodka till one was stupefied and did not feel the passing of the long hours and days. Upon me, a native of the north, the steppe produced the effect of a deserted Tatar cemetery. In the summer the steppe with its solemn calm, the monotonous chur of the grasshoppers, the transparent moonlight from which one could not hide, reduced me to listless melancholy; and in the winter the irreproachable whiteness of the steppe, its cold distance, long nights, and howling wolves oppressed me like a heavy nightmare. There were several people living at the station: my wife and I, a deaf and scrofulous telegraph clerk, and three watchmen. My assistant, a young man who was in consumption, used to go for treatment to the town, where he stayed for months at a time, leaving his duties to me together with the right of pocketing his salary. I had no children, no cake would have tempted visitors to come and see me, and I could only visit other officials on the line, and that no oftener than once a month.

I remember my wife and I saw the New Year in. We sat at table, chewed lazily, and heard the deaf telegraph clerk monotonously tapping on his apparatus in the next room. I had already drunk five glasses of drugged vodka, and, propping my heavy head on my fist, thought of my overpowering boredom from which there was no escape, while my wife sat beside me and did not take her eyes off me. She looked at me as no one can look but a woman who has nothing in this world but a handsome husband. She loved me madly, slavishly, and not merely my good looks, or my soul, but my sins, my ill-humour and boredom, and even my cruelty when, in drunken fury, not knowing how to vent my ill-humour, I tormented her with reproaches.

In spite of the boredom which was consuming me, we were preparing to see the New Year in with exceptional festiveness, and were awaiting midnight with some impatience. The fact is, we had in reserve two bottles of champagne, the real thing, with the label of Veuve Clicquot; this treasure I had won the previous autumn in a bet with the station-master of D. when I was drinking with him at a christening. It sometimes happens during a lesson in mathematics, when the very air is still with boredom, a butterfly flutters into the class-room; the boys toss their heads and begin watching its flight with interest, as though they saw before them not a butterfly but something new and strange; in the same way ordinary champagne, chancing to come into our dreary station, roused us. We sat in silence looking alternately at the clock and at the bottles.

When the hands pointed to five minutes to twelve I slowly began uncorking a bottle. I don't know whether I was affected by the vodka, or whether the bottle was wet, but all I remember is that when the cork flew up to the ceiling with a bang, my bottle slipped out of my hands and fell on the floor. Not more than a glass of the wine was spilt, as I managed to catch the bottle and put my thumb over the foaming neck.

"Well, may the New Year bring you happiness!" I said, filling two glasses. "Drink!"

My wife took her glass and fixed her frightened eyes on me. Her face was pale and wore a look of horror.

"Did you drop the bottle?" she asked.

"Yes. But what of that?"

"It's unlucky," she said, putting down her glass and turning paler still. "It's a bad omen. It means that some misfortune will happen to us this year."

"What a silly thing you are," I sighed. "You are a clever woman, and yet you talk as much nonsense as an old nurse. Drink."

"God grant it is nonsense, but . . . something is sure to happen! You'll see."

She did not even sip her glass, she moved away and sank into thought. I uttered a few stale commonplaces about superstition, drank half a bottle, paced up and down, and then went out of the room.

Outside there was the still frosty night in all its cold, inhospitable beauty. The moon and two white fluffy clouds beside it hung just over the station, motionless as though glued to the spot, and looked as though waiting for something. A faint transparent light came from them and touched the white earth softly, as though afraid of wounding her modesty, and lighted up everything—the snowdrifts, the embankment. . . . It was still.

I walked along the railway embankment.

"Silly woman," I thought, looking at the sky spangled with brilliant stars. "Even if one admits that omens sometimes tell the truth, what evil can happen to us? The misfortunes we have endured already, and which are facing us now, are so great that it is difficult to imagine anything worse. What further harm can you do a fish which has been caught and fried and served up with sauce?"

A poplar covered with hoar frost looked in the bluish darkness like a giant wrapt in a shroud. It looked at me sullenly and dejectedly, as though like me it realized its loneliness. I stood a long while looking at it.

"My youth is thrown away for nothing, like a useless cigarette end," I went on musing. "My parents died when I was a little child; I was expelled from the high school, I was born of a noble family, but I have received neither education nor breeding, and I have no more knowledge than the humblest mechanic. I have no refuge, no relations, no friends, no work I like. I am not fitted for anything, and in the prime of my powers I am good for nothing but to be stuffed into this little station; I have known nothing but trouble and failure all my life. What can happen worse?"

Red lights came into sight in the distance. A train was moving towards me. The slumbering steppe listened to the sound of it. My thoughts were so bitter that it seemed to me that I was thinking aloud, and that the moan of the telegraph wire and the rumble of the train were expressing my thoughts.

"What can happen worse? The loss of my wife?" I wondered.

"Even that is not terrible. It's no good hiding it from my conscience: I don't love my wife. I married her when I was only a wretched boy; now I am young and vigorous, and she has gone off and grown older and sillier, stuffed from her head to her heels with conventional ideas. What charm is there in her maudlin love, in her hollow chest, in her lusterless eyes? I put up with her, but I don't love her. What can happen? My youth is being wasted, as the saying is, for a pinch of snuff. Women flit before my eyes only in the carriage windows, like falling stars. Love I never had and have not. My manhood, my courage, my power of feeling are going to ruin. . . . Everything is being thrown away like dirt, and all my wealth here in the steppe is not worth a farthing."

The train rushed past me with a roar and indifferently cast the glow of its red lights upon me. I saw it stop by the green lights of the station, stop for a minute and rumble off again. After walking a mile and a half I went back. Melancholy thoughts haunted me still. Painful as it was to me, yet I remember I tried as it were to make my thoughts still gloomier and more melancholy. You know people who are vain and not very clever have moments when the consciousness that they are miserable affords them positive satisfaction, and they even coquet with their misery for their own entertainment. There was a great deal of truth in what I thought, but there was also a great deal that was absurd and conceited, and there was something boyishly defiant in my question: "What could happen worse?"

"And what is there to happen?" I asked myself. "I think I have endured everything. I've been ill, I've lost money, I get reprimanded by my superiors every day, and I go hungry, and a mad wolf has run into the station yard. What more is there? I have been insulted, humiliated, . . . and I have insulted others in my time. I have not been a criminal, it is true, but I don't think I am capable of crime— I am not afraid of being hauled up for it."

The two little clouds had moved away from the moon and stood at a little distance, looking as though they were whispering about something which the moon must not know. A light breeze was racing across the steppe, bringing the faint rumble of the retreating train.

My wife met me at the doorway. Her eyes were laughing gaily and her whole face was beaming with good-humour.

"There is news for you!" she whispered. "Make haste, go to your room and put on your new coat; we have a visitor."

"What visitor?"

"Aunt Natalya Petrovna has just come by the train."

"What Natalya Petrovna?"

"The wife of my uncle Semyon Fyodoritch. You don't know her. She is a very nice, good woman."

Probably I frowned, for my wife looked grave and whispered rapidly:

"Of course it is queer her having come, but don't be cross, Nikolay, and don't be hard on her. She is unhappy, you know; Uncle Semyon Fyodoritch really is ill-natured and tyrannical, it is difficult to live with him. She says she will only stay three days with us, only till she gets a letter from her brother."

My wife whispered a great deal more nonsense to me about her despotic uncle; about the weakness of mankind in general and of young wives in particular; about its being our duty to give shelter to all, even great sinners, and so on. Unable to make head or tail of it, I put on my new coat and went to make acquaintance with my "aunt."

A little woman with large black eyes was sitting at the table. My table, the grey walls, my roughly-made sofa, everything to the tiniest grain of dust seemed to have grown younger and more cheerful in the presence of this new, young, beautiful, and dissolute creature, who had a most subtle perfume about her. And that our visitor was a lady of easy virtue I could see from her smile, from her scent, from the peculiar way in which she glanced and made play with her eyelashes, from the tone in which she talked with my wife—a respectable woman. There was no need to tell me she had run away from her husband, that her husband was old and despotic, that she was good-natured and lively; I took it all in at the first glance. Indeed, it is doubtful whether there is a man in all Europe who cannot spot at the first glance a woman of a certain temperament.

"I did not know I had such a big nephew!" said my aunt, holding out her hand to me and smiling.

"And I did not know I had such a pretty aunt," I answered.

Supper began over again. The cork flew with a bang out of the second bottle, and my aunt swallowed half a glassful at a gulp, and when my wife went out of the room for a moment my aunt did not scruple to drain a full glass. I was drunk both with the wine and with the presence of a woman. Do you remember the song?

> "Eyes black as pitch, eyes full of passion,
> Eyes burning bright and beautiful,
> How I love you,
> How I fear you!"

I don't remember what happened next. Anyone who wants to know how love begins may read novels and long stories; I will put it shortly and in the words of the same silly song:

> "It was an evil hour
> When first I met you."

Everything went head over heels to the devil. I remember a fearful, frantic whirlwind which sent me flying round like a feather. It lasted a long while, and swept from the face of the earth my wife and my aunt herself and my strength. From the little station in the steppe it has flung me, as you see, into this dark street.

Now tell me what further evil can happen to me?

1887

Enemies

Between nine and ten on a dark September evening the only son of the district doctor, Kirilov, a child of six, called Andrey, died of diphtheria. Just as the doctor's wife sank on her knees by the dead child's bedside and was overwhelmed by the first rush of despair there came a sharp ring at the bell in the entry.

All the servants had been sent out of the house that morning on account of the diphtheria. Kirilov went to open the door just as he was, without his coat on, with his waistcoat unbuttoned, without wiping his wet face or his hands which were scalded with carbolic. It was dark in the entry and nothing could be distinguished in the man who came in but medium height, a white scarf, and a large, extremely pale face, so pale that its entrance seemed to make the passage lighter.

"Is the doctor at home?" the newcomer asked quickly.

"I am at home," answered Kirilov. "What do you want?"

"Oh, it's you? I am very glad," said the stranger in a tone of relief, and he began feeling in the dark for the doctor's hand, found it and squeezed it tightly in his own. "I am very . . . very glad! We are acquainted. My name is Abogin, and I had the honour of meeting you in the summer at Gnutchev's. I am very glad I have found you at home. . . . For God's sake don't refuse to come back with me at once. . . . My wife has been taken dangerously ill. . . . And the carriage is waiting. . . ."

From the voice and gestures of the speaker it could be seen that he was in a state of great excitement. Like a man terrified by a house on fire or a mad dog, he could hardly restrain his rapid breathing and spoke quickly in a shaking voice, and there was a note of unaffected sincerity and childish alarm in his voice. As people always do who are frightened and overwhelmed, he spoke in brief, jerky sentences and uttered a great many unnecessary, irrelevant words.

"I was afraid I might not find you in," he went on. "I was in a perfect agony as I drove here. Put on your things and let us go, for God's sake. . . . This is how it happened. Alexandr Semyonovitch

Paptchinsky, whom you know, came to see me. . . . We talked a little and then we sat down to tea; suddenly my wife cried out, clutched at her heart, and fell back on her chair. We carried her to bed and . . . and I rubbed her forehead with ammonia and sprinkled her with water . . . she lay as though she were dead. . . . I am afraid it is aneurism. . . . Come along . . . her father died of aneurism."

Kirilov listened and said nothing, as though he did not understand Russian.

When Abogin mentioned again Paptchinsky and his wife's father and once more began feeling in the dark for his hand the doctor shook his head and said apathetically, dragging out each word:

"Excuse me, I cannot come . . . my son died . . . five minutes ago!"

"Is it possible!" whispered Abogin, stepping back a pace. "My God, at what an unlucky moment I have come! A wonderfully unhappy day . . . wonderfully. What a coincidence. . . . It's as though it were on purpose!"

Abogin took hold of the door-handle and bowed his head. He was evidently hesitating and did not know what to do—whether to go away or to continue entreating the doctor.

"Listen," he said fervently, catching hold of Kirilov's sleeve. "I well understand your position! God is my witness that I am ashamed of attempting at such a moment to intrude on your attention, but what am I to do? Only think, to whom can I go? There is no other doctor here, you know. For God's sake come! I am not asking you for myself. . . . I am not the patient!"

A silence followed. Kirilov turned his back on Abogin, stood still a moment, and slowly walked into the drawing-room. Judging from his unsteady, mechanical step, from the attention with which he set straight the fluffy shade on the unlighted lamp in the drawing-room and glanced into a thick book lying on the table, at that instant he had no intention, no desire, was thinking of nothing and most likely did not remember that there was a stranger in the entry. The twilight and stillness of the drawing-room seemed to increase his numbness. Going out of the drawing-room into his study he raised his right foot higher than was necessary, and felt for the doorposts with his hands, and as he did so there was an air of perplexity about his whole figure as though he were in somebody else's house, or were drunk for the first time in his life and were now abandoning himself with surprise to the new sensation. A broad streak of light stretched across the bookcase on one wall of the study; this light came together with the close, heavy smell of carbolic and ether from the door into the bedroom, which stood a little way open. . . . The doctor sank into a low chair in front of the table; for a minute he stared drowsily at his books, which lay with the light on them, then got up and went into the bedroom.

Here in the bedroom reigned a dead silence. Everything to the smallest detail was eloquent of the storm that had been passed through, of exhaustion, and everything was at rest. A candle standing among a crowd of bottles, boxes, and pots on a stool and a big lamp on the chest of drawers threw a brilliant light over all the room. On the bed under the window lay a boy with open eyes and a look of wonder on his face. He did not move, but his open eyes seemed every moment growing darker and sinking further into his head. The mother was kneeling by the bed with her arms on his body and her head hidden in the bedclothes. Like the child, she did not stir; but what throbbing life was suggested in the curves of her body and in her arms! She leaned against the bed with all her being, pressing against it greedily with all her might, as though she were afraid of disturbing the peaceful and comfortable attitude she had found at last for her exhausted body. The bedclothes, the rags and bowls, the splashes of water on the floor, the little paintbrushes and spoons thrown down here and there, the white bottle of lime water, the very air, heavy and stifling—were all hushed and seemed plunged in repose.

The doctor stopped close to his wife, thrust his hands in his trouser pockets, and slanting his head on one side fixed his eyes on his son. His face bore an expression of indifference, and only from the drops that glittered on his beard it could be seen that he had just been crying.

That repellent horror which is thought of when we speak of death was absent from the room. In the numbness of everything, in the mother's attitude, in the indifference on the doctor's face there was something that attracted and touched the heart, that subtle, almost elusive beauty of human sorrow which men will not for a long time learn to understand and describe, and which it seems only music can convey. There was a feeling of beauty, too, in the austere stillness. Kirilov and his wife were silent and not weeping, as though besides the bitterness of their loss they were conscious, too, of all the tragedy of their position; just as once their youth had passed away, so now together with this boy their right to have children had gone for ever to all eternity! The doctor was forty-four, his hair was grey and he looked like an old man; his faded and invalid wife was thirty-five. Andrey was not merely the only child, but also the last child.

In contrast to his wife the doctor belonged to the class of people who at times of spiritual suffering feel a craving for movement. After standing for five minutes by his wife, he walked, raising his right foot high, from the bedroom into a little room which was half filled up by a big sofa; from there he went into the kitchen. After wandering by the stove and the cook's bed he bent down and went by a little door into the passage.

There he saw again the white scarf and the white face.

"At last," sighed Abogin, reaching towards the door-handle. "Let us go, please."

The doctor started, glanced at him, and remembered. . . .

"Why, I have told you already that I can't go!" he said, growing more animated. "How strange!"

"Doctor, I am not a stone, I fully understand your position . . . I feel for you," Abogin said in an imploring voice, laying his hand on his scarf. "But I am not asking you for myself. My wife is dying. If you had heard that cry, if you had seen her face, you would understand my pertinacity. My God, I thought you had gone to get ready! Doctor, time is precious. Let us go, I entreat you."

"I cannot go," said Kirilov emphatically, and he took a step into the drawing-room.

Abogin followed him and caught hold of his sleeve.

"You are in sorrow, I understand. But I'm not asking you to a case of toothache, or to a consultation, but to save a human life!" he went on entreating like a beggar. "Life comes before any personal sorrow! Come, I ask for courage, for heroism! For the love of humanity!"

"Humanity—that cuts both ways," Kirilov said irritably. "In the name of humanity I beg you not to take me. And how queer it is, really! I can hardly stand and you talk to me about humanity! I am fit for nothing just now. . . . Nothing will induce me to go, and I can't leave my wife alone. No, no. . . ."

Kirilov waved his hands and staggered back.

"And . . . and don't ask me," he went on in a tone of alarm. "Excuse me. By No. XIII of the regulations I am obliged to go and you have the right to drag me by my collar . . . drag me if you like, but . . . I am not fit . . . I can't even speak . . . excuse me."

"There is no need to take that tone to me, doctor!" said Abogin, again taking the doctor by his sleeve. "What do I care about No. XIII! To force you against your will I have no right whatever. If you will, come; if you will not—God forgive you; but I am not appealing to your will, but to your feelings. A young woman is dying. You were just speaking of the death of your son. Who should understand my horror if not you?"

Abogin's voice quivered with emotion; that quiver and his tone were far more persuasive than his words. Abogin was sincere, but it was remarkable that whatever he said his words sounded stilted, soulless, and inappropriately flowery, and even seemed an outrage on the atmosphere of the doctor's home and on the woman who was somewhere dying. He felt this himself, and so, afraid of not being understood, did his utmost to put softness and tenderness into his voice so that the sincerity of his tone might prevail if his words did not. As a rule, however fine and deep a phrase may be, it only affects the indifferent, and cannot fully satisfy those who are happy or unhappy; that is why dumbness is most often the highest expression of happiness or unhappiness; lovers understand each other better when they are silent, and a fervent, passionate speech delivered by the grave only touches outsiders, while to the widow and children of the dead man it seems cold and trivial.

Kirilov stood in silence. When Abogin uttered a few more phrases concerning the noble calling of a doctor, self-sacrifice, and so on, the doctor asked sullenly: "Is it far?"

"Something like eight or nine miles. I have capital horses, doctor! I give you my word of honour that I will get you there and back in an hour. Only one hour."

These words had more effect on Kirilov than the appeals to humanity or the noble calling of the doctor. He thought a moment and said with a sigh: "Very well, let us go!"

He went rapidly with a more certain step to his study, and afterwards came back in a long frock-coat. Abogin, greatly relieved, fidgeted round him and scraped with his feet as he helped him on with his overcoat, and went out of the house with him.

It was dark out of doors, though lighter than in the entry. The tall, stooping figure of the doctor, with his long, narrow beard and aquiline nose, stood out distinctly in the darkness. Abogin's big head and the little student's cap that barely covered it could be seen now as well as his pale face. The scarf showed white only in front, behind it was hidden by his long hair.

"Believe me, I know how to appreciate your generosity," Abogin muttered as he helped the doctor into the carriage. "We shall get there quickly. Drive as fast as you can, Luka, there's a good fellow! Please!"

The coachman drove rapidly. At first there was a row of indistinct buildings that stretched alongside the hospital yard; it was dark everywhere except for a bright light from a window that gleamed through the fence into the furthest part of the yard while three windows of the upper storey of the hospital looked paler than the surrounding air. Then the carriage drove into dense shadow; here there was the smell of dampness and mushrooms, and the sound of rustling trees; the crows, awakened by the noise of the wheels, stirred among the foliage and uttered prolonged plaintive cries as though they knew the doctor's son was dead and that Abogin's wife was ill. Then came glimpses of separate trees, of bushes; a pond, on which great black shadows were slumbering, gleamed with a sullen light— and the carriage rolled over a smooth level ground. The clamour of the crows sounded dimly far away and soon ceased altogether.

Kirilov and Abogin were silent almost all the way. Only once Abogin heaved a deep sigh and muttered:

"It's an agonizing state! One never loves those who are near one so much as when one is in danger of losing them."

And when the carriage slowly drove over the river, Kirilov started all at once as though the splash of the water had frightened him, and made a movement.

"Listen—let me go," he said miserably. "I'll come to you later. I must just send my assistant to my wife. She is alone, you know!"

Abogin did not speak. The carriage swaying from side to side and crunching over the stones drove up the sandy bank and rolled on its way. Kirilov moved restlessly and looked about him in misery. Behind them in the dim light of the stars the road could be seen and the riverside willows vanishing into the darkness. On the right lay a plain as uniform and as boundless as the sky; here and there in the distance, probably on the peat marches, dim lights were glimmering. On the left, parallel with the road, ran a hill tufted with small bushes, and above the hill stood motionless a big, red half-moon, slightly veiled with mist and encircled by tiny clouds, which seemed to be looking round at it from all sides and watching that it did not go away.

In all nature there seemed to be a feeling of hopelessness and pain. The earth, like a ruined woman sitting alone in a dark room and trying not to think of the past, was brooding over memories of spring and summer and apathetically waiting for the inevitable winter. Wherever one looked, on all sides, nature seemed like a dark, infinitely deep, cold pit from which neither Kirilov nor Abogin nor the red half-moon could escape. . . .

The nearer the carriage got to its goal the more impatient Abogin became. He kept moving, leaping up, looking over the coachman's shoulder. And when at last the carriage stopped before the entrance, which was elegantly curtained with striped linen, and when he looked at the lighted windows of the second storey there was an audible catch in his breath.

"If anything happens . . . I shall not survive it," he said, going into the hall with the doctor, and rubbing his hands in agitation. "But there is no commotion, so everything must be going well so far," he added, listening in the stillness.

There was no sound in the hall of steps or voices and all the house seemed asleep in spite of the lighted windows. Now the doctor and Abogin, who till then had been in darkness, could see each other clearly. The doctor was tall and stooped, was untidily dressed and not good-looking. There was an unpleasantly harsh, morose, and unfriendly look about his lips, thick as a negro's, his aquiline nose, and listless, apathetic eyes. His unkempt head and sunken temples, the premature greyness of his long, narrow beard through which his chin was visible, the pale grey hue of his skin and his careless, uncouth manners—the harshness of all this was suggestive of years of poverty, of ill fortune, of weariness with life and with men. Looking at his frigid figure one could hardly believe that this man had a wife, that he was capable of weeping over his child. Abogin presented a very different appearance. He was a thick-set, sturdy-looking, fair man with a big head and large, soft features; he was elegantly dressed in the very latest fashion. In his carriage, his closely buttoned coat, his long hair, and his face there was a suggestion of something generous, leonine; he walked with his head erect and his chest squared, he spoke in an agreeable baritone, and there was a shade of refined almost feminine elegance in the manner in which he took off his scarf and smoothed his hair. Even his paleness and the childlike terror with which he looked up at the stairs as he took off his coat did not detract from his dignity nor diminish the air of sleekness, health, and aplomb which characterized his whole figure.

"There is nobody and no sound," he said going up the stairs. "There is no commotion. God grant all is well."

He led the doctor through the hall into a big drawing-room where there was a black piano and a chandelier in a white cover; from there they both went into a very snug, pretty little drawing-room full of an agreeable, rosy twilight.

"Well, sit down here, doctor, and I . . . will be back directly. I will go and have a look and prepare them."

Kirilov was left alone. The luxury of the drawing-room, the agreeably subdued light and his own presence in the stranger's unfamiliar house, which had something of the character of an adventure, did not apparently affect him. He sat in a low chair and scrutinized his hands, which were burnt with carbolic. He only caught a passing glimpse of the bright red lamp-shade and the violoncello case, and glancing in the direction where the clock was ticking he noticed a stuffed wolf as substantial and sleek-looking as Abogin himself.

It was quiet. . . . Somewhere far away in the adjoining rooms someone uttered a loud exclamation: "Ah!" There was a clang of a glass door, probably of a cupboard, and again all was still. After waiting five minutes Kirilov left off scrutinizing his hands and raised his eyes to the door by which Abogin had vanished.

In the doorway stood Abogin, but he was not the same as when he had gone out. The look of sleekness and refined elegance had disappeared—his face, his hands, his attitude were contorted by a revolting expression of something between horror and agonizing physical pain. His nose, his lips, his moustache, all his features were moving and seemed trying to tear themselves from his face, his eyes looked as though they were laughing with agony. . . .

Abogin took a heavy stride into the drawing-room, bent forward, moaned, and shook his fists.

"She has deceived me," he cried, with a strong emphasis on the second syllable of the verb. "Deceived me, gone away. She fell ill and sent me for the doctor only to run away with that clown Paptchinsky! My God!"

Abogin took a heavy step towards the doctor, held out his soft white fists in his face, and shaking them went on yelling:

"Gone away! Deceived me! But why this deception? My God! My God! What need of this dirty, scoundrelly trick, this diabolical, snakish farce? What have I done to her? Gone away!"

Tears gushed from his eyes. He turned on one foot and began pacing up and down the drawing-room. Now in his short coat, his fashionable narrow trousers which made his legs look disproportionately slim, with his big head and long mane he was extremely like a lion. A gleam of curiosity came into the apathetic face of the doctor. He got up and looked at Abogin.

"Excuse me, where is the patient?" he said.

"The patient! The patient!" cried Abogin, laughing, crying, and still brandishing his fists. "She is not ill, but accursed! The baseness! The vileness! The devil himself could not have imagined anything more loathsome! She sent me off that she might run away with a buffoon, a dull-witted clown, an Alphonse! Oh God, better she had died! I cannot bear it! I cannot bear it!"

The doctor drew himself up. His eyes blinked and filled with tears, his narrow beard began moving to right and to left together with his jaw.

"Allow me to ask what's the meaning of this?" he asked, looking round him with curiosity. "My child is dead, my wife is in grief alone in the whole house. . . . I myself can scarcely stand up, I have not slept for three nights. . . . And here I am forced to play a part in some vulgar farce, to play the part of a stage property! I don't . . . don't understand it!"

Abogin unclenched one fist, flung a crumpled note on the floor, and stamped on it as though it were an insect he wanted to crush.

"And I didn't see, didn't understand," he said through his clenched teeth, brandishing one fist before his face with an expression as though some one had trodden on his corns. "I did not notice that he came every day! I did not notice that he came today in a closed carriage! What did he come in a closed carriage for? And I did not see it! Noodle!"

"I don't understand . . ." muttered the doctor. "Why, what's the meaning of it? Why, it's an outrage on personal dignity, a mockery of human suffering! It's incredible. . . . It's the first time in my life I have had such an experience!"

With the dull surprise of a man who has only just realized that he has been bitterly insulted the doctor shrugged his shoulders, flung wide his arms, and not knowing what to do or to say sank helplessly into a chair.

"If you have ceased to love me and love another—so be it; but why this deceit, why this vulgar, treacherous trick?" Abogin said in a tearful voice. "What is the object of it? And what is there to justify it? And what have I done to you? Listen, doctor," he said hotly, going up to Kirilov. "You have been the involuntary witness of my misfortune and I am not going to conceal the truth from you. I swear that I loved the woman, loved her devotedly, like a slave! I have sacrificed everything for her; I have quarrelled with my own people, I have given up the service and music, I have forgiven her what I could not have forgiven my own mother or sister. . . . I have never looked askance at her. . . . I have never gainsaid her in anything. Why this deception? I do not demand love, but why this loathsome duplicity? If she did not love me, why did she not say so openly, honestly, especially as she knows my views on the subject? . . ."

With tears in his eyes, trembling all over, Abogin opened his heart to the doctor with perfect sincerity. He spoke warmly, pressing both hands on his heart, exposing the secrets of his private life without the faintest hesitation, and even seemed to be glad that at last these secrets were no longer pent up in his breast. If he had talked in this way for an hour or two, and opened his heart, he would undoubtedly have felt better. Who knows, if the doctor had listened to him and had sympathized with him like a friend, he might perhaps, as often happens, have reconciled himself to his trouble without protest, without doing anything needless and absurd. . . . But what happened was quite different. While Abogin was speaking the outraged doctor perceptibly changed. The indifference and wonder on his face gradually gave way to an expression of bitter resentment, indignation, and anger. The features of his face became even harsher, coarser, and more unpleasant. When Abogin held out before his eyes the photograph of a young woman with a handsome face as cold and expressionless as a nun's and asked him whether, looking at that face, one could conceive that it was capable of duplicity, the doctor suddenly flew out, and with flashing eyes said, rudely rapping out each word:

"What are you telling me all this for? I have no desire to hear it! I have no desire to!" he shouted and brought his fist down on the table. "I don't want your vulgar secrets! Damnation take them! Don't dare to tell me of such vulgar doings! Do you consider that I have not been insulted enough already? That I am a flunkey whom you can insult without restraint? Is that it?"

Abogin staggered back from Kirilov and stared at him in amazement.

"Why did you bring me here?" the doctor went on, his beard quivering. "If you are so puffed up with good living that you go and get married and then act a farce like this, how do I come in? What have I to do with your love affairs? Leave me in peace! Go on squeezing money out of the poor in your gentlemanly way. Make a display of humane ideas, play (the doctor looked sideways at the violoncello case) play the bassoon and the trombone, grow as fat as capons, but don't dare to insult personal dignity! If you cannot respect it, you might at least spare it your attention!"

"Excuse me, what does all this mean?" Abogin asked, flushing red.

"It means that it's base and low to play with people like this! I am a doctor; you look upon doctors and people generally who work and don't stink of perfume and prostitution as your menials and *mauvais ton*; well, you may look upon them so, but no one has given you the right to treat a man who is suffering as a stage property!"

"How dare you say that to me!" Abogin said quietly, and his face began working again, and this time unmistakably from anger.

"No, how dared you, knowing of my sorrow, bring me here to listen to these vulgarities!" shouted the doctor, and he again banged on the table with his fist. "Who has given you the right to make a mockery of another man's sorrow?"

"You have taken leave of your senses," shouted Abogin. "It is ungenerous. I am intensely unhappy myself and . . . and . . ."

"Unhappy!" said the doctor, with a smile of contempt. "Don't utter that word, it does not concern you. The spendthrift who cannot raise a loan calls himself unhappy, too. The capon, sluggish from over-feeding, is unhappy, too. Worthless people!"

"Sir, you forget yourself," shrieked Abogin. "For saying things like that . . . people are thrashed! Do you understand?"

Abogin hurriedly felt in his side pocket, pulled out a pocket-book, and extracting two notes flung them on the table.

"Here is the fee for your visit," he said, his nostrils dilating. "You are paid."

"How dare you offer me money?" shouted the doctor and he brushed the notes off the table on to the floor. "An insult cannot be paid for in money!"

Abogin and the doctor stood face to face, and in their wrath continued flinging undeserved insults at each other. I believe that never in their lives, even in delirium, had they uttered so much that was unjust, cruel, and absurd. The egoism of the unhappy was conspicuous in both. The unhappy are egoistic, spiteful, unjust, cruel, and less capable of understanding each other than fools. Unhappiness does not bring people together but draws them apart, and even where one would fancy people should be united by the similarity of their sorrow, far more injustice and cruelty is generated than in comparatively placid surroundings.

"Kindly let me go home!" shouted the doctor, breathing hard.

Abogin rang the bell sharply. When no one came to answer the bell he rang again and angrily flung the bell on the floor; it fell on the carpet with a muffled sound, and uttered a plaintive note as though at the point of death. A footman came in.

"Where have you been hiding yourself, the devil take you?" His master flew at him, clenching his fists. "Where were you just now? Go and tell them to bring the victoria round for this gentleman, and order the closed carriage to be got ready for me. Stay," he cried as the footman turned to go out. "I won't have a single traitor in the house by to-morrow! Away with you all! I will engage fresh servants! Reptiles!"

Abogin and the doctor remained in silence waiting for the carriage. The first regained his expression of sleekness and his refined elegance. He paced up and down the room, tossed his head elegantly, and was evidently meditating on something. His anger had not cooled, but he tried to appear not to notice his enemy. . . . The doctor stood, leaning with one hand on the edge of the table, and looked at Abogin with that profound and somewhat cynical, ugly contempt only to be found in the eyes of sorrow and indigence when they are confronted with well-nourished comfort and elegance.

When a little later the doctor got into the victoria and drove off there was still a look of contempt in his eyes. It was dark, much darker than it had been an hour before. The red half-moon had sunk behind the hill and the clouds that had been guarding it lay in dark patches near the stars. The carriage with red lamps rattled along the road and soon overtook the doctor. It was Abogin driving off to protest, to do absurd things. . . .

All the way home the doctor thought not of his wife, nor of his Andrey, but of Abogin and the people in the house he had just left. His thoughts were unjust and inhumanly cruel. He condemned Abogin and his wife and Paptchinsky and all who lived in rosy, sub-dued light among sweet perfumes, and all the way home he hated and despised them till his head ached. And a firm conviction concerning those people took shape in his mind.

Time will pass and Kirilov's sorrow will pass, but that conviction, unjust and unworthy of the human heart, will not pass, but will remain in the doctor's mind to the grave.

1887

The Kiss

At eight o'clock on the evening of the twentieth of May all the six
batteries of the N—— Reserve Artillery Brigade halted for the night
in the village of Myestetchki on their way to camp. When the general
commotion was at its height, while some officers were busily occu-
pied around the guns, while others, gathered together in the square
near the church enclosure, were listening to the quartermasters, a
man in civilian dress, riding a strange horse, came into sight round
the church. The little dun-coloured horse with a good neck and a
short tail came, moving not straight forward, but as it were sideways, with a sort of dance step, as though it were being lashed about
the legs. When he reached the officers the man on the horse took off
his hat and said:

"His Excellency Lieutenant-General von Rabbek invites the gentlemen to drink tea with him this minute. . . ."

The horse turned, danced, and retired sideways; the messenger
raised his hat once more, and in an instant disappeared with his
strange horse behind the church.

"What the devil does it mean?" grumbled some of the officers,
dispersing to their quarters. "One is sleepy, and here this Von Rabbek
with his tea! We know what tea means."

The officers of all the six batteries remembered vividly an incident
of the previous year, when during manœuvres they, together with the
officers of a Cossack regiment, were in the same way invited to tea
by a count who had an estate in the neighbourhood and was a retired
army officer: the hospitable and genial count made much of them, fed
them, and gave them drink, refused to let them go to their quarters in
the village and made them stay the night. All that, of course, was
very nice—nothing better could be desired, but the worst of it was,
the old army officer was so carried away by the pleasure of the young
men's company that till sunrise he was telling the officers anecdotes
of his glorious past, taking them over the house, showing them
expensive pictures, old engravings, rare guns, reading them

autograph letters from great people, while the weary and exhausted officers looked and listened, longing for their beds and yawning in their sleeves; when at last their host let them go, it was too late for sleep.

Might not this Von Rabbek be just such another? Whether he were or not, there was no help for it. The officers changed their uniforms, brushed themselves, and went all together in search of the gentleman's house. In the square by the church they were told they could get to His Excellency's by the lower path—going down behind the church to the river, going along the bank to the garden, and there an avenue would take them to the house; or by the upper way—straight from the church by the road which, half a mile from the village, led right up to His Excellency's granaries. The officers decided to go by the upper way.

"What Von Rabbek is it?" they wondered on the way. "Surely not the one who was in command of the N—— cavalry division at Plevna?"

"No, that was not Von Rabbek, but simply Rabbe and no 'von.' "

"What lovely weather!"

At the first of the granaries the road divided in two: one branch went straight on and vanished in the evening darkness, the other led to the owner's house on the right. The officers turned to the right and began to speak more softly. . . . On both sides of the road stretched stone granaries with red roofs, heavy and sullen-looking, very much like barracks of a district town. Ahead of them gleamed the windows of the manor-house.

"A good omen, gentlemen," said one of the officers. "Our setter is the foremost of all; no doubt he scents game ahead of us! . . ."

Lieutenant Lobytko, who was walking in front, a tall and stalwart fellow, though entirely without moustache (he was over five-and-twenty, yet for some reason there was no sign of hair on his round, well-fed face), renowned in the brigade for his peculiar faculty for divining the presence of women at a distance, turned round and said:

"Yes, there must be women here; I feel that by instinct."

On the threshold the officers were met by Von Rabbek himself, a comely-looking man of sixty in civilian dress. Shaking hands with his guests, he said that he was very glad and happy to see them, but begged them earnestly for God's sake to excuse him for not asking them to stay the night; two sisters with their children, some brothers, and some neighbours, had come on a visit to him, so that he had not one spare room left.

The General shook hands with every one, made his apologies, and smiled, but it was evident by his face that he was by no means so delighted as their last year's count, and that he had invited the officers simply because, in his opinion, it was a social obligation to do so. And the officers themselves, as they walked up the softly carpeted stairs, as they listened to him, felt that they had been invited to this house simply because it would have been awkward not to invite them; and at the sight of the footmen, who hastened to light the lamps in the entrance below and in the anteroom above, they began to feel as though they had brought uneasiness and discomfort into the house with them. In a house in which two sisters and their children, brothers, and neighbours were gathered together, probably on account of some family festivity, or event, how could the presence of nineteen unknown officers possibly be welcome?

At the entrance to the drawing-room the officers were met by a tall, graceful old lady with black eyebrows and a long face, very much like the Empress Eugénie. Smiling graciously and majestically, she said she was glad and happy to see her guests, and apologized that her husband and she were on this occasion unable to invite *messieurs les officiers* to stay the night. From her beautiful majestic smile, which instantly vanished from her face every time she turned away from her guests, it was evident that she had seen numbers of officers in her day, that she was in no humour for them now, and if she invited them to her house and apologized for not doing more, it was only because her breeding and position in society required it of her.

When the officers went into the big dining-room, there were about a dozen people, men and ladies, young and old, sitting at tea at the end of a long table. A group of men was dimly visible behind their chairs, wrapped in a haze of cigar smoke; and in the midst of them stood a lanky young man with red whiskers, talking loudly, with a lisp, in English. Through a door beyond the group could be seen a light room with pale blue furniture.

"Gentlemen, there are so many of you that it is impossible to introduce you all!" said the General in a loud voice, trying to sound very cheerful. "Make each other's acquaintance, gentlemen, without any ceremony!"

The officers—some with very serious and even stern faces, others with forced smiles, and all feeling extremely awkward—somehow made their bows and sat down to tea.

The most ill at ease of them all was Ryabovitch—a little officer in spectacles, with sloping shoulders, and whiskers like a lynx's. While some of his comrades assumed a serious expression, while others wore forced smiles, his face, his lynx-like whiskers, and spectacles seemed to say: "I am the shyest, most modest, and most undistinguished officer in the whole brigade!" At first, on going into the room and sitting down to the table, he could not fix his attention on any one face or object. The faces, the dresses, the cut-glass decanters of brandy, the steam from the glasses, the moulded cornices—all blended in one general impression that inspired in Ryabovitch alarm and a desire to hide his head. Like a lecturer making his first appearance before the public, he saw everything that was before his eyes, but apparently only had a dim understanding of it (among physiologists this condition, when the subject sees but does not understand, is called psychical blindness). After a little while, growing accustomed to his surroundings, Ryabovitch saw clearly and began to observe. As a shy man, unused to society, what struck him first was that in which he had always been deficient—namely, the extraordinary boldness of his new acquaintances. Von Rabbek, his wife, two elderly ladies, a young lady in a lilac dress, and the young man with the red whiskers, who was, it appeared, a younger son of Von Rabbek, very cleverly, as though they had rehearsed it beforehand, took seats between the officers, and at once got up a heated discussion in which the visitors could not help taking part. The lilac young lady hotly asserted that the artillery had a much better time than the cavalry and the infantry, while Von Rabbek and the elderly ladies maintained the opposite. A brisk interchange of talk followed. Ryabovitch watched the lilac young lady who argued so hotly about what was unfamiliar and utterly uninteresting to her, and watched artificial smiles come and go on her face.

Von Rabbek and his family skilfully drew the officers into the discussion, and meanwhile kept a sharp lookout over their glasses and mouths, to see whether all of them were drinking, whether all had enough sugar, why some one was not eating cakes or not drinking brandy. And the longer Ryabovitch watched and listened, the more he was attracted by this insincere but splendidly disciplined family.

After tea the officers went into the drawing-room. Lieutenant

Lobytko's instinct had not deceived him. There were a great number of girls and young married ladies. The "setter" lieutenant was soon standing by a very young, fair girl in a black dress, and, bending down to her jauntily, as though leaning on an unseen sword, smiled and shrugged his shoulders coquettishly. He probably talked very interesting nonsense, for the fair girl looked at his well-fed face condescendingly and asked indifferently, "Really?" And from that uninterested "Really?" the setter, had he been intelligent, might have concluded that she would never call him to heel.

The piano struck up; the melancholy strains of a valse floated out of the wide open windows, and every one, for some reason, remembered that it was spring, a May evening. Every one was conscious of the fragrance of roses, of lilac, and of the young leaves of the poplar. Ryabovitch, in whom the brandy he had drunk made itself felt, under the influence of the music stole a glance towards the window, smiled, and began watching the movements of the women, and it seemed to him that the smell of roses, of poplars, and lilac came not from the garden, but from the ladies' faces and dresses.

Von Rabbek's son invited a scraggy-looking young lady to dance, and waltzed round the room twice with her. Lobytko, gliding over the parquet floor, flew up to the lilac young lady and whirled her away. Dancing began. . . . Ryabovitch stood near the door among those who were not dancing and looked on. He had never once danced in his whole life, and he had never once in his life put his arm round the waist of a respectable woman. He was highly delighted that a man should in the sight of all take a girl he did not know round the waist and offer her his shoulder to put her hand on, but he could not imagine himself in the position of such a man. There were times when he envied the boldness and swagger of his companions and was inwardly wretched; the consciousness that he was timid, that he was round-shouldered and uninteresting, that he had a long waist and lynx-like whiskers, had deeply mortified him, but with years he had grown used to this feeling, and now, looking at his comrades dancing or loudly talking, he no longer envied them, but only felt touched and mournful.

When the quadrille began, young Von Rabbek came up to those who were not dancing and invited two officers to have a game of billiards. The officers accepted and went with him out of the drawing-room. Ryabovitch, having nothing to do and wishing to take part in the general movement, slouched after them. From the big drawing-room they went into the little drawing-room, then into a narrow corridor with a glass roof, and thence into a room in which on their entrance three sleepy-looking footmen jumped up quickly from the sofa. At last, after passing through a long succession of rooms, young Von Rabbek and the officers came into a small room where there was a billiard-table. They began to play.

Ryabovitch, who had never played any game but cards, stood near the billiard-table and looked indifferently at the players, while they in unbuttoned coats, with cues in their hands, stepped about, made puns, and kept shouting out unintelligible words.

The players took no notice of him, and only now and then one of them, shoving him with his elbow or accidentally touching him with the end of his cue, would turn round and say "Pardon!" Before the first game was over he was weary of it, and began to feel he was not wanted and in the way. . . . He felt disposed to return to the drawing-room, and he went out.

On his way back he met with a little adventure. When he had gone half-way he noticed he had taken a wrong turning. He distinctly remembered that he ought to meet three sleepy footmen on his way, but he had passed five or six rooms, and those sleepy figures seemed to have vanished into the earth. Noticing his mistake, he walked back a little way and turned to the right; he found himself in a little dark room which he had not seen on his way to the billiard-room. After standing there a little while, he resolutely opened the first door that met his eyes and walked into an absolutely dark room. Straight in front could be seen the crack in the doorway through which there was a gleam of vivid light; from the other side of the door came the muffled sound of a melancholy mazurka. Here, too, as in the drawing-room, the windows were wide open and there was a smell of poplars, lilac and roses. . . .

Ryabovitch stood still in hesitation. . . . At that moment, to his surprise, he heard hurried footsteps and the rustling of a dress, a breathless feminine voice whispered "At last!" And two soft, fragrant, unmistakably feminine arms were clasped about his neck; a warm cheek was pressed to his cheek, and simultaneously there was the sound of a kiss. But at once the bestower of the kiss uttered a faint shriek and skipped back from him, as it seemed to Ryabovitch, with aversion. He, too, almost shrieked and rushed towards the gleam of light at the door. . . .

When he went back into the drawing-room his heart was beating and his hands were trembling so noticeably that he made haste to hide them behind his back. At first he was tormented by shame and dread that the whole drawing-room knew that he had just been kissed and embraced by a woman. He shrank into himself and looked uneasily about him, but as he became convinced that people were dancing and talking as calmly as ever, he gave himself up entirely to the new sensation which he had never experienced before in his life. Something strange was happening to him. . . . His neck, round which soft, fragrant arms had so lately been clasped, seemed to him to be anointed with oil; on his left cheek near his moustache where the unknown had kissed him there was a faint chilly tingling sensation as from peppermint drops, and the more he rubbed the place the more distinct was the chilly sensation; all over, from head to foot, he was full of a strange new feeling which grew stronger and stronger. . . . He wanted to dance, to talk, to run into the garden, to laugh aloud. . . . He quite forgot that he was round-shouldered and uninteresting, that he had lynx-like whiskers and an "undistinguished appearance" (that was how his appearance had been described by some ladies whose conversation he had accidentally overheard). When Von Rabbek's wife happened to pass by him, he gave her such a broad and friendly smile that she stood still and looked at him inquiringly.

"I like your house immensely!" he said, setting his spectacles straight.

The General's wife smiled and said that the house had belonged to her father; then she asked whether his parents were living, whether he had long been in the army, why he was so thin, and so on. . . . After receiving answers to her questions, she went on, and after his conversation with her his smiles were more friendly than ever, and he thought he was surrounded by splendid people. . . .

At supper Ryabovitch ate mechanically everything offered him, drank, and without listening to anything, tried to understand what had just happened to him. . . . The adventure was of a mysterious and romantic character, but it was not difficult to explain it. No doubt some girl or young married lady had arranged a tryst with some one in the dark room; had waited a long time, and being nervous and excited had taken Ryabovitch for her hero; this was the more probable as Ryabovitch had stood still hesitating in the dark room, so that he, too, had seemed like a person expecting something. . . . This was how Ryabovitch explained to himself the kiss he had received.

"And who is she?" he wondered, looking round at the women's faces. "She must be young, for elderly ladies don't give rendezvous. That she was a lady, one could tell by the rustle of her dress, her perfume, her voice. . . ."

His eyes rested on the lilac young lady, and he thought her very attractive; she had beautiful shoulders and arms, a clever face, and a delightful voice. Ryabovitch, looking at her, hoped that she and no one else was his unknown. . . . But she laughed somehow artificially and wrinkled up her long nose, which seemed to him to make her look old. Then he turned his eyes upon the fair girl in a black dress. She was younger, simpler, and more genuine, had a charming brow, and drank very daintily out of her wineglass. Ryabovitch now hoped that it was she. But soon he began to think her face flat, and fixed his eyes upon the one next her.

"It's difficult to guess," he thought, musing. "If one takes the shoulders and arms of the lilac one only, adds the brow of the fair one and the eyes of the one on the left of Lobytko, then . . ."

He made a combination of these things in his mind and so formed the image of the girl who had kissed him, the image that he wanted her to have, but could not find at the table. . . .

After supper, replete and exhilarated, the officers began to take leave and say thank you. Von Rabbek and his wife began again apologizing that they could not ask them to stay the night.

"Very, very glad to have met you, gentlemen," said Von Rabbek, and this time sincerely (probably because people are far more sincere and good-humoured at speeding their parting guests than on meeting them). "Delighted. I hope you will come on your way back! Don't stand on ceremony! Where are you going? Do you want to go by the upper way? No, go across the garden; it's nearer here by the lower way."

The officers went out into the garden. After the bright light and the noise the garden seemed very dark and quiet. They walked in silence all the way to the gate. They were a little drunk, pleased, and in good spirits, but the darkness and silence made them thoughtful for a minute. Probably the same idea occurred to each one of them as to Ryabovitch: would there ever come a time for them when, like Von Rabbek, they would have a large house, a family, a garden—when they, too, would be able to welcome people, even though insincerely, feed them, make them drunk and contented?

Going out of the garden gate, they all began talking at once and laughing loudly about nothing. They were walking now along the little path that led down to the river, and then ran along the water's edge, winding round the bushes on the bank, the pools, and the willows that overhung the water. The bank and the path were scarcely visible, and the other bank was entirely plunged in darkness. Stars were reflected here and there on the dark water; they quivered and were broken up on the surface—and from that alone it could be seen that the river was flowing rapidly. It was still. Drowsy curlews cried plaintively on the further bank, and in one of the bushes on the nearest side a nightingale was trilling loudly, taking no notice of the crowd of officers. The officers stood round the bush, touched it, but the nightingale went on singing.

"What a fellow!" they exclaimed approvingly. "We stand beside him and he takes not a bit of notice! What a rascal!"

At the end of the way the path went uphill, and, skirting the church enclosure, turned into the road. Here the officers, tired with walking uphill, sat down and lighted their cigarettes. On the other side of the river a murky red fire came into sight, and having nothing better to do, they spent a long time in discussing whether it was a camp fire or a light in a window, or something else. . . . Ryabovitch, too, looked at the light, and he fancied that the light looked and winked at him, as though it knew about the kiss.

On reaching his quarters, Ryabovitch undressed as quickly as possible and got into bed. Lobytko and Lieutenant Merzlyakov—a peaceable, silent fellow, who was considered in his own circle a highly educated officer, and was always, whenever it was possible, reading the "Vyestnik Evropi," which he carried about with him everywhere—were quartered in the same hut with Ryabovitch. Lobytko undressed, walked up and down the room for a long while with the air of a man who has not been satisfied, and sent his orderly for beer. Merzlyakov got into bed, put a candle by his pillow and plunged into reading the "Vyestnik Evropi."

"Who was she?" Ryabovitch wondered, looking at the smoky ceiling.

His neck still felt as though he had been anointed with oil, and there was still the chilly sensation near his mouth as though from peppermint drops. The shoulders and arms of the young lady in lilac, the brow and the truthful eyes of the fair girl in black, waists, dresses, and brooches, floated through his imagination. He tried to fix his attention on these images, but they danced about, broke up and flickered. When these images vanished altogether from the broad dark background which every man sees when he closes his eyes, he began to hear hurried footsteps, the rustle of skirts, the sound of a kiss and—an intense groundless joy took possession of him. . . . Abandoning himself to this joy, he heard the orderly return and announce that there was no beer. Lobytko was terribly indignant, and began pacing up and down again.

"Well, isn't he an idiot?" he kept saying, stopping first before Ryabovitch and then before Merzlyakov. "What a fool and a dummy a man must be not to get hold of any beer! Eh? Isn't he a scoundrel?"

"Of course you can't get beer here," said Merzlyakov, not removing his eyes from the "Vyestnik Evropi."

"Oh! Is that your opinion?" Lobytko persisted. "Lord have mercy upon us, if you dropped me on the moon I'd find you beer and women directly! I'll go and find some at once. . . . You may call me an impostor if I don't!"

He spent a long time in dressing and pulling on his high boots, then finished smoking his cigarette in silence and went out.

"Rabbek, Grabbek, Labbek," he muttered, stopping in the outer room. "I don't care to go alone, damn it all! Ryabovitch, wouldn't you like to go for a walk? Eh?"

Receiving no answer, he returned, slowly undressed and got into bed. Merzlyakov sighed, put the "Vyestnik Evropi" away, and put out the light.

"H'm! . . ." muttered Lobytko, lighting a cigarette in the dark.

Ryabovitch pulled the bed-clothes over his head, curled himself up in bed, and tried to gather together the floating images in his mind and to combine them into one whole. But nothing came of it. He soon fell asleep, and his last thought was that some one had caressed him and made him happy—that something extraordinary, foolish, but joyful and delightful, had come into his life. The thought did not leave him even in his sleep.

When he woke up the sensations of oil on his neck and the chill of peppermint about his lips had gone, but joy flooded his heart just as the day before. He looked enthusiastically at the window-frames, gilded by the light of the rising sun, and listened to the movement of the passers-by in the street. People were talking loudly close to the window. Lebedetsky, the commander of Ryabovitch's battery, who had only just overtaken the brigade, was talking to his sergeant at the top of his voice, being always accustomed to shout.

"What else?" shouted the commander.

"When they were shoeing yesterday, your high nobility, they drove a nail into Pigeon's hoof. The vet. put on clay and vinegar; they are leading him apart now. And also, your honour, Artemyev got drunk yesterday, and the lieutenant ordered him to be put in the limber of a spare gun-carriage."

The sergeant reported that Karpov had forgotten the new cords for the trumpets and the rings for the tents, and that their honours, the officers, had spent the previous evening visiting General Von Rabbek. In the middle of this conversation the red-bearded face of Lebedetsky appeared in the window. He screwed up his short-sighted eyes, looking at the sleepy faces of the officers, and said good-morning to them.

"Is everything all right?" he asked.

"One of the horses has a sore neck from the new collar," answered Lobytko, yawning.

The commander sighed, thought a moment, and said in a loud voice:

"I am thinking of going to see Alexandra Yevgrafovna. I must call on her. Well, good-bye. I shall catch you up in the evening."

A quarter of an hour later the brigade set off on its way. When it was moving along the road by the granaries, Ryabovitch looked at the house on the right. The blinds were down in all the windows. Evidently the household was still asleep. The one who had kissed Ryabovitch the day before was asleep, too. He tried to imagine her asleep. The wide-open windows of the bedroom, the green branches peeping in, the morning freshness, the scent of the poplars, lilac, and roses, the bed, a chair, and on it the skirts that had rustled the day before, the little slippers, the little watch on the table—all this he pictured to himself clearly and distinctly, but the features of the face, the sweet sleepy smile, just what was characteristic and important, slipped through his imagination like quicksilver through the fingers. When he had ridden on half a mile, he looked back: the yellow church, the house, and the river, were all bathed in light; the river with its bright green banks, with the blue sky reflected in it and glints of silver in the sunshine here and there, was very beautiful. Ryabovitch gazed for the last time at Myestetchki, and he felt as sad as though he were parting with something very near and dear to him.

And before him on the road lay nothing but long familiar, uninteresting pictures. . . . To right and to left, fields of young rye and buckwheat with rooks hopping about in them. If one looked ahead, one saw dust and the backs of men's heads; if one looked back, one saw the same dust and faces. . . . Foremost of all marched four men with sabres—this was the vanguard. Next, behind, the crowd of singers, and behind them the trumpeters on horseback. The vanguard and the chorus of singers, like torch-bearers in a funeral procession, often forgot to keep the regulation distance and pushed a long way ahead. . . . Ryabovitch was with the first cannon of the fifth battery. He could see all the four batteries moving in front of him. For any one not a military man this long tedious procession of a moving brigade seems an intricate and unintelligible muddle; one cannot understand why there are so many people round one cannon, and why it is drawn by so many horses in such a strange network of harness, as though it really were so terrible and heavy. To Ryabovitch it was all perfectly comprehensible and therefore uninteresting. He had known for ever so long why at the head of each battery there rode a stalwart bombardier, and why he was called a bombardier; immediately behind this bombardier could be seen the horsemen of the first and then of the middle units. Ryabovitch knew that the horses on which they rode, those on the left, were called one name, while those on the right were called another—it was extremely uninteresting. Behind the horsemen came two shaft-horses. On one of them sat a rider with the dust of yesterday on his back and a clumsy and funny-looking piece of wood on his leg. Ryabovitch knew the object of this piece of wood, and did not think it funny. All the riders waved their whips mechanically and shouted from time to time. The cannon itself was ugly. On the fore part lay sacks of oats covered with canvas, and the cannon itself was hung all over with kettles, soldiers' knapsacks, bags, and looked like some small harmless animal surrounded for some unknown reason by men and horses. To the leeward of it marched six men, the gunners, swinging their arms. After the cannon there came again more bombardiers, riders, shaft-horses, and behind them another cannon, as ugly and unimpressive as the first. After the second followed a third, a fourth; near the fourth an officer, and so on. There were six batteries in all in the brigade, and four cannons in each battery. The procession covered half a mile; it ended in a string of wagons near which an extremely attractive creature—the ass, Magar, brought by a battery commander from Turkey—paced pensively with his long-eared head drooping.

Ryabovitch looked indifferently before and behind, at the backs of heads and at faces; at any other time he would have been half asleep, but now he was entirely absorbed in his new agreeable thoughts. At first when the brigade was setting off on the march he tried to persuade himself that the incident of the kiss could only be interesting as a mysterious little adventure, that it was in reality trivial, and to think of it seriously, to say the least of it, was stupid; but now he bade farewell to logic and gave himself up to dreams. . . . At one moment he imagined himself in Von Rabbek's drawing-room beside a girl who was like the young lady in lilac and the fair girl in black; then he would close his eyes and see himself with another, entirely unknown girl, whose features were very vague. In his imagination he talked, caressed her, leaned on her shoulder, pictured war, separation, then meeting again, supper with his wife, children. . . .

"Brakes on!" the word of command rang out every time they went downhill.

He, too, shouted "Brakes on!" and was afraid this shout would disturb his reverie and bring him back to reality. . . .

As they passed by some landowner's estate Ryabovitch looked over the fence into the garden. A long avenue, straight as a ruler, strewn with yellow sand and bordered with young birch-trees, met his eyes. . . . With the eagerness of a man given up to dreaming, he pictured to himself little feminine feet tripping along yellow sand, and quite unexpectedly had a clear vision in his imagination of the girl who had kissed him and whom he had succeeded in picturing to himself the evening before at supper. This image remained in his brain and did not desert him again.

At midday there was a shout in the rear near the string of wagons: "Easy! Eyes to the left! Officers!"

The general of the brigade drove by in a carriage with a pair of white horses. He stopped near the second battery, and shouted something which no one understood. Several officers, among them Ryabovitch, galloped up to them.

"Well?" asked the general, blinking his red eyes. "Are there any sick?"

Receiving an answer, the general, a little skinny man, chewed, thought for a moment and said, addressing one of the officers:

"One of your drivers of the third cannon has taken off his leg-guard and hung it on the fore part of the cannon, the rascal. Reprimand him."

He raised his eyes to Ryabovitch and went on:

"It seems to me your front strap is too long."

Making a few other tedious remarks, the general looked at Lobytko and grinned.

"You look very melancholy today, Lieutenant Lobytko," he said. "Are you pining for Madame Lopuhov? Eh? Gentlemen, he is pining for Madame Lopuhov."

The lady in question was a very stout and tall person who had long passed her fortieth year. The general, who had a predilection for solid ladies, whatever their ages, suspected a similar taste in his officers. The officers smiled respectfully. The general, delighted at having said something very amusing and biting, laughed loudly, touched his coachman's back, and saluted. The carriage rolled on. . . .

"All I am dreaming about now which seems to me so impossible and unearthly is really quite an ordinary thing," thought Ryabovitch, looking at the clouds of dust racing after the general's carriage. "It's all very ordinary, and every one goes through it. . . . That general, for instance, has once been in love; now he is married and has children. Captain Vahter, too, is married and beloved, though the nape of his neck is very red and ugly and he has no waist. . . . Salmanov is coarse and very Tatar, but he has had a love affair that has ended in marriage. . . . I am the same as every one else, and I, too, shall have the same experience as every one else, sooner or later. . . ."

And the thought that he was an ordinary person, and that his life was ordinary, delighted him and gave him courage. He pictured *her* and his happiness as he pleased, and put no rein on his imagination. . . .

When the brigade reached their halting-place in the evening, and the officers were resting in their tents, Ryabovitch, Merzlyakov, and Lobytko were sitting round a box having supper. Merzlyakov ate without haste, and, as he munched deliberately, read the "Vyestnik Evropi," which he held on his knees. Lobytko talked incessantly and kept filling up his glass with beer, and Ryabovitch, whose head was confused from dreaming all day long, drank and said nothing. After three glasses he got a little drunk, felt weak, and had an irresistible desire to impart his new sensations to his comrades.

"A strange thing happened to me at those Von Rabbeks'," he began, trying to put an indifferent and ironical tone into his voice. "You know I went into the billiard-room. . . ."

He began describing very minutely the incident of the kiss, and a moment later relapsed into silence. . . . In the course of that moment he had told everything, and it surprised him dreadfully to find how short a time it took him to tell it. He had imagined that he could have been telling the story of the kiss till next morning. Listening to him, Lobytko, who was a great liar and consequently believed no one, looked at him sceptically and laughed. Merzlyakov twitched his eyebrows and, without removing his eyes from the "Vyestnik Evropi," said:

"That's an odd thing! How strange! . . . throws herself on a man's neck, without addressing him by name. . . . She must be some sort of hysterical neurotic."

"Yes, she must," Ryabovitch agreed.

"A similar thing once happened to me," said Lobytko, assuming a scared expression. "I was going last year to Kovno. . . . I took a second-class ticket. The train was crammed, and it was impossible to sleep. I gave the guard half a rouble; he took my luggage and led me to another compartment. . . . I lay down and covered myself with a rug. . . . It was dark, you understand. Suddenly I felt some one touch me on the shoulder and breathe in my face. I made a movement with my hand and felt somebody's elbow. . . . I opened my eyes and only imagine—a woman. Black eyes, lips red as a prime salmon, nostrils breathing passionately—a bosom like a buffer. . . ."

"Excuse me," Merzlyakov interrupted calmly, "I understand about the bosom, but how could you see the lips if it was dark?"

Lobytko began trying to put himself right and laughing at Merzlyakov's unimaginativeness. It made Ryabovitch wince. He walked away from the box, got into bed, and vowed never to confide again.

Camp life began. . . . The days flowed by, one very much like another. All those days Ryabovitch felt, thought, and behaved as though he were in love. Every morning when his orderly handed him water to wash with, and he sluiced his head with cold water, he thought there was something warm and delightful in his life.

In the evenings when his comrades began talking of love and women, he would listen, and draw up closer; and he wore the expression of a soldier when he hears the description of a battle in which he has taken part. And on the evenings when the officers, out on the spree with the setter—Lobytko—at their head, made Don Juan excursions to the "suburb," and Ryabovitch took part in such excursions, he always was sad, felt profoundly guilty, and inwardly begged *her* forgiveness. . . . In hours of leisure or on sleepless nights, when he felt moved to recall his childhood, his father and mother—everything near and dear, in fact, he invariably thought of Myestetchki, the strange horse, Von Rabbek, his wife who was like the Empress Eugénie, the dark room, the crack of light at the door. . . .

On the thirty-first of August he went back from the camp, not with the whole brigade, but with only two batteries of it. He was dreaming and excited all the way, as though he were going back to his native place. He had an intense longing to see again the strange horse, the church, the insincere family of the Von Rabbeks, the dark room. The "inner voice," which so often deceives lovers, whispered to him for some reason that he would be sure to see her . . . and he was tortured by the questions, How he should meet her? What he would talk to her about? Whether she had forgotten the kiss? If the worst came to the worst, he thought, even if he did not meet her, it would be a pleasure to him merely to go through the dark room and recall the past.

Towards evening there appeared on the horizon the familiar church and white granaries. Ryabovitch's heart beat. . . . He did not hear the officer who was riding beside him and saying something to him, he forgot everything, and looked eagerly at the river shining in the distance, at the roof of the house, at the dovecote round which the pigeons were circling in the light of the setting sun.

When they reached the church and were listening to the billeting orders, he expected every second that a man on horseback would come round the church enclosure and invite the officers to tea, but . . . the billeting orders were read, the officers were in haste to go on to the village, and the man on horseback did not appear.

"Von Rabbek will hear at once from the peasants that we have come and will send for us," thought Ryabovitch, as he went into the hut, unable to understand why a comrade was lighting a candle and why the orderlies were hurriedly setting samovars. . . .

A painful uneasiness took possession of him. He lay down, then got up and looked out of the window to see whether the messenger were coming. But there was no sign of him.

He lay down again, but half an hour later he got up, and, unable to restrain his uneasiness, went into the street and strode towards the church. It was dark and deserted in the square near the church. . . . Three soldiers were standing silent in a row where the road began to go downhill. Seeing Ryabovitch, they roused themselves and saluted. He returned the salute and began to go down the familiar path.

On the further side of the river the whole sky was flooded with crimson: the moon was rising; two peasant women, talking loudly, were picking cabbage in the kitchen garden; behind the kitchen garden there were some dark huts. . . . And everything on the near side of the river was just as it had been in May: the path, the bushes, the willows overhanging the water . . . but there was no sound of the brave nightingale, and no scent of poplar and fresh grass.

Reaching the garden, Ryabovitch looked in at the gate. The garden was dark and still. . . . He could see nothing but the white stems of the nearest birch-trees and a little bit of the avenue; all the rest melted together into a dark blur. Ryabovitch looked and listened eagerly, but after waiting for a quarter of an hour without hearing a sound or catching a glimpse of a light, he trudged back. . . .

He went down to the river. The General's bath-house and the bath-sheets on the rail of the little bridge showed white before him. . . . He went on to the bridge, stood a little, and, quite unnecessarily, touched the sheets. They felt rough and cold. He looked down at the water. . . . The river ran rapidly and with a faintly audible gurgle round the piles of the bath-house. The red moon was reflected near the left bank; little ripples ran over the reflection, stretching it out, breaking it into bits, and seemed trying to carry it away. . . .

"How stupid, how stupid!" thought Ryabovitch, looking at the running water. "How unintelligent it all is!"

Now that he expected nothing, the incident of the kiss, his impatience, his vague hopes and disappointment, presented themselves in a clear light. It no longer seemed to him strange that he had not seen the General's messenger, and that he would never see the girl who had accidentally kissed him instead of some one else; on the contrary, it would have been strange if he had seen her. . . .

The water was running, he knew not where or why, just as it did in May. In May it had flowed into the great river, from the great river into the sea; then it had risen in vapour, turned into rain, and perhaps the very same water was running now before Ryabovitch's eyes again. . . . What for? Why?

And the whole world, the whole of life, seemed to Ryabovitch an unintelligible, aimless jest. . . . And turning his eyes from the water and looking at the sky, he remembered again how fate in the person of an unknown woman had by chance caressed him, he remembered his summer dreams and fancies, and his life struck him as extraordinarily meagre, poverty-stricken, and colourless. . . .

When he went back to his hut he did not find one of his comrades. The orderly informed him that they had all gone to "General von Rabbek's, who had sent a messenger on horseback to invite them. . . ."

For an instant there was a flash of joy in Ryabovitch's heart, but he quenched it at once, got into bed, and in his wrath with his fate, as though to spite it, did not go to the General's.

1887

Kashtanka

(*A Story*)

I

MISBEHAVIOUR

A young dog, a reddish mongrel, between a dachshund and a "yard-dog," very like a fox in face, was running up and down the pavement looking uneasily from side to side. From time to time she stopped and, whining and lifting first one chilled paw and then another, tried to make up her mind how it could have happened that she was lost.

She remembered very well how she had passed the day, and how, in the end, she had found herself on this unfamiliar pavement.

The day had begun by her master Luka Alexandritch's putting on his hat, taking something wooden under his arm wrapped up in a red handkerchief, and calling: "Kashtanka, come along!"

Hearing her name the mongrel had come out from under the work-table, where she slept on the shavings, stretched herself voluptuously and run after her master. The people Luka Alexandritch worked for lived a very long way off, so that, before he could get to any one of them, the carpenter had several times to step into a tavern to fortify himself. Kashtanka remembered that on the way she had behaved extremely improperly. In her delight that she was being taken for a walk she jumped about, dashed barking after the trams, ran into yards, and chased other dogs. The carpenter was continually losing sight of her, stopping, and angrily shouting at her. Once he had even, with an expression of fury in his face, taken her fox-like ear in his fist, smacked her, and said emphatically: "Pla-a-ague take you, you pest!"

After having left the work where it had been bespoken, Luka Alexandritch went into his sister's and there had something to eat and drink; from his sister's he had gone to see a bookbinder he knew;

from the bookbinder's to a tavern, from the tavern to another crony's, and so on. In short, by the time Kashtanka found herself on the unfamiliar pavement, it was getting dusk, and the carpenter was as drunk as a cobbler. He was waving his arms and, breathing heavily, muttered:

"In sin my mother bore me! Ah, sins, sins! Here now we are walking along the street and looking at the street lamps, but when we die, we shall burn in a fiery Gehenna. . . ."

Or he fell into a good-natured tone, called Kashtanka to him, and said to her: "You, Kashtanka, are an insect of a creature, and nothing else. Beside a man, you are much the same as a joiner beside a cabinet-maker. . . ."

While he talked to her in that way, there was suddenly a burst of music. Kashtanka looked round and saw that a regiment of soldiers was coming straight towards her. Unable to endure the music, which unhinged her nerves, she turned round and round and wailed. To her great surprise, the carpenter, instead of being frightened, whining and barking, gave a broad grin, drew himself up to attention, and saluted with all his five fingers. Seeing that her master did not protest, Kashtanka whined louder than ever, and dashed across the road to the opposite pavement.

When she recovered herself, the band was not playing and the regiment was no longer there. She ran across the road to the spot where she had left her master, but alas, the carpenter was no longer there. She dashed forward, then back again and ran across the road once more, but the carpenter seemed to have vanished into the earth. Kashtanka began sniffing the pavement, hoping to find her master by the scent of his tracks, but some wretch had been that way just before in new rubber goloshes, and now all delicate scents were mixed with an acute stench of india-rubber, so that it was impossible to make out anything.

Kashtanka ran up and down and did not find her master, and meanwhile it had got dark. The street lamps were lighted on both sides of the road, and lights appeared in the windows. Big, fluffy snow-flakes were falling and painting white the pavement, the horses' backs and the cabmen's caps, and the darker the evening grew the whiter were all these objects. Unknown customers kept walking incessantly to and fro, obstructing her field of vision and shoving against her with their feet. (All mankind Kashtanka divided into two uneven parts: masters and customers; between them there was an essential difference: the first had the right to beat her, and the second she had the right to nip by the calves of their legs.) These customers were hurrying off somewhere and paid no attention to her.

When it got quite dark, Kashtanka was overcome by despair and horror. She huddled up in an entrance and began whining piteously. The long day's journeying with Luka Alexandritch had exhausted her, her ears and her paws were freezing, and, what was more, she was terribly hungry. Only twice in the whole day had she tasted a morsel: she had eaten a little paste at the bookbinder's, and in one of the taverns she had found a sausage skin on the floor, near the counter—that was all. If she had been a human being she would have certainly thought: "No, it is impossible to live like this! I must shoot myself!"

II

A MYSTERIOUS STRANGER

But she thought of nothing, she simply whined. When her head and back were entirely plastered over with the soft feathery snow, and she had sunk into a painful doze of exhaustion, all at once the door of the entrance clicked, creaked, and struck her on the side. She jumped up. A man belonging to the class of customers came out. As Kashtanka whined and got under his feet, he could not help noticing her. He bent down to her and asked:

"Doggy, where do you come from? Have I hurt you? O, poor thing, poor thing. . . . Come, don't be cross. . . . I am sorry."

Kashtanka looked at the stranger through the snow-flakes that hung on her eyelashes, and saw before her a short, fat little man, with a plump, shaven face wearing a top hat and a fur coat that swung open.

"What are you whining for?" he went on, knocking the snow off her back with his fingers. "Where is your master? I suppose you are lost? Ah, poor doggy! What are we going to do now?"

Catching in the stranger's voice a warm, cordial note, Kashtanka licked his hand, and whined still more pitifully.

"Oh, you nice funny thing!" said the stranger. "A regular fox! Well, there's nothing for it, you must come along with me! Perhaps you will be of use for something. . . . Well!"

He clicked with his lips, and made a sign to Kashtanka with his hand, which could only mean one thing: "Come along!" Kashtanka went.

Not more than half an hour later she was sitting on the floor in a big, light room, and, leaning her head against her side, was looking with tenderness and curiosity at the stranger who was sitting at the table, dining. He ate and threw pieces to her. . . . At first he gave her bread and the green rind of cheese, then a piece of meat, half a pie and chicken bones, while through hunger she ate so quickly that she had not time to distinguish the taste, and the more she ate the more acute was the feeling of hunger.

"Your masters don't feed you properly," said the stranger, seeing with what ferocious greediness she swallowed the morsels without munching them. "And how thin you are! Nothing but skin and bones. . . ."

Kashtanka ate a great deal and yet did not satisfy her hunger, but she was simply stupefied with eating. After dinner she lay down in the middle of the room, stretched her legs and, conscious of an agreeable weariness all over her body, wagged her tail. While her new master, lounging in an easy-chair, smoked a cigar, she wagged her tail and considered the question, whether it was better at the stranger's or at the carpenter's. The stranger's surroundings were poor and ugly; besides the easy-chairs, the sofa, the lamps and the rugs, there was nothing, and the room seemed empty. At the carpenter's the whole place was stuffed full of things: he had a table, a bench, a heap of shavings, planes, chisels, saws, a cage with a goldfinch, a basin. . . . The stranger's room smelt of nothing, while there was always a thick fog in the carpenter's room, and a glorious smell of glue, varnish, and shavings. On the other hand, the stranger had one great superiority—he gave her a great deal to eat and, to do him full justice, when Kashtanka sat facing the table and looking wistfully at him, he did not once hit or kick her, and did not once shout: "Go away, damned brute!"

When he had finished his cigar her new master went out, and a minute later came back holding a little mattress in his hands.

"Hey, you dog, come here!" he said, laying the mattress in the corner near the dog. "Lie down here, go to sleep!"

Then he put out the lamp and went away. Kashtanka lay down on the mattress and shut her eyes; the sound of a bark rose from the street, and she would have liked to answer it, but all at once she was overcome with unexpected melancholy. She thought of Luka Alexandritch, of his son Fedyushka, and her snug little place under the bench. . . . She remembered on the long winter evenings, when the carpenter was planing or reading the paper aloud, Fedyushka usually played with her. . . . He used to pull her from under the bench by her hind legs, and play such tricks with her, that she saw green before her eyes, and ached in every joint. He would make her walk on her hind legs, use her as a bell, that is, shake her violently by the tail so that she squealed and barked, and give her tobacco to sniff. . . . The following trick was particularly agonising: Fedyushka would tie a piece of meat to a thread and give it to Kashtanka, and then, when she had swallowed it he would, with a loud laugh, pull it back again from her stomach, and the more lurid were her memories the more loudly and miserably Kashtanka whined.

But soon exhaustion and warmth prevailed over melancholy. She began to fall asleep. Dogs ran by in her imagination: among them a shaggy old poodle, whom she had seen that day in the street with a white patch on his eye and tufts of wool by his nose. Fedyushka ran after the poodle with a chisel in his hand, then all at once he too was covered with shaggy wool, and began merrily barking beside Kashtanka. Kashtanka and he good-naturedly sniffed each other's noses and merrily ran down the street. . . .

III

NEW AND VERY AGREEABLE ACQUAINTANCES

When Kashtanka woke up it was already light, and a sound rose from the street, such as only comes in the day-time. There was not a soul in the room. Kashtanka stretched, yawned and, cross and ill-humoured, walked about the room. She sniffed the corners and the furniture, looked into the passage and found nothing of interest there. Besides the door that led into the passage there was another door. After thinking a little Kashtanka scratched on it with both paws, opened it, and went into the adjoining room. Here on the bed, covered with a rug, a customer, in whom she recognised the stranger of yesterday, lay asleep.

"Rrrrr . . ." she growled, but recollecting yesterday's dinner, wagged her tail, and began sniffing.

She sniffed the stranger's clothes and boots and thought they smelt of horses. In the bedroom was another door, also closed. Kashtanka scratched at the door, leaned her chest against it, opened it, and was instantly aware of a strange and very suspicious smell. Foreseeing an unpleasant encounter, growling and looking about her, Kashtanka walked into a little room with a dirty wall-paper and drew back in alarm. She saw something surprising and terrible. A grey gander came straight towards her, hissing, with its neck bowed down to the floor and its wings outspread. Not far from him, on a little mattress, lay a white tom-cat; seeing Kashtanka, he jumped up, arched his back, wagged his tail with his hair standing on end and he, too, hissed at her. The dog was frightened in earnest, but not caring to betray her alarm, began barking loudly and dashed at the cat. . . . The cat arched his back more than ever, mewed and gave Kashtanka a smack on the head with his paw. Kashtanka jumped back, squatted on all four paws, and craning her nose towards the cat, went off into loud, shrill barks; meanwhile the gander came up behind and gave her a painful peck in the back. Kashtanka leapt up and dashed at the gander.

"What's this?" They heard a loud angry voice, and the stranger came into the room in his dressing-gown, with a cigar between his teeth. "What's the meaning of this? To your places!"

He went up to the cat, flicked him on his arched back, and said:

"Fyodor Timofeyitch, what's the meaning of this? Have you got up a fight? Ah, you old rascal! Lie down!"

And turning to the gander he shouted: "Ivan Ivanitch, go home!"

The cat obediently lay down on his mattress and closed his eyes. Judging from the expression of his face and whiskers, he was displeased with himself for having lost his temper and got into a fight. Kashtanka began whining resentfully, while the gander craned his neck and began saying something rapidly, excitedly, distinctly, but quite unintelligibly.

"All right, all right," said his master, yawning. "You must live in peace and friendship." He stroked Kashtanka and went on: "And you, red-hair, don't be frightened. . . . They are capital company, they won't annoy you. Stay, what are we to call you? You can't go on without a name, my dear."

The stranger thought a moment and said: "I tell you what . . . you shall be Auntie. . . . Do you understand? Auntie!"

And repeating the word "Auntie" several times he went out.

Kashtanka sat down and began watching. The cat sat motionless on his little mattress, and pretended to be asleep. The gander, craning his neck and stamping, went on talking rapidly and excitedly about something. Apparently it was a very clever gander; after every long tirade, he always stepped back with an air of wonder and made a show of being highly delighted with his own speech. . . . Listening to him and answering "R-r-r-r," Kashtanka fell to sniffing the corners. In one of the corners she found a little trough in which she saw some soaked peas and a sop of rye crusts. She tried the peas; they were not nice; she tried the sopped bread and began eating it. The gander was not at all offended that the strange dog was eating his food, but, on the contrary, talked even more excitedly, and to show his confidence went to the trough and ate a few peas himself.

IV

MARVELS ON A HURDLE

A little while afterwards the stranger came in again, and brought a strange thing with him like a hurdle, or like the figure II. On the crosspiece on the top of this roughly made wooden frame hung a bell, and a pistol was also tied to it; there were strings from the tongue of the bell, and the trigger of the pistol. The stranger put the frame in the middle of the room, spent a long time tying and untying something, then looked at the gander and said: "Ivan Ivanitch, if you please!"

The gander went up to him and stood in an expectant attitude.

"Now then," said the stranger, "let us begin at the very beginning. First of all, bow and make a curtsey! Look sharp!"

Ivan Ivanitch craned his neck, nodded in all directions, and scraped with his foot.

"Right. Bravo. . . . Now die!"

The gander lay on his back and stuck his legs in the air. After performing a few more similar, unimportant tricks, the stranger suddenly clutched at his head, and assuming an expression of horror, shouted: "Help! Fire! We are burning!"

Ivan Ivanitch ran to the frame, took the string in his beak, and set the bell ringing.

The stranger was very much pleased. He stroked the gander's neck and said:

"Bravo, Ivan Ivanitch! Now pretend that you are a jeweller selling gold and diamonds. Imagine now that you go to your shop and find thieves there. What would you do in that case?"

The gander took the other string in his beak and pulled it, and at once a deafening report was heard. Kashtanka was highly delighted with the bell ringing, and the shot threw her into so much ecstasy that she ran round the frame barking.

"Auntie, lie down!" cried the stranger; "be quiet!"

Ivan Ivanitch's task was not ended with the shooting. For a whole hour afterwards the stranger drove the gander round him on a cord, cracking a whip, and the gander had to jump over barriers and through hoops; he had to rear, that is, sit on his tail and wave his legs in the air. Kashtanka could not take her eyes off Ivan Ivanitch, wriggled with delight, and several times fell to running after him with shrill barks. After exhausting the gander and himself, the stranger wiped the sweat from his brow and cried:

"Marya, fetch Havronya Ivanovna here!"

A minute later there was the sound of grunting. . . . Kashtanka growled, assumed a very valiant air, and to be on the safe side, went nearer to the stranger. The door opened, an old woman looked in, and, saying something, led in a black and very ugly sow. Paying no attention to Kashtanka's growls, the sow lifted up her little hoof and grunted good-humouredly. Apparently it was very agreeable to her to see her master, the cat, and Ivan Ivanitch. When she went up to the cat and gave him a light tap on the stomach with her hoof, and then made some remark to the gander, a great deal of good-nature was expressed in her movements, and the quivering of her tail. Kashtanka realised at once that to growl and bark at such a character was useless.

The master took away the frame and cried: "Fyodor Timofeyitch, if you please!"

The cat stretched lazily, and reluctantly, as though performing a duty, went up to the sow.

"Come, let us begin with the Egyptian pyramid," began the master.

He spent a long time explaining something, then gave the word of command, "One . . . two . . . three!" At the word "three" Ivan Ivanitch flapped his wings and jumped onto the sow's back. . . . When, balancing himself with his wings and his neck, he got a firm foothold on the bristly back, Fyodor Timofeyitch listlessly and lazily, with manifest disdain, and with an air of scorning his art and not caring a pin for it, climbed on to the sow's back, then reluctantly mounted on to the gander, and stood on his hind legs. The result was what the stranger called the Egyptian pyramid. Kashtanka yapped with delight, but at that moment the old cat yawned and, losing his balance, rolled off the gander. Ivan Ivanitch lurched and fell off too. The stranger shouted, waved his hands, and began explaining something again. After spending an hour over the pyramid their indefatigable master proceeded to teach Ivan Ivanitch to ride on the cat, then began to teach the cat to smoke, and so on.

The lesson ended in the stranger's wiping the sweat off his brow and going away. Fyodor Timofeyitch gave a disdainful sniff, lay down on his mattress, and closed his eyes; Ivan Ivanitch went to the trough, and the pig was taken away by the old woman. Thanks to the number of her new impressions, Kashtanka hardly noticed how the day passed, and in the evening she was installed with her mattress in the room with the dirty wall-paper, and spent the night in the society of Fyodor Timofeyitch and the gander.

V

TALENT! TALENT!

A month passed.

Kashtanka had grown used to having a nice dinner every evening, and being called Auntie. She had grown used to the stranger too, and to her new companions. Life was comfortable and easy.

Every day began in the same way. As a rule, Ivan Ivanitch was the first to wake up, and at once went up to Auntie or to the cat, twisting his neck, and beginning to talk excitedly and persuasively, but, as before, unintelligibly. Sometimes he would crane up his head in the air and utter a long monologue. At first Kashtanka thought he talked so much because he was very clever, but after a little time had passed, she lost all her respect for him; when he went up to her with his long speeches she no longer wagged her tail, but treated him as a tiresome chatterbox, who would not let anyone sleep and, without the slightest ceremony, answered him with "R-r-r-r!"

Fyodor Timofeyitch was a gentleman of a very different sort. When he woke he did not utter a sound, did not stir, and did not even open his eyes. He would have been glad not to wake, for, as was evident, he was not greatly in love with life. Nothing interested him, he showed an apathetic and nonchalant attitude to everything, he disdained everything and, even while eating his delicious dinner, sniffed contemptuously.

When she woke Kashtanka began walking about the room and sniffing the corners. She and the cat were the only ones allowed to go all over the flat; the gander had not the right to cross the threshold of the room with the dirty wall-paper, and Havronya Ivanovna lived somewhere in a little outhouse in the yard and made her appearance only during the lessons. Their master got up late, and immediately after drinking his tea began teaching them their tricks. Every day the frame, the whip, and the hoop were brought in, and every day almost the same performance took place. The lesson lasted three or four hours, so that sometimes Fyodor Timofeyitch was so tired that he staggered about like a drunken man, and Ivan Ivanitch opened his beak and breathed heavily, while their master became red in the face and could not mop the sweat from his brow fast enough.

The lesson and the dinner made the day very interesting, but the evenings were tedious. As a rule, their master went off somewhere in the evening and took the cat and the gander with him. Left alone, Auntie lay down on her little mattress and began to feel sad. . . .

Melancholy crept on her imperceptibly and took possession of her by degrees, as darkness does of a room. It began with the dog's losing every inclination to bark, to eat, to run about the rooms, and even to look at things; then vague figures, half dogs, half human beings, with countenances attractive, pleasant, but incomprehensible, would appear in her imagination; when they came Auntie wagged her tail, and it seemed to her that she had somewhere, at some time, seen them and loved them. . . . And as she dropped asleep, she always felt that those figures smelt of glue, shavings, and varnish.

When she had grown quite used to her new life, and from a thin, long mongrel, had changed into a sleek, well-groomed dog, her master looked at her one day before the lesson and said:

"It's high time, Auntie, to get to business. You have kicked up your heels in idleness long enough. I want to make an artiste of you. . . . Do you want to be an artiste?"

And he began teaching her various accomplishments. At the first lesson he taught her to stand and walk on her hind legs, which she liked extremely. At the second lesson she had to jump on her hind legs and catch some sugar, which her teacher held high above her head. After that, in the following lessons she danced, ran tied to a cord, howled to music, rang the bell, and fired the pistol, and in a month could successfully replace Fyodor Timofeyitch in the "Egyptian Pyramid." She learned very eagerly and was pleased with her own success; running with her tongue out on the cord, leaping through the hoop, and riding on old Fyodor Timofeyitch, gave her the greatest enjoyment. She accompanied every successful trick with a shrill, delighted bark, while her teacher wondered, was also delighted, and rubbed his hands.

"It's talent! It's talent!" he said. "Unquestionable talent! You will certainly be successful!"

And Auntie grew so used to the word talent, that every time her master pronounced it, she jumped up as if it had been her name.

VI

AN UNEASY NIGHT

Auntie had a doggy dream that a porter ran after her with a broom, and she woke up in a fright.

It was quite dark and very stuffy in the room. The fleas were biting. Auntie had never been afraid of darkness before, but now, for some reason, she felt frightened and inclined to bark.

Her master heaved a loud sigh in the next room, then soon afterwards the sow grunted in her sty, and then all was still again. When one thinks about eating one's heart grows lighter, and Auntie began thinking how that day she had stolen the leg of a chicken from Fyodor Timofeyitch, and had hidden it in the drawing-room, between the cupboard and the wall, where there were a great many spiders' webs and a great deal of dust. Would it not be as well to go now and look whether the chicken leg were still there or not? It was very possible that her master had found it and eaten it. But she must not go out of the room before morning, that was the rule. Auntie shut her eyes to go to sleep as quickly as possible, for she knew by experience that the sooner you go to sleep the sooner the morning comes. But all at once there was a strange scream not far from her which made her start and jump up on all four legs. It was Ivan Ivanitch, and his cry was not babbling and persuasive as usual, but a wild, shrill, unnatural scream, like the squeak of a door opening. Unable to distinguish anything in the darkness, and not understanding what was wrong, Auntie felt still more frightened and growled: "R-r-r-r. . . ."

Some time passed, as long as it takes to eat a good bone; the scream was not repeated. Little by little Auntie's uneasiness passed off and she began to doze. She dreamed of two big black dogs with tufts of last year's coat left on their haunches and sides; they were eating out of a big basin some swill, from which there came a white steam and a most appetising smell; from time to time they looked round at Auntie, showed their teeth and growled: "We are not going to give you any!" But a peasant in a fur-coat ran out of the house and drove them away with a whip; then Auntie went up to the basin and began eating, but as soon as the peasant went out of the gate, the two black dogs rushed at her growling, and all at once there was again a shrill scream.

"K-gee! K-gee-gee!" cried Ivan Ivanitch.

Auntie woke, jumped up and, without leaving her mattress, went off into a yelping bark. It seemed to her that it was not Ivan Ivanitch that was screaming but someone else, and for some reason the sow again grunted in her sty.

Then there was the sound of shuffling slippers, and the master came into the room in his dressing-gown with a candle in his hand. The flickering light danced over the dirty wall-paper and the ceiling, and chased away the darkness. Auntie saw that there was no stranger in the room. Ivan Ivanitch was sitting on the floor and was not asleep. His wings were spread out and his beak was open, and altogether he looked as though he were very tired and thirsty. Old Fyodor Timofeyitch was not asleep either. He, too, must have been awakened by the scream.

"Ivan Ivanitch, what's the matter with you?" the master asked the gander. "Why are you screaming? Are you ill?"

The gander did not answer. The master touched him on the neck, stroked his back, and said: "You are a queer chap. You don't sleep yourself, and you don't let other people. . . ."

When the master went out, carrying the candle with him, there was darkness again. Auntie felt frightened. The gander did not scream, but again she fancied that there was some stranger in the room. What was most dreadful was that this stranger could not be bitten, as he was unseen and had no shape. And for some reason she thought that something very bad would certainly happen that night.

Fyodor Timofeyitch was uneasy too. Auntie could hear him shifting on his mattress, yawning and shaking his head.

Somewhere in the street there was a knocking at a gate and the sow grunted in her sty. Auntie began to whine, stretched out her front-paws and laid her head down upon them. She fancied that in the knocking at the gate, in the grunting of the sow, who was for some reason awake, in the darkness and the stillness, there was something as miserable and dreadful as in Ivan Ivanitch's scream. Everything was in agitation and anxiety, but why? Who was the stranger who could not be seen? Then two dim flashes of green gleamed for a minute near Auntie. It was Fyodor Timofeyitch, for the first time of their whole acquaintance coming up to her. What did he want? Auntie licked his paw, and not asking why he had come, howled softly and on various notes.

"K-gee!" cried Ivan Ivanitch, "K-g-ee!"

The door opened again and the master came in with a candle.

The gander was sitting in the same attitude as before, with his beak open, and his wings spread out, his eyes were closed.

"Ivan Ivanitch!" his master called him.

The gander did not stir. His master sat down before him on the floor, looked at him in silence for a minute, and said:

"Ivan Ivanitch, what is it? Are you dying? Oh, I remember now, I remember!" he cried out, and clutched at his head. "I know why it is! It's because the horse stepped on you to-day! My God! My God!"

Auntie did not understand what her master was saying, but she saw from his face that he, too, was expecting something dreadful. She stretched out her head towards the dark window, where it seemed to her some stranger was looking in, and howled.

"He is dying, Auntie!" said her master, and wrung his hands. "Yes, yes, he is dying! Death has come into your room. What are we to do?"

Pale and agitated, the master went back into his room, sighing and shaking his head. Auntie was afraid to remain in the darkness, and followed her master into his bedroom. He sat down on the bed and repeated several times: "My God, what's to be done?"

Auntie walked about round his feet, and not understanding why she was wretched and why they were all so uneasy, and trying to understand, watched every movement he made. Fyodor Timofeyitch, who rarely left his little mattress, came into the master's bedroom too, and began rubbing himself against his feet. He shook his head as though he wanted to shake painful thoughts out of it, and kept peeping suspiciously under the bed.

The master took a saucer, poured some water from his wash-stand into it, and went to the gander again.

"Drink, Ivan Ivanitch!" he said tenderly, setting the saucer before him; "drink, darling."

But Ivan Ivanitch did not stir and did not open his eyes. His master bent his head down to the saucer and dipped his beak into the water, but the gander did not drink, he spread his wings wider than ever, and his head remained lying in the saucer.

"No, there's nothing to be done now," sighed his master. "It's all over. Ivan Ivanitch is gone!"

And shining drops, such as one sees on the window-pane when it rains, trickled down his cheeks. Not understanding what was the matter, Auntie and Fyodor Timofeyitch snuggled up to him and looked with horror at the gander.

"Poor Ivan Ivanitch!" said the master, sighing mournfully. "And I was dreaming I would take you in the spring into the country, and would walk with you on the green grass. Dear creature, my good comrade, you are no more! How shall I do without you now?"

It seemed to Auntie that the same thing would happen to her, that is, that she too, there was no knowing why, would close her eyes, stretch out her paws, open her mouth, and everyone would look at her with horror. Apparently the same reflections were passing through the brain of Fyodor Timofeyitch. Never before had the old cat been so morose and gloomy.

It began to get light, and the unseen stranger who had so frightened Auntie was no longer in the room. When it was quite daylight, the porter came in, took the gander, and carried him away. And soon afterwards the old woman came in and took away the trough.

Auntie went into the drawing-room and looked behind the cupboard: her master had not eaten the chicken bone, it was lying in its place among the dust and spiders' webs. But Auntie felt sad and dreary and wanted to cry. She did not even sniff at the bone, but went under the sofa, sat down there, and began softly whining in a thin voice.

VII

AN UNSUCCESSFUL DÉBUT

One fine evening the master came into the room with the dirty wallpaper, and, rubbing his hands, said:

"Well. . . ."

He meant to say something more, but went away without saying it. Auntie, who during her lessons had thoroughly studied his face and intonations, divined that he was agitated, anxious and, she fancied, angry. Soon afterwards he came back and said:

"To-day I shall take with me Auntie and Fyodor Timofeyitch. To-day, Auntie, you will take the place of poor Ivan Ivanitch in the 'Egyptian Pyramid.' Goodness knows how it will be! Nothing is ready, nothing has been thoroughly studied, there have been few rehearsals! We shall be disgraced, we shall come to grief!"

Then he went out again, and a minute later, came back in his fur-coat and top hat. Going up to the cat he took him by the fore-paws and put him inside the front of his coat, while Fyodor Timofeyitch appeared completely unconcerned, and did not even trouble to open his eyes. To him it was apparently a matter of absolute indifference whether he remained lying down, or were lifted up by his paws, whether he rested on his mattress or under his master's fur-coat. . . .

"Come along, Auntie," said her master.

Wagging her tail, and understanding nothing, Auntie followed him. A minute later she was sitting in a sledge by her master's feet and heard him, shrinking with cold and anxiety, mutter to himself:

"We shall be disgraced! We shall come to grief!"

The sledge stopped at a big strange-looking house, like a soup-ladle turned upside down. The long entrance to this house, with its three glass doors, was lighted up with a dozen brilliant lamps. The doors opened with a resounding noise and, like jaws, swallowed up the people who were moving to and fro at the entrance. There were a great many people; horses, too, often ran up to the entrance, but no dogs were to be seen.

The master took Auntie in his arms and thrust her in his coat, where Fyodor Timofeyitch already was. It was dark and stuffy there, but warm. For an instant two green sparks flashed at her; it was the cat, who opened his eyes on being disturbed by his neighbour's cold rough paws. Auntie licked his ear, and, trying to settle herself as comfortably as possible, moved uneasily, crushed him under her cold paws, and casually poked her head out from under the coat, but at once growled angrily, and tucked it in again. It seemed to her that she had seen a huge, badly lighted room, full of monsters; from behind screens and gratings, which stretched on both sides of the room, horrible faces looked out: faces of horses with horns, with long ears, and one fat, huge countenance with a tail instead of a nose, and two long gnawed bones sticking out of his mouth.

The cat mewed huskily under Auntie's paws, but at that moment the coat was flung open, the master said, "Hop!" and Fyodor Timofeyitch and Auntie jumped to the floor. They were now in a little room with grey plank walls; there was no other furniture in it but a little table with a looking-glass on it, a stool, and some rags hung about the corners, and instead of a lamp or candles, there was a bright fan-shaped light attached to a little pipe fixed in the wall. Fyodor Timofeyitch licked his coat which had been ruffled by Auntie, went under the stool, and lay down. Their master, still agitated and rubbing his hands, began undressing. . . . He undressed as he usually did at home when he was preparing to get under the rug, that is, took off everything but his underlinen, then he sat down on the stool, and, looking in the looking-glass, began playing the most surprising tricks with himself. . . . First of all he put on his head a wig, with a parting and with two tufts of hair standing up like horns, then he smeared his face thickly with something white, and over the white colour painted his eyebrows, his moustaches, and red on his cheeks. His antics did not end with that. After smearing his face and neck, he began putting himself into an extraordinary and incongruous costume, such as Auntie had never seen before, either in houses or in the street. Imagine very full trousers, made of chintz covered with big flowers, such as is used in working-class houses for curtains and covering furniture, trousers which buttoned up just under his armpits. One trouser leg was made of brown chintz, the other of bright yellow. Almost lost in these, he then put on a short chintz jacket, with a big scalloped collar, and a gold star on the back, stockings of different colours, and green slippers. . . .

Everything seemed going round before Auntie's eyes and in her soul. The white-faced, sack-like figure smelt like her master, its voice, too, was the familiar master's voice, but there were moments when Auntie was tortured by doubts, and then she was ready to run away from the parti-coloured figure and to bark. The new place, the fan-shaped light, the smell, the transformation that had taken place in her master—all this aroused in her a vague dread and a foreboding that she would certainly meet with some horror such as the big face with the tail instead of a nose. And then, somewhere through the wall, some hateful band was playing, and from time to time she heard an incomprehensible roar. Only one thing reassured her—that was the imperturbability of Fyodor Timofeyitch. He dozed with the utmost tranquillity under the stool, and did not open his eyes even when it was moved.

A man in a dress coat and a white waistcoat peeped into the little room and said:

"Miss Arabella has just gone on. After her—you."

Their master made no answer. He drew a small box from under the table, sat down, and waited. From his lips and his hands it could be seen that he was agitated, and Auntie could hear how his breathing came in gasps.

"Monsieur George, come on!" someone shouted behind the door. Their master got up and crossed himself three times, then took the cat from under the stool and put him in the box.

"Come, Auntie," he said softly.

Auntie, who could make nothing out of it, went up to his hands, he kissed her on the head, and put her beside Fyodor Timofeyitch. Then followed darkness. . . . Auntie trampled on the cat, scratched at the walls of the box, and was so frightened that she could not utter a sound, while the box swayed and quivered, as though it were on the waves. . . .

"Here we are again!" her master shouted aloud: "here we are again!"

Auntie felt that after that shout the box struck against something hard and left off swaying. There was a loud deep roar, someone was being slapped, and that someone, probably the monster with the tail instead of a nose, roared and laughed so loud that the locks of the box trembled. In response to the roar, there came a shrill, squeaky laugh from her master, such as he never laughed at home.

"Ha!" he shouted, trying to shout above the roar. "Honoured friends! I have only just come from the station! My granny's kicked the bucket and left me a fortune! There is something very heavy in the box, it must be gold, ha! ha! I bet there's a million here! We'll open it and look. . . ."

The lock of the box clicked. The bright light dazzled Auntie's eyes, she jumped out of the box, and, deafened by the roar, ran quickly round her master, and broke into a shrill bark.

"Ha!" exclaimed her master. "Uncle Fyodor Timofeyitch! Beloved Aunt, dear relations! The devil take you!"

He fell on his stomach on the sand, seized the cat and Auntie, and fell to embracing them. While he held Auntie tight in his arms, she glanced round into the world into which fate had brought her and, impressed by its immensity, was for a minute dumbfounded with amazement and delight, then jumped out of her master's arms, and to express the intensity of her emotions, whirled round and round on one spot like a top. This new world was big and full of bright light; wherever she looked, on all sides, from floor to ceiling there were faces, faces, faces, and nothing else.

"Auntie, I beg you to sit down!" shouted her master. Remembering what that meant, Auntie jumped on to a chair, and sat down. She looked at her master. His eyes looked at her gravely and kindly as always, but his face, especially his mouth and teeth, were made grotesque by a broad immovable grin. He laughed, skipped about, twitched his shoulders, and made a show of being very merry in the presence of the thousands of faces. Auntie believed in his merriment, all at once felt all over her that those thousands of faces were looking at her, lifted up her fox-like head, and howled joyously.

"You sit there, Auntie," her master said to her, "while Uncle and I will dance the Kamarinsky."

Fyodor Timofeyitch stood looking about him indifferently, waiting to be made to do something silly. He danced listlessly, carelessly, sullenly, and one could see from his movements, his tail and his ears, that he had a profound contempt for the crowd, the bright light, his master and himself. When he had performed his allotted task, he gave a yawn and sat down.

"Now, Auntie!" said her master, "we'll have first a song, and then a dance, shall we?"

He took a pipe out of his pocket, and began playing. Auntie, who could not endure music, began moving uneasily in her chair and howled. A roar of applause rose from all sides. Her master bowed, and when all was still again, went on playing. . . . Just as he took one very high note, someone high up among the audience uttered a loud exclamation:

"Auntie!" cried a child's voice, "why it's Kashtanka!"

"Kashtanka it is!" declared a cracked drunken tenor. "Kashtanka! Strike me dead, Fedyushka, it is Kashtanka. Kashtanka! here!"

Someone in the gallery gave a whistle, and two voices, one a boy's and one a man's, called loudly: "Kashtanka! Kashtanka!"

Auntie started, and looked where the shouting came from. Two faces, one hairy, drunken and grinning, the other chubby, rosy-cheeked and frightened-looking, dazed her eyes as the bright light had dazed them before. . . . She remembered, fell off the chair, struggled on the sand, then jumped up, and with a delighted yap dashed towards those faces. There was a deafening roar, interspersed with whistles and a shrill childish shout: "Kashtanka! Kashtanka!"

Auntie leaped over the barrier, then across someone's shoulders. She found herself in a box: to get into the next tier she had to leap over a high wall. Auntie jumped, but did not jump high enough, and slipped back down the wall. Then she was passed from hand to hand, licked hands and faces, kept mounting higher and higher, and at last got into the gallery. . . .

Half an hour afterwards, Kashtanka was in the street, following the people who smelt of glue and varnish. Luka Alexandritch staggered and instinctively, taught by experience, tried to keep as far from the gutter as possible.

"In sin my mother bore me," he muttered. "And you, Kashtanka, are a thing of little understanding. Beside a man, you are like a joiner beside a cabinet-maker."

Fedyushka walked beside him, wearing his father's cap. Kashtanka looked at their backs, and it seemed to her that she had been following them for ages, and was glad that there had not been a break for a minute in her life.

She remembered the little room with dirty wall-paper, the gander, Fyodor Timofeyitch, the delicious dinners, the lessons, the circus, but all that seemed to her now like a long, tangled, oppressive dream.

1887

The Grasshopper

All Olga Ivanovna's friends and acquaintances were at her wedding.

"Look at him; isn't it true that there is something in him?" she said to her friends, with a nod towards her husband, as though she wanted to explain why she was marrying a simple, very ordinary, and in no way remarkable man.

Her husband, Osip Stepanitch Dymov, was a doctor, and only of the rank of a titular councillor. He was on the staff of two hospitals: in one a ward-surgeon and in the other a dissecting demonstrator. Every day from nine to twelve he saw patients and was busy in his ward, and after twelve o'clock he went by tram to the other hospital, where he dissected. His private practice was a small one, not worth more than five hundred roubles a year. That was all. What more could one say about him? Meanwhile, Olga Ivanovna and her friends and acquaintances were not quite ordinary people. Every one of them was remarkable in some way, and more or less famous; already had made a reputation and was looked upon as a celebrity; or if not yet a celebrity, gave brilliant promise of becoming one. There was an actor from the Dramatic Theatre, who was a great talent of established reputation, as well as an elegant, intelligent, and modest man, and a capital elocutionist, and who taught Olga Ivanovna to recite; there was a singer from the opera, a good-natured, fat man who assured Olga Ivanovna, with a sigh, that she was ruining herself, that if she would take herself in hand and not be lazy she might make a remarkable singer; then there were several artists, and chief among them Ryabovsky, a very handsome, fair young man of five-and-twenty who painted genre pieces, animal studies, and landscapes, was successful at exhibitions, and had sold his last picture for five hundred roubles. He touched up Olga Ivanovna's sketches, and used to say she might do something. Then a violoncellist, whose instrument used to sob, and who openly declared that of all the ladies of his acquaintance the only one who could accompany him was Olga Ivanovna; then there was a literary man, young but already well known, who had written stories, novels, and plays. Who else? Why, Vassily Vassilyitch, a landowner and amateur illustrator and vignettist, with a great feeling for the old Russian style, the old ballad and epic. On paper, on china, and on smoked plates, he produced literally marvels. In the midst of this free artistic company, spoiled by fortune, though refined and modest, who recalled the existence of doctors only in times of illness, and to whom the name of Dymov sounded in no way different from Sidorov or Tarasov—in the midst of this company Dymov seemed strange, not wanted, and small, though he was tall and broad-shouldered. He looked as though he had on somebody else's coat, and his beard was like a shopman's. Though if he had been a writer or an artist, they would have said that his beard reminded them of Zola.

An artist said to Olga Ivanovna that with her flaxen hair and in her wedding-dress she was very much like a graceful cherry-tree when it is covered all over with delicate white blossoms in spring.

"Oh, let me tell you," said Olga Ivanovna, taking his arm, "how it was it all came to pass so suddenly. Listen, listen! . . . I must tell you that my father was on the same staff at the hospital as Dymov. When my poor father was taken ill, Dymov watched for days and nights together at his bedside. Such self-sacrifice! Listen, Ryabovsky! You, my writer, listen; it is very interesting! Come nearer. Such self-sacrifice, such genuine sympathy! I sat up with my father, and did not sleep for nights, either. And all at once—the princess had won the hero's heart—my Dymov fell head over ears in love. Really, fate is so strange at times! Well, after my father's death he came to see me sometimes, met me in the street, and one fine evening, all at once he made me an offer . . . like snow upon my head. . . . I lay awake all night, crying, and fell hellishly in love myself. And here, as you see, I am his wife. There really is something strong, powerful, bearlike about him, isn't there? Now his face is turned three-quarters towards us in a bad light, but when he turns round look at his forehead. Ryabovsky, what do you say to that forehead? Dymov, we are talking about you!" she called to her husband. "Come here; hold out your honest hand to Ryabovsky. . . . That's right, be friends."

Dymov, with a naïve and good-natured smile, held out his hand to Ryabovsky, and said:

"Very glad to meet you. There was a Ryabovsky in my year at the medical school. Was he a relation of yours?"

II

Olga Ivanovna was twenty-two, Dymov was thirty-one. They got on splendidly together when they were married. Olga Ivanovna hung all her drawing-room walls with her own and other people's sketches, in frames and without frames, and near the piano and furniture arranged picturesque corners with Japanese parasols, easels, daggers, busts, photographs, and rags of many colours. . . . In the dining-room she papered the walls with peasant woodcuts, hung up bark shoes and sickles, stood in a corner a scythe and a rake, and so achieved a dining-room in the Russian style. In her bedroom she draped the ceiling and the walls with dark cloths to make it like a cavern, hung a Venetian lantern over the beds, and at the door set a figure with a halberd. And every one thought that the young people had a very charming little home.

When she got up at eleven o'clock every morning, Olga Ivanovna played the piano or, if it were sunny, painted something in oils. Then between twelve and one she drove to her dressmaker's. As Dymov and she had very little money, only just enough, she and her dressmaker were often put to clever shifts to enable her to appear constantly in new dresses and make a sensation with them. Very often out of an old dyed dress, out of bits of tulle, lace, plush, and silk, costing nothing, perfect marvels were created, something bewitching—not a dress, but a dream. From the dressmaker's Olga Ivanovna usually drove to some actress of her acquaintance to hear the latest theatrical gossip, and incidentally to try and get hold of tickets for the first night of some new play or for a benefit performance. From the actress's she had to go to some artist's studio or to some exhibition or to see some celebrity—either to pay a visit or to give an invitation or simply to have a chat. And everywhere she met with a gay and friendly welcome, and was assured that she was good, that she was sweet, that she was rare. . . . Those whom she called great and famous received her as one of themselves, as an equal, and predicted with one voice that, with her talents, her taste, and her intelligence, she would do great things if she concentrated herself. She sang, she played the piano, she painted in oils, she carved, she took part in amateur performances; and all this not just anyhow, but all with talent, whether she made lanterns for an illumination or dressed up or tied somebody's cravat—everything she did was exceptionally graceful, artistic, and charming. But her talents showed themselves in nothing so clearly as in her faculty for quickly becoming acquainted and on intimate terms with celebrated people. No sooner did any one become ever so little celebrated, and set people talking about him, than she made his acquaintance, got on friendly terms the same day, and invited him to her house. Every new acquaintance she made was a veritable fête for her. She adored celebrated people, was proud of them, dreamed of them every night. She craved for them, and never could satisfy her craving. The old ones departed and were forgotten, new ones came to replace them, but to these, too, she soon grew accustomed or was disappointed in them, and began eagerly seeking for fresh great men, finding them and seeking for them again. What for?

Between four and five she dined at home with her husband. His simplicity, good sense, and kindheartedness touched her and moved her up to enthusiasm. She was constantly jumping up, impulsively hugging his head and showering kisses on it.

"You are a clever, generous man, Dymov," she used to say, "but you have one very serious defect. You take absolutely no interest in art. You don't believe in music or painting."

"I don't understand them," he would say mildly. "I have spent all my life in working at natural science and medicine, and I have never had time to take an interest in the arts."

"But, you know, that's awful, Dymov!"

"Why so? Your friends don't know anything of science or medicine, but you don't reproach them with it. Every one has his own line. I don't understand landscapes and operas, but the way I look at it is that if one set of sensible people devote their whole lives to them, and other sensible people pay immense sums for them, they must be of use. I don't understand them, but not understanding does not imply disbelieving in them."

"Let me shake your honest hand!"

After dinner Olga Ivanovna would drive off to see her friends, then to a theatre or to a concert, and she returned home after midnight. So it was every day.

On Wednesdays she had "At Homes." At these "At Homes" the hostess and her guests did not play cards and did not dance, but entertained themselves with various arts. An actor from the Dramatic Theatre recited, a singer sang, artists sketched in the albums of which Olga Ivanovna had a great number, the violoncellist played, and the hostess herself sketched, carved, sang, and played accompaniments. In the intervals between the recitations, music, and singing, they talked and argued about literature, the theatre, and painting. There were no ladies, for Olga Ivanovna considered all ladies wearisome and vulgar except actresses and her dressmaker. Not one of these entertainments passed without the hostess starting at every ring at the bell, and saying, with a triumphant expression, "It is he," meaning by "he," of course, some new celebrity. Dymov was not in the drawing-room, and no one remembered his existence. But exactly at half-past eleven the door leading into the dining-room opened, and Dymov would appear with his good-natured, gentle smile and say, rubbing his hands:

"Come to supper, gentlemen."

They all went into the dining-room, and every time found on the table exactly the same things: a dish of oysters, a piece of ham or veal, sardines, cheese, caviare, mushrooms, vodka, and two decanters of wine.

"My dear *maître d'hôtel!*" Olga Ivanovna would say, clasping her hands with enthusiasm, "you are simply fascinating! My friends, look at his forehead! Dymov, turn your profile. Look! he has the face of a Bengal tiger and an expression as kind and sweet as a gazelle. Ah, the darling!"

The visitors ate, and, looking at Dymov, thought, "He really is a nice fellow"; but they soon forgot about him, and went on talking about the theatre, music, and painting.

The young people were happy, and their life flowed on without a hitch.

The third week of their honeymoon was spent, however, not quite happily—sadly, indeed. Dymov caught erysipelas in the hospital, was in bed for six days, and had to have his beautiful black hair cropped. Olga Ivanovna sat beside him and wept bitterly, but when he was better she put a white handkerchief on his shaven head and began to paint him as a Bedouin. And they were both in good spirits. Three days after he had begun to go back to the hospital he had another mischance.

"I have no luck, little mother," he said one day at dinner. "I had four dissections to do today, and I cut two of my fingers at one. And I did not notice it till I got home."

Olga Ivanovna was alarmed. He smiled, and told her that it did not matter, and that he often cut his hands when he was dissecting.

"I get absorbed, little mother, and grow careless."

Olga Ivanovna dreaded symptoms of blood-poisoning, and prayed about it every night, but all went well. And again life flowed on peaceful and happy, free from grief and anxiety. The present was happy, and to follow it spring was at hand, already smiling in the distance, and promising a thousand delights. There would be no end to their happiness. In April, May and June a summer villa a good distance out of town; walks, sketching, fishing, nightingales; and then from July right on to autumn an artist's tour on the Volga, and in this tour Olga Ivanovna would take part as an indispensable member of the society. She had already had made for her two travelling dresses of linen, had bought paints, brushes, canvases, and a new palette for the journey. Almost every day Ryabovsky visited her to see what progress she was making in her painting; when she showed him her painting, he used to thrust his hands deep into his pockets, compress his lips, sniff, and say:

"Ye—es . . . ! That cloud of yours is screaming: it's not in the evening light. The foreground is somehow chewed up, and there is something, you know, not the thing. . . . And your cottage is weighed down and whines pitifully. That corner ought to have been taken more in shadow, but on the whole it is not bad; I like it."

And the more incomprehensible he talked, the more readily Olga Ivanovna understood him.

III

After dinner on the second day of Trinity week, Dymov bought some sweets and some savouries and went down to the villa to see his wife. He had not seen her for a fortnight, and missed her terribly. As he sat in the train and afterwards as he looked for his villa in a big wood, he felt all the while hungry and weary, and dreamed of how he would have supper in freedom with his wife, then tumble into bed and to sleep. And he was delighted as he looked at his parcel, in which there was caviare, cheese, and white salmon.

The sun was setting by the time he found his villa and recognized it. The old servant told him that her mistress was not at home, but that most likely she would soon be in. The villa, very uninviting in appearance, with low ceilings papered with writing-paper and with uneven floors full of crevices, consisted only of three rooms. In one there was a bed, in the second there were canvases, brushes, greasy papers, and men's overcoats and hats lying about on the chairs and in the windows, while in the third Dymov found three unknown men; two were dark-haired and had beards, the other was clean-shaven and fat, apparently an actor. There was a samovar boiling on the table.

"What do you want?" asked the actor in a bass voice, looking at Dymov ungraciously. "Do you want Olga Ivanovna? Wait a minute; she will be here directly."

Dymov sat down and waited. One of the dark-haired men, looking sleepily and listlessly at him, poured himself out a glass of tea, and asked:

"Perhaps you would like some tea?"

Dymov was both hungry and thirsty, but he refused tea for fear of spoiling his supper. Soon he heard footsteps and a familiar laugh; a door slammed, and Olga Ivanovna ran into the room, wearing a wide-brimmed hat and carrying a box in her hand; she was followed by Ryabovsky, rosy and good-humoured, carrying a big umbrella and a campstool.

"Dymov!" cried Olga Ivanovna, and she flushed crimson with pleasure. "Dymov!" she repeated, laying her head and both arms on his bosom. "Is that you? Why haven't you come for so long? Why? Why?"

"When could I, little mother? I am always busy, and whenever I am free it always happens somehow that the train does not fit."

"But how glad I am to see you! I have been dreaming about you the whole night, the whole night, and I was afraid you must be ill. Ah! if you only knew how sweet you are! You have come in the nick of time! You will be my salvation! You are the only person who can save me! There is to be a most original wedding here tomorrow," she went on, laughing, and tying her husband's cravat. "A young telegraph clerk at the station, called Tchikeldyeev, is going to be married. He is a handsome young man and—well, not stupid, and you know there is something strong, bearlike in his face . . . you might paint him as a young Norman. We summer visitors take a great interest in him, and have promised to be at his wedding. . . . He is a lonely, timid man, not well off, and of course it would be a shame not to be sympathetic to him. Fancy! the wedding will be after the service; then we shall all walk from the church to the bride's lodgings . . . you see the wood, the birds singing, patches of sunlight on the grass, and all of us spots of different colours against the bright green background—very original, in the style of the French impressionists. But, Dymov, what am I to go to the church in?" said Olga Ivanovna, and she looked as though she were going to cry. "I have nothing here, literally nothing! no dress, no flowers, no gloves . . . you must save me. Since you have come, fate itself bids you save me. Take the keys, my precious, go home and get my pink dress from the wardrobe. You remember it; it hangs in front. . . . Then, in the storeroom, on the floor, on the right side, you will see two cardboard boxes. When you open the top one you will see tulle, heaps of tulle and rags of all sorts, and under them flowers. Take out all the flowers carefully, try not to crush them, darling; I will choose among them later. . . . And buy me some gloves."

"Very well," said Dymov; "I will go tomorrow and send them to you."

"Tomorrow?" asked Olga Ivanovna, and she looked at him surprised. "You won't have time tomorrow. The first train goes tomorrow at nine, and the wedding's at eleven. No, darling, it must be today; it absolutely must be today. If you won't be able to come tomorrow, send them by a messenger. Come, you must run along. . . . The passenger train will be in directly; don't miss it, darling."

"Very well."

"Oh, how sorry I am to let you go!" said Olga Ivanovna, and tears came into her eyes. "And why did I promise that telegraph clerk, like a silly?"

Dymov hurriedly drank a glass of tea, took a cracknel, and, smiling gently, went to the station. And the caviare, the cheese, and the white salmon were eaten by the two dark gentlemen and the fat actor.

IV

On a still moonlight night in July Olga Ivanovna was standing on the deck of a Volga steamer and looking alternately at the water and at the picturesque banks. Beside her was standing Ryabovsky, telling her the black shadows on the water were not shadows, but a dream, that it would be sweet to sink into forgetfulness, to die, to become a memory in the sight of that enchanted water with the fantastic glimmer, in sight of the fathomless sky and the mournful, dreamy shores that told of the vanity of our life and of the existence of something higher, blessed, and eternal. The past was vulgar and uninteresting, the future was trivial, and that marvellous night, unique in a lifetime, would soon be over, would blend with eternity; then, why live?

And Olga Ivanovna listened alternately to Ryabovsky's voice and the silence of the night, and thought of her being immortal and never dying. The turquoise colour of the water, such as she had never seen before, the sky, the river-banks, the black shadows, and the unaccountable joy that flooded her soul, all told her that she would make a great artist, and that somewhere in the distance, in the infinite space beyond the moonlight, success, glory, the love of the people, lay awaiting her. . . . When she gazed steadily without blinking into the distance, she seemed to see crowds of people, lights, triumphant strains of music, cries of enthusiasm, she herself in a white dress, and flowers showered upon her from all sides. She thought, too, that beside her, leaning with his elbows on the rail of the steamer, there was standing a real great man, a genius, one of God's elect. . . . All that he had created up to the present was fine, new, and extraordinary, but what he would create in time, when with maturity his rare talent reached its full development, would be astounding, immeasurably sublime; and that could be seen by his face, by his manner of expressing himself and his attitude to nature. He talked of shadows, of the tones of evening, of the moonlight, in a special way, in a language of his own, so that one could not help feeling the fascination of his power over nature. He was very handsome, original, and his life, free, independent, aloof from all common cares, was like the life of a bird.

"It's growing cooler," said Olga Ivanovna, and she gave a shudder.

Ryabovsky wrapped her in his cloak, and said mournfully:

"I feel that I am in your power; I am a slave. Why are you so enchanting today?"

He kept staring intently at her, and his eyes were terrible. And she was afraid to look at him.

"I love you madly," he whispered, breathing on her cheek. "Say one word to me and I will not go on living; I will give up art . . ." he muttered in violent emotion. "Love me, love . . ."

"Don't talk like that," said Olga Ivanovna, covering her eyes. "It's dreadful! How about Dymov?"

"What of Dymov? Why Dymov? What have I to do with Dymov? The Volga, the moon, beauty, my love, ecstasy, and there is no such thing as Dymov. . . . Ah! I don't know . . . I don't care about the past; give me one moment, one instant!"

Olga Ivanovna's heart began to throb. She tried to think about her husband, but all her past, with her wedding, with Dymov, and with her "At Homes," seemed to her petty, trivial, dingy, unnecessary, and far, far away. . . . Yes, really, what of Dymov? Why Dymov? What had she to do with Dymov? Had he any existence in nature, or was he only a dream?

"For him, a simple and ordinary man the happiness he has had already is enough," she thought, covering her face with her hands. "Let them condemn me, let them curse me, but in spite of them all I will go to my ruin; I will go to my ruin! . . . One must experience everything in life. My God! how terrible and how glorious!"

"Well? Well?" muttered the artist, embracing her, and greedily kissing the hands with which she feebly tried to thrust him from her. "You love me? Yes? Yes? Oh, what a night! marvellous night!"

"Yes, what a night!" she whispered, looking into his eyes, which were bright with tears.

Then she looked round quickly, put her arms round him, and kissed him on the lips.

"We are nearing Kineshmo!" said some one on the other side of the deck.

They heard heavy footsteps; it was a waiter from the refreshment-bar.

"Waiter," said Olga Ivanovna, laughing and crying with happiness, "bring us some wine."

The artist, pale with emotion, sat on the seat, looking at Olga Ivanovna with adoring, grateful eyes; then he closed his eyes, and said, smiling languidly:

"I am tired."

And he leaned his head against the rail.

V

On the second of September the day was warm and still, but overcast. In the early morning a light mist had hung over the Volga, and after nine o'clock it had begun to spout with rain. And there seemed no hope of the sky clearing. Over their morning tea Ryabovsky told Olga Ivanovna that painting was the most ungrateful and boring art, that he was not an artist, that none but fools thought that he had any talent, and all at once, for no rhyme or reason, he snatched up a knife and with it scraped over his very best sketch. After his tea he sat plunged in gloom at the window and gazed at the Volga. And now the Volga was dingy, all of one even colour without a gleam of light, cold-looking. Everything, everything recalled the approach of dreary, gloomy autumn. And it seemed as though nature had removed now from the Volga the sumptuous green covers from the banks, the brilliant reflections of the sunbeams, the transparent blue distance, and all its smart gala array, and had packed it away in boxes till the coming spring, and the crows were flying above the Volga and crying tauntingly, "Bare, bare!"

Ryabovsky heard their cawing, and thought he had already gone off and lost his talent, that everything in this world was relative, conditional, and stupid, and that he ought not to have taken up with this woman. . . In short, he was out of humour and depressed.

Olga Ivanovna sat behind the screen on the bed, and, passing her fingers through her lovely flaxen hair, pictured herself first in the drawing-room, then in the bedroom, then in her husband's study; her imagination carried her to the theatre, to the dressmaker, to her distinguished friends. Were they getting something up now? Did they think of her? The season had begun by now, and it would be time to think about her "At Homes." And Dymov? Dear Dymov? with what gentleness and childlike pathos he kept begging her in his letters to make haste and come home! Every month he sent her seventy-five roubles, and when she wrote him that she had lent the artists a hundred roubles, he sent that hundred too. What a kind, generous-hearted man! The travelling wearied Olga Ivanovna; she was bored; and she longed to get away from the peasants, from the damp smell of the river, and to cast off the feeling of physical uncleanliness of which she was conscious all the time, living in the peasants' huts and wandering from village to village. If Ryabovsky had not given his word to the artists that he would stay with them till the twentieth of September, they might have gone away that very day. And how nice that would have been!

"My God!" moaned Ryabovsky. "Will the sun ever come out? I can't go on with a sunny landscape without the sun. . . ."

"But you have a sketch with a cloudy sky," said Olga Ivanovna, coming from behind the screen. "Do you remember, in the right foreground forest trees, on the left a herd of cows and geese? You might finish it now."

"Aie!" the artist scowled. "Finish it! Can you imagine I am such a fool that I don't know what I want to do?"

"How you have changed to me!" sighed Olga Ivanovna.

"Well, a good thing too!"

Olga Ivanovna's face quivered; she moved away to the stove and began to cry.

"Well, that's the last straw—crying! Give over! I have a thousand reasons for tears, but I am not crying."

"A thousand reasons!" cried Olga Ivanovna. "The chief one is that you are weary of me. Yes!" she said, and broke into sobs. "If one is to tell the truth, you are ashamed of our love. You keep trying to prevent the artists from noticing it, though it is impossible to conceal it, and they have known all about it for ever so long."

"Olga, one thing I beg you," said the artist in an imploring voice, laying his hand on his heart—"one thing; don't worry me! I want nothing else from you!"

"But swear that you love me still!"

"This is agony!" the artist hissed through his teeth, and he jumped up. "It will end by my throwing myself in the Volga or going out of my mind! Let me alone!"

"Come, kill me, kill me!" cried Olga Ivanovna. "Kill me!"

She sobbed again, and went behind the screen. There was a swish of rain on the straw thatch of the hut. Ryabovsky clutched his head and strode up and down the hut; then with a resolute face, as though bent on proving something to somebody, put on his cap, slung his gun over his shoulder, and went out of the hut.

After he had gone, Olga Ivanovna lay a long time on the bed, crying. At first she thought it would be a good thing to poison herself, so that when Ryabovsky came back he would find her dead; then her imagination carried her to her drawing-room, to her husband's study, and she imagined herself sitting motionless beside Dymov and enjoying the physical peace and cleanliness, and in the evening sitting in the theatre, listening to Mazini. And a yearning for civilization, for the noise and bustle of the town, for celebrated people sent a pang to her heart. A peasant woman came into the hut and began in a leisurely way lighting the stove to get the dinner. There was a smell of charcoal fumes, and the air was filled with bluish smoke. The artists came in, in muddy high boots and with faces wet with rain, examined their sketches, and comforted themselves by saying that the Volga had its charms even in bad weather. On the wall the cheap clock went "tic-tic-tic." . . . The flies, feeling chilled, crowded round the ikon in the corner, buzzing, and one could hear the cockroaches scurrying about among the thick portfolios under the seats. . . .

Ryabovsky came home as the sun was setting. He flung his cap on the table, and, without removing his muddy boots, sank pale and exhausted on the bench and closed his eyes.

"I am tired . . ." he said, and twitched his eyebrows, trying to raise his eyelids.

To be nice to him and to show she was not cross, Olga Ivanovna went up to him, gave him a silent kiss, and passed the comb through his fair hair. She meant to comb it for him.

"What's that?" he said, starting as though something cold had touched him, and he opened his eyes. "What is it? Please let me alone."

He thrust her off, and moved away. And it seemed to her that there was a look of aversion and annoyance on his face.

At that time the peasant woman cautiously carried him, in both hands, a plate of cabbage-soup. And Olga Ivanovna saw how she wetted her fat fingers in it. And the dirty peasant woman, standing with her body thrust forward, and the cabbage-soup which Ryabovsky began eating greedily, and the hut, and their whole way of life, which she at first had so loved for its simplicity and artistic disorder, seemed horrible to her now. She suddenly felt insulted, and said coldly:

"We must part for a time, or else from boredom we shall quarrel in earnest. I am sick of this; I am going today."

"Going how? Astride on a broomstick?"

"Today is Thursday, so the steamer will be here at half-past nine."

"Eh? Yes, yes. . . . Well, go, then . . ." Ryabovsky said softly, wiping his mouth with a towel instead of a dinner napkin. "You are dull and have nothing to do here, and one would have to be a great egoist to try and keep you. Go home, and we shall meet again after the twentieth."

Olga Ivanovna packed in good spirits. Her cheeks positively glowed with pleasure. Could it really be true, she asked herself, that she would soon be writing in her drawing-room and sleeping in her bedroom, and dining with a cloth on the table? A weight was lifted from her heart, and she no longer felt angry with the artist.

"My paints and brushes I will leave with you, Ryabovsky," she said. "You can bring what's left. . . . Mind, now, don't be lazy here when I am gone; don't mope, but work. You are such a splendid fellow, Ryabovsky!"

At ten o'clock Ryabovsky gave her a farewell kiss, in order, as she thought, to avoid kissing her on the steamer before the artists, and went with her to the landing-stage. The steamer soon came up and carried her away.

She arrived home two and a half days later. Breathless with excitement, she went, without taking off her hat or waterproof, into the drawing-room and thence into the dining-room. Dymov, with his waistcoat unbuttoned and no coat, was sitting at the table sharpening a knife on a fork; before him lay a grouse on a plate. As Olga Ivanovna went into the flat she was convinced that it was essential to hide everything from her husband, and that she would have the strength and skill to do so; but now, when she saw his broad, mild, happy smile, and shining, joyful eyes, she felt that to deceive this man was as vile, as revolting, and as impossible and out of her power as to bear false witness, to steal, or to kill, and in a flash she resolved to tell him all that had happened. Letting him kiss and embrace her, she sank down on her knees before him and hid her face.

"What is it, what is it, little mother?" he asked tenderly. "Were you homesick?"

She raised her face, red with shame, and gazed at him with a guilty and imploring look, but fear and shame prevented her from telling him the truth.

"Nothing," she said; "it's just nothing. . . ."

"Let us sit down," he said, raising her and seating her at the table. "That's right, eat the grouse. You are starving, poor darling."

She eagerly breathed in the atmosphere of home and ate the grouse, while he watched her with tenderness and laughed with delight.

VI

Apparently, by the middle of the winter Dymov began to suspect that he was being deceived. As though his conscience was not clear, he could not look his wife straight in the face, did not smile with delight when he met her, and to avoid being left alone with her, he often brought in to dinner his colleague, Korostelev, a little close-cropped man, with a wrinkled face, who kept buttoning and unbuttoning his reefer jacket with embarrassment when he talked with Olga Ivanovna, and then with his right hand nipped his left moustache. At dinner the two doctors talked about the fact that a displacement of the diaphragm was sometimes accompanied by irregularities of the heart, or that a great number of neurotic complaints were met with of late, or that Dymov had the day before found a cancer of the lower abdomen while dissecting a corpse with the diagnosis of pernicious anaemia. And it seemed as though they were talking of medicine to give Olga Ivanovna a chance of being silent—that is, of not lying. After dinner Korostelev sat down to the piano, while Dymov sighed and said to him:

"Ech, brother—well, well! Play something melancholy."

Hunching up his shoulders and stretching his fingers wide apart, Korostelev played some chords and began singing in a tenor voice, "Show me the abode where the Russian peasant would not groan," while Dymov sighed once more, propped his head on his fist, and sank into thought.

Olga Ivanovna had been extremely imprudent in her conduct of late. Every morning she woke up in a very bad humour and with the thought that she no longer cared for Ryabovsky, and that, thank God, it was all over now. But as she drank her coffee she reflected that Ryabovsky had robbed her of her husband, and that now she was left with neither her husband nor Ryabovsky; then she remembered talks she had heard among her acquaintances of a picture Ryabovsky was preparing for the exhibition, something striking, a mixture of genre and landscape, in the style of Polyenov, about which every one who had been in his studio went into raptures; and this, of course, she mused, he had created under her influence, and altogether, thanks to her influence, he had greatly changed for the better. Her influence was so beneficent and essential that if she were to leave him he might perhaps go to ruin. And she remembered, too, that the last time he had come to see her in a great-coat with flecks on it and a new tie, he had asked her languidly:

"Am I beautiful?"

And with his elegance, his long curls, and his blue eyes, he really was very beautiful (or perhaps it only seemed so), and he had been affectionate to her.

Considering and remembering many things Olga Ivanovna dressed and in great agitation drove to Ryabovsky's studio. She found him in high spirits, and enchanted with his really magnificent picture. He was dancing about and playing the fool and answering serious questions with jokes. Olga Ivanovna was jealous of the picture and hated it, but from politeness she stood before the picture for five minutes in silence, and, heaving a sigh, as though before a holy shrine, said softly:

"Yes, you have never painted anything like it before. Do you know, it is positively awe-inspiring?"

And then she began beseeching him to love her and not to cast her off, to have pity on her in her misery and her wretchedness. She shed tears, kissed his hands, insisted on his swearing that he loved her, told him that without her good influence he would go astray and be ruined. And, when she had spoilt his good-humour, feeling herself humiliated, she would drive off to her dressmaker or to an actress of her acquaintance to try and get theatre tickets.

If she did not find him at his studio she left a letter in which she swore that if he did not come to see her that day she would poison herself. He was scared, came to see her, and stayed to dinner. Regardless of her husband's presence, he would say rude things to her, and she would answer him in the same way. Both felt they were a burden to each other, that they were tyrants and enemies, and were wrathful, and in their wrath did not notice that their behaviour was unseemly, and that even Korostelev, with his close-cropped head, saw it all. After dinner Ryabovsky made haste to say good-bye and get away.

"Where are you off to?" Olga Ivanovna would ask him in the hall, looking at him with hatred.

Scowling and screwing up his eyes, he mentioned some lady of their acquaintance, and it was evident that he was laughing at her jealousy and wanted to annoy her. She went to her bedroom and lay down on her bed; from jealousy, anger, a sense of humiliation and shame, she bit the pillow and began sobbing aloud. Dymov left

Korostelev in the drawing-room, went into the bedroom, and with a desperate and embarrassed face said softly:

"Don't cry so loud, little mother; there's no need. You must be quiet about it. You must not let people see. . . . You know what is done is done, and can't be mended."

Not knowing how to ease the burden of her jealousy, which actually set her temples throbbing with pain, and thinking still that things might be set right, she would wash, powder her tear-stained face, and fly off to the lady mentioned.

Not finding Ryabovsky with her, she would drive off to a second, then to a third. At first she was ashamed to go about like this, but afterwards she got used to it, and it would happen that in one evening she would make the round of all her female acquaintances in search of Ryabovsky, and they all understood it.

One day she said to Ryabovsky of her husband:

"That man crushes me with his magnanimity."

This phrase pleased her so much that when she met the artists who knew of her affair with Ryabovsky she said every time of her husband, with a vigorous movement of her arm:

"That man crushes me with his magnanimity."

Their manner of life was the same as it had been the year before. On Wednesdays they were "At Home"; an actor recited, the artists sketched. The violoncellist played, a singer sang, and invariably at half-past eleven the door leading to the dining-room opened and Dymov, smiling, said:

"Come to supper, gentlemen."

As before, Olga Ivanovna hunted celebrities, found them, was not satisfied, and went in pursuit of fresh ones. As before, she came back late every night; but now Dymov was not, as last year, asleep, but sitting in his study at work of some sort. He went to bed at three o'clock and got up at eight.

One evening when she was getting ready to go to the theatre and standing before the pier glass, Dymov came into her bedroom, wearing his dresscoat and a white tie. He was smiling gently and looked into his wife's face joyfully, as in old days; his face was radiant.

"I have just been defending my thesis," he said, sitting down and smoothing his knees.

"Defending?" asked Olga Ivanovna.

"Oh, oh!" he laughed, and he craned his neck to see his wife's face in the mirror, for she was still standing with her back to him, doing up her hair. "Oh, oh," he repeated, "do you know it's very possible they may offer me the Readership in General Pathology? It seems like it."

It was evident from his beaming, blissful face that if Olga Ivanovna had shared with him his joy and triumph he would have forgiven her everything, both the present and the future, and would have forgotten everything, but she did not understand what was meant by a "readership" or by "general pathology"; besides, she was afraid of being late for the theatre, and she said nothing.

He sat there another two minutes, and with a guilty smile went away.

VII

It had been a very troubled day.

Dymov had a very bad headache; he had no breakfast, and did not go to the hospital, but spent the whole time lying on his sofa in the study. Olga Ivanovna went as usual at midday to see Ryabovsky, to show him her still-life sketch, and to ask him why he had not been to see her the evening before. The sketch seemed to her worthless, and she had painted it only in order to have an additional reason for going to the artist.

She went in to him without ringing, and as she was taking off her goloshes in the entry she heard a sound as of something running softly in the studio, with a feminine rustle of skirts; and as she hastened to peep in she caught a momentary glimpse of a bit of brown petticoat, which vanished behind a big picture draped, together with the easel, with black calico, to the floor. There could be no doubt that a woman was hiding there. How often Olga Ivanovna herself had taken refuge behind that picture!

Ryabovsky, evidently much embarrassed, held out both hands to her, as though surprised at her arrival, and said with a forced smile:

"Aha! Very glad to see you! Anything nice to tell me?"

Olga Ivanovna's eyes filled with tears. She felt ashamed and bitter, and would not for a million roubles have consented to speak in the presence of the outsider, the rival, the deceitful woman who was standing now behind the picture, and probably giggling malignantly.

"I have brought you a sketch," she said timidly in a thin voice, and her lips quivered. *"Nature morte."*

"Ah—ah! . . . A sketch?"

The artist took the sketch in his hands, and as he examined it walked, as it were mechanically, into the other room.

Olga Ivanovna followed him humbly.

"*Nature morte* . . . first-rate sort," he muttered, falling into rhyme. "Kurort . . . sport . . . port . . ."

From the studio came the sound of hurried footsteps and the rustle of a skirt.

So she had gone. Olga Ivanovna wanted to scream aloud, to hit the artist on the head with something heavy, but she could see nothing through her tears, was crushed by her shame, and felt herself, not Olga Ivanovna, not an artist, but a little insect.

"I am tired . . ." said the artist languidly, looking at the sketch and tossing his head as though struggling with drowsiness. "It's very nice, of course, but here a sketch today, a sketch last year, another sketch in a month . . . I wonder you are not bored with them. If I were you I should give up painting and work seriously at music or something. You're not an artist, you know, but a musician. But you can't think how tired I am! I'll tell them to bring us some tea, shall I?"

He went out of the room, and Olga Ivanovna heard him give some order to his footman. To avoid farewells and explanations, and above all to avoid bursting into sobs, she ran as fast as she could, before Ryabovsky came back, to the entry, put on her goloshes, and went out into the street; then she breathed easily, and felt she was free for ever from Ryabovsky and from painting and from the burden of shame which had so crushed her in the studio. It was all over!

She drove to her dressmaker's; then to see Barnay, who had only arrived the day before; from Barnay to a music-shop, and all the time she was thinking how she would write Ryabovsky a cold, cruel letter full of personal dignity, and how in the spring or the summer she would go with Dymov to the Crimea, free herself finally from the past there, and begin a new life.

On getting home late in the evening she sat down in the drawing-room, without taking off her things, to begin the letter. Ryabovsky had told her she was not an artist, and to pay him out she wrote to him now that he painted the same thing every year, and said exactly the same thing every day; that he was at a standstill, and that nothing more would come of him than had come already. She wanted to write, too, that he owed a great deal to her good influence, and that if he was going wrong it was only because her influence was paralysed by various dubious persons like the one who had been hiding behind the picture that day.

"Little mother!" Dymov called from the study, without opening the door.

"What is it?"

"Don't come in to me, but only come to the door—that's right. . . . The day before yesterday I must have caught diphtheria at the hospital, and now . . . I am ill. Make haste and send for Korostelev."

Olga Ivanovna always called her husband by his surname, as she did all the men of her acquaintance; she disliked his Christian name, Osip, because it reminded her of the Osip in Gogol and the silly pun on his name. But now she cried:

"Osip, it cannot be!"

"Send for him; I feel ill," Dymov said behind the door, and she could hear him go back to the sofa and lie down. "Send!" she heard his voice faintly.

"Good Heavens!" thought Olga Ivanovna, turning chill with horror. "Why, it's dangerous!"

For no reason she took the candle and went into the bedroom, and there, reflecting what she must do, glanced casually at herself in the pier glass. With her pale, frightened face, in a jacket with sleeves high on the shoulders, with yellow ruches on her bosom, and with stripes running in unusual directions on her skirt, she seemed to herself horrible and disgusting. She suddenly felt poignantly sorry for Dymov, for his boundless love for her, for his young life, and even for the desolate little bed in which he had not slept for so long; and she remembered his habitual, gentle, submissive smile. She wept bitterly, and wrote an imploring letter to Korostelev. It was two o'clock in the night.

VIII

When towards eight o'clock in the morning Olga Ivanovna, her head heavy from want of sleep and her hair unbrushed, came out of her bedroom, looking unattractive and with a guilty expression on her face, a gentleman with a black beard, apparently the doctor, passed by her into the entry. There was a smell of drugs. Korostelev was standing near the study door, twisting his left moustache with his right hand.

"Excuse me, I can't let you go in," he said surlily to Olga Ivanovna; "it's catching. Besides, it's no use, really; he is delirious, anyway."

"Has he really got diphtheria?" Olga Ivanovna asked in a whisper.

"People who wantonly risk infection ought to be hauled up and punished for it," muttered Korostelev, not answering Olga Ivanovna's question. Do you know why he caught it? On Tuesday he was sucking up the mucus through a pipette from a boy with diphtheria. And what for? It was stupid. . . . Just from folly. . . ."

"Is it dangerous, very?" asked Olga Ivanovna.

"Yes; they say it is the malignant form. We ought to send for Shrek really."

A little red-haired man with a long nose and a Jewish accent arrived; then a tall, stooping, shaggy individual, who looked like a head deacon; then a stout young man with a red face and spectacles. These were doctors who came to watch by turns beside their colleague. Korostelev did not go home when his turn was over, but remained and wandered about the rooms like an uneasy spirit. The maid kept getting tea for the various doctors, and was constantly running to the chemist, and there was no one to do the rooms. There was a dismal stillness in the flat.

Olga Ivanovna sat in her bedroom and thought that God was punishing her for having deceived her husband. That silent, unrepining, uncomprehended creature, robbed by his mildness of all personality and will, weak from excessive kindness, had been suffering in obscurity somewhere on his sofa, and had not complained. And if he were to complain even in delirium, the doctors watching by his bedside would learn that diphtheria was not the only cause of his sufferings. They would ask Korostelev. He knew all about it, and it was not for nothing that he looked at his friend's wife with eyes that seemed to say that she was the real chief criminal and diphtheria was only her accomplice. She did not think now of the moonlight evening on the Volga, nor the words of love, nor their poetical life in the peasant's hut. She thought only that from an idle whim, from self-indulgence, she had sullied herself all over from head to foot in something filthy, sticky, which one could never wash off. . . .

"Oh, how fearfully false I've been!" she thought, recalling the troubled passion she had known with Ryabovsky. "Curse it all! . . ."

At four o'clock she dined with Korostelev. He did nothing but scowl and drink red wine, and did not eat a morsel. She ate nothing, either. At one minute she was praying inwardly and vowing to God that if Dymov recovered she would love him again and be a faithful wife to him. Then, forgetting herself for a minute, she would look at Korostelev, and think: "Surely it must be dull to be a humble, obscure person, not remarkable in any way, especially with such a wrinkled face and bad manners!" Then it seemed to her that God would strike her dead that minute for not having once been in her husband's study, for fear of infection. And altogether she had a dull, despondent feeling and a conviction that her life was spoilt, and that there was no setting it right anyhow. . . .

After dinner darkness came on. When Olga Ivanovna went into the drawing-room Korostelev was asleep on the sofa, with a gold-embroidered silk cushion under his head.

"Khee-poo-ah," he snored—"khee-poo-ah."

And the doctors as they came to sit up and went away again did not notice this disorder. The fact that a strange man was asleep and snoring in the drawing-room, and the sketches on the walls and the exquisite decoration of the room, and the fact that the lady of the house was dishevelled and untidy—all that aroused not the slightest interest now. One of the doctors chanced to laugh at something, and the laugh had a strange and timid sound that made one's heart ache.

When Olga Ivanovna went into the drawing-room next time, Korostelev was not asleep, but sitting up and smoking.

"He has diphtheria of the nasal cavity," he said in a low voice, "and the heart is not working properly now. Things are in a bad way, really."

"But you will send for Shrek?" said Olga Ivanovna.

"He has been already. It was he who noticed that the diphtheria had passed into the nose. What's the use of Shrek! Shrek's no use at all, really. He is Shrek, I am Korostelev, and nothing more."

The time dragged on fearfully slowly. Olga Ivanovna lay down in her clothes on her bed, that had not been made all day, and sank into a doze. She dreamed that the whole flat was filled up from floor to ceiling with a huge piece of iron, and that if they could only get the iron out they would all be light-hearted and happy. Waking, she realized that it was not the iron but Dymov's illness that was weighing on her.

"Nature morte, port . . ." she thought, sinking into forgetfulness again. "Sport . . . Kurort . . . and what of Shrek? Shrek . . . trek . . . wreck. . . . And where are my friends now? Do they know that we are in trouble? Lord, save . . . spare! Shrek . . . trek . . ."

And again the iron was there. . . . The time dragged on slowly, though the clock on the lower storey struck frequently. And bells were continually ringing as the doctors arrived. . . . The housemaid came in with an empty glass on a tray, and asked, "Shall I make the bed, madam?" and getting no answer, went away.

The clock below struck the hour. She dreamed of the rain on the Volga; and again some one came into her bedroom, she thought a stranger. Olga Ivanovna jumped up, and recognized Korostelev.

"What time is it?" she asked.

"About three."

"Well, what is it?"

"What, indeed! . . . I've come to tell you he is passing. . . ."

He gave a sob, sat down on the bed beside her, and wiped away the tears with his sleeve. She could not grasp it at once, but turned cold all over and began slowly crossing herself.

"He is passing," he repeated in a shrill voice, and again he gave a sob. "He is dying because he sacrificed himself. What a loss for science!" he said bitterly. "Compare him with all of us. He was a great man, an extraordinary man! What gifts! What hopes we all had of him!" Korostelev went on, wringing his hands: "Merciful God, he was a man of science; we shall never look on his like again. Osip Dymov, what have you done—aie, aie, my God!"

Korostelev covered his face with both hands in despair, and shook his head.

"And his moral force," he went on, seeming to grow more and more exasperated against some one. "Not a man, but a pure, good, loving soul, and clean as crystal. He served science and died for science. And he worked like an ox night and day—no one spared him—and with his youth and his learning he had to take a private practice and work at translations at night to pay for these . . . vile rags!"

Korostelev looked with hatred at Olga Ivanovna, snatched at the sheet with both hands and angrily tore it, as though it were to blame.

"He did not spare himself, and others did not spare him. Oh, what's the use of talking!"

"Yes, he was a rare man," said a bass voice in the drawing-room.

Olga Ivanovna remembered her whole life with him from the beginning to the end, with all its details, and suddenly she understood that he really was an extraordinary, rare, and, compared with every one else she knew, a great man. And remembering how her father, now dead, and all the other doctors had behaved to him, she realized that they really had seen in him a future celebrity. The walls, the ceiling, the lamp, and the carpet on the floor, seemed to be winking at her sarcastically, as though they would say, "You were blind! you were blind!" With a wail she flung herself out of the bedroom, dashed by some unknown man in the drawing-room, and ran into her husband's study. He was lying motionless on the sofa, covered to the waist with a quilt. His face was fearfully thin and sunken, and was of a greyish-yellow colour such as is never seen in the living; only from the forehead, from the black eyebrows and from the familiar smile, could he be recognized as Dymov. Olga Ivanovna hurriedly felt his chest, his forehead, and his hands. The chest was still warm, but the forehead and hands were unpleasantly cold, and the half-open eyes looked, not at Olga Ivanovna, but at the quilt.

"Dymov!" she called aloud, "Dymov!" She wanted to explain to him that it had been a mistake, that all was not lost, that life might still be beautiful and happy, that he was an extraordinary, rare, great man, and that she would all her life worship him and bow down in homage and holy awe before him. . . .

"Dymov!" she called him, patting him on the shoulder, unable to believe that he would never wake again. "Dymov! Dymov!"

In the drawing-room Korostelev was saying to the housemaid:

"Why keep asking? Go to the church beadle and enquire where they live. They'll wash the body and lay it out, and do everything that is necessary."

1892

Neighbours

Pyotr Mihalitch Ivashin was very much out of humour: his sister, a young girl, had gone away to live with Vlassitch, a married man. To shake off the despondency and depression which pursued him at home and in the fields, he called to his aid his sense of justice, his genuine and noble ideas—he had always defended free-love!—but this was of no avail, and he always came back to the same conclusion as their foolish old nurse, that his sister had acted wrongly and that Vlassitch had abducted his sister. And that was distressing.

His mother did not leave her room all day long; the old nurse kept sighing and speaking in whispers; his aunt had been on the point of taking her departure every day, and her trunks were continually being brought down to the hall and carried up again to her room. In the house, in the yard, and in the garden it was as still as though there were some one dead in the house. His aunt, the servants, and even the peasants, so it seemed to Pyotr Mihalitch, looked at him enigmatically and with perplexity, as though they wanted to say "Your sister has been seduced; why are you doing nothing?" And he reproached himself for inactivity, though he did not know precisely what action he ought to have taken.

So passed six days. On the seventh—it was Sunday afternoon—a messenger on horseback brought a letter. The address was in a familiar feminine handwriting: "Her Excy. Anna Nikolaevna Ivashin." Pyotr Mihalitch fancied that there was something defiant, provocative, in the handwriting and in the abbreviation "Excy." And advanced ideas in women are obstinate, ruthless, cruel.

"She'd rather die than make any concession to her unhappy mother, or beg her forgiveness," thought Pyotr Mihalitch, as he went to his mother with the letter.

His mother was lying on her bed, dressed. Seeing her son, she rose impulsively, and straightening her grey hair, which had fallen from under her cap, asked quickly:

"What is it? What is it?"

"This has come . . ." said her son, giving her the letter.

Zina's name, and even the pronoun "she" was not uttered in the house. Zina was spoken of impersonally: "This has come," "Gone away," and so on. . . . The mother recognised her daughter's handwriting, and her face grew ugly and unpleasant, and her grey hair escaped again from her cap.

"No!" she said, with a motion of her hands, as though the letter scorched her fingers. "No, no, never! Nothing would induce me!"

The mother broke into hysterical sobs of grief and shame; she evidently longed to read the letter, but her pride prevented her. Pyotr Mihalitch realised that he ought to open the letter himself and read it aloud, but he was overcome by anger such as he had never felt before; he ran out into the yard and shouted to the messenger:

"Say there will be no answer! There will be no answer! Tell them that, you beast!"

And he tore up the letter; then tears came into his eyes, and feeling that he was cruel, miserable, and to blame, he went out into the fields.

He was only twenty-seven, but he was already stout. He dressed like an old man in loose, roomy clothes, and suffered from asthma. He already seemed to be developing the characteristics of an elderly country bachelor. He never fell in love, never thought of marriage, and loved no one but his mother, his sister, his old nurse, and the gardener, Vassilitch. He was fond of good fare, of his nap after dinner, and of talking about politics and exalted subjects. He had in his day taken his degree at the university, but he now looked upon his studies as though in them he had discharged a duty incumbent upon young men between the ages of eighteen and twenty-five; at any rate, the ideas which now strayed every day through his mind had nothing in common with the university or the subjects he had studied there.

In the fields it was hot and still, as though rain were coming. It was steaming in the wood, and there was a heavy fragrant scent from the pines and rotting leaves. Pyotr Mihalitch stopped several times and wiped his wet brow. He looked at his winter corn and his spring oats, walked round the clover-field, and twice drove away a partridge with its chicks which had strayed in from the wood. And all the while he was thinking that this insufferable state of things could not go on for ever, and that he must end it one way or another. End it stupidly, madly, but he must end it.

"But how? What can I do?" he asked himself, and looked imploringly at the sky and at the trees, as though begging for their help.

But the sky and the trees were mute. His noble ideas were no help, and his common sense whispered that the agonising question could have no solution but a stupid one, and that to-day's scene with the messenger was not the last one of its kind. It was terrible to think what was in store for him!

As he returned home the sun was setting. By now it seemed to him that the problem was incapable of solution. He could not accept the accomplished fact, and he could not refuse to accept it, and there was no intermediate course. When, taking off his hat and fanning himself with his handkerchief, he was walking along the road, and had only another mile and a half to go before he would reach home, he heard bells behind him. It was a very choice and successful combination of bells, which gave a clear crystal note. No one had such bells on his horses but the police captain, Medovsky, formerly an officer in the hussars, a man in broken-down health, who had been a great rake and spendthrift, and was a distant relation of Pyotr Mihalitch. He was like one of the family at the Ivashins' and had a tender, fatherly affection for Zina, as well as a great admiration for her.

"I was coming to see you," he said, overtaking Pyotr Mihalitch. "Get in; I'll give you a lift."

He was smiling and looked cheerful. Evidently he did not yet know that Zina had gone to live with Vlassitch; perhaps he had been told of it already, but did not believe it. Pyotr Mihalitch felt in a difficult position.

"You are very welcome," he muttered, blushing till the tears came into his eyes, and not knowing how to lie or what to say. "I am delighted," he went on, trying to smile, "but . . . Zina is away and mother is ill."

"How annoying!" said the police captain, looking pensively at Pyotr Mihalitch. "And I was meaning to spend the evening with you. Where has Zinaida Mihalovna gone?"

"To the Sinitskys', and I believe she meant to go from there to the monastery. I don't quite know."

The police captain talked a little longer and then turned back. Pyotr Mihalitch walked home, and thought with horror what the police captain's feelings would be when he learned the truth. And

Pyotr Mihalitch imagined his feelings, and actually experiencing them himself, went into the house.

"Lord help us," he thought, "Lord help us!"

At evening tea the only one at the table was his aunt. As usual, her face wore the expression that seemed to say that though she was a weak, defenceless woman, she would allow no one to insult her. Pyotr Mihalitch sat down at the other end of the table (he did not like his aunt) and began drinking tea in silence.

"Your mother has had no dinner again to-day," said his aunt. "You ought to do something about it, Petrusha. Starving oneself is no help in sorrow."

It struck Pyotr Mihalitch as absurd that his aunt should meddle in other people's business and should make her departure depend on Zina's having gone away. He was tempted to say something rude to her, but restrained himself. And as he restrained himself he felt the time had come for action, and that he could not bear it any longer. Either he must act at once or fall on the ground, and scream and bang his head upon the floor. He pictured Vlassitch and Zina, both of them progressive and self-satisfied, kissing each other somewhere under a maple tree, and all the anger and bitterness that had been accumulating in him for the last seven days fastened upon Vlassitch.

"One has seduced and abducted my sister," he thought, "another will come and murder my mother, a third will set fire to the house and sack the place. . . . And all this under the mask of friendship, lofty ideas, unhappiness!"

"No, it shall not be!" Pyotr Mihalitch cried suddenly, and he brought his fist down on the table.

He jumped up and ran out of the dining-room. In the stable the steward's horse was standing ready saddled. He got on it and galloped off to Vlassitch.

There was a perfect tempest within him. He felt a longing to do something extraordinary, startling, even if he had to repent of it all his life afterwards. Should he call Vlassitch a blackguard, slap him in the face, and then challenge him to a duel? But Vlassitch was not one of those men who do fight duels; being called a blackguard and slapped in the face would only make him more unhappy, and would make him shrink into himself more than ever. These unhappy, defenceless people are the most insufferable, the most tiresome creatures in the world.

They can do anything with impunity. When the luckless man responds to well-deserved reproach by looking at you with eyes full of deep and guilty feeling, and with a sickly smile bends his head submissively, even justice itself could not lift its hand against him.

"No matter. I'll horsewhip him before her eyes and tell him what I think of him," Pyotr Mihalitch decided.

He was riding through his wood and waste land, and he imagined Zina would try to justify her conduct by talking about the rights of women and individual freedom, and about there being no difference between legal marriage and free union. Like a woman, she would argue about what she did not understand. And very likely at the end she would ask, "How do you come in? What right have you to inter-fere?"

"No, I have no right," muttered Pyotr Mihalitch. "But so much the better. . . . The harsher I am, the less right I have to interfere, the better."

It was sultry. Clouds of gnats hung over the ground and in the waste places the peewits called plaintively. Everything betokened rain, but he could not see a cloud in the sky. Pyotr Mihalitch crossed the boundary of his estate and galloped over a smooth, level field. He often went along this road and knew every bush, every hollow in it. What now in the far distance looked in the dusk like a dark cliff was a red church; he could picture it all down to the smallest detail, even the plaster on the gate and the calves that were always grazing in the church enclosure. Three-quarters of a mile to the right of the church there was a copse like a dark blur—it was Count Koltonovitch's. And beyond the church Vlassitch's estate began.

From behind the church and the count's copse a huge black storm-cloud was rising, and there were ashes of white lightning.

"Here it is!" thought Pyotr Mihalitch. "Lord help us, Lord help us!"

The horse was soon tired after its gallop, and Pyotr Mihalitch was tired too. The storm-cloud looked at him angrily and seemed to advise him to go home. He felt a little scared.

"I will prove to them they are wrong," he tried to reassure himself. "They will say that it is free-love, individual freedom; but freedom means self-control and not subjection to passion. It's not liberty but license!"

He reached the count's big pond; it looked dark blue and frowning under the cloud, and a smell of damp and slime rose from it. Near the dam, two willows, one old and one young, drooped tenderly towards one another. Pyotr Mihalitch and Vlassitch had been walking near this very spot only a fortnight before, humming a students' song:

" 'Youth is wasted, life is nought, when the heart is cold and loveless.' "

A wretched song!

It was thundering as Pyotr Mihalitch rode through the copse, and the trees were bending and rustling in the wind. He had to make haste. It was only three-quarters of a mile through a meadow from the copse to Vlassitch's house. Here there were old birch-trees on each side of the road. They had the same melancholy and unhappy air as their owner Vlassitch, and looked as tall and lanky as he. Big drops of rain pattered on the birches and on the grass; the wind had suddenly dropped, and there was a smell of wet earth and poplars. Before him he saw Vlassitch's fence with a row of yellow acacias, which were tall and lanky too; where the fence was broken he could see the neglected orchard.

Pyotr Mihalitch was not thinking now of the horsewhip or of a slap in the face, and did not know what he would do at Vlassitch's. He felt nervous. He felt frightened on his own account and on his sister's, and was terrified at the thought of seeing her. How would she behave with her brother? What would they both talk about? And had he not better go back before it was too late? As he made these reflections, he galloped up the avenue of lime-trees to the house, rode round the big clumps of lilacs, and suddenly saw Vlassitch.

Vlassitch, wearing a cotton shirt, and top-boots, bending forward, with no hat on in the rain, was coming from the corner of the house to the front door. He was followed by a workman with a hammer and a box of nails. They must have been mending a shutter which had been banging in the wind. Seeing Pyotr Mihalitch, Vlassitch stopped.

"It's you!" he said, smiling. "That's nice."

"Yes, I've come, as you see," said Pyotr Mihalitch, brushing the rain off himself with both hands.

"Well, that's capital! I'm very glad," said Vlassitch, but he did not hold out his hand: evidently he did not venture, but waited for Pyotr Mihalitch to hold out his. "It will do the oats good," he said, looking at the sky.

"Yes."

They went into the house in silence. To the right of the hall was a door leading to another hall and then to the drawing-room, and on the left was a little room which in winter was used by the steward. Pyotr Mihalitch and Vlassitch went into this little room.

"Where were you caught in the rain?"

"Not far off, quite close to the house."

Pyotr Mihalitch sat down on the bed. He was glad of the noise of the rain and the darkness of the room. It was better: it made it less dreadful, and there was no need to see his companion's face. There was no anger in his heart now, nothing but fear and vexation with himself. He felt he had made a bad beginning, and that nothing would come of this visit.

Both were silent for some time and affected to be listening to the rain.

"Thank you, Petrusha," Vlassitch began, clearing his throat. "I am very grateful to you for coming. It's generous and noble of you. I understand it, and, believe me, I appreciate it. Believe me."

He looked out of the window and went on, standing in the middle of the room:

"Everything happened so secretly, as though we were concealing it all from you. The feeling that you might be wounded and angry has been a blot on our happiness all these days. But let me justify myself. We kept it secret not because we did not trust you. To begin with, it all happened suddenly, by a kind of inspiration; there was no time to discuss it. Besides, it's such a private, delicate matter, and it was awkward to bring a third person in, even some one as intimate as you. Above all, in all this we reckoned on your generosity. You are a very noble and generous person. I am infinitely grateful to you. If you ever need my life, come and take it."

Vlassitch talked in a quiet, hollow bass, always on the same droning note; he was evidently agitated. Pyotr Mihalitch felt it was his turn to speak, and that to listen and keep silent would really mean playing the part of a generous and noble simpleton, and that had not been his idea in coming. He got up quickly and said, breathlessly in an undertone:

"Listen, Grigory. You know I liked you and could have desired no better husband for my sister; but what has happened is awful! It's terrible to think of it!"

"Why is it terrible?" asked Vlassitch, with a quiver in his voice. "It would be terrible if we had done wrong, but that isn't so."

"Listen, Grigory. You know I have no prejudices; but, excuse my frankness, to my mind you have both acted selfishly. Of course, I shan't say so to my sister—it will distress her; but you ought to know: mother is miserable beyond all description."

"Yes, that's sad," sighed Vlassitch. "We foresaw that, Petrusha, but what could we have done? Because one's actions hurt other people, it doesn't prove that they are wrong. What's to be done! Every important step one takes is bound to distress somebody. If you went to fight for freedom, that would distress your mother, too. What's to be done! Any one who puts the peace of his family before everything has to renounce the life of ideas completely."

There was a vivid flash of lightning at the window, and the lightning seemed to change the course of Vlassitch's thoughts. He sat down beside Pyotr Mihalitch and began saying what was utterly beside the point.

"I have such a reverence for your sister, Petrusha," he said. "When I used to come and see you, I felt as though I were going to a holy shrine, and I really did worship Zina. Now my reverence for her grows every day. For me she is something higher than a wife—yes, higher!" Vlassitch waved his hands. "She is my holy of holies. Since she is living with me, I enter my house as though it were a temple. She is an extraordinary, rare, most noble woman!"

"Well, he's off now!" thought Pyotr Mihalitch; he disliked the word "woman."

"Why shouldn't you be married properly?" he asked. "How much does your wife want for a divorce?"

"Seventy-five thousand."

"It's rather a lot. But if we were to negotiate with her?"

"She won't take a farthing less. She is an awful woman, brother," sighed Vlassitch. "I've never talked to you about her before—it was unpleasant to think of her; but now that the subject has come up, I'll tell you about her. I married her on the impulse of the moment—a fine, honourable impulse. An officer in command of a battalion of our regiment—if you care to hear the details—had an affair with a girl of eighteen; that is, to put it plainly, he seduced her, lived with her for two months, and abandoned her. She was in an awful position, brother. She was ashamed to go home to her parents; besides, they wouldn't have received her. Her lover had abandoned her; there was nothing left for her but to go to the barracks and sell herself. The other officers in the regiment were indignant. They were by no means saints themselves, but the baseness of it was so striking. Besides, no one in the regiment could endure the man. And to spite him, you understand, the indignant lieutenants and ensigns began getting up a subscription for the unfortunate girl. And when we subalterns met together and began to subscribe five or ten roubles each, I had a sudden inspiration. I felt it was an opportunity to do something fine. I hastened to the girl and warmly expressed my sympathy. And while I was on my way to her, and while I was talking to her, I loved her fervently as a woman insulted and injured. Yes. . . . Well, a week later I made her an offer. The colonel and my comrades thought my marriage out of keeping with the dignity of an officer. That roused me more than ever. I wrote a long letter, do you know, in which I proved that my action ought to be inscribed in the annals of the regiment in letters of gold, and so on. I sent the letter to my colonel and copies to my comrades. Well, I was excited, and, of course, I could not avoid being rude. I was asked to leave the regiment. I have a rough copy of it put away somewhere; I'll give it to you to read sometime. It was written with great feeling. You will see what lofty and noble sentiments I was experiencing. I resigned my commission and came here with my wife. My father had left a few debts, I had no money, and from the first day my wife began making acquaintances, dressing herself smartly, and playing cards, and I was obliged to mortgage the estate. She led a bad life, you understand, and you are the only one of the neighbours who hasn't been her lover. After two years I gave her all I had to set me free and she went off to town. Yes. . . . And now I pay her twelve hundred roubles a year. She is an awful woman! There is a fly, brother, which lays an egg in the back of a spider so that the spider can't shake it off: the grub fastens upon the spider and drinks its heart's blood. That was how this woman fastened upon me and sucks the blood of my heart. She hates and despises me for being so stupid; that is, for marrying a woman like her. My chivalry seems to her despicable. 'A wise man cast me off,' she says, 'and a fool picked me up.' To her thinking no one but a pitiful idiot could have behaved as I did. And that is insufferably bitter to me, brother. Altogether, I may say in parenthesis, fate has been hard upon me, very hard."

Pyotr Mihalitch listened to Vlassitch and wondered in perplexity what it was in this man that had so charmed his sister. He was not young—he was forty-one—lean and lanky, narrow-chested, with a long nose, and grey hairs in his beard. He talked in a droning voice, had a sickly smile, and waved his hands awkwardly as he talked. He had neither health, nor pleasant, manly manners, nor *savoir-faire*, nor gaiety, and in all his exterior there was something colourless and indefinite. He dressed without taste, his surroundings were depressing, he did not care for poetry or painting because "they have no answer to give to the questions of the day"—that is, he did not understand them; music did not touch him. He was a poor farmer.

His estate was in a wretched condition and was mortgaged; he was paying twelve per cent. on the second mortgage and owed ten thousand on personal securities as well. When the time came to pay the interest on the mortgage or to send money to his wife, he asked every one to lend him money with as much agitation as though his house were on fire, and, at the same time losing his head, he would sell the whole of his winter store of fuel for five roubles and a stack of straw for three roubles, and then have his garden fence or old cucumber-frames chopped up to heat his stoves. His meadows were ruined by pigs, the peasants' cattle strayed in the undergrowth in his woods, and every year the old trees were fewer and fewer: beehives and rusty pails lay about in his garden and kitchen-garden. He had neither talents nor abilities, nor even ordinary capacity for living like other people. In practical life he was a weak, naïve man, easy to deceive and to cheat, and the peasants with good reason called him "simple."

He was a Liberal, and in the district was regarded as a "Red," but even his progressiveness was a bore. There was no originality nor moving power about his independent views: he was revolted, indignant, and delighted always on the same note; it was always spiritless and ineffective. Even in moments of strong enthusiasm he never raised his head or stood upright. But the most tiresome thing of all was that he managed to express even his best and finest ideas so that they seemed in him commonplace and out of date. It reminded one of something old one had read long ago, when slowly and with an air of profundity he would begin discoursing of his noble, lofty moments, of his best years; or when he went into raptures over the younger generation, which has always been, and still is, in advance of society; or abused Russians for donning their dressing-gowns at thirty and forgetting the principles of their *alma mater*. If you stayed the night with him, he would put Pissarev or Darwin on your bedroom table; if you said you had read it, he would go and bring Dobrolubov.

In the district this was called free-thinking, and many people looked upon this free-thinking as an innocent and harmless eccentricity; it made him profoundly unhappy, however. It was for him the maggot of which he had just been speaking; it had fastened upon him and was sucking his life-blood. In his past there had been the strange marriage in the style of Dostoevsky; long letters and copies written in a bad, unintelligible hand-writing, but with great feeling, endless misunderstandings, explanations, disappointments, then debts, a second mortgage, the allowance to his wife, the monthly borrowing of money—and all this for no benefit to any one, either himself or others. And in the present, as in the past, he was still in a nervous flurry, on the lookout for heroic actions, and poking his nose into other people's affairs; as before, at every favourable opportunity there were long letters and copies, wearisome, stereotyped conversations about the village community, or the revival of handicrafts or the establishment of cheese factories—conversations as like one another as though he had prepared them, not in his living brain, but by some mechanical process. And finally this scandal with Zina of which one could not see the end!

And meanwhile Zina was young—she was only twenty-two— good-looking, elegant, gay; she was fond of laughing, chatter, argument, a passionate musician; she had good taste in dress, in furniture, in books, and in her own home she would not have put up with a room like this, smelling of boots and cheap vodka. She, too, had advanced ideas, but in her free-thinking one felt the overflow of energy, the vanity of a young, strong, spirited girl, passionately eager to be better and more original than others. . . . How had it happened that she had fallen in love with Vlassitch?

"He is a Quixote, an obstinate fanatic, a maniac," thought Pyotr

Mihalitch, "and she is as soft, yielding, and weak in character as I am. . . . She and I give in easily, without resistance. She loves him; but, then, I, too, love him in spite of everything."

Pyotr Mihalitch considered Vlassitch a good, straightforward man, but narrow and one-sided. In his perturbations and his sufferings, and in fact in his whole life, he saw no lofty aims, remote or immediate; he saw nothing but boredom and incapacity for life. His self-sacrifice and all that Vlassitch himself called heroic actions or noble impulses seemed to him a useless waste of force, unnecessary blank shots which consumed a great deal of powder. And Vlassitch's fanatical belief in the extraordinary loftiness and faultlessness of his own way of thinking struck him as naïve and even morbid; and the fact that Vlassitch all his life had contrived to mix the trivial with the exalted, that he had made a stupid marriage and looked upon it as an act of heroism, and then had affairs with other women and regarded that as a triumph of some idea or other was simply incomprehensible.

Nevertheless, Pyotr Mihalitch was fond of Vlassitch; he was conscious of a sort of power in him, and for some reason he had never had the heart to contradict him.

Vlassitch sat down quite close to him for a talk in the dark, to the accompaniment of the rain, and he had cleared his throat as a prelude to beginning on something lengthy, such as the history of his marriage. But it was intolerable for Pyotr Mihalitch to listen to him; he was tormented by the thought that he would see his sister directly.

"Yes, you've had bad luck," he said gently; "but, excuse me, we've been wandering from the point. That's not what we are talking about."

"Yes, yes, quite so. Well, let us come back to the point," said Vlassitch, and he stood up. "I tell you, Petrusha, our conscience is clear. We are not married, but there is no need for me to prove to you that our marriage is perfectly legitimate. You are as free in your ideas as I am, and, happily, there can be no disagreement between us on that point. As for our future, that ought not to alarm you. I'll work in the sweat of my brow, I'll work day and night—in fact, I will strain every nerve to make Zina happy. Her life will be a splendid one! You may ask, am I able to do it. I am, brother! When a man devotes every minute to one thought, it's not difficult for him to attain his object. But let us go to Zina; it will be a joy to her to see you."

Pyotr Mihalitch's heart began to beat. He got up and followed Vlassitch into the hall, and from there into the drawing-room. There was nothing in the huge gloomy room but a piano and a long row of old chairs ornamented with bronze, on which no one ever sat. There was a candle alight on the piano. From the drawing-room they went in silence into the dining-room. This room, too, was large and comfortless; in the middle of the room there was a round table with two leaves with six thick legs, and only one candle. A clock in a large mahogany case like an ikon stand pointed to half-past two.

Vlassitch opened the door into the next room and said:

"Zina, here is Petrusha come to see us!"

At once there was the sound of hurried footsteps and Zina came into the dining-room. She was tall, plump, and very pale, and, just as when he had seen her for the last time at home, she was wearing a black skirt and a red blouse, with a large buckle on her belt. She flung one arm round her brother and kissed him on the temple.

"What a storm!" she said. "Grigory went off somewhere and I was left quite alone in the house."

She was not embarrassed, and looked at her brother as frankly and candidly as at home; looking at her, Pyotr Mihalitch, too, lost his embarrassment.

"But you are not afraid of storms," he said, sitting down at the table.

"No," she said, "but here the rooms are so big, the house is so old, and when there is thunder it all rattles like a cupboard full of crockery. It's a charming house altogether," she went on, sitting down opposite her brother. "There's some pleasant memory in every room. In my room, only fancy, Grigory's grandfather shot himself."

"In August we shall have the money to do up the lodge in the garden," said Vlassitch.

"For some reason when it thunders I think of that grandfather," Zina went on. "And in this dining-room somebody was flogged to death."

"That's an actual fact," said Vlassitch, and he looked with wide-open eyes at Pyotr Mihalitch. "Sometime in the forties this place was let to a Frenchman called Olivier. The portrait of his daughter is lying in an attic now—a very pretty girl. This Olivier, so my father told me, despised Russians for their ignorance and treated them with cruel derision. Thus, for instance, he insisted on the priest walking without his hat for half a mile round his house, and on the church bells being rung when the Olivier family drove through the village. The serfs and altogether the humble of this world, of course, he treated with even less ceremony. Once there came along this road one of the simple-hearted sons of wandering Russia, somewhat after the style of Gogol's divinity student, Homa Brut. He asked for a night's lodging, pleased the bailiffs, and was given a job at the office of the estate. There are many variations of the story. Some say the divinity student stirred up the peasants, others that Olivier's daughter fell in love with him. I don't know which is true, only one fine evening Olivier called him in here and cross-examined him, then ordered him to be beaten. Do you know, he sat here at this table drinking claret while the stable-boys beat the man. He must have tried to wring something out of him. Towards morning the divinity student died of the torture and his body was hidden. They say it was thrown into Koltovitch's pond. There was an inquiry, but the Frenchman paid some thousands to some one in authority and went away to Alsace. His lease was up just then, and so the matter ended."

"What scoundrels!" said Zina, shuddering.

"My father remembered Olivier and his daughter well. He used to say she was remarkably beautiful and eccentric. I imagine the divinity student had done both—stirred up the peasants and won the daughter's heart. Perhaps he wasn't a divinity student at all, but some one travelling incognito."

Zina grew thoughtful; the story of the divinity student and the beautiful French girl had evidently carried her imagination far away. It seemed to Pyotr Mihalitch that she had not changed in the least during the last week, except that she was a little paler. She looked calm and just as usual, as though she had come with her brother to visit Vlassitch. But Pyotr Mihalitch felt that some change had taken place in himself. Before, when she was living at home, he could have spoken to her about anything, and now he did not feel equal to asking her the simple question, "How do you like being here?" The question seemed awkward and unnecessary. Probably the same change had taken place in her. She was in no haste to turn the conversation to her mother, to her home, to her relations with Vlassitch;

she did not defend herself, she did not say that free unions are better than marriages in the church; she was not agitated, and calmly brooded over the story of Olivier. . . . And why had they suddenly begun talking of Olivier?

"You are both of you wet with the rain," said Zina, and she smiled joyfully; she was touched by this point of resemblance between her brother and Vlassitch.

And Pyotr Mihalitch felt all the bitterness and horror of his position. He thought of his deserted home, the closed piano, and Zina's bright little room into which no one went now; he thought there were no prints of little feet on the garden-paths, and that before tea no one went off, laughing gaily, to bathe. What he had clung to more and more from his childhood upwards, what he had loved thinking about when he used to sit in the stuffy class-room or the lecture theatre—brightness, purity, and joy, everything that filled the house with life and light, had gone never to return, had vanished, and was mixed up with a coarse, clumsy story of some battalion officer, a chivalrous lieutenant, a depraved woman and a grandfather who had shot himself. . . . And to begin to talk about his mother or to think that the past could ever return would mean not understanding what was clear.

Pyotr Mihalitch's eyes filled with tears and his hand began to tremble as it lay on the table. Zina guessed what he was thinking about, and her eyes, too, glistened and looked red.

"Grigory, come here," she said to Vlassitch.

They walked away to the window and began talking of something in a whisper. From the way that Vlassitch stooped down to her and the way she looked at him, Pyotr Mihalitch realised again that everything was irreparably over, and that it was no use to talk of anything. Zina went out of the room.

"Well, brother!" Vlassitch began, after a brief silence, rubbing his hands and smiling. "I called our life happiness just now, but that was, so to speak, poetical license. In reality, there has not been a sense of happiness so far. Zina has been thinking all the time of you, of her mother, and has been worrying; looking at her, I, too, felt worried. Hers is a bold, free nature, but, you know, it's difficult when you're not used to it, and she is young, too. The servants call her 'Miss'; it seems a trifle, but it upsets her. There it is, brother."

Zina brought in a plateful of strawberries. She was followed by a little maidservant, looking crushed and humble, who set a jug of milk on the table and made a very low bow: she had something about her that was in keeping with the old furniture, something petrified and dreary.

The sound of the rain had ceased. Pyotr Mihalitch ate strawberries while Vlassitch and Zina looked at him in silence. The moment of the inevitable but useless conversation was approaching, and all three felt the burden of it. Pyotr Mihalitch's eyes filled with tears again; he pushed away his plate and said that he must be going home, or it would be getting late, and perhaps it would rain again. The time had come when common decency required Zina to speak of those at home and of her new life.

"How are things at home?" she asked rapidly, and her pale face quivered. "How is mother?"

"You know mother . . ." said Pyotr Mihalitch, not looking at her.

"Petrusha, you've thought a great deal about what has happened," she said, taking hold of her brother's sleeve, and he knew how hard it was for her to speak. "You've thought a great deal: tell me, can we reckon on mother's accepting Grigory . . . and the whole position, one day?"

She stood close to her brother, face to face with him, and he was astonished that she was so beautiful, and that he seemed not to have noticed it before. And it seemed to him utterly absurd that his sister, so like his mother, pampered, elegant, should be living with Vlassitch and in Vlassitch's house, with the petrified servant, and the table with six legs—in the house where a man had been flogged to death, and that she was not going home with him, but was staying here to sleep.

"You know mother," he said, not answering her question. "I think you ought to have . . . to do something, to ask her forgiveness or something. . . ."

"But to ask her forgiveness would mean pretending we had done wrong. I'm ready to tell a lie to comfort mother, but it won't lead anywhere. I know mother. Well, what will be, must be!" said Zina, growing more cheerful now that the most unpleasant had been said. "We'll wait for five years, ten years, and be patient, and then God's will be done."

She took her brother's arm, and when she walked through the dark hall she squeezed close to him. They went out on the steps.

Pyotr Mihalitch said good-bye, got on his horse, and set off at a walk; Zina and Vlassitch walked a little way with him. It was still and warm, with a delicious smell of hay; stars were twinkling brightly between the clouds. Vlassitch's old garden, which had seen so many gloomy stories in its time, lay slumbering in the darkness, and for some reason it was mournful riding through it.

"Zina and I to-day after dinner spent some really exalted moments," said Vlassitch. "I read aloud to her an excellent article on the question of emigration. You must read it, brother! You really must. It's remarkable for its lofty tone. I could not resist writing a letter to the editor to be forwarded to the author. I wrote only a single line: 'I thank you and warmly press your noble hand.' "

Pyotr Mihalitch was tempted to say, "Don't meddle in what does not concern you," but he held his tongue.

Vlassitch walked by his right stirrup and Zina by the left; both seemed to have forgotten that they had to go home. It was damp, and they had almost reached Koltovitch's copse. Pyotr Mihalitch felt that they were expecting something from him, though they hardly knew what it was, and he felt unbearably sorry for them. Now as they walked by the horse with submissive faces, lost in thought, he had a deep conviction that they were unhappy, and could not be happy, and their love seemed to him a melancholy, irreparable mistake. Pity and the sense that he could do nothing to help them reduced him to that state of spiritual softening when he was ready to make any sacrifice to get rid of the painful feeling of sympathy.

"I'll come over sometimes for a night," he said.

But it sounded as though he were making a concession, and did not satisfy him. When they stopped near Koltovitch's copse to say good-bye, he bent down to Zina, touched her shoulder, and said:

"You are right, Zina! You have done well." To avoid saying more and bursting into tears, he lashed his horse and galloped into the wood. As he rode into the darkness, he looked round and saw Vlassitch and Zina walking home along the road—he taking long strides, while she walked with a hurried, jerky step beside him— talking eagerly about something.

"I am an old woman!" thought Pyotr Mihalitch. "I went to solve the question and I have only made it more complicated—there it is!"

He was heavy at heart. When he got out of the copse he rode at a walk and then stopped his horse near the pond. He wanted to sit and think without moving. The moon was rising and was reflected in a streak of red on the other side of the pond. There were low rumbles of thunder in the distance. Pyotr Mihalitch looked steadily at the water and imagined his sister's despair, her martyr-like pallor, the tearless eyes with which she would conceal her humiliation from others. He imagined her with child, imagined the death of their mother, her funeral, Zina's horror. . . . The proud, superstitious old woman would be sure to die of grief. Terrible pictures of the future rose before him on the background of smooth, dark water, and among pale feminine figures he saw himself, a weak, cowardly man with a guilty face.

A hundred paces off on the right bank of the pond, something dark was standing motionless: was it a man or a tall post? Pyotr Mihalitch thought of the divinity student who had been killed and thrown into the pond.

"Olivier behaved inhumanly, but one way or another he did settle the question, while I have settled nothing and have only made it worse," he thought, gazing at the dark figure that looked like a ghost. "He said and did what he thought right while I say and do what I don't think right; and I don't know really what I do think. . . ."

He rode up to the dark figure: it was an old rotten post, the relic of some shed.

From Koltovitch's copse and garden there came a strong fragrant scent of lilies of the valley and honey-laden flowers. Pyotr Mihalitch rode along the bank of the pond and looked mournfully into the water. And thinking about his life, he came to the conclusion he had never said or acted upon what he really thought, and other people had repaid him in the same way. And so the whole of life seemed to him as dark as this water in which the night sky was reflected and water-weeds grew in a tangle. And it seemed to him that nothing could ever set it right.

1892

Ward No. 6

I

In the hospital yard there stands a small lodge surrounded by a perfect forest of burdocks, nettles, and wild hemp. Its roof is rusty, the chimney is tumbling down, the steps at the front-door are rotting away and overgrown with grass, and there are only traces left of the stucco. The front of the lodge faces the hospital; at the back it looks out into the open country, from which it is separated by the grey hospital fence with nails on it. These nails, with their points upwards, and the fence, and the lodge itself, have that peculiar, desolate, God-forsaken look which is only found in our hospital and prison buildings.

If you are not afraid of being stung by the nettles, come by the narrow footpath that leads to the lodge, and let us see what is going on inside. Opening the first door, we walk into the entry. Here along the walls and by the stove every sort of hospital rubbish lies littered about. Mattresses, old tattered dressing-gowns, trousers, blue striped shirts, boots and shoes no good for anything—all these remnants are piled up in heaps, mixed up and crumpled, mouldering and giving out a sickly smell.

The porter, Nikita, an old soldier wearing rusty good-conduct stripes, is always lying on the litter with a pipe between his teeth. He has a grim, surly, battered-looking face, overhanging eyebrows which give him the expression of a sheep-dog of the steppes, and a red nose; he is short and looks thin and scraggy, but he is of imposing deportment and his fists are vigorous. He belongs to the class of simple-hearted, practical, and dull-witted people, prompt in carrying out orders, who like discipline better than anything in the world, and so are convinced that it is their duty to beat people. He showers blows on the face, on the chest, on the back, on whatever comes first, and is convinced that there would be no order in the place if he did not.

Next you come into a big, spacious room which fills up the whole lodge except for the entry. Here the walls are painted a dirty blue, the ceiling is as sooty as in a hut without a chimney—it is evident that in the winter the stove smokes and the room is full of fumes. The windows are disfigured by iron gratings on the inside. The wooden floor is grey and full of splinters. There is a stench of sour cabbage, of smouldering wicks, of bugs, and of ammonia, and for the first minute this stench gives you the impression of having walked into a menagerie. . . .

There are bedsteads screwed to the floor. Men in blue hospital dressing-gowns, and wearing night-caps in the old style, are sitting and lying on them. These are the lunatics.

There are five of them in all here. Only one is of the upper class, the rest are all artisans. The one nearest the door—a tall, lean workman with shining red whiskers and tear-stained eyes—sits with his head propped on his hand, staring at the same point. Day and night he grieves, shaking his head, sighing and smiling bitterly. He rarely takes a part in conversation and usually makes no answer to questions; he eats and drinks mechanically when food is offered him. From his agonizing, throbbing cough, his thinness, and the flush on his cheeks, one may judge that he is in the first stage of consumption. Next to him is a little, alert, very lively old man, with a pointed beard and curly black hair like a negro's. By day he walks up and down the ward from window to window, or sits on his bed, cross-legged like a Turk, and, ceaselessly as a bullfinch whistles, softly sings and titters. He shows his childish gaiety and lively character at night also when he gets up to say his prayers—that is, to beat himself on the chest with his fists, and to scratch with his fingers at the door. This is the Jew Moiseika, an imbecile, who went crazy twenty years ago when his hat factory was burnt down.

And of all the inhabitants of Ward No. 6, he is the only one who is allowed to go out of the lodge, and even out of the yard into the street. He has enjoyed this privilege for years, probably because he is an old inhabitant of the hospital—a quiet, harmless imbecile, the buffoon of the town, where people are used to seeing him surrounded by boys and dogs. In his wretched gown, in his absurd night-cap, and in slippers, sometimes with bare legs and even without trousers, he walks about the streets, stopping at the gates and little shops, and begging for a copper. In one place they will give him some kvass, in another some bread, in another a copper, so that he generally goes back to the ward feeling rich and well fed. Everything that he brings back Nikita takes from him for his own benefit. The soldier does this roughly, angrily turning the Jew's pockets inside out, and calling God to witness that he will not let him go into the street again, and that breach of the regulations is worse to him than anything in the world.

Moiseika likes to make himself useful. He gives his companions water, and covers them up when they are asleep; he promises each of them to bring him back a kopeck, and to make him a new cap; he feeds with a spoon his neighbour on the left, who is paralyzed. He acts in this way, not from compassion nor from any considerations of a humane kind, but through imitation, unconsciously dominated by Gromov, his neighbour on the right hand.

Ivan Dmitritch Gromov, a man of thirty-three, who is a gentleman by birth, and has been a court usher and provincial secretary, suffers from the mania of persecution. He either lies curled up in bed, or walks from corner to corner as though for exercise; he very rarely sits down. He is always excited, agitated, and overwrought by a sort of vague, undefined expectation. The faintest rustle in the entry or shout in the yard is enough to make him raise his head and begin listening: whether they are coming for him, whether they are looking for him. And at such times his face expresses the utmost uneasiness and repulsion.

I like his broad face with its high cheek-bones, always pale and unhappy, and reflecting, as though in a mirror, a soul tormented by conflict and long-continued terror. His grimaces are strange and abnormal, but the delicate lines traced on his face by profound, genuine suffering show intelligence and sense, and there is a warm and healthy light in his eyes. I like the man himself, courteous, anxious to be of use, and extraordinarily gentle to everyone except Nikita. When anyone drops a button or a spoon, he jumps up from his bed quickly and picks it up; every day he says good-morning to his companions, and when he goes to bed he wishes them good-night.

Besides his continually overwrought condition and his grimaces, his madness shows itself in the following way also. Sometimes in the evenings he wraps himself in his dressing-gown, and, trembling all over, with his teeth chattering, begins walking rapidly from corner to corner and between the bedsteads. It seems as though he is in a violent fever. From the way he suddenly stops and glances at his companions, it can be seen that he is longing to say something very important, but, apparently reflecting that they would not listen, or would not understand him, he shakes his head impatiently and goes on pacing up and down. But soon the desire to speak gets the upper hand of every consideration, and he will let himself go and speak fervently and passionately. His talk is disordered and feverish like delirium, disconnected, and not always intelligible, but, on the other hand, something extremely fine may be felt in it, both in the words and the voice. When he talks you recognize in him the lunatic and the man. It is difficult to reproduce on paper his insane talk. He speaks of the baseness of mankind, of violence trampling on justice, of the glorious life which will one day be upon earth, of the window-gratings, which remind him every minute of the stupidity and cruelty of oppressors. It makes a disorderly, incoherent potpourri of themes old but not yet out of date.

II

Some twelve or fifteen years ago an official called Gromov, a highly respectable and prosperous person, was living in his own house in the principal street of the town. He had two sons, Sergey and Ivan. When Sergey was a student in his fourth year he was taken ill with galloping consumption and died, and his death was, as it were, the first of a whole series of calamities which suddenly showered on the Gromov family. Within a week of Sergey's funeral the old father was put on his trial for fraud and misappropriation, and he died of typhoid in the prison hospital soon afterwards. The house, with all their belongings, was sold by auction, and Ivan Dmitritch and his mother were left entirely without means.

Hitherto in his father's lifetime, Ivan Dmitritch, who was studying in the University of Petersburg, had received an allowance of sixty or seventy roubles a month, and had had no conception of poverty; now he had to make an abrupt change in his life. He had to spend his time from morning to night giving lessons for next to nothing, to work at copying, and with all that to go hungry, as all his earnings were sent to keep his mother. Ivan Dmitritch could not stand such a life; he lost heart and strength, and, giving up the university, went home.

Here, through interest, he obtained the post of teacher in the district school, but could not get on with his colleagues, was not liked by the boys, and soon gave up the post. His mother died. He was for six months without work, living on nothing but bread and water; then he became a court usher. He kept this post until he was dismissed owing to his illness.

He had never even in his young student days given the impression of being perfectly healthy. He had always been pale, thin, and given to catching cold; he ate little and slept badly. A single glass of wine went to his head and made him hysterical. He always had a craving for society, but, owing to his irritable temperament and suspiciousness, he never became very intimate with anyone, and had no friends. He always spoke with contempt of his fellow-townsmen, saying that their coarse ignorance and sleepy animal existence seemed to him loathsome and horrible. He spoke in a loud tenor, with heat, and invariably either with scorn and indignation, or with wonder and enthusiasm, and always with perfect sincerity. Whatever one talked to him about he always brought it round to the same subject: that life was dull and stifling in the town; that the townspeople had no lofty interests, but lived a dingy, meaningless life, diversified by violence, coarse profligacy, and hypocrisy; that scoundrels were well fed and clothed, while honest men lived from hand to mouth; that they needed schools, a progressive local paper, a theatre, public lectures, the co-ordination of the intellectual elements; that society must see its failings and be horrified. In his criticisms of people he laid on the colours thick, using only black and white, and no fine shades; mankind was divided for him into honest men and scoundrels: there was nothing in between. He always spoke with passion and enthusiasm of women and of love, but he had never been in love.

In spite of the severity of his judgments and his nervousness, he was liked, and behind his back was spoken of affectionately as Vanya. His innate refinement and readiness to be of service, his good breeding, his moral purity, and his shabby coat, his frail appearance and family misfortunes, aroused a kind, warm, sorrowful feeling. Moreover, he was well educated and well read; according to the townspeople's notions, he knew everything, and was in their eyes something like a walking encyclopædia.

He had read a great deal. He would sit at the club, nervously pulling at his beard and looking through the magazines and books; and from his face one could see that he was not reading, but devouring the pages without giving himself time to digest what he read. It must be supposed that reading was one of his morbid habits, as he fell upon anything that came into his hands with equal avidity, even last

year's newspapers and calendars. At home he always read lying
down.

III

One autumn morning Ivan Dmitritch, turning up the collar of
his greatcoat and splashing through the mud, made his way by side-
streets and back lanes to see some artisan, and to collect some
payment that was owing. He was in a gloomy mood, as he always was
in the morning. In one of the side-streets he was met by two convicts
in fetters and four soldiers with rifles in charge of them. Ivan
Dmitritch had very often met convicts before, and they had always
excited feelings of compassion and discomfort in him; but now this
meeting made a peculiar, strange impression on him. It suddenly
seemed to him for some reason that he, too, might be put into fetters
and led through the mud to prison like that. After visiting the artisan,
on the way home he met near the post office a police superintendent
of his acquaintance, who greeted him and walked a few paces along
the street with him, and for some reason this seemed to him suspicious. At home he could not get the convicts or the soldiers with
their rifles out of his head all day, and an unaccountable inward agitation prevented him from reading or concentrating his mind. In the
evening he did not light his lamp, and at night he could not sleep, but
kept thinking that he might be arrested, put into fetters, and thrown
into prison. He did not know of any harm he had done, and could be
certain that he would never be guilty of murder, arson, or theft in the
future either; but was it not easy to commit a crime by accident,
unconsciously, and was not false witness always possible, and, indeed,
miscarriage of justice? It was not without good reason that the age-
long experience of the simple people teaches that beggary and prison
are ills none can be safe from. A judicial mistake is very possible as
legal proceedings are conducted nowadays, and there is nothing to be
wondered at in it. People who have an official, professional
relation to other men's sufferings—for instance, judges, police officers, doctors—in course of time, through habit, grow so callous that
they cannot, even if they wish it, take any but a formal attitude to
their clients; in this respect they are not different from the peasant
who slaughters sheep and calves in the back-yard, and does not notice
the blood. With this formal, soulless attitude to human personality

the judge needs but one thing—time—in order to deprive an innocent man of all rights of property, and to condemn him to penal servitude. Only the time spent on performing certain formalities for which the judge is paid his salary, and then—it is all over. Then you may look in vain for justice and protection in this dirty, wretched little town a hundred and fifty miles from a railway station! And, indeed, is it not absurd even to think of justice when every kind of violence is accepted by society as a rational and consistent necessity, and every act of mercy—for instance, a verdict of acquittal—calls forth a perfect outburst of dissatisfied and revengeful feeling?

In the morning Ivan Dmitritch got up from his bed in a state of horror, with cold perspiration on his forehead, completely convinced that he might be arrested any minute. Since his gloomy thoughts of yesterday had haunted him so long, he thought, it must be that there was some truth in them. They could not, indeed, have come into his mind without any grounds whatever.

A policeman walking slowly passed by the windows: that was not for nothing. Here were two men standing still and silent near the house. Why were they silent? And agonizing days and nights followed for Ivan Dmitritch. Everyone who passed by the windows or came into the yard seemed to him a spy or a detective. At midday the chief of the police usually drove down the street with a pair of horses; he was going from his estate near the town to the police department; but Ivan Dmitritch fancied every time that he was driving especially quickly, and that he had a peculiar expression: it was evident that he was in haste to announce that there was a very important criminal in the town. Ivan Dmitritch started at every ring at the bell and knock at the gate, and was agitated whenever he came upon anyone new at his landlady's; when he met police officers and gendarmes he smiled and began whistling so as to seem unconcerned. He could not sleep for whole nights in succession expecting to be arrested, but he snored loudly and sighed as though in deep sleep, that his landlady might think he was asleep; for if he could not sleep it meant that he was tormented by the stings of conscience—what a piece of evidence! Facts and common sense persuaded him that all these terrors were nonsense and morbidity, that if one looked at the matter more broadly there was nothing really terrible in arrest and imprisonment—so long as the conscience is at ease; but the more sensibly and logically he reasoned, the more acute and agonizing his mental distress became. It might be compared with the story of a hermit who tried to cut a dwelling-place for himself in a virgin forest; the more zealously he worked with his axe, the thicker the forest grew. In the end Ivan Dmitritch, seeing it was useless, gave up reasoning altogether, and abandoned himself entirely to despair and terror.

He began to avoid people and to seek solitude. His official work had been distasteful to him before: now it became unbearable to him. He was afraid they would somehow get him into trouble, would put a bribe in his pocket unnoticed and then denounce him, or that he would accidentally make a mistake in official papers that would appear to be fraudulent, or would lose other people's money. It is strange that his imagination had never at other times been so agile and inventive as now, when every day he thought of thousands of different reasons for being seriously anxious over his freedom and honour; but, on the other hand, his interest in the outer world, in books in particular, grew sensibly fainter, and his memory began to fail him.

In the spring when the snow melted there were found in the ravine near the cemetery two half-decomposed corpses—the bodies of an old woman and a boy bearing the traces of death by violence. Nothing was talked of but these bodies and their unknown murderers. That people might not think he had been guilty of the crime, Ivan Dmitritch walked about the streets, smiling, and when he met acquaintances he turned pale, flushed, and began declaring that there was no greater crime than the murder of the weak and defenceless. But this duplicity soon exhausted him, and after some reflection he decided that in his position the best thing to do was to hide in his landlady's cellar. He sat in the cellar all day and then all night, then another day, was fearfully cold, and waiting till dusk, stole secretly like a thief back to his room. He stood in the middle of the room till daybreak, listening without stirring. Very early in the morning, before sunrise, some workmen came into the house. Ivan Dmitritch knew perfectly well that they had come to mend the stove in the kitchen, but terror told him that they were police officers disguised as workmen. He slipped stealthily out of the flat, and, overcome by terror, ran along the street without his cap and coat. Dogs raced after him barking, a peasant shouted somewhere behind him, the wind whistled in his ears, and it seemed to Ivan Dmitritch that the force and violence of the whole world was massed together behind his back and was chasing after him.

He was stopped and brought home, and his landlady sent for a doctor. Doctor Andrey Yefimitch, of whom we shall have more to say hereafter, prescribed cold compresses on his head and laurel drops, shook his head, and went away, telling the landlady he should not come again, as one should not interfere with people who are going out of their minds. As he had not the means to live at home and be nursed, Ivan Dmitritch was soon sent to the hospital, and was there put into the ward for venereal patients. He could not sleep at night, was full of whims and fancies, and disturbed the patients, and was soon afterwards, by Andrey Yefimitch's orders, transferred to Ward No. 6.

Within a year Ivan Dmitritch was completely forgotten in the town, and his books, heaped up by his landlady in a sledge in the shed, were pulled to pieces by boys.

IV

Ivan Dmitritch's neighbour on the left hand is, as I have said already, the Jew Moiseika; his neighbour on the right hand is a peasant so rolling in fat that he is almost spherical, with a blankly stupid face, utterly devoid of thought. This is a motionless, gluttonous, unclean animal who has long ago lost all powers of thought or feeling. An acrid, stifling stench always comes from him.

Nikita, who has to clean up after him, beats him terribly with all his might, not sparing his fists; and what is dreadful is not his being beaten—that one can get used to—but the fact that this stupefied creature does not respond to the blows with a sound or a movement, nor by a look in the eyes, but only sways a little like a heavy barrel.

The fifth and last inhabitant of Ward No. 6 is a man of the artisan class who has once been a sorter in the post office, a thinnish, fair little man with a good-natured but rather sly face. To judge from the clear, cheerful look in his calm and intelligent eyes, he has some pleasant idea in his mind, and has some very important and agreeable secret. He has under his pillow and under his mattress something that he never shows anyone, not from fear of its being taken from him and stolen, but from modesty. Sometimes he goes to the window, and turning his back to his companions, puts something on his breast, and bending his head, looks at it; if you go up to him at such a moment, he is overcome with confusion and snatches something off his breast. But it is not difficult to guess his secret.

"Congratulate me," he often says to Ivan Dmitritch; "I have been presented with the Stanislav order of the second degree with the star. The second degree with the star is only given to foreigners, but for some reason they want to make an exception for me," he says with a smile, shrugging his shoulders in perplexity. "That I must confess I did not expect."

"I don't understand anything about that," Ivan Dmitritch replies morosely.

"But do you know what I shall attain to sooner or later?" the former sorter persists, screwing up his eyes slily. "I shall certainly get the Swedish 'Polar Star.' That's an order it is worth working for, a white cross with a black ribbon. It's very beautiful."

Probably in no other place is life so monotonous as in this ward. In the morning the patients, except the paralytic and the fat peasant, wash in the entry at a big tub and wipe themselves with the skirts of their dressing-gowns; after that they drink tea out of tin mugs which Nikita brings them out of the main building. Everyone is allowed one mugful. At midday they have soup made out of sour cabbage and boiled grain, in the evening their supper consists of grain left from dinner. In the intervals they lie down, sleep, look out of window, and walk from one corner to the other. And so every day. Even the former sorter always talks of the same orders.

Fresh faces are rarely seen in Ward No. 6. The doctor has not taken in any new mental cases for a long time, and the people who are fond of visiting lunatic asylums are few in this world. Once every two months Semyon Lazaritch, the barber, appears in the ward. How he cuts the patients' hair, and how Nikita helps him to do it, and what a trepidation the lunatics are always thrown into by the arrival of the drunken, smiling barber, we will not describe.

No one even looks into the ward except the barber. The patients are condemned to see day after day no one but Nikita.

A rather strange rumour has, however, been circulating in the hospital of late.

It is rumoured that the doctor has begun to visit Ward No. 6.

V

A strange rumour!

Dr. Andrey Yefimitch Ragin is a strange man in his way. They say that when he was young he was very religious, and prepared himself for a clerical career, and that when he had finished his studies at the high school in 1863 he intended to enter a theological academy, but that his father, a surgeon and doctor of medicine, jeered at him and declared point-blank that he would disown him if he became a priest. How far this is true I don't know, but Andrey Yefimitch himself has more than once confessed that he has never had a natural bent for medicine or science in general.

However that may have been, when he finished his studies in the medical faculty he did not enter the priesthood. He showed no special devoutness, and was no more like a priest at the beginning of his medical career than he is now.

His exterior is heavy, coarse like a peasant's, his face, his beard, his flat hair, and his coarse, clumsy figure, suggest an overfed, intemperate, and harsh innkeeper on the highroad. His face is surly-looking and covered with blue veins, his eyes are little and his nose is red. With his height and broad shoulders he has huge hands and feet; one would think that a blow from his fist would knock the life out of anyone, but his step is soft, and his walk is cautious and insinuating; when he meets anyone in a narrow passage he is always the first to stop and make way, and to say, not in a bass, as one would expect, but in a high, soft tenor: "I beg your pardon!" He has a little swelling on his neck which prevents him from wearing stiff starched collars, and so he always goes about in soft linen or cotton shirts. Altogether he does not dress like a doctor. He wears the same suit for ten years, and the new clothes, which he usually buys at a Jewish shop, look as shabby and crumpled on him as his old ones; he sees patients and dines and pays visits all in the same coat; but this is not due to niggardliness, but to complete carelessness about his appearance.

When Andrey Yefimitch came to the town to take up his duties the "institution founded to the glory of God" was in a terrible condition. One could hardly breathe for the stench in the wards, in the passages, and in the courtyards of the hospital. The hospital servants, the nurses, and their children slept in the wards together with the patients. They complained that there was no living for beetles, bugs, and mice. The surgical wards were never free from erysipelas. There were only two scalpels and not one thermometer in the whole hospital; potatoes were kept in the baths. The superintendent, the housekeeper, and the medical assistant robbed the patients, and of the old doctor, Andrey Yefimitch's predecessor, people declared that he secretly sold the hospital alcohol, and that he kept a regular harem consisting of nurses and female patients. These disorderly proceedings were perfectly well known in the town, and were even exaggerated, but people took them calmly; some justified them on the ground that there were only peasants and working men in the hospital, who could not be dissatisfied, since they were much worse off at home than in the hospital—they couldn't be fed on woodcocks! Others said in excuse that the town alone, without help from the Zemstvo, was not equal to maintaining a good hospital; thank God for having one at all, even a poor one. And the newly formed Zemstvo did not open infirmaries either in the town or the neighbourhood, relying on the fact that the town already had its hospital.

After looking over the hospital Andrey Yefimitch came to the conclusion that it was an immoral institution and extremely prejudicial to the health of the townspeople. In his opinion the most sensible thing that could be done was to let out the patients and close the hospital. But he reflected that his will alone was not enough to do this, and that it would be useless; if physical and moral impurity were driven out of one place, they would only move to another; one must wait for it to wither away of itself. Besides, if people open a hospital and put up with having it, it must be because they need it; superstition and all the nastiness and abominations of daily life were necessary, since in process of time they worked out to something sensible, just as manure turns into black earth. There was nothing on earth so good that it had not something nasty about its first origin.

When Andrey Yefimitch undertook his duties he was apparently not greatly concerned about the irregularities at the hospital. He only asked the attendants and nurses not to sleep in the wards, and had two cupboards of instruments put up; the superintendent, the housekeeper, the medical assistant, and the erysipelas remained unchanged.

Andrey Yefimitch loved intelligence and honesty intensely, but he had no strength of will nor belief in his right to organize an intelligent and honest life about him. He was absolutely unable to give orders, to forbid things, and to insist. It seemed as though he had taken a vow never to raise his voice and never to make use of the imperative. It was difficult for him to say "Fetch" or "Bring"; when he wanted his meals he would cough hesitatingly and say to the cook: "How about tea? . . ." or "How about dinner? . . ." To dismiss the superintendent or to tell him to leave off stealing, or to abolish the unnecessary parasitic post altogether, was absolutely beyond his powers. When Andrey Yefimitch was deceived or flattered, or accounts he knew to be cooked were brought him to sign, he would turn as red as a crab and feel guilty, but yet he would sign the accounts. When the patients complained to him of being hungry or of the roughness of the nurses, he would be confused and mutter guiltily: "Very well, very well, I will go into it later. . . . Most likely there is some misunderstanding. . . ."

At first Andrey Yefimitch worked very zealously. He saw patients every day from morning till dinnertime, performed operations, and even attended confinements. The ladies said of him that he was attentive and clever at diagnosing diseases, especially those of women and children. But in process of time the work unmistakably wearied him by its monotony and obvious uselessness. To-day one sees thirty patients, and to-morrow they have increased to thirty-five, the next day forty, and so on from day to day, from year to year, while the mortality in the town did not decrease and the patients did not leave off coming. To be any real help to forty patients between morning and dinner was not physically possible, so it could but lead to deception. If twelve thousand patients were seen in a year it meant, if one looked at it simply, that twelve thousand men were deceived. To put those who were seriously ill into wards, and to treat them according to the principles of science, was impossible, too, because though there were principles there was no science; if he were to put aside philosophy and pedantically follow the rules as other doctors did, the things above all necessary were cleanliness and ventilation instead of dirt, wholesome nourishment instead of broth made of stinking, sour cabbage, and good assistants instead of thieves; and, indeed, why hinder people dying if death is the normal and legitimate end of everyone? What is gained if some shopkeeper or clerk lives an extra five or ten years? If the aim of medicine is by drugs to alleviate suffering, the question forces itself on one: why alleviate it? In the first place, they say that suffering leads man to perfection; and in the second, if mankind really learns to alleviate its sufferings with pills and drops, it will completely abandon religion and philosophy, in which it has hitherto found not merely protection from all sorts of trouble, but even happiness. Pushkin suffered terrible agonies before his death, poor Heine lay paralyzed for several years; why, then, should not some Andrey Yefimitch or Matryona Savishna be ill, since their lives had nothing of importance in them, and would have been entirely empty and like the life of an amœba except for suffering?

Oppressed by such reflections, Andrey Yefimitch relaxed his efforts and gave up visiting the hospital every day.

VI

His life was passed like this. As a rule he got up at eight o'clock in the morning, dressed, and drank his tea. Then he sat down in his study to read, or went to the hospital. At the hospital the out-patients were sitting in the dark, narrow little corridor waiting to be seen by the doctor. The nurses and the attendants, tramping with their boots over the brick floors, ran by them; gaunt-looking patients in dressing-gowns passed; dead bodies and vessels full of filth were carried by; the children were crying, and there was a cold draught. Andrey Yefimitch knew that such surroundings were torture to feverish, consumptive, and impressionable patients; but what could be done? In the consulting-room he was met by his assistant, Sergey Sergeyitch— a fat little man with a plump, well-washed shaven face, with soft, smooth manners, wearing a new loosely cut suit, and looking more like a senator than a medical assistant. He had an immense practice in the town, wore a white tie, and considered himself more proficient than the doctor, who had no practice. In the corner of the consulting-room there stood a huge ikon in a shrine with a heavy lamp in front of it, and near it a candle-stand with a white cover on it. On the walls hung portraits of bishops, a view of the Svyatogorsky Monastery, and wreaths of dried cornflowers. Sergey Sergeyitch was religious, and liked solemnity and decorum. The ikon had been put up at his expense; at his instructions some one of the patients read the hymns of praise in the consulting-room on Sundays, and after the reading Sergey Sergeyitch himself went through the wards with a censer and burned incense.

There were a great many patients, but the time was short, and so the work was confined to the asking of a few brief questions and the administration of some drugs, such as castor-oil or volatile ointment. Andrey Yefimitch would sit with his cheek resting in his hand, lost in thought and asking questions mechanically. Sergey Sergeyitch sat down too, rubbing his hands, and from time to time putting in his word.

"We suffer pain and poverty," he would say, "because we do not pray to the merciful God as we should. Yes!"

Andrey Yefimitch never performed any operations when he was seeing patients; he had long ago given up doing so, and the sight of blood upset him. When he had to open a child's mouth in order to look at its throat, and the child cried and tried to defend itself with its little hands, the noise in his ears made his head go round and brought tears into his eyes. He would make haste to prescribe a drug, and motion to the woman to take the child away.

He was soon wearied by the timidity of the patients and their incoherence, by the proximity of the pious Sergey Sergeyitch, by the portraits on the walls, and by his own questions which he had asked over and over again for twenty years. And he would go away after seeing five or six patients. The rest would be seen by his assistant in his absence.

With the agreeable thought that, thank God, he had no private practice now, and that no one would interrupt him, Andrey Yefimitch sat down to the table immediately on reaching home and took up a book. He read a great deal and always with enjoyment. Half his salary went on buying books, and of the six rooms that made up his abode three were heaped up with books and old magazines. He liked best of all works on history and philosophy; the only medical publication to which he subscribed was *The Doctor*, of which he always read the last pages first. He would always go on reading for several hours without a break and without being weary. He did not read as rapidly and impulsively as Ivan Dmitritch had done in the past, but slowly and with concentration, often pausing over a passage which he liked or did not find intelligible. Near the books there always stood a decanter of vodka, and a salted cucumber or a pickled apple lay beside it, not on a plate, but on the baize table-cloth. Every half-hour he would pour himself out a glass of vodka and drink it without taking his eyes off the book. Then without looking at it he would feel for the cucumber and bite off a bit.

At three o'clock he would go cautiously to the kitchen door, cough, and say: "Daryushka, what about dinner? . . ."

After his dinner—a rather poor and untidily served one—Andrey Yefimitch would walk up and down his rooms with his arms folded, thinking. The clock would strike four, then five, and still he would be walking up and down thinking. Occasionally the kitchen door would creak, and the red and sleepy face of Daryushka would appear.

"Andrey Yefimitch, isn't it time for you to have your beer?" she would ask anxiously.

"No, it is not time yet . . ." he would answer. "I'll wait a little. . . . I'll wait a little. . . ."

Towards the evening the postmaster, Mihail Averyanitch, the only man in the town whose society did not bore Andrey Yefimitch, would come in. Mihail Averyanitch had once been a very rich landowner, and had served in the cavalry, but had come to ruin, and was forced by poverty to take a job in the post office late in life. He had a hale and hearty appearance, luxuriant grey whiskers, the manners of a well-bred man, and a loud, pleasant voice. He was good-natured and emotional, but hot-tempered. When anyone in the post office made a protest, expressed disagreement, or even began to argue, Mihail Averyanitch would turn crimson, shake all over, and shout in a voice of thunder, "Hold your tongue!" so that the post office had long enjoyed the reputation of an institution which it was terrible to visit. Mihail Averyanitch liked and respected Andrey Yefimitch for his culture and the loftiness of his soul; he treated the other inhabitants of the town superciliously, as though they were his subordinates.

"Here I am," he would say, going in to Andrey Yefimitch. "Good-evening, my dear fellow! I'll be bound, you are getting sick of me, aren't you?"

"On the contrary, I am delighted," said the doctor. "I am always glad to see you."

The friends would sit down on the sofa in the study and for some time would smoke in silence.

"Daryushka, what about the beer?" Andrey Yefimitch would say.

They would drink their first bottle still in silence, the doctor brooding and Mihail Averyanitch with a gay and animated face, like a man who has something very interesting to tell. The doctor was always the one to begin the conversation.

"What a pity," he would say quietly and slowly, not looking his friend in the face (he never looked anyone in the face)—"what a great pity it is that there are no people in our town who are capable of carrying on intelligent and interesting conversation, or care to do so. It is an immense privation for us. Even the educated class do not rise above vulgarity; the level of their development, I assure you, is not a bit higher than that of the lower orders."

"Perfectly true. I agree."

"You know, of course," the doctor went on quietly and deliberately, "that everything in this world is insignificant and uninteresting except the higher spiritual manifestations of the human mind. Intellect draws a sharp line between the animals and man, suggests the divinity of the latter, and to some extent even takes the place of the immortality which does not exist. Consequently the intellect is the only possible source of enjoyment. We see and hear of no trace of intellect about us, so we are deprived of enjoyment. We have books, it is true, but that is not at all the same as living talk and converse. If you will allow me to make a not quite apt comparison: books are the printed score, while talk is the singing."

"Perfectly true."

A silence would follow. Daryushka would come out of the kitchen and with an expression of blank dejection would stand in the doorway to listen, with her face propped on her fist.

"Eh!" Mihail Averyanitch would sigh. "To expect intelligence of this generation!"

And he would describe how wholesome, entertaining, and interesting life had been in the past. How intelligent the educated class in Russia used to be, and what lofty ideas it had of honour and friendship; how they used to lend money without an IOU, and it was thought a disgrace not to give a helping hand to a comrade in need; and what campaigns, what adventures, what skirmishes, what comrades, what women! And the Caucasus, what a marvellous country! The wife of a battalion commander, a queer woman, used to put on an officer's uniform and drive off into the mountains in the evening, alone, without a guide. It was said that she had a love affair with some princeling in the native village.

"Queen of Heaven, Holy Mother . . ." Daryushka would sigh.

"And how we drank! And how we ate! And what desperate liberals we were!"

Andrey Yefimitch would listen without hearing; he was musing as he sipped his beer.

"I often dream of intellectual people and conversation with them," he said suddenly, interrupting Mihail Averyanitch. "My father gave me an excellent education, but under the influence of the ideas of the sixties made me become a doctor. I believe if I had not obeyed him then, by now I should have been in the very centre of the intellectual movement. Most likely I should have become a member of some university. Of course, intellect, too, is transient and not eternal, but you know why I cherish a partiality for it. Life is a vexatious trap; when a thinking man reaches maturity and attains to full conscious- ness he cannot help feeling that he is in a trap from which there is no escape. Indeed, he is summoned without his choice by fortuitous cir- cumstances from non-existence into life . . . what for? He tries to find out the meaning and object of his existence; he is told nothing, or he is told absurdities; he knocks and it is not opened to him; death comes to him—also without his choice. And so, just as in prison men held together by common misfortune feel more at ease when they are together, so one does not notice the trap in life when people with a bent for analysis and generalization meet together and pass their time in the interchange of proud and free ideas. In that sense the intellect is the source of an enjoyment nothing can replace."

"Perfectly true."

Not looking his friend in the face, Andrey Yefimitch would go on, quietly and with pauses, talking about intellectual people and con- versation with them, and Mihail Averyanitch would listen attentively and agree: "Perfectly true."

"And you do not believe in the immortality of the soul?" he would ask suddenly.

"No, honoured Mihail Averyanitch; I do not believe it, and have no grounds for believing it."

"I must own I doubt it too. And yet I have a feeling as though I should never die. Oh, I think to myself: 'Old fogey, it is time you were dead!' But there is a little voice in my soul says: 'Don't believe it; you won't die.' "

Soon after nine o'clock Mihail Averyanitch would go away. As he put on his fur coat in the entry he would say with a sigh:

"What a wilderness fate has carried us to, though, really! What's most vexatious of all is to have to die here. Ech! . . ."

VII

After seeing his friend out Andrey Yefimitch would sit down at the table and begin reading again. The stillness of the evening, and afterwards of the night, was not broken by a single sound, and it seemed as though time were standing still and brooding with the doctor over the book, and as though there were nothing in existence but the books and the lamp with the green shade. The doctor's coarse peasant-like face was gradually lighted up by a smile of delight and enthusiasm over the progress of the human intellect. Oh, why is not man immortal? he thought. What is the good of the brain centres and convolutions, what is the good of sight, speech, self-consciousness, genius, if it is all destined to depart into the soil, and in the end to grow cold together with the earth's crust, and then for millions of years to fly with the earth round the sun with no meaning and no object? To do that there was no need at all to draw man with his lofty, almost godlike intellect out of non-existence, and then, as though in mockery, to turn him into clay. The transmutation of substances! But what cowardice to comfort oneself with that cheap substitute for immortality! The unconscious processes that take place in nature are lower even than the stupidity of man, since in stupidity there is, anyway, consciousness and will, while in those processes there is absolutely nothing. Only the coward who has more fear of death than dignity can comfort himself with the fact that his body will in time live again in the grass, in the stones, in the toad. To find one's immortality in the transmutation of substances is as strange as to prophesy a brilliant future for the case after a precious violin has been broken and become useless.

When the clock struck, Andrey Yefimitch would sink back into his chair and close his eyes to think a little. And under the influence of the fine ideas of which he had been reading he would, unawares, recall his past and his present. The past was hateful—better not to think of it. And it was the same in the present as in the past. He knew that at the very time when his thoughts were floating together with the cooling earth round the sun, in the main building beside his abode people were suffering in sickness and physical impurity: someone perhaps could not sleep and was making war upon the insects, someone was being infected by erysipelas, or moaning over too tight a bandage; perhaps the patients were playing cards with the nurses and drinking vodka. According to the yearly return, twelve thousand people had been deceived; the whole hospital rested as it had done twenty years ago on thieving, filth, scandals, gossip, on gross quackery, and, as before, it was an immoral institution extremely injurious to the health of the inhabitants. He knew that Nikita knocked the patients about behind the barred windows of Ward No. 6, and that Moiseika went about the town every day begging alms.

On the other hand, he knew very well that a magical change had taken place in medicine during the last twenty-five years. When he was studying at the university he had fancied that medicine would soon be overtaken by the fate of alchemy and metaphysics; but now when he was reading at night the science of medicine touched him and excited his wonder, and even enthusiasm. What unexpected brilliance, what a revolution! Thanks to the antiseptic system operations were performed such as the great Pirogov had considered impossible even *in spe*. Ordinary Zemstvo doctors were venturing to perform the resection of the kneecap; of abdominal operations only one per cent. was fatal; while stone was considered such a trifle that they did not even write about it. A radical cure for syphilis had been discovered. And the theory of heredity, hypnotism, the discoveries of Pasteur and of Koch, hygiene based on statistics, and the work of our Zemstvo doctors!

Psychiatry with its modern classification of mental diseases, methods of diagnosis, and treatment, was a perfect Elborus in comparison with what had been in the past. They no longer poured cold water on the heads of lunatics nor put strait-waistcoats upon them; they treated them with humanity, and even, so it was stated in the papers, got up balls and entertainments for them. Andrey Yefimitch knew that with modern tastes and views such an abomination as Ward No. 6 was possible only a hundred and fifty miles from a railway in a little town where the mayor and all the town council were half-illiterate tradesmen who looked upon the doctor as an oracle who must be believed without any criticism even if he had poured molten lead into their mouths; in any other place the public and the newspapers would long ago have torn this little Bastille to pieces.

"But, after all, what of it?" Andrey Yefimitch would ask himself, opening his eyes. "There is the antiseptic system, there is Koch, there is Pasteur, but the essential reality is not altered a bit; ill-health and mortality are still the same. They get up balls and entertainments for the mad, but still they don't let them go free; so it's all nonsense and vanity, and there is no difference in reality between the best Vienna clinic and my hospital." But depression and a feeling akin to envy prevented him from feeling indifferent; it must have been owing to exhaustion. His heavy head sank on to the book, he put his hands under his face to make it softer, and thought: "I serve in a pernicious institution and receive a salary from people whom I am deceiving. I am not honest, but then, I of myself am nothing, I am only part of an inevitable social evil: all local officials are pernicious and receive their salary for doing nothing. . . . And so for my dishonesty it is not I who am to blame, but the times. . . . If I had been born two hundred years later I should have been different. . . ."

When it struck three he would put out his lamp and go into his bedroom; he was not sleepy.

VIII

Two years before, the Zemstvo in a liberal mood had decided to allow three hundred roubles a year to pay for additional medical service in the town till the Zemstvo hospital should be opened, and the district doctor, Yevgeny Fyodoritch Hobotov, was invited to the town to assist Andrey Yefimitch. He was a very young man—not yet thirty—tall and dark, with broad cheek-bones and little eyes; his forefathers had probably come from one of the many alien races of Russia. He arrived in the town without a farthing, with a small portmanteau, and a plain young woman whom he called his cook. This woman had a baby at the breast. Yevgeny Fyodoritch used to go about in a cap with a peak, and in high boots, and in the winter wore a sheepskin. He made great friends with Sergey Sergeyitch, the medical assistant, and with the treasurer, but held aloof from the other officials, and for some reason called them aristocrats. He had only one book in his lodgings, "The Latest Prescriptions of the Vienna Clinic for 1881." When he went to a patient he always took this book with him. He played billiards in the evening at the club: he did not like cards. He was very fond of using in conversation such expressions as "endless bobbery," "canting soft soap," "shut up with your finicking. . . ."

He visited the hospital twice a week, made the round of the wards, and saw out-patients. The complete absence of antiseptic treatment and the cupping roused his indignation, but he did not introduce any new system, being afraid of offending Andrey Yefimitch. He regarded his colleague as a sly old rascal, suspected him of being a man of large means, and secretly envied him. He would have been very glad to have his post.

IX

On a spring evening towards the end of March, when there was no snow left on the ground and the starlings were singing in the hospital garden, the doctor went out to see his friend the postmaster as far as the gate. At that very moment the Jew Moiseika, returning with his booty, came into the yard. He had no cap on, and his bare feet were thrust into goloshes; in his hand he had a little bag of coppers.

"Give me a kopeck!" he said to the doctor, smiling, and shivering with cold. Andrey Yefimitch, who could never refuse anyone anything, gave him a ten-kopeck piece.

"How bad that is!" he thought, looking at the Jew's bare feet with their thin red ankles. "Why, it's wet."

And stirred by a feeling akin both to pity and disgust, he went into the lodge behind the Jew, looking now at his bald head, now at his ankles. As the doctor went in, Nikita jumped up from his heap of litter and stood at attention.

"Good-day, Nikita," Andrey Yefimitch said mildly. "That Jew should be provided with boots or something, he will catch cold."

"Certainly, your honour. I'll inform the superintendent."

"Please do; ask him in my name. Tell him that I asked."

The door into the ward was open. Ivan Dmitritch, lying propped on his elbow on the bed, listened in alarm to the unfamiliar voice, and suddenly recognized the doctor. He trembled all over with anger, jumped up, and with a red and wrathful face, with his eyes starting out of his head, ran out into the middle of the road.

"The doctor has come!" he shouted, and broke into a laugh. "At last! Gentlemen, I congratulate you. The doctor is honouring us with a visit! Cursed reptile!" he shrieked, and stamped in a frenzy such as had never been seen in the ward before. "Kill the reptile! No, killing's too good. Drown him in the midden-pit!"

Andrey Yefimitch, hearing this, looked into the ward from the entry and asked gently: "What for?"

"What for?" shouted Ivan Dmitritch, going up to him with a menacing air and convulsively wrapping himself in his dressing-gown.

"What for? Thief!" he said with a look of repulsion, moving his lips a though he would spit at him. "Quack! hangman!"

"Calm yourself," said Andrey Yefimitch, smiling guiltily. "I assure you I have never stolen anything; and as to the rest, most likely you greatly exaggerate. I see you are angry with me. Calm yourself, I beg, if you can, and tell me coolly what are you angry for?"

"What are you keeping me here for?"

"Because you are ill."

"Yes, I am ill. But you know dozens, hundreds of madmen are walking about in freedom because your ignorance is incapable of distinguishing them from the sane. Why am I and these poor wretches to be shut up here like scapegoats for all the rest? You, your assistant, the superintendent, and all your hospital rabble, are immeasurably inferior to every one of us morally; why then are we shut up and you not? Where's the logic of it?"

"Morality and logic don't come in, it all depends on chance. If anyone is shut up he has to stay, and if anyone is not shut up he can walk about, that's all. There is neither morality nor logic in my being a doctor and your being a mental patient, there is nothing but idle chance."

"That twaddle I don't understand . . ." Ivan Dmitritch brought out in a hollow voice, and he sat down on his bed.

Moiseika, whom Nikita did not venture to search in the presence of the doctor, laid out on his bed pieces of bread, bits of paper, and little bones, and, still shivering with cold, began rapidly in a singsong voice saying something in Yiddish. He most likely imagined that he had opened a shop.

"Let me out," said Ivan Dmitritch, and his voice quivered.

"I cannot."

"But why, why?"

"Because it is not in my power. Think, what use will it be to you if I do let you out? Go. The townspeople or the police will detain you or bring you back."

"Yes, yes, that's true," said Ivan Dmitritch, and he rubbed his forehead. "It's awful! But what am I to do, what?"

Andrey Yefimitch liked Ivan Dmitritch's voice and his intelligent young face with its grimaces. He longed to be kind to the young man and soothe him; he sat down on the bed beside him, thought, and said:

"You ask me what to do. The very best thing in your position would be to run away. But, unhappily, that is useless. You would be taken up. When society protects itself from the criminal, mentally deranged, or otherwise inconvenient people, it is invincible. There is only one thing left for you: to resign yourself to the thought that your presence here is inevitable."

"It is no use to anyone."

"So long as prisons and madhouses exist someone must be shut up in them. If not you, I. If not I, some third person. Wait till in the distant future prisons and madhouses no longer exist, and there will be neither bars on the windows nor hospital gowns. Of course, that time will come sooner or later."

Ivan Dmitritch smiled ironically.

"You are jesting," he said, screwing up his eyes. "Such gentlemen as you and your assistant Nikita have nothing to do with the future, but you may be sure, sir, better days will come! I may express myself cheaply, you may laugh, but the dawn of a new life is at hand; truth and justice will triumph, and—our turn will come! I shall not live to see it, I shall perish, but some people's great-grandsons will see it. I greet them with all my heart and rejoice, rejoice with them! Onward! God be your help, friends!"

With shining eyes Ivan Dmitritch got up, and stretching his hands towards the window, went on with emotion in his voice:

"From behind these bars I bless you! Hurrah for truth and justice! I rejoice!"

"I see no particular reason to rejoice," said Andrey Yefimitch, who thought Ivan Dmitritch's movement theatrical, though he was delighted by it. "Prisons and madhouses there will not be, and truth, as you have just expressed it, will triumph; but the reality of things, you know, will not change, the laws of nature will still remain the same. People will suffer pain, grow old, and die just as they do now. However magnificent a dawn lighted up your life, you would yet in the end be nailed up in a coffin and thrown into a hole."

"And immortality?"

"Oh, come, now!"

"You don't believe in it, but I do. Somebody in Dostoevsky or Voltaire said that if there had not been a God men would have invented him. And I firmly believe that if there is no immortality the great intellect of man will sooner or later invent it."

"Well said," observed Andrey Yefimitch, smiling with pleasure; "it's a good thing you have faith. With such a belief one may live happily even shut up within walls. You have studied somewhere, I presume?"

"Yes, I have been at the university, but did not complete my studies."

"You are a reflecting and a thoughtful man. In any surroundings you can find tranquility in yourself. Free and deep thinking which strives for the comprehension of life, and complete contempt for the foolish bustle of the world—those are two blessings beyond any that man has ever known. And you can possess them even though you lived behind threefold bars. Diogenes lived in a tub, yet he was happier than all the kings of the earth."

"Your Diogenes was a blockhead," said Ivan Dmitritch morosely. "Why do you talk to me about Diogenes and some foolish comprehension of life?" he cried, growing suddenly angry and leaping up. "I love life; I love it passionately. I have the mania of persecution, a continual agonizing terror; but I have moments when I am overwhelmed by the thirst for life, and then I am afraid of going mad. I want dreadfully to live, dreadfully!"

He walked up and down the ward in agitation, and said, dropping his voice:

"When I dream I am haunted by phantoms. People come to me, I hear voices and music, and I fancy I am walking through woods or by the seashore, and I long so passionately for movement, for interests. . . . Come, tell me, what news is there?" asked Ivan Dmitritch; "what's happening?"

"Do you wish to know about the town or in general?"

"Well, tell me first about the town, and then in general."

"Well, in the town it is appallingly dull. . . . There's no one to say a word to, no one to listen to. There are no new people. A young doctor called Hobotov has come here recently."

"He had come in my time. Well, he is a low cad, isn't he?"

"Yes, he is a man of no culture. It's strange, you know. . . . Judging by every sign, there is no intellectual stagnation in our capital cities; there is a movement—so there must be real people there too; but for some reason they always send us such men as I would rather not see. It's an unlucky town!"

"Yes, it is an unlucky town," sighed Ivan Dmitritch, and he

laughed. "And how are things in general? What are they writing in the papers and reviews?"

It was by now dark in the ward. The doctor got up, and, standing, began to describe what was being written abroad and in Russia, and the tendency of thought that could be noticed now. Ivan Dmitritch listened attentively and put questions, but suddenly, as though recalling something terrible, clutched at his head and lay down on the bed with his back to the doctor.

"What's the matter?" asked Andrey Yefimitch.

"You will not hear another word from me," said Ivan Dmitritch rudely. "Leave me alone."

"Why so?"

"I tell you, leave me alone. Why the devil do you persist?"

Andrey Yefimitch shrugged his shoulders, heaved a sigh, and went out. As he crossed the entry he said: "You might clear up here, Nikita . . . there's an awfully stuffy smell."

"Certainly, your honour."

"What an agreeable young man!" thought Andrey Yefimitch, going back to his flat. "In all the years I have been living here I do believe he is the first I have met with whom one can talk. He is capable of reasoning and is interested in just the right things."

While he was reading, and afterwards, while he was going to bed, he kept thinking about Ivan Dmitritch, and when he woke next morning he remembered that he had the day before made the acquaintance of an intelligent and interesting man, and determined to visit him again as soon as possible.

X

Ivan Dmitritch was lying in the same position as on the previous day, with his head clutched in both hands and his legs drawn up. His face was not visible.

"Good-day, my friend," said Andrey Yefimitch. "You are not asleep, are you?"

"In the first place, I am not your friend," Ivan Dmitritch articulated into the pillow; "and in the second, your efforts are useless; you will not get one word out of me."

"Strange," muttered Andrey Yefimitch in confusion. "Yesterday we talked peacefully, but suddenly for some reason you took offence and broke off all at once. . . . Probably I expressed myself awkwardly, or perhaps gave utterance to some idea which did not fit in with your convictions. . . ."

"Yes, a likely idea!" said Ivan Dmitritch, sitting up and looking at the doctor with irony and uneasiness. His eyes were red. "You can go and spy and probe somewhere else, it's no use your doing it here. I knew yesterday what you had come for."

"A strange fancy," laughed the doctor. "So you suppose me to be a spy?"

"Yes, I do. . . . A spy or a doctor who has been charged to test me—it's all the same—"

"Oh, excuse me, what a queer fellow you are really!"

The doctor sat down on the stool near the bed and shook his head reproachfully.

"But let us suppose you are right," he said, "let us suppose that I am treacherously trying to trap you into saying something so as to betray you to the police. You would be arrested and then tried. But would you be any worse off being tried and in prison than you are here? If you are banished to a settlement, or even sent to penal servitude, would it be worse than being shut up in this ward? I imagine it would be no worse. . . . What, then, are you afraid of?"

These words evidently had an effect on Ivan Dmitritch. He sat down quietly.

It was between four and five in the afternoon—the time when Andrey Yefimitch usually walked up and down his rooms, and Daryushka asked whether it was not time for his beer. It was a still, bright day.

"I came out for a walk after dinner, and here I have come, as you see," said the doctor. "It is quite spring."

"What month is it? March?" asked Ivan Dmitritch.

"Yes, the end of March."

"Is it very muddy?"

"No, not very. There are already paths in the garden."

"It would be nice now to drive in an open carriage somewhere into the country," said Ivan Dmitritch, rubbing his red eyes as though he were just awake, "then to come home to a warm, snug study, and . . . and to have a decent doctor to cure one's headache. . . . It's so long since I have lived like a human being. It's disgusting here! Insufferably disgusting!"

After his excitement of the previous day he was exhausted and listless, and spoke unwillingly. His fingers twitched, and from his face it could be seen that he had a splitting headache.

"There is no real difference between a warm, snug study and this ward," said Andrey Yefimitch. "A man's peace and contentment do not lie outside a man, but in himself."

"What do you mean?"

"The ordinary man looks for good and evil in external things—that is, in carriages, in studies—but a thinking man looks for it in himself."

"You should go and preach that philosophy in Greece, where it's warm and fragrant with the scent of pomegranates, but here it is not suited to the climate. With whom was it I was talking of Diogenes? Was it with you?'

"Yes, with me yesterday."

"Diogenes did not need a study or a warm habitation; it's hot there without. You can lie in your tub and eat oranges and olives. But bring him to Russia to live: he'd be begging to be let indoors in May, let alone December. He'd be doubled up with the cold."

"No. One can be insensible to cold as to every other pain. Marcus Aurelius says: 'A pain is a vivid idea of pain; make an effort of will to change that idea, dismiss it, cease to complain, and the pain will disappear.' That is true. The wise man, or simply the reflecting, thoughtful man, is distinguished precisely by his contempt for suffering; he is always contented and surprised at nothing."

"Then I am in idiot, since I suffer and am discontented and surprised at the baseness of mankind."

"You are wrong in that; if you will reflect more on the subject you will understand how insignificant is all that external world that agitates us. One must strive for the comprehension of life, and in that is true happiness."

"Comprehension . . ." repeated Ivan Dmitritch frowning. "External, internal. . . . Excuse me, but I don't understand it. I only know," he said, getting up and looking angrily at the doctor—"I only know that God has created me of warm blood and nerves, yes, indeed! If organic tissue is capable of life it must react to every stimulus. And I do! To pain I respond with tears and outcries, to baseness with indignation, to filth with loathing. To my mind, that is just what is called life. The lower the organism, the less sensitive it is, and the more feebly it reacts to stimulus; and the higher it is, the more responsively and vigorously it reacts to reality. How is it you don't know that? A doctor, and not know such trifles! To despise suffering, to be always contented, and to be surprised at nothing, one must reach this condition"—and Ivan Dmitritch pointed to the peasant who was a mass of fat—"or to harden oneself by suffering to such a point that one loses all sensibility to it—that is, in other words, to cease to live. You must excuse me, I am not a sage or a philosopher," Ivan Dmitritch continued with irritation, "and I don't understand anything about it. I am not capable of reasoning."

"On the contrary, your reasoning is excellent."

"The Stoics, whom you are parodying, were remarkable people, but their doctrine crystallized two thousand years ago and has not advanced, and will not advance, an inch forward, since it is not practical or living. It had a success only with the minority which spends its life in savouring all sorts of theories and ruminating over them; the majority did not understand it. A doctrine which advocates indifference to wealth and to the comforts of life, and a contempt for suffering and death, is quite unintelligible to the vast majority of men, since that majority has never known wealth or the comforts of life; and to despise suffering would mean to it despising life itself, since the whole existence of man is made up of the sensations of hunger, cold, injury, loss, and a Hamlet-like dread of death. The whole of life lies in these sensations; one may be oppressed by it, one may hate it, but one cannot despise it. Yes, so, I repeat, the doctrine of the Stoics can never have a future; from the beginning of time up to to-day you see continually increasing the struggle, the sensibility to pain, the capacity of responding to stimulus."

Ivan Dmitritch suddenly lost the thread of his thoughts, stopped, and rubbed his forehead with vexation.

"I meant to say something important, but I have lost it," he said. "What was I saying? Oh, yes! This is what I mean: one of the Stoics sold himself into slavery to redeem his neighbour, so, you see, even a Stoic did react to stimulus, since, for such a generous act as the destruction of oneself for the sake of one's neighbour, he must have had a soul capable of pity and indignation. Here in prison I have forgotten everything I have learned, or else I could have recalled something else. Take Christ, for instance: Christ responded to reality by weeping, smiling, being sorrowful and moved to wrath, even overcome by misery. He did not go to meet His sufferings with a smile, He did not despise death, but prayed in the Garden of Gethsemane that this cup might pass Him by."

Ivan Dmitritch laughed and sat down.

"Granted that a man's peace and contentment lie not outside but in himself," he said, "granted that one must despise suffering and not be surprised at anything, yet on what ground do you preach the theory? Are you a sage? A philosopher?"

"No, I am not a philosopher, but everyone ought to preach it because it is reasonable."

"No, I want to know how it is that you consider yourself competent to judge of 'comprehension,' contempt for suffering, and so on. Have you ever suffered? Have you any idea of suffering? Allow me to ask you, were you ever thrashed in your childhood?"

"No, my parents had an aversion for corporal punishment."

"My father used to flog me cruelly; my father was a harsh, sickly Government clerk with a long nose and a yellow neck. But let us talk of you. No one has laid a finger on you all your life, no one has scared you nor beaten you; you are as strong as a bull. You grew up under your father's wing and studied at his expense, and then you dropped at once into a sinecure. For more than twenty years you have lived rent free with heating, lighting, and service all provided, and had the right to work how you pleased and as much as you pleased, even to do nothing. You were naturally a flabby, lazy man, and so you have tried to arrange your life so that nothing should disturb you or make you move. You have handed over your work to the assistant and the rest of the rabble while you sit in peace and warmth, save money, read, amuse yourself with reflections, with all sorts of lofty nonsense, and" (Ivan Dmitritch looked at the doctor's red nose) "with boozing; in fact, you have seen nothing of life, you know absolutely nothing of it, and are only theoretically acquainted with reality; you despise suffering and are surprised at nothing for a very simple reason: vanity of vanities, the external and the internal, contempt for life, for suffering and for death, comprehension, true happiness—that's the philosophy that suits the Russian sluggard best. You see a peasant beating his wife, for instance. Why interfere? Let him beat her, they will both die sooner or later, anyway; and, besides, he who beats injures by his blows, not the person he is beating, but himself. To get drunk is stupid and unseemly, but if you drink you die, and if you don't drink you die. A peasant woman comes with toothache . . . well, what of it? Pain is the idea of pain, and besides 'there is no living in this world without illness; we shall all die, and so, go away, woman, don't hinder me from thinking and drinking vodka.' A young man asks advice, what he is to do, how he is to live; anyone else would think before answering, but you have got the answer ready: strive for 'comprehension' or for true happiness. And what is that fantastic 'true happiness'? There's no answer, of course. We are kept here behind barred windows, tortured, left to rot; but that is very good and reasonable, because there is no difference at all between this ward and a warm, snug study. A convenient philosophy. You can do nothing, and your conscience is clear, and you feel you are wise. . . . No, sir, it is not philosophy, it's not thinking, it's not breadth of vision, but laziness, fakirism, drowsy stupefaction. Yes," cried Ivan Dmitritch, getting angry again, "you despise suffering, but I'll be bound if you pinch your finger in the door you will howl at the top of your voice."

"And perhaps I shouldn't howl," said Andrey Yefimitch, with a gentle smile.

"Oh, I dare say! Well, if you had a stroke of paralysis, or supposing some fool or bully took advantage of his position and rank to insult you in public, and if you knew he could do it with impunity, then you would understand what it means to put people off with comprehension and true happiness."

"That's original," said Andrey Yefimitch, laughing with pleasure and rubbing his hands. "I am agreebly struck by your inclination for drawing generalizations, and the sketch of my character you have just drawn is simply brilliant. I must confess that talking to you gives me great pleasure. Well, I've listened to you, and now you must graciously listen to me."

XI

The conversation went on for about an hour longer, and apparently made a deep impression on Andrey Yefimitch. He began going to the ward every day. He went there in the mornings and after dinner, and often the dusk of evening found him in conversation with Ivan Dmitritch. At first Ivan Dmitritch held aloof from him, suspected him of evil designs, and openly expressed his hostility. But afterwards he got used to him, and his abrupt manner changed to one of condescending irony.

Soon it was all over the hospital that the doctor, Andrey Yefimitch, had taken to visiting Ward No. 6. No one—neither Sergey Sergeyitch, nor Nikita, nor the nurses—could conceive why he went there, why he stayed there for hours together, what he was talking about, and why he did not write prescriptions. His actions seemed strange. Often Mihail Averyanitch did not find him at home, which had never happened in the past, and Daryushka was greatly perturbed, for the doctor drank his beer now at no definite time, and sometimes was even late for dinner.

One day—it was at the end of June—Dr. Hobotov went to see Andrey Yefimitch about something. Not finding him at home, he proceeded to look for him in the yard; there he was told that the old doctor had gone to see the mental patients. Going into the lodge and stopping in the entry, Hobotov heard the following conversation:

"We shall never agree, and you will not succeed in converting me to your faith," Ivan Dmitritch was saying irritably; "you are utterly ignorant of reality, and you have never known suffering, but have only like a leech fed beside the sufferings of others, while I have been in continual suffering from the day of my birth till to-day. For that reason, I tell you frankly, I consider myself superior to you and more competent in every respect. It's not for you to teach me."

"I have absolutely no ambition to convert you to my faith," said Andrey Yefimitch gently, and with regret that the other refused to understand him. "And that is not what matters, my friend; what matters is not that you have suffered and I have not. Joy and suffering are passing; let us leave them, never mind them. What matters is that you and I think; we see in each other people who are capable of thinking and reasoning, and that is a common bond between us however different our views. If you knew, my friend, how sick I am of the universal senselessness, ineptitude, stupidity, and with what delight I always talk with you! You are an intelligent man, and I enjoy your company."

Hobotov opened the door an inch and glanced into the ward; Ivan Dmitritch in his night-cap and the doctor Andrey Yefimitch were sitting side by side on the bed. The madman was grimacing, twitching, and convulsively wrapping himself in his gown, while the doctor sat motionless with bowed head, and his face was red and looked helpless and sorrowful. Hobotov shrugged his shoulders, grinned, and glanced at Nikita. Nikita shrugged his shoulders too.

Next day Hobotov went to the lodge, accompanied by the assistant. Both stood in the entry and listened.

"I fancy our old man has gone clean off his chump!" said Hobotov as he came out of the lodge.

"Lord have mercy upon us sinners!" sighed the decorous Sergey Sergeyitch, scrupulously avoiding the puddles that he might not muddy his polished boots. "I must own, honoured Yevgeny Fyodoritch, I have been expecting it for a long time."

XII

After this Andrey Yefimitch began to notice a mysterious air in all around him. The attendants, the nurses, and the patients looked at him inquisitively when they met him, and then whispered together. The superintendent's little daughter Masha, whom he liked to meet in the hospital garden, for some reason ran away from him now when he went up with a smile to stroke her on the head. The postmaster no longer said, "Perfectly true," as he listened to him, but in unaccountable confusion muttered, "Yes, yes, yes . . ." and looked at him with a grieved and thoughtful expression; for some reason he took to advising his friend to give up vodka and beer, but as a man of delicate feeling he did not say this directly, but hinted it, telling him first about the commanding officer of his battalion, an excellent man, and then about the priest of the regiment, a capital fellow, both of whom drank and fell ill, but on giving up drinking completely regained their health. On two or three occasions Andrey Yefimitch was visited by his colleague Hobotov, who also advised him to give up spirituous liquors, and for no apparent reason recommended him to take bromide.

In August Andrey Yefimitch got a letter from the mayor of the town asking him to come on very important business. On arriving at the town hall at the time fixed, Andrey Yefimitch found there the military commander, the superintendent of the district school, a member of the town council, Hobotov, and a plump, fair gentleman who was introduced to him as a doctor. This doctor, with a Polish surname difficult to pronounce, lived at a pedigree stud-farm twenty miles away, and was now on a visit to the town.

"There's something that concerns you," said the member of the town council, addressing Andrey Yefimitch after they had all greeted one another and sat down to the table. "Here Yevgeny Fyodoritch says that there is not room for the dispensary in the main building, and that it ought to be transferred to one of the lodges. That's of no consequence—of course it can be transferred, but the point is that the lodge wants doing up."

"Yes, it would have to be done up," said Andrey Yefimitch after a moment's thought. "If the corner lodge, for instance, were fitted up as a dispensary, I imagine it would cost at least five hundred roubles. An unproductive expenditure!"

Everyone was silent for a space.

"I had the honour of submitting to you ten years ago," Andrey Yefimitch went on in a low voice, "that the hospital in its present form is a luxury for the town beyond its means. It was built in the forties, but things were different then. The town spends too much on unnecessary buildings and superfluous staff. I believe with a different system two model hospitals might be maintained for the same money."

"Well, let us have a different system, then!" the member of the town council said briskly.

"I have already had the honour of submitting to you that the medical department should be transferred to the supervision of the Zemstvo."

"Yes, transfer the money to the Zemstvo and they will steal it," laughed the fair-haired doctor.

"That's what it always comes to," the member of the council assented, and he also laughed.

Andrey Yefimitch looked with apathetic, lustreless eyes at the fair-haired doctor and said: "One should be just."

Again there was silence. Tea was brought in. The military commander, for some reason much embarrassed, touched Andrey Yefimitch's hand across the table and said: "You have quite forgotten us, doctor. But of course you are a hermit: you don't play cards and don't like women. You would be dull with fellows like us."

They all began saying how boring it was for a decent person to live in such a town. No theatre, no music, and at the last dance at the club there had been about twenty ladies and only two gentlemen. The young men did not dance, but spent all the time crowding round the refreshment bar or playing cards.

Not looking at anyone and speaking slowly in a low voice, Andrey Yefimitch began saying what a pity, what a terrible pity it was that the townspeople should waste their vital energy, their hearts, and their minds on cards and gossip, and should have neither the power nor the inclination to spend their time in interesting conversation and reading, and should refuse to take advantage of the enjoyments of the mind. The mind alone was interesting and worthy of attention, all the rest was low and petty. Hobotov listened to his colleague attentively and suddenly asked:

"Andrey Yefimitch, what day of the month is it?"

Having received an answer, the fair-haired doctor and he, in the tone of examiners conscious of their lack of skill, began asking Andrey Yefimitch what was the day of the week, how many days there were in the year, and whether it was true that there was a remarkable prophet living in Ward No. 6.

In response to the last question Andrey Yefimitch turned rather red and said: "Yes, he is mentally deranged, but he is an interesting young man."

They asked him no other questions.

When he was putting on his overcoat in the entry, the military commander laid a hand on his shoulder and said with a sigh:

"It's time for us old fellows to rest!"

As he came out of the hall, Andrey Yefimitch understood that it had been a committee appointed to enquire into his mental condition. H recalled the questions that had been asked him, flushed crimson, and for some reason, for the first time in his life, felt bitterly grieved for medical science.

"My God . . ." he thought, remembering how these doctors had just examined him; "why, they have only lately been hearing lectures on mental pathology; they had passed an examination—what's the explanation of this crass ignorance? They have not a conception of mental pathology!"

And for the first time in his life he felt insulted and moved to anger.

In the evening of the same day Mihail Averyanitch came to see him. The postmaster went up to him without waiting to greet him, took him by both hands, and said in an agitated voice:

"My dear fellow, my dear friend, show me that you believe in my genuine affection and look on me as your friend!" And preventing Andrey Yefimitch from speaking, he went on, growing excited: "I love you for your culture and nobility of soul. Listen to me, my dear fellow. The rules of their profession compel the doctors to conceal the truth from you, but I blurt out the plain truth like a soldier. You are not well! Excuse me, my dear fellow, but it is the truth; everyone about you has been noticing it for a long time. Dr. Yevgeny Fyodoritch has just told me that it is essential for you to rest and distract your mind for the sake of your health. Perfectly true! Excellent! In a day or two I am taking a holiday and am going away for a sniff of a different atmosphere. Show that you are a friend to me, let us go together! Let us go for a jaunt as in the good old days."

"I feel perfectly well," said Andrey Yefimitch after a moment's thought. "I can't go away. Allow me to show you my friendship in some other way."

To go off with no object, without his books, without his Daryushka, without his beer, to break abruptly through the routine of life, established for twenty years—the idea for the first minute struck him as wild and fantastic, but he remembered the conversation at the Zemstvo committee and the depressing feelings with which he had returned home, and the thought of a brief absence from the town in which stupid people looked on him as a madman was pleasant to him.

"And where precisely do you intend to go?" he asked.

"To Moscow, to Petersburg, to Warsaw. . . . I spent the five happiest years of my life in Warsaw. What a marvellous town! Let us go, my dear fellow!"

XIII

A week later it was suggested to Andrey Yefimitch that he should have a rest—that is, send in his resignation—a suggestion he received with indifference, and a week later still, Mihail Averyanitch and he were sitting in a posting carriage driving to the nearest railway station. The days were cool and bright, with a blue sky and a transparent distance. They were two days driving the hundred and fifty miles to the railway station, and stayed two nights on the way. When at the posting station the glasses given them for their tea had not been properly washed, or the drivers were slow in harnessing the horses, Mihail Averyanitch would turn crimson, and quivering all over would shout:

"Hold your tongue! Don't argue!"

And in the carriage he talked without ceasing for a moment,

describing his campaigns in the Caucasus and in Poland. What adventures he had had, what meetings! He talked loudly and opened his eyes so wide with wonder that he might well be thought to be lying. Moreover, as he talked he breathed in Andrey Yefimitch's face and laughed into his ear. This bothered the doctor and prevented him from thinking or concentrating his mind.

In the train they travelled, from motives of economy, third-class in a non-smoking compartment. Half the passengers were decent people. Mihail Averyanitch soon made friends with everyone, and moving from one seat to another, kept saying loudly that they ought not to travel by these appalling lines. It was a regular swindle! A very different thing riding on a good horse: one could do over seventy miles a day and feel fresh and well after it. And our bad harvests were due to the draining of the Pinsk marshes; altogether, the way things were done was dreadful. He got excited, talked loudly, and would not let others speak. This endless chatter to the accompaniment of loud laughter and expressive gestures wearied Andrey Yefimitch.

"Which of us is the madman?" he thought with vexation. "I, who try not to disturb my fellow-passengers in any way, or this egoist who thinks that he is cleverer and more interesting than anyone here, and so will leave no one in peace?"

In Moscow Mihail Averyanitch put on a military coat without epaulettes and trousers with red braid on them. He wore a military cap and overcoat in the street, and soldiers saluted him. It seemed to Andrey Yefimitch, now, that his companion was a man who had flung away all that was good and kept only what was bad of all the characteristics of a country gentleman that he had once possessed. He liked to be waited on even when it was quite unnecessary. The matches would be lying before him on the table, and he would see them and shout to the waiter to give him the matches; he did not hesitate to appear before a maidservant in nothing but his underclothes; he used the familiar mode of address to all footmen indiscriminately, even old men, and when he was angry called them fools and blockheads. This, Andrey Yefimitch thought, was like a gentleman, but disgusting.

First of all Mihail Averyanitch led his friend to the Iversky Madonna. He prayed fervently, shedding tears and bowing down to the earth, and when he had finished, heaved a deep sigh and said:

"Even though one does not believe it makes one somehow easier when one prays a little. Kiss the ikon, my dear fellow."

Andrey Yefimitch was embarrassed and he kissed the image, while Mihail Averyanitch pursed up his lips and prayed in a whisper, and again tears came into his eyes. Then they went to the Kremlin and looked there at the Tsar-cannon and the Tsar-bell, and even touched them with their fingers, admired the view over the river, visited St. Saviour's and the Rumyantsev museum.

They dined at Tyestov's. Mihail Averyanitch looked a long time at the menu, stroking his whiskers, and said in the tone of the gourmand accustomed to dine in restaurants:

"We shall see what you give us to eat to-day, angel!"

XIV

The doctor walked about, looked at things, ate and drank, but he had all the while one feeling: annoyance with Mihail Averyanitch. He longed to have a rest from his friend, to get away from him, to hide himself, while the friend thought it his duty not to let the doctor move a step away from him, and to provide him with as many distractions as possible. When there was nothing to look at he entertained him with conversation. For two days Andrey Yefimitch endured it, but on the third he announced to his friend that he was ill and wanted to stay at home for the whole day; his friend replied that in that case he would stay too—that really he needed rest, for he was run off his legs already. Andrey Yefimitch lay on the sofa, with his face to the back, and clenching his teeth, listened to his friend, who assured him with heat that sooner or later France would certainly thrash Germany, that there were a great many scoundrels in Moscow, and that it was impossible to judge of a horse's quality by its outward appearance. The doctor began to have a buzzing in his ears and palpitations of the heart, but out of delicacy could not bring himself to beg his friend to go away or hold his tongue. Fortunately Mihail Averyanitch grew weary of sitting in the hotel room, and after dinner he went out for a walk.

As soon as he was alone Andrey Yefimitch abandoned himself to a feeling of relief. How pleasant to lie motionless on the sofa and to know that one is alone in the room! Real happiness is impossible without solitude. The fallen angel betrayed God probably because he longed for solitude, of which the angels know nothing. Andrey Yefimitch wanted to think about what he had seen and heard during the last few days, but he could not get Mihail Averyanitch out of his head.

"Why, he has taken a holiday and come with me out of friendship, out of generosity," thought the doctor with vexation; "nothing could be worse than this friendly supervision. I suppose he is good-natured and generous and a lively fellow, but he is a bore. An insufferable bore. In the same way there are people who never say anything but what is clever and good, yet one feels that they are dull-witted people."

For the following days Andrey Yefimitch declared himself ill and would not leave the hotel room; he lay with his face to the back of the sofa, and suffered agonies of weariness when his friend entertained him with conversation, or rested when his friend was absent. He was vexed with himself for having come, and with his friend, who grew every day more talkative and more free-and-easy; he could not succeed in attuning his thoughts to a serious and lofty level.

"This is what I get from the real life Ivan Dmitritch talked about," he thought, angry at his own pettiness. "It's of no consequence, though. . . . I shall go home, and everything will go on as before. . . ."

It was the same thing in Petersburg too; for whole days together he did not leave the hotel room, but lay on the sofa and only got up to drink beer.

Mihail Averyanitch was all haste to get to Warsaw.

"My dear man, what should I go there for?" said Andrey Yefimitch in an imploring voice. "You go alone and let me get home! I entreat you!"

"On no account," protested Mihail Averyanitch. "It's a marvellous town."

Andrey Yefimitch had not the strength of will to insist on his own way, and much against his inclination went to Warsaw. There he did not leave the hotel room, but lay on the sofa, furious with himself, with his friend, and with the waiters, who obstinately refused to understand Russian; while Mihail Averyanitch, healthy, hearty, and full of spirits as usual, went about the town from morning to night, looking for his old acquaintances. Several times he did not return home at night. After one night spent in some unknown haunt he returned home early in the morning, in a violently excited condition, with a red face and tousled hair. For a long time he walked up and down the rooms muttering something to himself, then stopped and said:

"Honour before everything."

After walking up and down a little longer he clutched his head in both hands and pronounced in a tragic voice: "Yes, honour before everything! Accursed be the moment when the idea first entered my head to visit this Babylon! My dear friend," he added, addressing the doctor, "you may despise me, I have played and lost; lend me five hundred roubles!"

Andrey Yefimitch counted out five hundred roubles and gave them to his friend without a word. The latter, still crimson with shame and anger, incoherently articulated some useless vow, put on his cap, and went out. Returning two hours later he flopped into an easy-chair, heaved a loud sigh, and said:

"My honour is saved. Let us go, my friend; I do not care to remain another hour in this accursed town. Scoundrels! Austrian spies!"

By the time the friends were back in their own town it was November, and deep snow was lying in the streets. Dr. Hobotov had Andrey Yefimitch's post; he was still living in his old lodgings, waiting for Andrey Yefimitch to arrive and clear out of the hospital apartments. The plain woman whom he called his cook was already established in one of the lodges.

Fresh scandals about the hospital were going the round of the town. It was said that the plain woman had quarrelled with the superintendent, and that the latter had crawled on his knees before her begging forgiveness. On the very first day he arrived Andrey Yefimitch had to look out for lodgings.

"My friend," the postmaster said to him timidly, "excuse an indiscreet question: what means have you at your disposal?"

Andrey Yefimitch, without a word, counted out his money and said: "Eighty-six roubles."

"I don't mean that," Mihail Averyanitch brought out in confusion, misunderstanding him; "I mean, what have you to live on?"

"I tell you, eighty-six roubles . . . I have nothing else."

Mihail Averyanitch looked upon the doctor as an honourable man, yet he suspected that he had accumulated a fortune of at least twenty thousand. Now learning that Andrey Yefimitch was a beggar, that he had nothing to live on he was for some reason suddenly moved to tears and embraced his friend.

XV

Andrey Yefimitch now lodged in a little house with three windows. There were only three rooms besides the kitchen in the little house. The doctor lived in two of them which looked into the street, while Daryushka and the landlady with her three children lived in the third room and the kitchen. Sometimes the landlady's lover, a drunken peasant who was rowdy and reduced the children and Daryushka to terror, would come for the night. When he arrived and established himself in the kitchen and demanded vodka, they all felt very uncomfortable, and the doctor would be moved by pity to take the crying children into his room and let them lie on his floor, and this gave him great satisfaction.

He got up as before at eight o'clock, and after his morning tea sat down to read his old books and magazines: he had no money for new ones. Either because the books were old, or perhaps because of the change in his surroundings, reading exhausted him, and did not grip his attention as before. That he might not spend his time in idleness he made a detailed catalogue of his books and gummed little labels on their backs, and this mechanical, tedious work seemed to him more interesting than reading. The monotonous, tedious work lulled his thoughts to sleep in some unaccountable way, and the time passed quickly while he thought of nothing. Even sitting in the kitchen, peeling potatoes with Daryushka or picking over the buckwheat grain, seemed to him interesting. On Saturdays and Sundays he went to church. Standing near the wall and half closing his eyes, he listened to the singing and thought of his father, of his mother, of the university, of the religions of the world; he felt calm and melancholy, and as he went out of the church afterwards he regretted that the service was so soon over. He went twice to the hospital to talk to Ivan Dmitritch. But on both occasions Ivan Dmitritch was unusually excited and ill-humoured; he bade the doctor leave him in peace, as he had long been sick of empty chatter, and declared, to make up for all his sufferings, he asked from the damned scoundrels only one favour—solitary confinement. Surely they would not refuse him even that? On both occasions when Andrey Yefimitch was taking leave of him and wishing him good-night, he answered rudely and said:

"Go to hell!"

And Andrey Yefimitch did not know now whether to go to him for the third time or not. He longed to go.

In old days Andrey Yefimitch used to walk about his rooms and think in the interval after dinner, but now from dinner-time till evening tea he lay on the sofa with his face to the back and gave himself up to trivial thoughts which he could not struggle against. He was mortified that after more than twenty years of service he had been given neither a pension nor any assistance. It is true that he had not done his work honestly, but, then, all who are in the Service get a pension without distinction whether they are honest or not. Contemporary justice lies precisely in the bestowal of grades, orders, and pensions, not for moral qualities or capacities, but for service whatever it may have been like. Why was he alone to be an exception? He had no money at all. He was ashamed to pass by the shop and look at the woman who owned it. He owed thirty-two roubles for beer already. There was money owing to the landlady also. Daryushka sold old clothes and books on the sly, and told lies to the landlady, saying that the doctor was just going to receive a large sum of money.

He was angry with himself for having wasted on travelling the thousand roubles he had saved up. How useful that thousand roubles would have been now! He was vexed that people would not leave him in peace. Hobotov thought it his duty to look in on his sick colleague from time to time. Everything about him was revolting to Andrey Yefimitch—his well-fed face and vulgar, condescending tone, and his use of the word "colleague," and his high top-boots; the most revolting thing was that he thought it was his duty to treat Andrey Yefimitch, and thought that he really was treating him. On every visit he brought a bottle of bromide and rhubarb pills.

Mihail Averyanitch, too, thought it his duty to visit his friend and entertain him. Every time he went in to Andrey Yefimitch with an affectation of ease, laughed constrainedly, and began assuring him that he was looking very well to-day, and that, thank God, he was on the highroad to recovery, and from this it might be concluded that he looked on his friend's condition as hopeless. He had not yet repaid his Warsaw debt, and was overwhelmed by shame; he was constrained, and so tried to laugh louder and talk more amusingly. His anecdotes and descriptions seemed endless now, and were an agony both to Andrey Yefimitch and himself.

In his presence Andrey Yefimitch usually lay on the sofa with his face to the wall, and listened with his teeth clenched; his soul was oppressed with rankling disgust, and after every visit from his friend he felt as though this disgust had risen higher, and was mounting into his throat.

To stifle petty thoughts he made haste to reflect that he himself, and Hobotov, and Mihail Averyanitch, would all sooner or later perish without leaving any trace on the world. If one imagined some spirit flying by the earthly globe in space in a million years he would see nothing but clay and bare rocks. Everything—culture and the moral law—would pass away and not even a burdock would grow out of them. Of what consequence was shame in the presence of a shopkeeper, of what consequence was the insignificant Hobotov or the wearisome friendship of Mihail Averyanitch? It was all trivial and nonsensical.

But such reflections did not help him now. Scarcely had he imagined the earthly globe in a million years, when Hobotov in his high top-boots or Mihail Averyanitch with his forced laugh would appear from behind a bare rock, and he even heard the shamefaced whisper: "The Warsaw debt. . . . I will repay it in a day or two, my dear fellow, without fail. . . ."

XVI

One day Mihail Averyanitch came after dinner when Andrey Yefimitch was lying on the sofa. It so happened that Hobotov arrived at the same time with his bromide. Andrey Yefimitch got up heavily and sat down, leaning both arms on the sofa.

"You have a much better colour to-day than you had yesterday, my dear man," began Mihail Averyanitch. "Yes, you look jolly. Upon my soul, you do!"

"It's high time you were well, colleague," said Hobotov, yawning. "I'll be bound, you are sick of this bobbery."

"And we shall recover," said Mihail Averyanitch cheerfully. "We shall live another hundred years! To be sure!"

"Not a hundred years, but another twenty," Hobotov said

reassuringly. "It's all right, all right, colleague; don't lose heart. . . . Don't go piling it on!"

"We'll show what we can do," laughed Mihail Averyanitch, and he slapped his friend on the knee. "We'll show them yet! Next summer, please God, we shall be off to the Caucasus, and we will ride all over it on horseback—trot, trot, trot! And when we are back from the Caucasus I shouldn't wonder if we will all dance at the wedding." Mihail Averyanitch gave a sly wink. "We'll marry you, my dear boy, we'll marry you. . . ."

Andrey Yefimitch felt suddenly that the rising disgust had mounted to his throat, his heart began beating violently.

"That's vulgar," he said, getting up quickly and walking away to the window. "Don't you understand that you are talking vulgar nonsense?"

He meant to go on softly and politely, but against his will he suddenly clenched his fists and raised them above his head.

"Leave me alone," he shouted in a voice unlike his own, flushing crimson and shaking all over. "Go away, both of you!"

Mihail Averyanitch and Hobotov got up and stared at him first with amazement and then with alarm.

"Go away, both!" Andrey Yefimitch went on shouting. "Stupid people! Foolish people! I don't want either your friendship or your medicines, stupid man! Vulgar! Nasty!"

Hobotov and Mihail Averyanitch, looking at each other in bewilderment, staggered to the door and went out. Andrey Yefimitch snatched up the bottle of bromide and flung it after them; the bottle broke with a crash on the door-frame.

"Go to the devil!" he shouted in a tearful voice, running out into the passage. "To the devil!"

When his guests were gone Andrey Yefimitch lay down on the sofa, trembling as though in a fever, and went on for a long while repeating: "Stupid people! Foolish people!"

When he was calmer, what occurred to him first of all was the thought that poor Mihail Averyanitch must be feeling fearfully ashamed and depressed now, and that it was all dreadful. Nothing like this had ever happened to him before. Where was his intelligence and his tact? Where was his comprehension of things and his philosophical indifference?

The doctor could not sleep all night for shame and vexation with himself, and at ten o'clock next morning he went to the post office and apologized to the postmaster.

"We won't think again of what has happened," Mihail Averyanitch, greatly touched, said with a sigh, warmly pressing his hand. "Let bygones be bygones. Lyubavkin," he suddenly shouted so loud that all the postmen and other persons present started, "hand a chair; and you wait," he shouted to a peasant woman who was stretching out a registered letter to him through the grating. "Don't you see that I am busy? We will not remember the past," he went on, affectionately addressing Andrey Yefimitch; "sit down, I beg you, my dear fellow."

For a minute he stroked his knees in silence, and then said:

"I have never had a thought of taking offence. Illness is no joke, I understand. Your attack frightened the doctor and me yesterday, and we had a long talk about you afterwards. My dear friend, why won't you treat your illness seriously? You can't go on like this. . . . Excuse me speaking openly as a friend," whispered Mihail Averyanitch. "You live in the most unfavourable surroundings, in a crowd, in uncleanliness, no one to look after you, no money for proper treatment. . . . My dear friend, the doctor and I implore you with all our hearts, listen to our advice: go into the hospital! There you will have wholesome food and attendance and treatment. Though, between ourselves, Yevgeny Fyodoritch is *mauvais ton*, yet he does understand his work, you can fully rely upon him. He has promised me he will look after you."

Andrey Yefimitch was touched by the postmaster's genuine sympathy and the tears which suddenly glittered on his cheeks.

"My honoured friend, don't believe it!" he whispered, laying his hand on his heart; "don't believe them. It's all a sham. My illness is only that in twenty years I have only found one intelligent man in the whole town, and he is mad. I am not ill at all, it's simply that I have got into an enchanted circle which there is no getting out of. I don't care; I am ready for anything."

"Go into the hospital, my dear fellow."

"I don't care if it were into the pit."

"Give me your word, my dear man, that you will obey Yevgeny Fyodoritch in everything."

"Certainly I will give you my word. But I repeat, my honoured friend, I have got into an enchanted circle. Now everything, even the genuine sympathy of my friends, leads to the same thing—to my ruin. I am going to my ruin, and I have the manliness to recognize it."

"My dear fellow, you will recover."

"What's the use of saying that?" said Andrey Yefimitch, with irritation. "There are few men who at the end of their lives do not experience what I am experiencing now. When you are told that you have something such as diseased kidneys or enlarged heart, and you begin being treated for it, or are told you are mad or a criminal—that is, in fact, when people suddenly turn their attention to you—you may be sure you have got into an enchanted circle from which you will not escape. You will try to escape and make things worse. You had better give in, for no human efforts can save you. So it seems to me."

Meanwhile the public was crowding at the grating. That he might not be in their way, Andrey Yefimitch got up and began to take leave. Mihail Averyanitch made him promise on his honour once more, and escorted him to the outer door.

Towards evening on the same day Hobotov, in his sheepskin and his high top-boots, suddenly made his appearance, and said to Andrey Yefimitch in a tone as though nothing had happened the day before:

"I have come on business, colleague. I have come to ask you whether you would not join me in a consultation. Eh?"

Thinking that Hobotov wanted to distract his mind with an outing, or perhaps really to enable him to earn something, Andrey Yefimitch put on his coat and hat, and went out with him into the street. He was glad of the opportunity to smooth over his fault of the previous day and to be reconciled, and in his heart thanked Hobotov, who did not even allude to yesterday's scene and was evidently sparing him. One would never have expected such delicacy from this uncultured man.

"Where is your invalid?" asked Andrey Yefimitch.

"In the hospital. . . . I have long wanted to show him to you. A very interesting case."

They went into the hospital yard, and going round the main building, turned towards the lodge where the mental cases were kept, and all this, for some reason, in silence. When they went into the lodge Nikita as usual jumped up and stood at attention.

"One of the patients here has a lung complication," Hobotov said in an undertone, going into the ward with Andrey Yefimitch. "You wait here, I'll be back directly. I am going for a stethoscope."

And he went away.

XVII

It was getting dusk. Ivan Dmitritch was lying on his bed with his face thrust into his pillow; the paralytic was sitting motionless, crying quietly and moving his lips. The fat peasant and the former sorter were asleep. It was quiet.

Andrey Yefimitch sat down on Ivan Dmitritch's bed and waited. But half an hour passed, and instead of Hobotov, Nikita came into the ward with a dressing-gown, some underlinen, and a pair of slippers in a heap on his arm.

"Please change your things, your honour," he said softly. "Here is your bed; come this way," he added, pointing to an empty bedstead which had obviously been recently brought into the ward. "It's all right; please God, you will recover."

Andrey Yefimitch understood it all. Without saying a word he crossed to the bed to which Nikita pointed and sat down; seeing that Nikita was standing waiting, he undressed entirely and he felt ashamed. Then he put on the hospital clothes; the drawers were very short, the shirt was long, and the dressing-gown smelt of smoked fish.

"Please God, you will recover," repeated Nikita, and he gathered up Andrey Yefimitch's clothes into his arms, went out, and shut the door after him.

"No matter . . ." thought Andrey Yefimitch, wrapping himself in his dressing-gown in a shame faced way and feeling that he looked like a convict in his new costume. "It's no matter. . . . It does not matter whether it's a dress-coat or a uniform or this dressing-gown. . . ."

But how about his watch? And the notebook that was in the side-pocket? And his cigarettes? Where had Nikita taken his clothes? Now perhaps to the day of his death he would not put on trousers, a waistcoat, and high boots. It was all somehow strange and even incomprehensible at first. Andrey Yefimitch was even now convinced that there was no difference between his landlady's house and Ward No. 6, that everything in this world was nonsense and vanity of vanities. And yet his hands were trembling, his feet were cold, and he was filled with dread at the thought that soon Ivan Dmitritch would get up and see that he was in a dressing-gown. He got up and walked across the room and sat down again.

Here he had been sitting already half an hour, an hour, and he was miserably sick of it: was it really possible to live here a day, a week, and even years like these people? Why, he had been sitting here, had walked about and sat down again; he could get up and look out of window and walk from corner to corner again, and then what? Sit so all the time, like a post, and think? No, that was scarcely possible.

Andrey Yefimitch lay down, but at once got up, wiped the cold sweat from his brow with his sleeve, and felt that his whole face smelt of smoked fish. He walked about again.

"It's some misunderstanding . . ." he said, turning out the palms of his hands in perplexity. "It must be cleared up. There is a misunderstanding. . . ."

Meanwhile Ivan Dmitritch woke up; he sat up and propped his cheeks on his fists. He spat. Then he glanced lazily at the doctor, and apparently for the first minute did not understand; but soon his sleepy face grew malicious and mocking.

"Aha! so they have put you in here, too, old fellow?" he said in a voice husky from sleepiness, screwing up one eye. "Very glad to see you. You sucked the blood of others, and now they will suck yours. Excellent!"

"It's a misunderstanding . . ." Andrey Yefimitch brought out, frightened by Ivan Dmitritch's words; he shrugged his shoulders and repeated:

"It's some misunderstanding. . . ."

Ivan Dmitritch spat again and lay down.

"Cursed life," he grumbled, "and what's bitter and insulting, this life will not end in compensation for our sufferings, it will not end with apotheosis as it would in an opera, but with death; peasants will come and drag one's dead body by the arms and the legs to the cellar. Ugh! Well, it does not matter. . . . We shall have our good time in the other world. . . . I shall come here as a ghost from the other world and frighten these reptiles. I'll turn their hair grey."

Moiseika returned, and, seeing the doctor, held out his hand.

"Give me one little kopeck," he said.

XVIII

Andrey Yefimitch walked away to the window and looked out into the open country. It was getting dark, and on the horizon to the right a cold crimson moon was mounting upwards. Not far from the hospital fence, not much more than two hundred yards away, stood a tall white house shut in by a stone wall. This was the prison.

"So this is real life," thought Andrey Yefimitch, and he felt frightened.

The moon and the prison, and the nails on the fence, and the faraway flames at the bone-charring factory were all terrible. Behind him there was the sound of a sigh. Andrey Yefimitch looked round and saw a man with glittering stars and orders on his breast, who was smiling and slily winking. And this, too, seemed terrible.

Andrey Yefimitch assured himself that there was nothing special about the moon or the prison, that even sane persons wear orders, and that everything in time will decay and turn to earth, but he was suddenly overcome with despair; he clutched at the grating with both hands and shook it with all his might. The strong grating did not yield.

Then that it might not be so dreadful he went to Ivan Dmitritch's bed and sat down.

"I have lost heart, my dear fellow," he muttered, trembling and wiping away the cold sweat, "I have lost heart."

"You should be philosophical," said Ivan Dmitritch ironically.

"My God, my God. . . . Yes, yes. . . . You were pleased to say once that there was no philosophy in Russia, but that all people, even the paltriest, talk philosophy. But you know the philosophizing of the paltriest does not harm anyone," said Andrey Yefimitch in a tone as if he wanted to cry and complain. "Why, then, that malignant laugh, my friend, and how can these paltry creatures help philosophizing if they are not satisfied? For an intelligent, educated man, made in God's image, proud and loving freedom, to have no alternative but to be a doctor in a filthy, stupid, wretched little town, and to spend his whole life among bottles, leeches, mustard plasters! Quackery, narrowness, vulgarity! Oh, my God!"

"You are talking nonsense. If you don't like being a doctor you should have gone in for being a statesman."

"I could not, I could not do anything. We are weak, my dear friend. . . . I used to be indifferent. I reasoned boldly and soundly, but

at the first coarse touch of life upon me I have lost heart. . . .
Prostration. . . . We are weak, we are poor creatures . . . and you, too,
my dear friend, you are intelligent, generous, you drew in good
impulses with your mother's milk, but you had hardly entered upon
life when you were exhausted and fell ill. . . . Weak, weak!"

Andrey Yefimitch was all the while at the approach of evening
tormented by another persistent sensation besides terror and the feeling of resentment. At last he realized that he was longing for a smoke
and for beer.

"I am going out, my friend," he said. "I will tell them to bring a
light; I can't put up with this. . . . I am not equal to it. . . ."

Andrey Yefimitch went to the door and opened it, but at once
Nikita jumped up and barred his way.

"Where are you going? You can't, you can't!" he said. "It's bed-
time."

"But I'm only going out for a minute to walk about the yard," said
Andrey Yefimitch.

"You can't, you can't; it's forbidden. You know that yourself."

"But what difference will it make to anyone if I do go out?" asked
Andrey Yefimitch, shrugging his shoulders. "I don't understand.
Nikita, I must go out!" he said in a trembling voice. "I must."

"Don't be disorderly, it's not right," Nikita said peremptorily.

"This is beyond everything," Ivan Dmitritch cried suddenly, and
he jumped up. "What right has he not to let you out? How dare they
keep us here? I believe it is clearly laid down in the law that no one
can be deprived of freedom without trial! It's an outrage! It's
tyranny!"

"Of course it's tyranny," said Andrey Yefimitch, encouraged by
Ivan Dmitritch's outburst. "I must go out, I want to. He has no right!
Open, I tell you."

"Do you hear, you dull-witted brute?" cried Ivan Dmitritch, and
he banged on the door with his fist. "Open the door, or I will break
it open! Torturer!"

"Open the door," cried Andrey Yefimitch, trembling all over; "I
insist!"

"Talk away!" Nikita answered through the door, "talk away. . . ."

"Anyhow, go and call Yevgeny Fyodoritch! Say that I beg him to
come for a minute!"

"His honour will come of himself to-morrow."

"They will never let us out," Ivan Dmitritch was going on meanwhile. "They will leave us to rot here! Oh, Lord, can there really be no hell in the next world, and will these wretches be forgiven? Where is justice? Open the door, you wretch! I am choking!" he cried in a hoarse voice, and flung himself upon the door. "I'll dash out my brains, murderers!"

Nikita opened the door quickly, and roughly with both his hands and his knee shoved Andrey Yefimitch back, then swung his arm and punched him in the face with his fist. It seemed to Andrey Yefimitch as though a huge salt wave enveloped him from his head downwards and dragged him to the bed; there really was a salt taste in his mouth: most likely the blood was running from his teeth. He waved his arms as though he were trying to swim out and clutched at a bedstead, and at the same moment felt Nikita hit him twice on the back.

Ivan Dmitritch gave a loud scream. He must have been beaten too.

Then all was still, the faint moonlight came through the grating, and a shadow like a net lay on the floor. It was terrible. Andrey Yefimitch lay and held his breath: he was expecting with horror to be struck again. He felt as though someone had taken a sickle, thrust it into him, and turned it round several times in his breast and bowels. He bit the pillow from pain and clenched his teeth, and all at once through the chaos in his brain there flashed the terrible unbearable thought that these people, who seemed now like black shadows in the moonlight, had to endure such pain day by day for years. How could it have happened that for more than twenty years he had not known it and had refused to know it? He knew nothing of pain, had no conception of it, so he was not to blame, but his conscience, as inexorable and as rough as Nikita, made him turn cold from the crown of his head to his heels. He leaped up, tried to cry out with all his might, and to run in haste to kill Nikita, and then Hobotov, the superintendent and the assistant, and then himself; but no sound came from his chest, and his legs would not obey him. Gasping for breath, he tore at the dressing-gown and the shirt on his breast, rent them, and fell senseless on the bed.

XIX

Next morning his head ached, there was a droning in his ears and a feeling of utter weakness all over. He was not ashamed at recalling his weakness the day before. He had been cowardly, had even been afraid of the moon, had openly expressed thoughts and feelings such as he had not expected in himself before; for instance, the thought that the paltry people who philosophized were really dissatisfied. But now nothing mattered to him.

He ate nothing, he drank nothing. He lay motionless and silent.

"It is all the same to me," he thought when they asked him questions. "I am not going to answer. . . . It's all the same to me."

After dinner Mihail Averyanitch brought him a quarter of a pound of tea and a pound of fruit pastilles. Daryushka came too and stood for a whole hour by the bed with an expression of dull grief on her face. Dr. Hobotov visited him. He brought a bottle of bromide and told Nikita to fumigate the ward with something.

Towards evening Andrey Yefimitch died of an apoplectic stroke. At first he had a violent shivering fit and a feeling of sickness; something revolting as it seemed, penetrating through his whole body, even to his finger-tips, strained from his stomach to his head and flooded his eyes and ears. There was a greenness before his eyes. Andrey Yefimitch understood that his end had come, and remembered that Ivan Dmitritch, Mihail Averyanitch, and millions of people believed in immortality. And what if it really existed? But he did not want immortality, and he thought of it only for one instant. A herd of deer, extraordinarily beautiful and graceful, of which he had been reading the day before, ran by him; then a peasant woman stretched out her hand to him with a registered letter. . . . Mihail Averyanitch said something, then it all vanished, and Andrey Yefimitch sank into oblivion for ever.

The hospital porters came, took him by his arms and his legs, and carried him away to the chapel.

There he lay on the table, with open eyes, and the moon shed its light upon him at night. In the morning Sergey Sergeyitch came, prayed piously before the crucifix, and closed his former chief's eyes.

Next day Andrey Yefimitch was buried. Mihail Averyanitch and Daryushka were the only people at the funeral.

1892

An Anonymous Story

I

Through causes which it is not the time to go into in detail, I had to enter the service of a Petersburg official called Orlov, in the capacity of a footman. He was about five and thirty, and was called Georgy* Ivanitch.

I entered this Orlov's service on account of his father, a prominent political man, whom I looked upon as a serious enemy of my cause. I reckoned that, living with the son, I should—from the conversations I should hear, and from the letters and papers I should find on the table—learn every detail of the father's plans and intentions.

As a rule at eleven o'clock in the morning the electric bell rang in my footman's quarters to let me know that my master was awake. When I went into the bedroom with his polished shoes and brushed clothes, Georgy Ivanitch would be sitting in his bed with a face that looked, not drowsy, but rather exhausted by sleep, and he would gaze off in one direction without any sign of satisfaction at having waked. I helped him to dress, and he let me do it with an air of reluctance without speaking or noticing my presence; then with his head wet with washing, smelling of fresh scent, he used to go into the dining-room to drink his coffee. He used to sit at the table, sipping his coffee and glancing through the newspapers, while the maid Polya and I stood respectfully at the door gazing at him. Two grown-up persons had to stand watching with the gravest attention a third drinking coffee and munching rusks. It was probably ludicrous and grotesque, but I saw nothing humiliating in having to stand near the door, though I was quite as well born and well educated as Orlov himself.

I was in the first stage of consumption, and was suffering from something else, possibly even more serious than consumption. I don't

* Both *g*'s hard, as in "Gorgon"; *e* like *ai* in *rain*.

know whether it was the effect of my illness or of an incipient change in my philosophy of life of which I was not conscious at the time, but I was, day by day, more possessed by a passionate, irritating longing for ordinary everyday life. I yearned for mental tranquillity, health, fresh air, good food. I was becoming a dreamer, and, like a dreamer, I did not know exactly what I wanted. Sometimes I felt inclined to go into a monastery, to sit there for days together by the window and gaze at the trees and the fields; sometimes I fancied I would buy fifteen acres of land and settle down as a country gentleman; sometimes I inwardly vowed to take up science and become a professor at some provincial university. I was a retired navy lieutenant; I dreamed of the sea, of our squadron, and of the corvette in which I had made the cruise round the world. I longed to experience again the indescribable feeling when, walking in the tropical forest or looking at the sunset in the Bay of Bengal, one is thrilled with ecstasy and at the same time homesick. I dreamed of mountains, women, music, and, with the curiosity of a child, I looked into people's faces, listened to their voices. And when I stood at the door and watched Orlov sipping his coffee, I felt not a footman, but a man interested in everything in the world, even in Orlov.

In appearance Orlov was a typical Petersburger, with narrow shoulders, a long waist, sunken temples, eyes of an indefinite colour, and scanty, dingy-coloured hair, beard and moustaches. His face had a stale, unpleasant look, though it was studiously cared for. It was particularly unpleasant when he was asleep or lost in thought. It is not worth while describing a quite ordinary appearance; besides, Petersburg is not Spain, and a man's appearance is not of much consequence even in love affairs, and is only of value to a handsome footman or coachman. I have spoken of Orlov's face and hair only because there was something in his appearance worth mentioning. When Orlov took a newspaper or book, whatever it might be, or met people, whoever they might be, an ironical smile began to come into his eyes, and his whole countenance assumed an expression of light mockery in which there was no malice. Before reading or hearing anything he always had his irony in readiness, as a savage has his shield. It was an habitual irony, like some old liquor brewed years ago, and now it came into his face probably without any participation of his will, as it were by reflex action. But of that later.

Soon after midday he took his portfolio, full of papers, and drove

to his office. He dined away from home and returned after eight
o'clock. I used to light the lamp and candles in his study, and he
would sit down in a low chair with his legs stretched out on another
chair, and, reclining in that position, would begin reading. Almost
every day he brought in new books with him or received parcels of
them from the shops, and there were heaps of books in three languages, to say nothing of Russian, which he had read and thrown
away, in the corners of my room and under my bed. He read with
extraordinary rapidity. They say: "Tell me what you read, and I'll tell
you who you are." That may be true, but it was absolutely impossible to judge of Orlov by what he read. It was a regular hotchpotch.
Philosophy, French novels, political economy, finance, new poets,
and publications of the firm *Posrednik**—and he read it all with the
same rapidity and with the same ironical expression in his eyes.

After ten o'clock he carefully dressed, often in evening dress, very
rarely in his *kammer-junker's* uniform, and went out, returning in the
morning.

Our relations were quiet and peaceful, and we never had any misunderstanding. As a rule he did not notice my presence, and when he
talked to me there was no expression of irony on his face—he evidently did not look upon me as a human being.

I only once saw him angry. One day—it was a week after I had
entered his service—he came back from some dinner at nine o'clock;
his face looked ill-humoured and exhausted. When I followed him
into his study to light the candles, he said to me:

"There's a nasty smell in the flat."

"No, the air is fresh," I answered.

"I tell you, there's a bad smell," he answered irritably.

"I open the movable panes every day."

"Don't argue, blockhead!" he shouted.

I was offended, and was on the point of answering, and goodness
knows how it would have ended if Polya, who knew her master
better than I did, had not intervened.

"There really is a disagreeable smell," she said, raising her eyebrows. "What can it be from? Stepan, open the pane in the
drawing-room, and light the fire."

I.e., Tchertkov and others, publishers of Tolstoy, who issued good literature for peasants' reading.

With much bustle and many exclamations, she went through all the rooms, rustling her skirts and squeezing the sprayer with a hissing sound. And Orlov was still out of humour; he was obviously restraining himself not to vent his ill-temper aloud. He was sitting at the table and rapidly writing a letter. After writing a few lines he snorted angrily and tore it up, then he began writing again.

"Damn them all!" he muttered. "They expect me to have an abnormal memory!"

At last the letter was written; he got up from the table and said, turning to me:

"Go to Znamensky Street and deliver this letter to Zinaida Fyodorovna Krasnovsky in person. But first ask the porter whether her husband—that is, Mr. Krasnovsky—has returned yet. If he has returned, don't deliver the letter, but come back. Wait a minute! . . . If she asks whether I have any one here, tell her that there have been two gentlemen here since eight o'clock, writing something."

I drove to Znamensky Street. The porter told me that Mr. Krasnovsky had not yet come in, and I made my way to the third storey. The door was opened by a tall, stout, drab-coloured flunkey with black whiskers, who in a sleepy, churlish, and apathetic voice, such as only flunkeys use in addressing other flunkeys, asked me what I wanted. Before I had time to answer, a lady dressed in black came hurriedly into the hall. She screwed up her eyes and looked at me.

"Is Zinaida Fyodorovna at home?" I asked.

"That is me," said the lady.

"A letter from Georgy Ivanitch."

She tore the letter open impatiently, and holding it in both hands, so that I saw her sparkling diamond rings, she began reading. I made out a pale face with soft lines, a prominent chin, and long dark lashes. From her appearance I should not have judged the lady to be more than five and twenty.

"Give him my thanks and my greetings," she said when she had finished the letter. "Is there any one with Georgy Ivanitch?" she asked softly, joyfully, and as though ashamed of her mistrust.

"Two gentlemen," I answered. "They're writing something."

"Give him my greetings and thanks," she repeated, bending her head sideways, and, reading the letter as she walked, she went noiselessly out.

I saw few women at that time, and this lady of whom I had a passing glimpse made an impression on me. As I walked home I recalled her face and the delicate fragrance about her, and fell to dreaming. By the time I got home Orlov had gone out.

II

And so my relations with my employer were quiet and peaceful, but still the unclean and degrading element which I so dreaded on becoming a footman was conspicuous and made itself felt every day. I did not get on with Polya. She was a well-fed and pampered hussy who adored Orlov because he was a gentleman and despised me because I was a footman. Probably, from the point of view of a real flunkey or cook, she was fascinating, with her red cheeks, her turned-up nose, her coquettish glances, and the plumpness, one might almost say fatness, of her person. She powdered her face, coloured her lips and eyebrows, laced herself in, and wore a bustle, and a bangle made of coins. She walked with little tripping steps; as she walked she swayed, or, as they say, wriggled her shoulders and back. The rustle of her skirts, the creaking of her stays, the jingle of her bangle and the vulgar smell of lip salve, toilet vinegar, and scent stolen from her master, aroused in me whilst I was doing the rooms with her in the morning a sensation as though I were taking part with her in some abomination.

Either because I did not steal as she did, or because I displayed no desire to become her lover, which she probably looked upon as an insult, or perhaps because she felt that I was a man of a different order, she hated me from the first day. My inexperience, my appearance—so unlike a flunkey—and my illness, seemed to her pitiful and excited her disgust. I had a bad cough at that time, and sometimes at night I prevented her from sleeping, as our rooms were only divided by a wooden partition, and every morning she said to me:

"Again you didn't let me sleep. You ought to be in hospital instead of in service."

She so genuinely believed that I was hardly a human being, but something infinitely below her, that, like the Roman matrons who were not ashamed to bathe before their slaves, she sometimes went about in my presence in nothing but her chemise.

Once when I was in a happy, dreamy mood, I asked her at dinner (we had soup and roast meat sent in from a restaurant every day):

"Polya, do you believe in God?"

"Why, of course!"

"Then," I went on, "you believe there will be a day of judgment, and that we shall have to answer to God for every evil action?"

She gave me no reply, but simply made a contemptuous grimace, and, looking that time at her cold eyes and over-fed expression, I realised that for her complete and finished personality no God, no conscience, no laws existed, and that if I had had to set fire to the house, to murder or to rob, I could not have hired a better accomplice.

In my novel surroundings I felt very uncomfortable for the first week at Orlov's before I got used to being addressed as "thou," and being constantly obliged to tell lies (saying "My master is not at home" when he was). In my flunkey's swallow-tail I felt as though I were in armour. But I grew accustomed to it in time. Like a genuine footman, I waited at table, tidied the rooms, ran and drove about on errands of all sorts. When Orlov did not want to keep an appointment with Zinaida Fyodorovna, or when he forgot that he had promised to go and see her, I drove to Znamensky Street, put a letter into her hands and told a lie. And the result of it all was quite different from what I had expected when I became a footman. Every day of this new life of mine was wasted for me and my cause, as Orlov never spoke of his father, nor did his visitors, and all I could learn of the stateman's doings was, as before, what I could glean from the newspapers or from correspondence with my comrades. The hundreds of notes and papers I used to find in the study and read had not the remotest connection with what I was looking for. Orlov was absolutely uninterested in his father's political work, and looked as though he had never heard of it, or as though his father had long been dead.

III

Every Thursday we had visitors.

I ordered a piece of roast beef from the restaurant and telephoned to Eliseyev's to send us caviare, cheese, oysters, and so on. I bought playing-cards. Polya was busy all day getting ready the tea-things and the dinner service. To tell the truth, this spurt of activity came as a pleasant change in our idle life, and Thursdays were for us the most interesting days.

Only three visitors used to come. The most important and perhaps the most interesting was the one called Pekarsky—a tall, lean man of five and forty, with a long hooked nose, with a big black beard, and a bald patch on his head. His eyes were large and prominent, and his expression was grave and thoughtful like that of a Greek philosopher. He was on the board of management of some railway, and also had some post in a bank; he was a consulting lawyer in some important Government institution, and had business relations with a large number of private persons as a trustee, chairman of committees, and so on. He was of quite a low grade in the service, and modestly spoke of himself as a lawyer, but he had a vast influence. A note or card from him was enough to make a celebrated doctor, a director of a railway, or a great dignitary see any one without waiting; and it was said that through his protection one might obtain even a post of the Fourth Class, and get any sort of unpleasant business hushed up. He was looked upon as a very intelligent man, but his was a strange, peculiar intelligence. He was able to multiply 213 by 373 in his head instantaneously, or turn English pounds into German marks without help of pencil or paper; he understood finance and railway business thoroughly, and the machinery of Russian administration had no secrets for him; he was a most skilful pleader in civil suits, and it was not easy to get the better of him at law. But that exceptional intelligence could not grasp many things which are understood even by some stupid people. For instance, he was absolutely unable to understand why people are depressed, why they weep, shoot themselves, and even kill others; why they fret about things that do not affect them personally, and why they laugh when they read Gogol or Shtchedrin. . . . Everything abstract, everything belonging to the domain of thought and feeling, was to him boring and incomprehensible, like music to one who has no ear. He looked at people simply from the business point of view, and divided them into competent and incompetent. No other classification existed for him. Honesty and rectitude were only signs of competence. Drinking, gambling, and debauchery were permissible, but must not be allowed to interfere with business. Believing in God was rather stupid, but religion ought to be safeguarded, as the common people must have some principle to restrain them, otherwise they would not work. Punishment is only necessary as a deterrent. There was no need to go away for holidays, as it was just as nice in town. And so on. He was a widower and had no children, but lived on a large scale, as though he had a family, and paid three thousand roubles a year for his flat.

The second visitor, Kukushkin, an actual civil councillor though a young man, was short, and was conspicuous for his extremely unpleasant appearance, which was due to the disproportion between his fat, puffy body and his lean little face. His lips were puckered up suavely, and his little trimmed moustaches looked as though they had been fixed on with glue. He was a man with the manners of a lizard. He did not walk, but, as it were, crept along with tiny steps, squirming and sniggering, and when he laughed he showed his teeth. He was a clerk on special commissions, and did nothing, though he received a good salary, especially in the summer, when special and lucrative jobs were found for him. He was a man of personal ambition, not only to the marrow of his bones, but more fundamentally—to the last drop of his blood; but even in his ambitions he was petty and did not rely on himself, but was building his career on the chance favour flung him by his superiors. For the sake of obtaining some foreign decoration, or for the sake of having his name mentioned in the newspapers as having been present at some special service in the company of other great personages, he was ready to submit to any kind of humiliation, to beg, to flatter, to promise. He flattered Orlov and Pekarsky from cowardice, because he thought they were powerful; he flattered Polya and me because we were in the service of a powerful man. Whenever I took off his fur coat he tittered and asked me: "Stepan, are you married?" and then unseemly vulgarities followed—by way of showing me special attention. Kukushkin flattered Orlov's weaknesses, humoured his corrupted and blasé ways; to please him he affected malicious raillery and atheism, in his company criticised persons before whom in other places he would slavishly grovel. When at supper they talked of love and women, he pretended to be a subtle and perverse voluptuary. As a rule, one may say, Petersburg rakes are fond of talking of their abnormal tastes. Some young actual civil councillor is perfectly satisfied with the embraces of his cook or of some unhappy street-walker on the Nevsky Prospect, but to listen to him you would think he was contaminated by all the vices of East and West combined, that he was an honourary member of a dozen iniquitous secret societies and was already marked by the police. Kukushkin lied about himself in an unconscionable way, and they did not exactly disbelieve him, but paid little heed to his incredible stories.

The third guest was Gruzin, the sun of a worthy and learned general; a man of Orlov's age, with long hair, short-sighted eyes, and gold spectacles. I remember his long white fingers, that looked like a pianist's; and, indeed, there was something of a musician, of a virtuoso, about his whole figure. The first violins in orchestras look just like that. He used to cough, suffered from migraine, and seemed altogether invalidish and delicate. Probably at home he was dressed and undressed like a baby. He had finished at the College of Jurisprudence, and had at first served in the Department of Justice, then he was transferred to the Senate; he left that, and through patronage had received a post in the Department of Crown Estates, and had soon afterwards given that up. In my time he was serving in Orlov's department; he was his head-clerk, but he said that he should soon exchange into the Department of Justice again. He took his duties and his shifting about from one post to another with exceptional levity, and when people talked before him seriously of grades in the service, decorations, salaries, he smiled good-naturedly and repeated Prutkov's aphorism: "It's only in the Government of service you learn the truth." He had a little wife with a wrinkled face, who was very jealous of him, and five weedy-looking children. He was unfaithful to his wife, he was only fond of his children when he saw them, and on the whole was rather indifferent to his family, and made fun of them. He and his family existed on credit, borrowing wherever they could at every opportunity, even from his superiors in the office and porters in people's houses. His was a flabby nature; he was so lazy that he did not care what became of himself, and drifted along heedless where or why he was going. He went where he was taken. If he was taken to some low haunt, he went; if wine was set before him, he drank—if it were not put before him, he abstained; if wives were abused in his presence, he abused his wife, declaring she had ruined his life—when wives were praised, he praised his and said quite sincerely: "I am very fond of her, poor thing!" He had no fur coat and always wore a rug which smelt of the nursery. When at supper he rolled balls of bread and drank a great deal of red wine, absorbed in thought, strange to say, I used to feel almost certain that there was something in him of which perhaps he had a vague sense, though in the bustle and vulgarity of his daily life he had not time to understand and appreciate it. He played a little on the piano. Sometimes he would sit down at the piano, play a chord or two, and begin singing softly:

"What does the coming day bring to me?"

But at once, as though afraid, he would get up and walk from the piano.

The visitors usually arrived about ten o'clock. They played cards in Orlov's study, and Polya and I handed them tea. It was only on these occasions that I could gauge the full sweetness of a flunkey's life. Standing for four or five hours at the door, watching that no one's glass should be empty, changing the ash-trays, running to the table to pick up the chalk or a card when it was dropped, and, above all, standing, waiting, being attentive without venturing to speak, to cough, to smile—is harder, I assure you, is harder than the hardest of field labour. I have stood on watch at sea for four hours at a stretch on stormy winter nights, and to my thinking it is an infinitely easier duty.

They used to play cards till two, sometimes till three o'clock at night, and then, stretching, they would go into the dining-room to supper, or, as Orlov said, for a snack of something. At supper there was conversation. It usually began by Orlov's speaking with laughing eyes of some acquaintance, of some book he had lately been reading, of a new appointment or Government scheme. Kukushkin, always ingratiating, would fall into his tone, and what followed was to me, in my mood at that time, a revolting exhibition. The irony of Orlov and his friends knew no bounds, and spared no one and nothing. If they spoke of religion, it was with irony; they spoke of philosophy, of the significance and object of life—irony again, if any one began about the peasantry, it was with irony.

There is in Petersburg a species of men whose speciality it is to jeer at every aspect of life; they cannot even pass by a starving man or a suicide without saying something vulgar. But Orlov and his friends did not jeer or make jokes, they talked ironically. They used to say that there was no God, and personality was completely lost at death; the immortals only existed in the French Academy. Real good did not and could not possibly exist, as its existence was conditional upon human perfection, which was a logical absurdity. Russia was a country as poor and dull as Persia. The intellectual class was hopeless; in Pekarsky's opinion the overwhelming majority in it were incompetent persons, good for nothing. The people were drunken, lazy, thievish, and degenerate. We had no science, our literature was uncouth, our commerce rested on swindling—"No selling without cheating." And everything was in that style, and everything was a subject for laughter.

Towards the end of supper the wine made them more good-humoured, and they passed to more lively conversation. They laughed over Gruzin's family life, over Kukushkin's conquests, or at Pekarsky, who had, they said, in his account book one page headed *Charity* and another *Physiological Necessities*. They said that no wife was faithful; that there was no wife from whom one could not, with practice, obtain caresses without leaving her drawing-room while her husband was sitting in his study close by; that girls in their teens were perverted and knew everything. Orlov had preserved a letter of a schoolgirl of fourteen: on her way home from school she had "hooked an officer on the Nevsky," who had, it appears, taken her home with him, and had only let her go late in the evening; and she hastened to write about this to her school friend to share her joy with her. They maintained that there was not and never had been such a thing as moral purity, and that evidently it was unnecessary; mankind had so far done very well without it. The harm done by so-called vice was undoubtedly exaggerated. Vices which are punished by our legal code had not prevented Diogenes from being a philosopher and a teacher. Caesar and Cicero were profligates and at the same time great men. Cato in his old age married a young girl, and yet he was regarded as a great ascetic and a pillar of morality.

At three or four o'clock the party broke up or they went off together out of town, or to Officers' Street, to the house of a certain Varvara Ossipovna, while I retired to my quarters, and was kept awake a long while by coughing and headache.

IV

Three weeks after I entered Orlov's service—it was Sunday morning, I remember—somebody rang the bell. It was not yet eleven, and Orlov was still asleep. I went to open the door. You can imagine my astonishment when I found a lady in a veil standing at the door on the landing.

"Is Georgy Ivanitch up?" she asked.

From her voice I recognised Zinaida Fyodorovna, to whom I had taken letters in Znamensky Street. I don't remember whether I had time or self-possession to answer her—I was taken aback at seeing her. And, indeed, she did not need my answer. In a flash she had darted by me, and, filling the hall with the fragrance of her perfume, which I remember to this day, she went on, and her footsteps died away. For at least half an hour afterwards I heard nothing. But again some one rang. This time it was a smartly dressed girl, who looked like a maid in a wealthy family, accompanied by our house porter. Both were out of breath, carrying two trunks and a dress-basket.

"These are for Zinaida Fyodorovna," said the girl.

And she went down without saying another word. All this was mysterious, and made Polya, who had a deep admiration for the pranks of her betters, smile slyly to herself; she looked as though she would like to say, "So that's what we're up to," and she walked about the whole time on tiptoe. At last we heard footsteps; Zinaida Fyodorovna came quickly into the hall, and seeing me at the door of my room, said:

"Stepan, take Georgy Ivanitch his things."

When I went in to Orlov with his clothes and his boots, he was sitting on the bed with his feet on the bearskin rug. There was an air of embarrassment about his whole figure. He did not notice me, and my menial opinion did not interest him; he was evidently perturbed and embarrassed before himself, before his inner eye. He dressed, washed, and used his combs and brushes silently and deliberately, as though allowing himself time to think over his position and to reflect, and even from his back one could see he was troubled and dissatisfied with himself.

They drank coffee together. Zinaida Fyodorovna poured out coffee for herself and for Orlov, then she put her elbows on the table and laughed.

"I still can't believe it," she said. "When one has been a long while on one's travels and reaches a hotel at last, it's difficult to believe that one hasn't to go on. It is pleasant to breathe freely."

With the expression of a child who very much wants to be mischievous, she sighed with relief and laughed again.

"You will excuse me," said Orlov, nodding towards the coffee. "Reading at breakfast is a habit I can't get over. But I can do two things at once—read and listen."

"Read away. . . . You shall keep your habits and your freedom. But why do you look so solemn? Are you always like that in the morning, or is it only to-day? Aren't you glad?"

"Yes, I am. But I must own I am a little overwhelmed."

"Why? You had plenty of time to prepare yourself for my descent upon you. I've been threatening to come every day."

"Yes, but I didn't expect you to carry out your threat to-day."

"I didn't expect it myself, but that's all the better. It's all the better, my dear. It's best to have an aching tooth out and have done with it."

"Yes, of course."

"Oh, my dear," she said, closing her eyes, "all is well that ends well; but before this happy ending, what suffering there has been! My laughing means nothing; I am glad, I am happy, but I feel more like crying than laughing. Yesterday I had to fight a regular battle," she went on in French. "God alone knows how wretched I was. But I laugh because I can't believe in it. I keep fancying that my sitting here drinking coffee with you is not real, but a dream."

Then, still speaking French, she described how she had broken with her husband the day before, and her eyes were alternately full of tears and of laughter while she gazed with rapture at Orlov. She told him her husband had long suspected her, but had avoided explanations; they had frequent quarrels, and usually at the most heated moment he would suddenly subside into silence and depart to his study for fear that in his exasperation he might give utterance to his suspicions or she might herself begin to speak openly. And she had felt guilty, worthless, incapable of taking a bold and serious step, and that had made her hate herself and her husband more every day, and she had suffered the torments of hell. But the day before, when during a quarrel he had cried out in a tearful voice, "My God, when will it end?" and had walked off to his study, she had run after him like a cat after a mouse, and, preventing him from shutting the door, she had cried that she hated him with her whole soul. Then he let her come into the study and she had told him everything, had confessed that she loved some one else, that that some one else was her real, most lawful husband, and that she thought it her true duty to go away to him that very day, whatever might happen, if she were to be shot for it.

"There's a very romantic streak in you," Orlov interrupted, keeping his eyes fixed on the newspaper.

She laughed and went on talking without touching her coffee. Her cheeks glowed and she was a little embarrassed by it, and she looked in confusion at Polya and me. From what she went on to say I learnt that her husband had answered her with threats, reproaches, and finally tears, and that it would have been more accurate to say that she, and not he, had been the attacking party.

"Yes, my dear, so long as I was worked up, everything went all right," she told Orlov; "but as night came on, my spirits sank. You don't believe in God, *George*, but I do believe a little, and I fear retribution. God requires of us patience, magnanimity, self-sacrifice, and here I am refusing to be patient and want to remodel my life to suit myself. Is that right? What if from the point of view of God it's wrong? At two o'clock in the night my husband came to me and said: 'You dare not go away. I'll fetch you back through the police and make a scandal.' And soon afterwards I saw him like a shadow at my door. 'Have mercy on me! Your elopement may injure me in the service.' Those words had a coarse effect upon me and made me feel stiff all over. I felt as though the retribution were beginning already; I began crying and trembling with terror. I felt as though the ceiling would fall upon me, that I should be dragged off to the police-station at once, that you would grow cold to me—all sorts of things, in fact! I thought I would go into a nunnery or become a nurse, and give up all thought of happiness, but then I remembered that you loved me, and that I had no right to dispose of myself without your knowledge; and everything in my mind was in a tangle—I was in despair and did not know what to do or think. But the sun rose and I grew happier. As soon as it was morning I dashed off to you. Ah, what I've been through, dear one! I haven't slept for two nights!"

She was tired out and excited. She was sleepy, and at the same time she wanted to talk endlessly, to laugh and to cry, and to go to a restaurant to lunch that she might feel her freedom.

"You have a cosy flat, but I am afraid it may be small for the two of us," she said, walking rapidly through all the rooms when they had finished breakfast. "What room will you give me? I like this one because it is next to your study."

At one o'clock she changed her dress in the room next to the study, which from that time she called hers, and she went off with

Orlov to lunch. They dined, too, at a restaurant, and spent the long interval between lunch and dinner in shopping. Till late at night I was opening the door to messengers and errand-boys from the shops. They bought, among other things, a splendid pier-glass, a dressing-table, a bedstead, and a gorgeous tea service which we did not need. They bought a regular collection of copper saucepans, which we set in a row on the shelf in our cold, empty kitchen. As we were unpacking the tea service Polya's eyes gleamed, and she looked at me two or three times with hatred and fear that I, not she, would be the first to steal one of these charming cups. A lady's writing-table, very expensive and inconvenient, came too. It was evident that Zinaida Fyodorovna contemplated settling with us for good, and meant to make the flat her home.

She came back with Orlov between nine and ten. Full of proud consciousness that she had done something bold and out of the common, passionately in love, and, as she imagined, passionately loved, exhausted, looking forward to a sweet sound sleep, Zinaida Fyodorovna was revelling in her new life. She squeezed her hands together in the excess of her joy, declared that everything was delightful, and swore that she would love Orlov for ever; and these vows, and the naïve, almost childish confidence that she too was deeply loved and would be loved for ever, made her at least five years younger. She talked charming nonsense and laughed at herself.

"There's no other blessing greater than freedom!" she said, forcing herself to say something serious and edifying. "How absurd it is when you think of it! We attach no value to our own opinion even when it is wise, but tremble before the opinion of all sorts of stupid people. Up to the last minute I was afraid of what other people would say, but as soon as I followed my own instinct and made up my mind to go my own way, my eyes were opened, I overcame my silly fears, and now I am happy and wish every one could be as happy!"

But her thoughts immediately took another turn, and she began talking of another flat, of wallpapers, horses, a trip to Switzerland and Italy. Orlov was tired by the restaurants and the shops, and was still suffering from the same uneasiness that I had noticed in the morning. He smiled, but more from politeness than pleasure, and when she spoke of anything seriously, he agreed ironically: "Oh, yes."

"Stepan, make haste and find us a good cook," she said to me.

"There's no need to be in a hurry over the kitchen arrangements," said Orlov, looking at me coldly. "We must first move into another flat."

We had never had cooking done at home nor kept horses, because, as he said, "he did not like disorder about him," and only put up with having Polya and me in his flat from necessity. The so-called domestic hearth with its everyday joys and its petty cares offended his taste as vulgarity; to be with child, or to have children and talk about them, was bad form, like a petty bourgeois. And I began to feel very curious to see how these two creatures would get on together in one flat—she, domestic and home-loving with her copper saucepans and her dreams of a good cook and horses; and he, fond of saying to his friends that a decent and orderly man's flat ought, like a warship, to have nothing in it superfluous—no women, no children, no rags, no kitchen utensils.

V

Then I will tell you what happened the following Thursday. That day Zinaida Fyodorovna dined at Content's or Donon's. Orlov returned home alone, and Zinaida Fyodorovna, as I learnt afterwards, went to the Petersburg Side to spend with her old governess the time visitors were with us. Orlov did not care to show her to his friends. I realised that at breakfast, when he began assuring her that for the sake of her peace of mind it was essential to give up his Thursday evenings.

As usual the visitors arrived at almost the same time.

"Is your mistress at home, too?" Kukushkin asked me in a whisper.

"No, sir," I answered.

He went in with a sly, oily look in his eyes, smiling mysteriously, rubbing his hands, which were cold from the frost.

"I have the honour to congratulate you," he said to Orlov, shaking all over with ingratiating, obsequious laughter. "May you increase and multiply like the cedars of Lebanon."

The visitors went into the bedroom, and were extremely jocose on the subject of a pair of feminine slippers, the rug that had been put down between the two beds, and a grey dressing-jacket that hung at the foot of the bedstead. They were amused that the obstinate man who despised all the common place details of love had been caught in feminine snares in such a simple and ordinary way.

"He who pointed the finger of scorn is bowing the knee in homage," Kukushkin repeated several times. He had, I may say in parenthesis, an unpleasant habit of adorning his conversation with texts in Church Slavonic. "Sh-sh!" he said as they went from the bedroom into the room next to the study. "Sh-sh! Here Gretchen is dreaming of her Faust."

He went off into a peal of laughter as though he had said something very amusing. I watched Gruzin, expecting that his musical soul would not endure this laughter, but I was mistaken. His thin, good-natured face beamed with pleasure. When they sat down to play cards, he, lisping and choking with laughter, said that all that "dear George" wanted to complete his domestic felicity was a cherry-wood pipe and a guitar. Pekarsky laughed sedately, but from his serious expression one could see that Orlov's new love affair was distasteful to him. He did not understand what had happened exactly.

"But how about the husband?" he asked in perplexity, after they had played three rubbers.

"I don't know," answered Orlov.

Pekarsky combed his big beard with his fingers and sank into thought, and he did not speak again till supper-time. When they were seated at supper, he began deliberately, drawling every word:

"Altogether, excuse my saying so, I don't understand either of you. You might love each other and break the seventh commandment to your heart's content—that I understand. Yes, that's comprehensible. But why make the husband a party to your secrets? Was there any need for that?"

"But does it make any difference?"

"Hm! . . ." Pekarsky mused. "Well, then, let me tell you this, my friend," he went on, evidently thinking hard: "if I ever marry again and you take it into your head to seduce my wife, please do it so that I don't notice it. It's much more honest to deceive a man than to break up his family life and injure his reputation. I understand. You both imagine that in living together openly you are doing something exceptionally honourable and advanced, but I can't agree with that . . . what shall I call it? . . . romantic attitude?"

Orlov made no reply. He was out of humour and disinclined to talk. Pekarsky, still perplexed, drummed on the table with his fingers, thought a little, and said:

"I don't understand you, all the same. You are not a student and she is not a dressmaker. You are both of you people with means. I should have thought you might have arranged a separate flat for her."

"No, I couldn't. Read Turgenev."

"Why should I read him? I have read him already."

"Turgenev teaches us in his novels that every exalted, noble-minded girl should follow the man she loves to the ends of the earth, and should serve his idea," said Orlov, screwing up his eyes ironically. "The ends of the earth are poetic license; the earth and all its ends can be reduced to the flat of the man she loves. . . . And so not to live in the same flat with the woman who loves you is to deny her her exalted vocation and to refuse to share her ideals. Yes, my dear fellow, Turgenev wrote, and I have to suffer for it."

"What Turgenev has got to do with it I don't understand," said Gruzin softly, and he shrugged his shoulders. "Do you remember, *George*, how in 'Three Meetings' he is walking late in the evening somewhere in Italy, and suddenly hears, *'Vieni pensando a me segretamente,'*" Gruzin hummed. "It's fine."

"But she hasn't come to settle with you by force," said Pekarsky. "It was your own wish."

"What next! Far from wishing it, I never imagined that this would ever happen. When she said she was coming to live with me, I thought it was a charming joke on her part."

Everybody laughed.

"I couldn't have wished for such a thing," said Orlov in the tone of a man compelled to justify himself. "I am not a Turgenev hero, and if I ever wanted to free Bulgaria I shouldn't need a lady's company. I look upon love primarily as a necessity of my physical nature, degrading and antagonistic to my spirit; it must either be satisfied with discretion or renounced altogether, otherwise it will bring into one's life elements as unclean as itself. For it to be an enjoyment and not a torment, I will try to make it beautiful and to surround it with a mass of illusions. I should never go and see a woman unless I were sure beforehand that she would be beautiful and fascinating; and I should never go unless I were in the mood. And it is only in that way that we succeed in deceiving one another, and fancying that we are in love and happy. But can I wish for copper saucepans and untidy hair, or like to be seen myself when I am unwashed or out of humour? Zinaida Fyodorovna in the simplicity of her heart wants me to love what I have been shunning all my life. She wants my flat to smell of cooking and washing up; she wants all the fuss of moving into another flat, of driving about with her own horses; she wants to count over my linen and to look after my health; she wants to meddle in my personal life at every instant, and to watch over every step; and at the same time she assures me genuinely that my habits and my freedom will be untouched. She is persuaded that, like a young couple, we shall very soon go for a honeymoon—that is, she wants to be with me all the time in trains and hotels, while I like to read on the journey and cannot endure talking in trains."

"You should give her a talking to," said Pekarsky.

"What! Do you suppose she would understand me? Why, we think so differently. In her opinion, to leave one's papa and mamma or one's husband for the sake of the man one loves is the height of civic virtue, while I look upon it as childish. To fall in love and run away with a man to her means beginning a new life, while to my mind it means nothing at all. Love and man constitute the chief interest of her life, and possibly it is the philosophy of the unconscious at work in her. Try and make her believe that love is only a simple physical need, like the need of food or clothes; that it doesn't mean the end of the world if wives and husbands are unsatisfactory; that a man may be a profligate and a libertine, and yet a man of honour and a genius; and that, on the other hand, one may abstain from the pleasures of love and at the same time be a stupid, vicious animal! The civilised man of to-day, even among the lower classes—for instance, the French workman—spends ten *sous* on dinner, five *sous* on his wine, and five or ten *sous* on woman, and devotes his brain and nerves entirely to his work. But Zinaida Fyodorovna assigns to love not so many *sous*, but her whole soul. I might give her a talking to, but she would raise a wail in answer, and declare in all sincerity that I had ruined her, that she had nothing left to live for."

"Don't say anything to her," said Pekarsky, "but simply take a separate flat for her, that's all."

"That's easy to say. . . ."

There was a brief silence.

"But she is charming," said Kukushkin. "She is exquisite. Such women imagine that they will be in love for ever, and abandon themselves with tragic intensity."

"But one must keep a head on one's shoulders," said Orlov; "one must be reasonable. All experience gained from everyday life and handed down in innumerable novels and plays, uniformly confirms the fact that adultery and cohabitation of any sort between decent people never lasts longer than two or at most three years, however great the love may have been at the beginning. That she ought to know. And so all this business of moving, of saucepans, hopes of eternal love and harmony, are nothing but a desire to delude herself and me. She is charming and exquisite—who denies it? But she has turned my life upside down; what I have regarded as trivial and nonsensical till now she has forced me to raise to the level of a serious problem; I serve an idol whom I have never looked upon as God. She is charming—exquisite, but for some reason now when I am going home, I feel uneasy, as though I expected to meet with something inconvenient at home, such as workmen pulling the stove to pieces and blocking up the place with heaps of bricks. In fact, I am no longer giving up to love a *sous*, but part of my peace of mind and my nerves. And that's bad."

"And she doesn't hear this villain!" sighed Kukushkin. "My dear sir," he said theatrically, "I will relieve you from the burdensome obligation to love that adorable creature! I will wrest Zinaida Fyodorovna from you!"

"You may . . ." said Orlov carelessly.

For half a minute Kukushkin laughed a shrill little laugh, shaking all over, then he said:

"Look out; I am in earnest! Don't you play the Othello afterwards!"

They all began talking of Kukushkin's indefatigable energy in love affairs, how irresistible he was to women, and what a danger he was to husbands; and how the devil would roast him in the other world for his immorality in this. He screwed up his eyes and remained silent, and when the names of ladies of their acquaintance were mentioned, he held up his little finger—as though to say they mustn't give away other people's secrets.

Orlov suddenly looked at his watch.

His friends understood, and began to take their leave. I remember that Gruzin, who was a little drunk, was wearisomely long in getting off. He put on his coat, which was cut like children's coats in poor families, pulled up the collar, and began telling some long-winded story; then, seeing he was not listened to, he flung the rug that smelt of the nursery over one shoulder, and with a guilty and imploring face begged me to find his hat.

"*George,* my angel," he said tenderly. "Do as I ask you, dear boy; come out of town with us!"

"You can go, but I can't. I am in the position of a married man now."

"She is a dear, she won't be angry. My dear chief, come along! It's glorious weather; there's snow and frost. . . . Upon my word, you want shaking up a bit; you are out of humour. I don't know what the devil is the matter with you. . . ."

Orlov stretched, yawned, and looked at Pekarsky.

"Are you going?" he said, hesitating.

"I don't know. Perhaps."

"Shall I get drunk? All right, I'll come," said Orlov after some hesitation. "Wait a minute; I'll get some money."

He went into the study, and Gruzin slouched in, too, dragging his rug after him. A minute later both came back into the hall. Gruzin, a little drunk and very pleased, was crumpling a ten-rouble note in his hands.

"We'll settle up to-morrow," he said. "And she is kind, she won't be cross. . . . She is my Lisotchka's godmother; I am fond of her, poor thing! Ah, my dear fellow!" he laughed joyfully, and pressing his forehead on Pekarsky's back. "Ah, Pekarsky, my dear soul! Advocatissimus—as dry as a biscuit, but you bet he is fond of women. . . ."

"Fat ones," said Orlov, putting on his fur coat. "But let us get off, or we shall be meeting her on the doorstep."

" '*Vieni pensando a me segretamente,* ' " hummed Gruzin.

At last they drove off: Orlov did not sleep at home, and returned next day at dinner-time.

VI

Zinaida Fyodorovna had lost her gold watch, a present from her father. This loss surprised and alarmed her. She spent half a day going through the rooms, looking helplessly on all the tables and on all the windows. But the watch had disappeared completely.

Only three days afterwards Zinaida Fyodorovna, on coming in, left her purse in the hall. Luckily for me, on that occasion it was not I but Polya who helped her off with her coat. When the purse was missed, it could not be found in the hall.

"Strange," said Zinaida Fyodorovna in bewilderment. "I distinctly remember taking it out of my pocket to pay the cabman . . . and then I put it here near the looking-glass. It's very odd!"

I had not stolen it, but I felt as though I had stolen it and had been caught in the theft. Tears actually came into my eyes. When they were seated at dinner, Zinaida Fyodorovna said to Orlov in French:

"There seem to be spirits in the flat. I lost my purse in the hall to-day, and now, lo and behold, it is on my table. But it's not quite a disinterested trick of the spirits. They took out a gold coin and twenty roubles in notes."

"You are always losing something; first it's your watch and then it's your money . . ." said Orlov. "Why is it nothing of the sort ever happens to me?"

A minute later Zinaida Fyodorovna had forgotten the trick played by the spirits, and was telling with a laugh how the week before she had ordered some notepaper and had forgotten to give her new address, and the shop had sent the paper to her old home at her husband's, who had to pay twelve roubles for it. And suddenly she turned her eyes on Polya and looked at her intently. She blushed as she did so, and was so confused that she began talking of something else.

When I took in the coffee to the study, Orlov was standing with his back to the fire and she was sitting in an arm-chair facing him.

"I am not in a bad temper at all," she was saying in French. "But I have been putting things together, and now I see it clearly. I can give you the day and the hour when she stole my watch. And the purse? There can be no doubt about it. Oh!" she laughed as she took the coffee from me. "Now I understand why I am always losing my handkerchiefs and gloves. Whatever you say, I shall dismiss the magpie to-morrow and send Stepan for my Sofya. She is not a thief and has not got such a . . . repulsive appearance."

"You are out of humour. To-morrow you will feel differently, and will realise that you can't discharge people simply because you suspect them."

"It's not suspicion; it's certainty," said Zinaida Fyodorovna. "So long as I suspected that unhappy-faced, poor-looking valet of yours, I said nothing. It's too bad of you not to believe me, *George*."

"If we think differently about anything, it doesn't follow that I don't believe you. You may be right," said Orlov, turning round and flinging his cigarette-end into the fire, "but there is no need to be excited about it, anyway. In fact, I must say, I never expected my humble establishment would cause you so much serious worry and agitation. You've lost a gold coin: never mind—you may have a hundred of mine; but to change my habits, to pick up a new housemaid, to wait till she is used to the place—all that's a tedious, tiring business and does not suit me. Our present maid certainly is fat, and has, perhaps, a weakness for gloves and handkerchiefs, but she is perfectly well behaved, well trained, and does not shriek when Kukushkin pinches her."

"You mean that you can't part with her? . . . Why don't you say so?"

"Are you jealous?"

"Yes, I am," said Zinaida Fyodorovna, decidedly.

"Thank you."

"Yes, I am jealous," she repeated, and tears glistened in her eyes. "No, it's something worse . . . which I find it difficult to find a name for." She pressed her hands on her temples, and went on impulsively. "You men are so disgusting! It's horrible!"

"I see nothing horrible about it."

"I've not seen it; I don't know; but they say that you men begin with housemaids as boys, and get so used to it that you feel no repugnance. I don't know, I don't know, but I have actually read . . . *George*, of course you are right," she said, going up to Orlov and changing to a caressing and imploring tone. "I really am out of humour to-day. But, you must understand, I can't help it. She disgusts me and I am afraid of her. It makes me miserable to see her."

"Surely you can rise above such paltriness?" said Orlov, shrugging his shoulders in perplexity, and walking away from the fire. "Nothing could be simpler: take no notice of her, and then she won't disgust you, and you won't need to make a regular tragedy out of a trifle."

I went out of the study, and I don't know what answer Orlov received. Whatever it was, Polya remained. After that Zinaida Fyodorovna never applied to her for anything, and evidently tried to dispense with her services. When Polya handed her anything or even passed by her, jingling her bangle and rustling her skirts, she shuddered.

I believe that if Gruzin or Pekarsky had asked Orlov to dismiss Polya he would have done so without the slightest hesitation, without troubling about any explanations. He was easily persuaded, like all indifferent people. But in his relations with Zinaida Fyodorovna he displayed for some reason, even in trifles, an obstinacy which sometimes was almost irrational. I knew beforehand that if Zinaida Fyodorovna liked anything, it would be certain not to please Orlov. When on coming in from shopping she made haste to show him with pride some new purchase, he would glance at it and say coldly that the more unnecessary objects they had in the flat, the less airy it would be. It sometimes happened that after putting on his dress clothes to go out somewhere, and after saying good-bye to Zinaida Fyodorovna, he would suddenly change his mind and remain at home from sheer perversity. I used to think that he remained at home then simply in order to feel injured.

"Why are you staying?" said Zinaida Fyodorovna, with a show of vexation, though at the same time she was radiant with delight. "Why do you? You are not accustomed to spending your evenings at home, and I don't want you to alter your habits on my account. Do go out as usual, if you don't want me to feel guilty."

"No one is blaming you," said Orlov.

With the air of a victim he stretched himself in his easy-chair in the study, and shading his eyes with his hand, took up a book. But soon the book dropped from his hand, he turned heavily in his chair, and again screened his eyes as though from the sun. Now he felt annoyed that he had not gone out.

"May I come in?" Zinaida Fyodorovna would say, coming irresolutely into the study. "Are you reading? I felt dull by myself, and have come just for a minute . . . to have a peep at you."

I remember one evening she went in like that, irresolutely and inappropriately, and sank on the rug at Orlov's feet, and from her soft, timid movements one could see that she did not understand his mood and was afraid.

"You are always reading . . ." she said cajolingly, evidently wishing to flatter him. "Do you know, *George*, what is one of the secrets of your success? You are very clever and well-read. What book have you there?"

Orlov answered. A silence followed for some minutes which seemed to me very long. I was standing in the drawing-room, from which I could watch them, and was afraid of coughing.

"There is something I wanted to tell you," said Zinaida Fyodorovna, and she laughed; "shall I? Very likely you'll laugh and say that I flatter myself. You know I want, I want horribly to believe that you are staying at home to-night for my sake . . . that we might spend the evening together. Yes? May I think so?"

"Do," he said, screening his eyes. "The really happy man is he who thinks not only of what is, but of what is not."

"That was a long sentence which I did not quite understand. You mean happy people live in their imagination. Yes, that's true. I love to sit in your study in the evening and let my thoughts carry me far, far away. . . . It's pleasant sometimes to dream. Let us dream aloud, *George*."

"I've never been at a girl's boarding-school; I never learnt the art."

"You are out of humour?" said Zinaida Fyodorovna, taking Orlov's hand. "Tell me why. When you are like that, I'm afraid. I don't know whether your head aches or whether you are angry with me. . . ."

Again there was a silence lasting several long minutes.

"Why have you changed?" she said softly. "Why are you never so tender or so gay as you used to be at Znamensky Street? I've been with you almost a month, but it seems to me as though we had not yet begun to live, and have not yet talked of anything as we ought to. You always answer me with jokes or else with a long cold lecture like a teacher. And there is something cold in your jokes. . . . Why have you given up talking to me seriously?"

"I always talk seriously."

"Well, then, let us talk. For God's sake, *George*. . . . Shall we?"

"Certainly, but about what?"

"Let us talk of our life, of our future," said Zinaida Fyodorovna dreamily. "I keep making plans for our life, plans and plans—and I enjoy doing it so! *George*, I'll begin with the question, when are you going to give up your post?"

"What for?" asked Orlov, taking his hand from his forehead.

"With your views you cannot remain in the service. You are out of place there."

"My views?" Orlov repeated. "My views? In conviction and temperament I am an ordinary official, one of Shtchedrin's heroes. You take me for something different, I venture to assure you."

"Joking again, *George*!"

"Not in the least. The service does not satisfy me, perhaps; but, anyway, it is better for me than anything else. I am used to it, and in it I meet men of my own sort; I am in my place there and find it tolerable."

"You hate the service and it revolts you."

"Indeed? If I resign my post, take to dreaming aloud and letting myself be carried away into another world, do you suppose that that world would be less hateful to me than the service?"

"You are ready to libel yourself in order to contradict me." Zinaida Fyodorovna was offended and got up. "I am sorry I began this talk."

"Why are you angry? I am not angry with you for not being an official. Every one lives as he likes best."

"Why, do you live as you like best? Are you free? To spend your life writing documents that are opposed to your own ideas," Zinaida Fyodorovna went on, clasping her hands in despair: "to submit to authority, congratulate your superiors at the New Year, and then cards and nothing but cards: worst of all, to be working for a system which must be distasteful to you—no, *George*, no! You should not make such horrid jokes. It's dreadful. You are a man of ideas, and you ought to be working for your ideas and nothing else."

"You really take me for quite a different person from what I am," sighed Orlov.

"Say simply that you don't want to talk to me. You dislike me, that's all," said Zinaida Fyodorovna through her tears.

"Look here, my dear," said Orlov admonishingly, sitting up in his chair. "You were pleased to observe yourself that I am a clever, well-read man, and to teach one who knows does nothing but harm. I know very well all the ideas, great and small, which you mean when you call me a man of ideas. So if I prefer the service and cards to those ideas, you may be sure I have good grounds for it. That's one thing. Secondly, you have, so far as I know, never been in the service, and can only have drawn your ideas of Government service from anecdotes and indifferent novels. So it would not be amiss for us to make a compact, once for all, not to talk of things we know already or of things about which we are not competent to speak."

"Why do you speak to me like that?" said Zinaida Fyodorovna, stepping back as though in horror. "What for? *George,* for God's sake, think what you are saying!"

Her voice quivered and broke; she was evidently trying to restrain her tears, but she suddenly broke into sobs.

"*George,* my darling, I am perishing!" she said in French, dropping down before Orlov, and laying her head on his knees. "I am miserable, I am exhausted. I can't bear it, I can't bear it. . . . In my childhood my hateful, depraved stepmother, then my husband, now you . . . you! . . . You meet my mad love with coldness and irony. . . . And that horrible, insolent servant," she went on, sobbing. "Yes, yes, I see: I am not your wife nor your friend, but a woman you don't respect because she has become your mistress. . . . I shall kill myself!"

I had not expected that her words and her tears would make such an impression on Orlov. He flushed, moved uneasily in his chair, and instead of irony, his face wore a look of stupid, school-boyish dismay.

"My darling, you misunderstood me," he muttered helplessly, touching her hair and her shoulders. "Forgive me, I entreat you. I was unjust . . . and I hate myself."

"I insult you with my whining and complaints. . . . You are a true, generous . . . rare man—I am conscious of it every minute; but I've been horribly depressed for the last few days. . . ."

Zinaida Fyodorovna impulsively embraced Orlov and kissed him on the cheek.

"Only please don't cry," he said.

"No, no. . . . I've had my cry, and now I am better."

"As for the servant, she shall be gone to-morrow," he said, still moving uneasily in his chair.

"No, she must stay, *George!* Do you hear? I am not afraid of her now. . . . One must rise above trifles and not imagine silly things. You are right! You are a wonderful, rare person!"

She soon left off crying. With tears glistening on her eyelashes, sitting on Orlov's knee, she told him in a low voice something touching, something like a reminiscence of childhood and youth. She stroked his face, kissed him, and carefully examined his hands with the rings on them and the charms on his watch-chain. She was carried away by what she was saying, and by being near the man she loved, and probably because her tears had cleared and refreshed her soul, there was a note of wonderful candour and sincerity in her voice. And Orlov played with her chestnut hair and kissed her hands, noiselessly pressing them to his lips.

Then they had tea in the study, and Zinaida Fyodorovna read aloud some letters. Soon after midnight they went to bed.

I had a fearful pain in my side that night, and could not get warm or go to sleep till morning. I could hear Orlov go from the bedroom into his study. After sitting there about an hour, he rang the bell. In my pain and exhaustion I forgot all the rules and conventions, and went to his study in my night attire, barefooted. Orlov, in his dressing-gown and cap, was standing in the doorway, waiting for me.

"When you are sent for you should come dressed," he said sternly. "Bring some fresh candles."

I was about to apologise, but suddenly broke into a violent cough, and clutched at the side of the door to save myself from falling.

"Are you ill?" said Orlov.

I believe it was the first time of our acquaintance that he addressed me not in the singular—goodness knows why. Most likely, in my night clothes and with my face distorted by coughing, I played my part poorly, and was very little like a flunkey.

"If you are ill, why do you take a place?" he said.

"That I may not die of starvation," I answered.

"How disgusting it all is, really!" he said softly, going up to his table.

While hurriedly getting into my coat, I put up and lighted fresh candles. He was sitting at the table, with feet stretched out on a low chair, cutting a book.

I left him deeply engrossed, and the book did not drop out of his hands as it had done in the evening.

VII

Now that I am writing these lines I am restrained by that dread of appearing sentimental and ridiculous, in which I have been trained from childhood; when I want to be affectionate or to say anything tender, I don't know how to be natural. And it is that dread, together with lack of practice, that prevents me from being able to express with perfect clearness what was passing in my soul at that time.

I was not in love with Zinaida Fyodorovna, but in the ordinary human feeling I had for her, there was far more youth, freshness, and joyousness than in Orlov's love.

As I worked in the morning, cleaning boots or sweeping the rooms, I waited with a thrill at my heart for the moment when I should hear her voice and her footsteps. To stand watching her as she drank her coffee in the morning or ate her lunch, to hold her fur coat for her in the hall, and to put the goloshes on her little feet while she rested her hand on my shoulder; then to wait till the hall porter rang up for me, to meet her at the door, cold, and rosy, powdered with the snow, to listen to her brief exclamations about the frost or the cabman—if only you knew how much all that meant to me! I longed to be in love, to have a wife and child of my own. I wanted my future wife to have just such a face, such a voice. I dreamed of it at dinner, and in the street when I was sent on some errand, and when I lay awake at night. Orlov rejected with disgust children, cooking, copper saucepans, and feminine knickknacks, and I gathered them all up, tenderly cherished them in my dreams, loved them, and begged them of destiny. I had visions of a wife, a nursery, a little house with garden paths. . . .

I knew that if I did love her I could never dare to hope for the miracle of her returning my love, but that reflection did not worry me. In my quiet, modest feeling akin to ordinary affection, there was no jealousy of Orlov or even envy of him, since I realised that for a wreck like me happiness was only to be found in dreams.

When Zinaida Fyodorovna sat up night after night for her *George*, looking immovably at a book of which she never turned a page, or when she shuddered and turned pale at Polya's crossing the room, I suffered with her, and the idea occurred to me to lance this festering wound as quickly as possible by letting her know what was said here at supper on Thursdays; but—how was it to be done? More and more often I saw her tears. For the first weeks she laughed and sang to herself, even when Orlov was not at home, but by the second month there was a mournful stillness in our flat broken only on Thursday evenings.

She flattered Orlov, and to wring from him a counterfeit smile or kiss, was ready to go on her knees to him, to fawn on him like a dog.

Even when her heart was heaviest, she could not resist glancing into a looking-glass if she passed one and straightening her hair. It seemed strange to me that she could still take an interest in clothes and go into ecstasies over her purchases. It did not seem in keeping with her genuine grief. She paid attention to the fashions and ordered expensive dresses. What for? On whose account? I particularly remember one dress which cost four hundred roubles. To give four hundred roubles for an unnecessary, useless dress while women for their hard day's work get only twenty kopecks a day without food, and the makers of Venice and Brussels lace are only paid half a franc a day on the supposition that they can earn the rest by immorality! And it seemed strange to me that Zinaida Fyodorovna was not conscious of it; it vexed me. But she had only to go out of the house for me to find excuses and explanations for everything, and to be waiting eagerly for the hall porter to ring for me.

She treated me as a flunkey, a being of a lower order. One may pat a dog, and yet not notice it; I was given orders and asked questions, but my presence was not observed. My master and mistress thought it unseemly to say more to me than is usually said to servants; if when waiting at dinner I had laughed or put in my word in the conversation, they would certainly have thought I was mad and have dismissed me. Zinaida Fyodorovna was favourably disposed to me, all the same. When she was sending me on some errand or explaining to me the working of a new lamp or anything of that sort, her face was extraordinarily kind, frank, and cordial, and her eyes looked me straight in the face. At such moments I always fancied she remembered with gratitude how I used to bring her letters to Znamensky Street. When she rang the bell, Polya, who considered me her favourite and hated me for it, used to say with a jeering smile:

"Go along, *your* mistress wants you."

Zinaida Fyodorovna considered me as a being of a lower order, and did not suspect that if any one in the house were in a humiliating position it was she. She did not know that I, a footman, was unhappy on her account, and used to ask myself twenty times a day what was in store for her and how it would all end. Things were growing visibly worse day by day. After the evening on which they had talked of his official work, Orlov, who could not endure tears, unmistakably began to avoid conversation with her; whenever Zinaida Fyodorovna began to argue, or to beseech him, or seemed on the point of crying, he seized some plausible excuse for retreating to his study or going out. He more and more rarely slept at home, and still more rarely dined there: on Thursdays he was the one to suggest some expedition to his friends. Zinaida Fyodorovna was still dreaming of having the cooking done at home, of moving to a new flat, of travelling abroad, but her dreams remained dreams. Dinner was sent in from the restaurant. Orlov asked her not to broach the question of moving until after they had come back from abroad, and apropos of their foreign tour, declared that they could not go till his hair had grown long, as one could not go trailing from hotel to hotel and serving the idea without long hair.

To crown it all, in Orlov's absence, Kukushkin began calling at the flat in the evening. There was nothing exceptional in his behaviour, but I could never forget the conversation in which he had offered to cut Orlov out. He was regaled with tea and red wine, and he used to titter and, anxious to say something pleasant, would declare that a free union was superior in every respect to legal marriage, and that all decent people ought really to come to Zinaida Fyodorovna and fall at her feet.

VIII

Christmas was spent drearily in vague anticipations of calamity. On New Year's Eve Orlov unexpectedly announced at breakfast that he was being sent to assist a senator who was on a revising commission in a certain province.

"I don't want to go, but I can't find an excuse to get off," he said with vexation. "I must go; there's nothing for it."

Such news instantly made Zinaida Fyodorovna's eyes look red. "Is it for long?" she asked.

"Five days or so."

"I am glad, really, you are going," she said after a moment's thought. "It will be a change for you. You will fall in love with some one on the way, and tell me about it afterwards."

At every opportunity she tried to make Orlov feel that she did not restrict his liberty in any way, and that he could do exactly as he liked, and this artless, transparent strategy deceived no one, and only unnecessarily reminded Orlov that he was not free.

"I am going this evening," he said, and began reading the paper.

Zinaida Fyodorovna wanted to see him off at the station, but he dissuaded her, saying that he was not going to America, and not going to be away five years, but only five days—possibly less.

The parting took place between seven and eight. He put one arm round her, and kissed her on the lips and on the forehead.

"Be a good girl, and don't be depressed while I am away," he said in a warm, affectionate tone which touched even me. "God keep you!"

She looked greedily into his face, to stamp his dear features on her memory, then she put her arms gracefully round his neck and laid her head on his breast.

"Forgive me our misunderstandings," she said in French. "Husband and wife cannot help quarrelling if they love each other, and I love you madly. Don't forget me. . . . Wire to me often and fully."

Orlov kissed her once more, and, without saying a word, went out in confusion. When he heard the click of the lock as the door closed, he stood still in the middle of the staircase in hesitation and glanced upwards. It seemed to me that if a sound had reached him at that moment from above, he would have turned back. But all was quiet. He straightened his coat and went downstairs irresolutely.

The sledges had been waiting a long while at the door. Orlov got into one, I got into the other with two portmanteaus. It was a hard frost and there were fires smoking at the cross-roads. The cold wind nipped my face and hands, and took my breath away as we drove rapidly along; and, closing my eyes, I thought what a splendid woman she was. How she loved him! Even useless rubbish is collected in the courtyards nowadays and used for some purpose, even broken glass is considered a useful commodity, but something so precious, so rare, as the love of a refined, young, intelligent, and good woman is utterly thrown away and wasted. One of the early sociologists regarded every evil passion as a force which might by judicious management be turned to good, while among us even a fine, noble passion springs up and dies away in impotence, turned to no account, misunderstood or vulgarised. Why is it?

The sledges stopped unexpectedly. I opened my eyes and I saw that we had come to a standstill in Sergievsky Street, near a big house where Pekarsky lived. Orlov got out of the sledge and vanished into the entry. Five minutes later Pekarsky's footman came out, bareheaded, and, angry with the frost, shouted to me:

"Are you deaf? Pay the cabmen and go upstairs. You are wanted!"

At a complete loss, I went to the first storey. I had been to Pekarsky's flat before—that is, I had stood in the hall and looked into the drawing-room, and, after the damp, gloomy street, it always struck me by the brilliance of its picture-frames, its bronzes and expensive furniture. To-day in the midst of this splendour I saw Gruzin, Kukushkin, and, after a minute, Orlov.

"Look here, Stepan," he said, coming up to me. "I shall be staying here till Friday or Saturday. If any letters or telegrams come, you must bring them here every day. At home, of course you will say that I have gone, and send my greetings. Now you can go."

When I reached home Zinaida Fyodorovna was lying on the sofa in the drawing-room, eating a pear. There was only one candle burning in the candelabra.

"Did you catch the train?" asked Zinaida Fyodorovna.

"Yes, madam. His honour sends his greetings."

I went into my room and I, too, lay down. I had nothing to do, and I did not want to read. I was not surprised and I was not indignant. I only racked my brains to think why this deception was necessary. It is only boys in their teens who deceive their mistresses like that. How was it that a man who had thought and read so much could not imagine anything more sensible? I must confess I had by no means a poor opinion of his intelligence. I believe if he had had to deceive his minister or any other influential person he would have put a great deal of skill and energy into doing so; but to deceive a woman, the first idea that occurred to him was evidently good enough. If it succeeded—well and good; if it did not, there would be no harm done—he could tell some other lie just as quickly and simply, with no mental effort.

At midnight when the people on the floor overhead were moving their chairs and shouting hurrah to welcome the New Year, Zinaida Fyodorovna rang for me from the room next to the study. Languid from lying down so long, she was sitting at the table, writing something on a scrap of paper.

"I must send a telegram," she said, with a smile. "Go to the station as quick as you can and ask them to send it after him."

Going out into the street, I read on the scrap of paper:

"May the New Year bring new happiness. Make haste and telegraph; I miss you dreadfully. It seems an eternity. I am only sorry I can't send a thousand kisses and my very heart by telegraph. Enjoy yourself, my darling.—ZINA."

I sent the telegram, and next morning I gave her the receipt.

IX

The worst of it was that Orlov had thoughtlessly let Polya, too, into the secret of his deception, telling her to bring his shirts to Sergievsky Street. After that, she looked at Zinaida Fyodorovna with a malignant joy and hatred I could not understand, and was never tired of snorting with delight to herself in her own room and in the hall.

"She's outstayed her welcome; it's time she took herself off!" she would say with zest. "She ought to realise that herself. . . ."

She already divined by instinct that Zinaida Fyodorovna would not be with us much longer, and, not to let the chance slip, carried off everything she set her eyes on—smelling-bottles, tortoise-shell hairpins, handkerchiefs, shoes! On the day after New Year's Day, Zinaida Fyodorovna summoned me to her room and told me in a low voice that she missed her black dress. And then she walked through all the rooms, with a pale, frightened, and indignant face, talking to herself:

"It's too much! It's beyond everything. Why, it's unheard-of insolence!"

At dinner she tried to help herself to soup, but could not—her hands were trembling. Her lips were trembling, too. She looked helplessly at the soup and at the little pies, waiting for the trembling to pass off, and suddenly she could not resist looking at Polya.

"You can go, Polya," she said. "Stepan is enough by himself."

"I'll stay; I don't mind," answered Polya.

"There's no need for you to stay. You go away altogether," Zinaida Fyodorovna went on, getting up in great agitation. "You may look out for another place. You can go at once."

"I can't go away without the master's orders. He engaged me. It must be as he orders."

"You can take orders from me, too! I am mistress here!" said Zinaida Fyodorovna, and she flushed crimson.

"You may be the mistress, but only the master can dismiss me. It was he engaged me."

"You dare not stay here another minute!" cried Zinaida

Fyodorovna, and she struck the plate with her knife. "You are a thief! Do you hear?"

Zinaida Fyodorovna flung her dinner-napkin on the table, and with a pitiful, suffering face, went quickly out of the room. Loudly sobbing and wailing something indistinct, Polya, too, went away. The soup and the grouse got cold. And for some reason all the restaurant dainties on the table struck me as poor, thievish, like Polya. Two pies on a plate had a particularly miserable and guilty air. "We shall be taken back to the restaurant to-day," they seemed to be saying, "and to-morrow we shall be put on the table again for some official or celebrated singer."

"She is a fine lady, indeed," I heard uttered in Polya's room. "I could have been a lady like that long ago, but I have some self-respect! We'll see which of us will be the first to go!"

Zinaida Fyodorovna rang the bell. She was sitting in her room, in the corner, looking as though she had been put in the corner as a punishment.

"No telegram has come?" she asked.

"No, madam."

"Ask the porter; perhaps there is a telegram. And don't leave the house," she called after me. "I am afraid to be left alone."

After that I had to run down almost every hour to ask the porter whether a telegram had come. I must own it was a dreadful time! To avoid seeing Polya, Zinaida Fyodorovna dined and had tea in her own room; it was here that she slept, too, on a short sofa like a half-moon, and she made her own bed. For the first days I took the telegrams; but, getting no answer, she lost her faith in me and began telegraphing herself. Looking at her, I, too, began impatiently hoping for a telegram. I hoped he would contrive some deception, would make arrangements, for instance, that a telegram should be sent to her from some station. If he were too much engrossed with cards or had been attracted by some other woman, I thought that both Gruzin and Kukushkin would remind him of us. But our expectations were vain. Five times a day I would go in to Zinaida Fyodorovna, intending to tell her the truth, but her eyes looked piteous as a fawn's, her shoulders seemed to droop, her lips were moving, and I went away again without saying a word. Pity and sympathy seemed to rob me of all manliness. Polya, as cheerful and well satisfied with herself as though nothing had happened, was tidying the master's study and the bedroom, rummaging in the cupboards, and making the crockery jingle, and when she passed Zinaida Fyodorovna's door, she hummed something and coughed. She was pleased that her mistress was hiding from her. In the evening she would go out somewhere, and rang at two or three o'clock in the morning, and I had to open the door to her and listen to remarks about my cough. Immediately afterwards I would hear another ring; I would run to the room next to the study, and Zinaida Fyodorovna, putting her head out of the door, would ask, "Who was it rung?" while she looked at my hands to see whether I had a telegram.

When at last on Saturday the bell rang below and she heard the familiar voice on the stairs, she was so delighted that she broke into sobs. She rushed to meet him, embraced him, kissed him on the breast and sleeves, said something one could not understand. The hall porter brought up the portmanteaus; Polya's cheerful voice was heard. It was as though some one had come home for the holidays.

"Why didn't you wire?" asked Zinaida Fyodorovna, breathless with joy. "Why was it? I have been in misery; I don't know how I've lived through it. . . . Oh, my God!"

"It was very simple! I returned with the senator to Moscow the very first day, and didn't get your telegrams," said Orlov. "After dinner, my love, I'll give you a full account of my doings, but now I must sleep and sleep. . . . I am worn out with the journey."

It was evident that he had not slept all night; he had probably been playing cards and drinking freely. Zinaida Fyodorovna put him to bed, and we all walked about on tiptoe all that day. The dinner went off quite satisfactorily, but when they went into the study and had coffee the explanation began. Zinaida Fyodorovna began talking of something rapidly in a low voice; she spoke in French, and her words flowed like a stream. Then I heard a loud sigh from Orlov, and his voice.

"My God!" he said in French. "Have you really nothing fresher to tell me than this everlasting tale of your servant's misdeeds?"

"But, my dear, she robbed me and said insulting things to me."

"But why is it she doesn't rob me or say insulting things to me? Why is it I never notice the maids nor the porters nor the footmen? My dear, you are simply capricious and refuse to know your own mind. . . . I really begin to suspect that you must be in a certain condition. When I offered to let her go, you insisted on her remaining, and now you want me to turn her away. I can be obstinate, too, in such cases. You want her to go, but I want her to remain. That's the only way to cure you of your nerves."

"Oh, very well, very well," said Zinaida Fyodorovna in alarm. "Let us say no more about that. . . . Let us put it off till to-morrow. . . . Now tell me about Moscow. . . . What is going on in Moscow?"

X

After lunch next day—it was the seventh of January, St. John the Baptist's Day—Orlov put on his black dress coat and his decoration to go to visit his father and congratulate him on his name day. He had to go at two o'clock, and it was only half-past one when he had finished dressing. What was he to do for that half-hour? He walked about the drawing-room, declaiming some congratulatory verses which he had recited as a child to his father and mother.

Zinaida Fyodorovna, who was just going out to a dressmaker's or to the shops, was sitting, listening to him with a smile. I don't know how their conversation began, but when I took Orlov his gloves, he was standing before her with a capricious, beseeching face, saying:

"For God's sake, in the name of everything that's holy, don't talk of things that everybody knows! What an unfortunate gift our intel-lectual thoughtful ladies have for talking with enthusiasm and an air of profundity of things that every schoolboy is sick to death of! Ah, if only you would exclude from our conjugal programme all these serious questions! How grateful I should be to you!"

"We women may not dare, it seems, to have views of our own."

"I give you full liberty to be as liberal as you like, and quote from any authors you choose, but make me one concession: don't hold forth in my presence on either of two subjects: the corruption of the upper classes and the evils of the marriage system. Do understand me, at last. The upper class is always abused in contrast with the world of tradesmen, priests, workmen and peasants, Sidors and Nikitas of all sorts. I detest both classes, but if I had honesty to choose between the two, I should without hesitation, prefer the upper class, and there would be no falsity or affectation about it, since all my tastes are in that direction. Our world is trivial and empty, but at any rate we speak French decently, read something, and don't punch each other in the ribs even in our most violent quarrels, while the Sidors and the Nikitas and their worships in trade talk about 'being quite agreeable,' 'in a jiffy,' 'blast your eyes,' and display the utmost license of pothouse manners and the most degrading superstition."

"The peasant and the tradesman feed you."

"Yes, but what of it? That's not only to my discredit, but to theirs too. They feed me and take off their caps to me, so it seems they have not the intelligence and honesty to do otherwise. I don't blame or praise any one: I only mean that the upper class and the lower are as bad as one another. My feelings and my intelligence are opposed to both, but my tastes lie more in the direction of the former. Well, now for the evils of marriage," Orlov went on, glancing at his watch. "It's high time for you to understand that there are no evils in the system itself; what is the matter is that you don't know yourselves what you want from marriage. What is it you want? In legal and illegal cohabitation, in every sort of union and cohabitation, good or bad, the underlying reality is the same. You ladies live for that underlying reality alone: for you it's everything; your existence would have no meaning for you without it. You want nothing but that, and you get it; but since you've taken to reading novels you are ashamed of it: you rush from pillar to post, you recklessly change your men, and to justify this turmoil you have begun talking of the evils of marriage. So long as you can't and won't renounce what underlies it all, your chief foe, your devil—so long as you serve that slavishly, what use is there in discussing the matter seriously? Everything you may say to me will be falsity and affectation. I shall not believe you."

I went to find out from the hall porter whether the sledge was at the door, and when I came back I found it had become a quarrel. As sailors say, a squall had blown up.

"I see you want to shock me by your cynicism today," said Zinaida Fyodorovna, walking about the drawing-room in great emotion. "It revolts me to listen to you. I am pure before God and man, and have nothing to repent of. I left my husband and came to you, and am proud of it. I swear, on my honour, I am proud of it!"

"Well, that's all right, then!"

"If you are a decent, honest man, you, too, ought to be proud of what I did. It raises you and me above thousands of people who would like to do as we have done, but do not venture through cowardice or petty prudence. But you are not a decent man. You are afraid of freedom, and you mock the promptings of genuine feeling, from fear that some ignoramus may suspect you of being sincere. You are afraid to show me to your friends; there's no greater infliction for you than to go about with me in the street. . . . Isn't that true? Why haven't you introduced me to your father or your cousin all this time? Why is it? No, I am sick of it at last," cried Zinaida Fyodorovna, stamping. "I demand what is mine by right. You must present me to your father."

"If you want to know him, go and present yourself. He receives visitors every morning from ten till half-past."

"How base you are!" said Zinaida Fyodorovna, wringing her hands in despair. "Even if you are not sincere, and are not saying what you think, I might hate you for your cruelty. Oh, how base you are!"

"We keep going round and round and never reach the real point. The real point is that you made a mistake, and you won't acknowledge it aloud. You imagined that I was a hero, and that I had some extraordinary ideas and ideals, and it has turned out that I am a most ordinary official, a cardplayer, and have no partiality for ideas of any sort. I am a worthy representative of the rotten world from which you have run away because you were revolted with its triviality and emptiness. Recognise it and be just: don't be indignant with me, but with yourself, as it is your mistake, and not mine."

"Yes, I admit I was mistaken."

"Well, that's all right, then. We've reached that point at last, thank God. Now hear something more, if you please: I can't rise to your level—I am too depraved; you can't descend to my level, either, for you are too exalted. So there is only one thing left to do. . . ."

"What?" Zinaida Fyodorovna asked quickly, holding her breath and turning suddenly as white as a sheet of paper.

"To call logic to our aid. . . ."

"Georgy, why are you torturing me?" Zinaida Fyodorovna said suddenly in Russian in a breaking voice. "What is it for? Think of my misery. . . ."

Orlov, afraid of tears, went quickly into his study, and I don't know why—whether it was that he wished to cause her extra pain, or whether he remembered it was usually done in such cases—he locked the door after him. She cried out and ran after him with a rustle of her skirt.

"What does this mean?" she cried, knocking at his door. "What . . . what does this mean?" she repeated in a shrill voice breaking with indignation. "Ah, so this is what you do! Then let me tell you I hate you, I despise you! Everything is over between us now."

I heard hysterical weeping mingled with laughter. Something small in the drawing-room fell off the table and was broken. Orlov went out into the hall by another door, and, looking round him nervously, he hurriedly put on his great-coat and went out.

Half an hour passed, an hour, and she was still weeping. I remembered that she had no father or mother, no relations, and here she was living between a man who hated her and Polya, who robbed her—and how desolate her life seemed to me! I do not know why, but I went into the drawing-room to her. Weak and helpless, looking with her lovely hair like an embodiment of tenderness and grace, she was in anguish, as though she were ill; she was lying on a couch, hiding her face, and quivering all over.

"Madam, shouldn't I fetch a doctor?" I asked gently.

"No, there's no need . . . it's nothing," she said, and she looked at me with her tear-stained eyes. "I have a little headache. . . . Thank you."

I went out, and in the evening she was writing letter after letter, and sent me out first to Pekarsky, then to Gruzin, then to Kukushkin, and finally anywhere I chose, if only I could find Orlov and give him the letter. Every time I came back with the letter she scolded me, entreated me, thrust money into my hand—as though she were in a fever. And all the night she did not sleep, but sat in the drawing-room, talking to herself.

Orlov returned to dinner next day, and they were reconciled.

The first Thursday afterwards Orlov complained to his friends of the intolerable life he led; he smoked a great deal, and said with irritation:

"It is no life at all; it's the rack. Tears, wailing, intellectual conversations, begging for forgiveness, again tears and wailing; and the long and the short of it is that I have no flat of my own now. I am wretched, and I make her wretched. Surely I haven't to live another month or two like this? How can I? But yet I may have to."

"Why don't you speak, then?" said Pekarsky.

"I've tried, but I can't. One can boldly tell the truth, whatever it may be, to an independent, rational man; but in this case one has to do with a creature who has no will, no strength of character, and no logic. I cannot endure tears; they disarm me. When she cries, I am ready to swear eternal love and cry myself."

Pekarsky did not understand; he scratched his broad forehead in perplexity and said:

"You really had better take another flat for her. It's so simple!"

"She wants me, not the flat. But what's the good of talking?" sighed Orlov. "I only hear endless conversations, but no way out of my position. It certainly is a case of 'being guilty without guilt.' I don't claim to be a mushroom, but it seems I've got to go into the basket. The last thing I've ever set out to be is a hero. I never could endure Turgenev's novels; and now, all of a sudden, as though to spite me, I've heroism forced upon me. I assure her on my honour that I'm not a hero at all, I adduce irrefutable proofs of the same, but she doesn't believe me. Why doesn't she believe me? I suppose I really must have something of the appearance of a hero."

"You go off on a tour of inspection in the provinces," said Kukushkin, laughing.

"Yes, that's the only thing left for me."

A week after this conversation Orlov announced that he was again ordered to attend the senator, and the same evening he went off with his portmanteaus to Pekarsky.

XI

An old man of sixty, in a long fur coat reaching to the ground, and a beaver cap, was standing at the door.

"Is Georgy Ivanitch at home?" he asked.

At first I thought it was one of the moneylenders, Gruzin's creditors, who sometimes used to come to Orlov for small payments on account; but when he came into the hall and flung open his coat, I saw the thick brows and the characteristically compressed lips which I knew so well from the photographs, and two rows of stars on the uniform. I recognised him: it was Orlov's father, the distinguished statesman.

I answered that Georgy Ivanitch was not at home. The old man pursed up his lips tightly and looked into space, reflecting, showing me his dried-up, toothless profile.

"I'll leave a note," he said; "show me in."

He left his goloshes in the hall, and, without taking off his long, heavy fur coat, went into the study. There he sat down before the table, and, before taking up the pen, for three minutes he pondered, shading his eyes with his hand as though from the sun—exactly as his son did when he was out of humour. His face was sad, thoughtful, with that look of resignation which I have only seen on the faces of the old and religious. I stood behind him, gazed at his bald head and at the hollow at the nape of his neck, and it was clear as daylight to me that this weak old man was now in my power. There was not a soul in the flat except my enemy and me. I had only to use a little physical violence, then snatch his watch to disguise the object of the crime, and to get off by the back way, and I should have gained infinitely more than I could have imagined possible when I took up the part of a footman. I thought that I could hardly get a better opportunity. But instead of acting, I looked quite unconcernedly, first at his bald patch and then at his fur, and calmly meditated on this man's relation to his only son, and on the fact that people spoiled by power and wealth probably don't want to die. . . .

"Have you been long in my son's service?" he asked, writing a large hand on the paper.

"Three months, your High Excellency."

He finished the letter and stood up. I still had time. I urged myself on and clenched my fists, trying to wring out of my soul some trace of my former hatred; I recalled what a passionate, implacable, obstinate hate I had felt for him only a little while before. . . . But it is difficult to strike a match against a crumbling stone. The sad old face and the cold glitter of his stars roused in me nothing but petty, cheap, unnecessary thoughts of the transitoriness of everything earthly, of the nearness of death. . . .

"Good-day, brother," said the old man. He put on his cap and went out.

There could be no doubt about it: I had undergone a change; I had become different. To convince myself, I began to recall the past, but at once I felt uneasy, as though I had accidentally peeped into a dark, damp corner. I remembered my comrades and friends, and my first thought was how I should blush in confusion if ever I met any of them. What was I now? What had I to think of and to do? Where was I to go? What was I living for?

I could make nothing of it. I only knew one thing—that I must make haste to pack my things and be off. Before the old man's visit my position as a flunkey had a meaning; now it was absurd. Tears dropped into my open portmanteau; I felt insufferably sad; but how I longed to live! I was ready to embrace and include in my short life every possibility open to man. I wanted to speak, to read, and to hammer in some big factory, and to stand on watch, and to plough. I yearned for the Nevsky Prospect, for the sea and the fields—for every place to which my imagination travelled. When Zinaida Fyodorovna came in, I rushed to open the door for her, and with peculiar tenderness took off her fur coat. The last time!

We had two other visitors that day besides the old man. In the evening when it was quite dark, Gruzin came to fetch some papers for Orlov. He opened the table-drawer, took the necessary papers, and, rolling them up, told me to put them in the hall beside his cap while he went in to see Zinaida Fyodorovna. She was lying on the sofa in the drawing-room, with her arms behind her head. Five or six days had already passed since Orlov went on his tour of inspection, and no one knew when he would be back, but this time she did not send telegrams and did not expect them. She did not seem to notice the presence of Polya, who was still living with us. "So be it, then," was what I read on her passionless and very pale face. Like Orlov, she wanted to be unhappy out of obstinacy. To spite herself and everything in the world, she lay for days together on the sofa, desiring and expecting nothing but evil for herself. Probably she was picturing to herself Orlov's return and the inevitable quarrels with him; then his growing indifference to her, his infidelities; then how they would separate; and perhaps these agonising thoughts gave her satisfaction. But what would she have said if she found out the actual truth?

"I love you, Godmother," said Gruzin, greeting her and kissing her hand. "You are so kind! And so dear *George* has gone away," he lied. "He has gone away, the rascal!"

He sat down with a sigh and tenderly stroked her hand.

"Let me spend an hour with you, my dear," he said. "I don't want to go home, and it's too early to go to the Birshovs'. The Birshovs are keeping their Katya's birthday to-day. She is a nice child!"

I brought him a glass of tea and a decanter of brandy. He slowly and with obvious reluctance drank the tea, and returning the glass to me, asked timidly:

"Can you give me . . . something to eat, my friend? I have had no dinner."

We had nothing in the flat. I went to the restaurant and brought him the ordinary rouble dinner.

"To your health, my dear," he said to Zinaida Fyodorovna, and he tossed off a glass of vodka. "My little girl, your godchild, sends you her love. Poor child! she's rickety. Ah, children, children!" he sighed. "Whatever you may say, Godmother, it is nice to be a father. Dear *George* can't understand that feeling."

He drank some more. Pale and lean, with his dinner-napkin over his chest like a little pinafore, he ate greedily, and raising his eyebrows, kept looking guiltily, like a little boy, first at Zinaida Fyodorovna and then at me. It seemed as though he would have begun crying if I had not given him the grouse or the jelly. When he had satisfied his hunger he grew more lively, and began laughingly telling some story about the Birshov household, but perceiving that it was tiresome and that Zinaida Fyodorovna was not laughing, he ceased. And there was a sudden feeling of dreariness. After he had finished his dinner they sat in the drawing-room by the light of a single lamp, and did not speak; it was painful to him to lie to her, and she wanted to ask him something, but could not make up her mind to. So passed half an hour. Gruzin glanced at his watch.

"I suppose it's time for me to go."

"No, stay a little. . . . We must have a talk."

Again they were silent. He sat down to the piano, struck one chord, then began playing, and sang softly. "What does the coming day bring me?" but as usual he got up suddenly and tossed his head.

"Play something," Zinaida Fyodorovna asked him.

"What shall I play?" he asked, shrugging his shoulders. "I have forgotten everything. I've given it up long ago."

Looking at the ceiling as though trying to remember, he played two pieces of Tchaikovsky with exquisite expression, with such warmth, such insight! His face was just as usual—neither stupid nor intelligent—and it seemed to me a perfect marvel that a man whom I was accustomed to see in the midst of the most degrading, impure surroundings, was capable of such purity, of rising to a feeling so lofty, so far beyond my reach. Zinaida Fyodorovna's face glowed, and she walked about the drawing-room in emotion.

"Wait a bit, Godmother; if I can remember it, I will play you something," he said; "I heard it played on the violoncello."

Beginning timidly and picking out the notes, and then gathering confidence, he played Saint-Saëns's "Swan Song." He played it through, and then played it a second time.

"It's nice, isn't it?" he said.

Moved by the music, Zinaida Fyodorovna stood beside him and asked:

"Tell me honestly, as a friend, what do you think about me?"

"What am I to say?" he said, raising his eyebrows. "I love you and think nothing but good of you. But if you wish that I should speak generally about the question that interests you," he went on, rubbing his sleeve near the elbow and frowning, "then, my dear, you know. . . . To follow freely the promptings of the heart does not always give good people happiness. To feel free and at the same time to be happy, it seems to me, one must not conceal from oneself that life is coarse, cruel, and merciless in its conservatism, and one must retaliate with what it deserves—that is, be as coarse and as merciless in one's striving for freedom. That's what I think."

"That's beyond me," said Zinaida Fyodorovna, with a mournful smile. "I am exhausted already. I am so exhausted that I wouldn't stir a finger for my own salvation."

"Go into a nunnery."

He said this in jest, but after he had said it, tears glistened in Zinaida Fyodorovna's eyes and then in his.

"Well," he said, "we've been sitting and sitting, and now we must go. Good-bye, dear Godmother. God give you health."

He kissed both her hands, and stroking them tenderly, said that he should certainly come to see her again in a day or two. In the hall, as he was putting on his overcoat, that was so like a child's pelisse, he fumbled long in his pockets to find a tip for me, but found nothing there.

"Good-bye, my dear fellow," he said sadly, and went away.

I shall never forget the feeling that this man left behind him.

Zinaida Fyodorovna still walked about the room in her excitement. That she was walking about and not still lying down was so much to the good. I wanted to take advantage of this mood to speak to her openly and then to go away, but I had hardly seen Gruzin out when I heard a ring. It was Kukushkin.

"Is Georgy Ivanitch at home?" he said. "Has he come back? You say no? What a pity! In that case, I'll go in and kiss your mistress's hand, and so away. Zinaida Fyodorovna, may I come in?" he cried. "I want to kiss your hand. Excuse my being so late."

He was not long in the drawing-room, not more than ten minutes, but I felt as though he were staying a long while and would never go away. I bit my lips from indignation and annoyance, and already hated Zinaida Fyodorovna. "Why does she not turn him out?" I thought indignantly, though it was evident that she was bored by his company.

When I held his fur coat for him he asked me, as a mark of special good-will, how I managed to get on without a wife.

"But I don't suppose you waste your time," he said, laughingly. "I've no doubt Polya and you are as thick as thieves. . . . You rascal!"

In spite of my experience of life, I knew very little of mankind at that time, and it is very likely that I often exaggerated what was of little consequence and failed to observe what was important. It seemed to me it was not without motive that Kukushkin tittered and flattered me. Could it be that he was hoping that I, like a flunkey, would gossip in other kitchens and servants' quarters of his coming to see us in the evenings when Orlov was away, and staying with Zinaida Fyodorovna till late at night? And when my tittle-tattle came to the ears of his acquaintance, he would drop his eyes in confusion and shake his little finger. And would not he, I thought, looking at his little honeyed face, this very evening at cards pretend and perhaps declare that he had already won Zinaida Fyodorovna from Orlov?

That hatred which failed me at midday when the old father had come, took possession of me now. Kukushkin went away at last, and as I listened to the shuffle of his leather goloshes, I felt greatly tempted to fling after him, as a parting shot, some coarse word of abuse, but I restrained myself. And when the steps had died away on the stairs, I went back to the hall, and, hardly conscious of what I was doing, took up the roll of papers that Gruzin had left behind, and ran headlong downstairs. Without cap or overcoat, I ran down into the street. It was not cold, but big flakes of snow were falling and it was windy.

"Your Excellency!" I cried, catching up Kukushkin. "Your Excellency!"

He stopped under a lamp-post and looked round with surprise.

"Your Excellency!" I said breathless, "your Excellency!"

And not able to think of anything to say, I hit him two or three times on the face with the roll of paper. Completely at a loss, and hardly wondering—I had so completely taken him by surprise—he leaned his back against the lamp-post and put up his hands to protect his face. At that moment an army doctor passed, and saw how I was beating the man, but he merely looked at us in astonishment and went on. I felt ashamed and I ran back to the house.

XII

With my head wet from the snow, and gasping for breath, I ran to my room, and immediately flung off my swallow-tails, put on a reefer jacket and an overcoat, and carried my portmanteau out into the passage; I must get away! But before going I hurriedly sat down and began writing to Orlov:

"I leave you my false passport," I began. "I beg you to keep it as a memento, you false man, you Petersburg official!

"To steal into another man's house under a false name, to watch under the mask of a flunkey this person's intimate life, to hear everything, to see everything in order later on, unasked, to accuse a man of lying—all this, you will say, is on a level with theft. Yes, but I care nothing for fine feelings now. I have endured dozens of your dinners and suppers when you said and did what you liked, and I had to hear, to look on, and be silent. I don't want to make you a present of my silence. Besides, if there is not a living soul at hand who dares to tell you the truth without flattery, let your flunkey Stepan wash your magnificent countenance for you."

I did not like this beginning, but I did not care to alter it. Besides, what did it matter?

The big windows with their dark curtains, the bed, the crumpled dress coat on the floor, and my wet footprints, looked gloomy and forbidding. And there was a peculiar stillness.

Possibly because I had run out into the street without my cap and goloshes I was in a high fever. My face burned, my legs ached. . . . My heavy head drooped over the table, and there was that kind of division in my thought when every idea in the brain seemed dogged by its shadow.

"I am ill, weak, morally cast down," I went on; "I cannot write to you as I should like to. For the first moment I desired to insult and humiliate you, but now I do not feel that I have the right to do so. You and I have both fallen, and neither of us will ever rise up again; and even if my letter were eloquent, terrible, and passionate, it would still seem like beating on the lid of a coffin: however one knocks upon it, one will not wake up the dead! No efforts could warm your accursed cold blood, and you know that better than I do. Why write? But my mind and heart are burning, and I go on writing; for some reason I am moved as though this letter still might save you and me. I am so feverish that my thoughts are disconnected, and my pen scratches the paper without meaning; but the question I want to put to you stands before me as clear as though in letters of flame.

"Why I am prematurely weak and fallen is not hard to explain. Like Samson of old, I have taken the gates of Gaza on my shoulders to carry them to the top of the mountain, and only when I was exhausted, when youth and health were quenched in me forever, I noticed that that burden was not for my shoulders, and that I had deceived myself. I have been, moreover, in cruel and continual pain. I have endured cold, hunger, illness, and loss of liberty. Of personal happiness I know and have known nothing. I have no home; my memories are bitter, and my conscience is often in dread of them. But why have you fallen—you? What fatal, diabolical causes hindered your life from blossoming into full flower? Why, almost before beginning life, were you in such haste to cast off the image and likeness of God, and to become a cowardly beast who backs and scares others because he is afraid himself? You are afraid of life—as afraid of it as an Oriental who sits all day on a cushion smoking his hookah. Yes, you read a great deal, and a European coat fits you well, but yet with what tender, purely Oriental, pasha-like care you protect yourself from hunger, cold, physical effort, from pain and uneasiness! How early your soul has taken to its dressing-gown! What a cowardly part you have played towards real life and nature, with which every healthy and normal man struggles! How soft, how snug, how warm, how comfortable—and how bored you are! Yes, it is deathly boredom, unrelieved by one ray of light, as in solitary confinement; but you try to hide from that enemy, too, you play cards eight hours out of twenty-four.

"And your irony? Oh, but how well I understand it! Free, bold, living thought is searching and dominating; for an indolent, sluggish mind it is intolerable. That it may not disturb your peace, like thousands of your contemporaries, you made haste in youth to put it under bar and bolt. Your ironical attitude to life, or whatever you like to call it, is your armour; and your thought, fettered and frightened, dare not leap over the fence you have put round it; and when you jeer at ideas which you pretend to know all about, you are like the deserter fleeing from the field of battle, and, to stifle his shame, sneering at war and at valour. Cynicism stifles pain. In some novel of Dostoevsky's an old man tramples underfoot the portrait of his dearly loved daughter because he had been unjust to her, and you vent your foul and vulgar jeers upon the ideas of goodness and truth because you have not the strength to follow them. You are frightened of every honest and truthful hint at your degradation, and you purposely surround yourself with people who do nothing but flatter your weaknesses. And you may well, you may well dread the sight of tears!

"By the way, your attitude to women. Shamelessness has been handed down to us in our flesh and blood, and we are trained to shamelessness; but that is what we are men for—to subdue the beast in us. When you reached manhood and *all* ideas became known to you, you could not have failed to see the truth; you knew it, but you did not follow it; you were afraid of it, and to deceive your conscience you began loudly assuring yourself that it was not you but woman that was to blame, that she was as degraded as your attitude to her. Your cold, scabrous anecdotes, your coarse laughter, all your innumerable theories concerning the underlying reality of marriage and the indefinite demands made upon it, concerning the ten *sous* the French workman pays his woman; your everlasting attacks on female logic, lying, weakness and so on—doesn't it all look like a desire at all costs to force woman down into the mud that she may be on the same level as your attitude to her? You are a weak, unhappy, unpleasant person!"

Zinaida Fyodorovna began playing the piano in the drawing-room, trying to recall the song of Saint-Saëns that Gruzin had played. I went and lay on my bed, but remembering that it was time for me to go, I got up with an effort and with a heavy, burning head went to the table again.

"But this is the question," I went on. "Why are we worn out? Why are we, at first so passionate, so bold, so noble, and so full of faith, complete bankrupts at thirty or thirty-five? Why does one waste in consumption, another put a bullet through his brains, a third seeks forgetfulness in vodka and cards, while the fourth tries to stifle his fear and misery by cynically trampling underfoot the pure image of his fair youth? Why is it that, having once fallen, we do not try to rise up again, and, losing one thing, do not seek something else? Why is it?

"The thief hanging on the Cross could bring back the joy of life and the courage of confident hope, though perhaps he had not more than an hour to live. You have long years before you, and I shall probably not die so soon as one might suppose. What if by a miracle the present turned out to be a dream, a horrible nightmare, and we should wake up renewed, pure, strong, proud of our righteousness? Sweet visions fire me, and I am almost breathless with emotion. I have a terrible longing to live. I long for our life to be holy, lofty, and majestic as the heavens above. Let us live! The sun doesn't rise twice a day, and life is not given us again—clutch at what is left of your life and save it. . . ."

I did not write another word. I had a multitude of thoughts in my mind, but I could not connect them and get them on to paper. Without finishing the letter, I signed it with my name and rank, and went into the study. It was dark. I felt for the table and put the letter on it. I must have stumbled against the furniture in the dark and made a noise.

"Who is there?" I heard an alarmed voice in the drawing-room.

And the clock on the table softly struck one at the moment.

XIII

For at least half a minute I fumbled at the door in the dark, feeling for the handle; then I slowly opened it and walked into the drawing-room. Zinaida Fyodorovna was lying on the couch, and raising herself on her elbow, she looked towards me. Unable to bring myself to speak, I walked slowly by, and she followed me with her eyes. I stood for a little time in the dining-room and then walked by her again, and she looked at me intently and with perplexity, even with alarm. At last I stood still and said with an effort:

"He is not coming back."

She quickly got on to her feet, and looked at me without understanding.

"He is not coming back," I repeated, and my heart beat violently. "He will not come back, for he has not left Petersburg. He is staying at Pekarsky's."

She understood and believed me—I saw that from her sudden pallor, and from the way she laid her arms upon her bosom in terror and entreaty. In one instant all that had happened of late flashed through her mind; she reflected, and with pitiless clarity she saw the whole truth. But at the same time she remembered that I was a flunkey, a being of a lower order. . . . A casual stranger, with hair ruffled, with face flushed with fever, perhaps drunk, in a common overcoat, was coarsely intruding into her intimate life, and that offended her. She said to me sternly:

"It's not your business: go away."

"Oh, believe me!" I cried impetuously, holding out my hands to her. "I am not a footman; I am as free as you."

I mentioned my name, and, speaking very rapidly that she might not interrupt me or go away, explained to her who I was and why I was living there. This new discovery struck her more than the first. Till then she had hoped that her footman had lied or made a mistake or been silly, but now after my confession she had no doubts left. From the expression of her unhappy eyes and face, which suddenly lost its softness and beauty and looked old, I saw that she was insufferably miserable, and that the conversation would lead to no good; but I went on impetuously:

"The senator and the tour of inspection were invented to deceive you. In January, just as now, he did not go away, but stayed at Pekarsky's, and I saw him every day and took part in the deception. He was weary of you, he hated your presence here, he mocked at you. . . . If you could have heard how he and his friends here jeered at you and your love, you would not have remained here one minute! Go away from here! Go away."

"Well," she said in a shaking voice, and moved her hand over her hair. "Well, so be it."

Her eyes were full of tears, her lips were quivering, and her whole face was strikingly pale and distorted with anger. Orlov's coarse, petty lying revolted her and seemed to her contemptible, ridiculous: she smiled and I did not like that smile.

"Well," she repeated, passing her hand over her hair again, "so be it. He imagines that I shall die of humiliation, and instead of that I am . . . amused by it. There's no need for him to hide." She walked away from the piano and said, shrugging her shoulders: "There's no need. . . . It would have been simpler to have it out with me instead of keeping in hiding in other people's flats. I have eyes; I saw it myself long ago. . . . I was only waiting for him to come back to have things out once for all."

Then she sat down on a low chair by the table, and, leaning her head on the arm of the sofa, wept bitterly. In the drawing-room there was only one candle burning in the candelabra, and the chair where she was sitting was in darkness; but I saw how her head and shoulders were quivering, and how her hair, escaping from her combs, covered her neck, her face, her arms. . . . Her quiet, steady weeping, which was not hysterical but a woman's ordinary weeping, expressed a sense of insult, of wounded pride, of injury, and of something helpless, hopeless, which one could not set right and to which one could not get used. Her tears stirred an echo in my troubled and suffering heart; I forgot my illness and everything else in the world; I walked about the drawing-room and muttered distractedly:

"Is this life? . . . Oh, one can't go on living like this, one can't. . . . Oh, it's madness, wickedness, not life."

"What humiliation!" she said through her tears. "To live together, to smile at me at the very time when I was burdensome to him, ridiculous in his eyes! Oh, how humiliating!"

She lifted up her head, and looking at me with tear-stained eyes through her hair, wet with her tears, and pushing it back as it prevented her seeing me, she asked:

"They laughed at me?"

"To these men you were laughable—you and your love and Turgenev; they said your head was full of him. And if we both die at once in despair, that will amuse them, too; they will make a funny anecdote of it and tell it at your requiem service. But why talk of them?" I said impatiently. "We must get away from here—I cannot stay here one minute longer."

She began crying again, while I walked to the piano and sat down.

"What are we waiting for?" I asked dejectedly. "It's two o'clock."

"I am not waiting for anything," she said. "I am utterly lost."

"Why do you talk like that? We had better consider together what we are to do. Neither you nor I can stay here. Where do you intend to go?"

Suddenly there was a ring at the bell. My heart stood still. Could it be Orlov, to whom perhaps Kukushkin had complained of me? How should we meet? I went to open the door. It was Polya. She came in shaking the snow off her pelisse, and went into her room without saying a word to me. When I went back to the drawing-room, Zinaida Fyodorovna, pale as death, was standing in the middle of the room, looking towards me with big eyes.

"Who was it?" she asked softly.

"Polya," I answered.

She passed her hand over her hair and closed her eyes wearily.

"I will go away at once," she said. "Will you be kind and take me to the Petersburg Side? What time is it now?"

"A quarter to three."

XIV

When, a little afterwards, we went out of the house, it was dark and deserted in the street. Wet snow was falling and a damp wind lashed in one's face. I remember it was the beginning of March; a thaw had set in, and for some days past the cabmen had been driving on wheels. Under the impression of the back stairs, of the cold, of the midnight darkness, and the porter in his sheepskin who had questioned us before letting us out of the gate, Zinaida Fyodorovna was utterly cast down and dispirited. When we got into the cab and the hood was put up, trembling all over, she began hurriedly saying how grateful she was to me.

"I do not doubt your good-will, but I am ashamed that you should be troubled," she muttered. "Oh, I understand, I understand. . . . When Gruzin was here to-day, I felt that he was lying and concealing something. Well, so be it. But I am ashamed, anyway, that you should be troubled."

She still had her doubts. To dispel them finally, I asked the cabman to drive through Sergievsky Street; stopping him at Pekarsky's door, I got out of the cab and rang. When the porter came to the door, I asked aloud, that Zinaida Fyodorovna might hear, whether Georgy Ivanitch was at home.

"Yes," was the answer, "he came in half an hour ago. He must be in bed by now. What do you want?"

Zinaida Fyodorovna could not refrain from putting her head out.

"Has Georgy Ivanitch been staying here long?" she asked.

"Going on for three weeks."

"And he's not been away?"

"No," answered the porter, looking at me with surprise.

"Tell him, early to-morrow," I said, "that his sister has arrived from Warsaw. Good-bye."

Then we drove on. The cab had no apron, the snow fell on us in big flakes, and the wind, especially on the Neva, pierced us through and through. I began to feel as though we had been driving for a long time, that for ages we had been suffering, and that for ages I had been listening to Zinaida Fyodorovna's shuddering breath. In semi-delirium, as though half asleep, I looked back upon my strange, incoherent life, and for some reason recalled a melodrama, "The Parisian Beggars," which I had seen once or twice in my childhood. And when to shake off that semi-delirium I peeped out from the hood and saw the dawn, all the images of the past, all my misty thoughts, for some reason, blended in me into one distinct, over-powering thought: everything was irrevocably over for Zinaida Fyodorovna and for me. This was as certain a conviction as though the cold blue sky contained a prophecy, but a minute later I was already thinking of something else and believed differently.

"What am I now?" said Zinaida Fyodorovna, in a voice husky with the cold and the damp. "Where am I to go? What am I to do? Gruzin told me to go into a nunnery. Oh, I would! I would change my dress, my face, my name, my thoughts . . . everything—everything, and would hide myself for ever. But they will not take me into a nunnery. I am with child."

"We will go abroad together to-morrow," I said.

"That's impossible. My husband won't give me a passport."

"I will take you without a passport."

The cabman stopped at a wooden house of two storeys, painted a dark colour. I rang. Taking from me her small light basket—the only luggage we had brought with us—Zinaida Fyodorovna gave a wry smile and said:

"These are my *bijoux*."

But she was so weak that she could not carry these *bijoux*.

It was a long while before the door was opened. After the third or fourth ring a light gleamed in the windows, and there was a sound of steps, coughing and whispering; at last the key grated in the lock, and a stout peasant woman with a frightened red face appeared at the door. Some distance behind her stood a thin little old woman with short grey hair, carrying a candle in her hand. Zinaida Fyodorovna ran into the passage and flung her arms round the old woman's neck.

"Nina, I've been deceived," she sobbed loudly. "I've been coarsely, foully deceived! Nina, Nina!"

I handed the basket to the peasant woman. The door was closed, but still I heard her sobs and the cry "Nina!"

I got into the cab and told the man to drive slowly to the Nevsky Prospect. I had to think of a night's lodging for myself.

Next day towards evening I went to see Zinaida Fyodorovna. She was terribly changed. There were no traces of tears on her pale, terribly sunken face, and her expression was different. I don't know whether it was that I saw her now in different surroundings, far from luxurious, and that our relations were by now different, or perhaps that intense grief had already set its mark upon her; she did not strike me as so elegant and well dressed as before. Her figure seemed smaller; there was an abruptness and excessive nervousness about her as though she were in a hurry, and there was not the same softness even in her smile. I was dressed in an expensive suit which I had bought during the day. She looked first of all at that suit and at the hat in my hand, then turned an impatient, searching glance upon my face as though studying it.

"Your transformation still seems to me a sort of miracle," she said. "Forgive me for looking at you with such curiosity. You are an extraordinary man, you know."

I told her again who I was, and why I was living at Orlov's, and I told her at greater length and in more detail than the day before. She listened with great attention, and said without letting me finish:

"Everything there is over for me. You know, I could not refrain from writing a letter. Here is the answer."

On the sheet which she gave there was written in Orlov's hand:

"I am not going to justify myself. But you must own that it was your mistake, not mine. I wish you happiness, and beg you to make haste and forget.

Yours sincerely,
G.O."

"P.S.—I am sending on your things."

The trunks and baskets despatched by Orlov were standing in the passage, and my poor little portmanteau was there beside them,

"So . . ." Zinaida Fyodorovna began, but she did not finish.

We were silent. She took the note and held it for a couple of minutes before her eyes, and during that time her face wore the same haughty, contemptuous, proud, and harsh expression as the day before at the beginning of our explanation; tears came into her eyes—not timid, bitter tears, but proud, angry tears.

"Listen," she said, getting up abruptly and moving away to the window that I might not see her face. "I have made up my mind to go abroad with you tomorrow."

"I am very glad. I am ready to go to-day."

"Accept me as a recruit. Have you read Balzac?" she asked suddenly, turning round. "Have you? At the end of his novel 'Père Goriot' the hero looks down upon Paris from the top of a hill and threatens the town: 'Now we shall settle our account,' and after this he begins a new life. So when I look out of the train window at Petersburg for the last time, I shall say, 'Now we shall settle our account!' "

Saying this, she smiled at her jest, and for some reason shuddered all over.

XV

At Venice I had an attack of pleurisy. Probably I had caught cold in the evening when we were rowing from the station to the Hotel Bauer. I had to take to my bed and stay there for a fortnight. Every morning while I was ill Zinaida Fyodorovna came from her room to drink coffee with me, and afterwards read aloud to me French and Russian books, of which we had bought a number at Vienna. These books were either long, long familiar to me or else had no interest for me, but I had the sound of a sweet, kind voice beside me, so that the meaning of all of them was summed up for me in the one thing—I was not alone. She would go out for a walk, come back in her light grey dress, her light straw hat, gay, warmed by the spring sun; and sitting by my bed, bending low down over me, would tell me something about Venice or read me those books—and I was happy.

At night I was cold, ill, and dreary, but by day I revelled in life—I can find no better expression for it. The brilliant warm sunshine beating in at the open windows and at the door upon the balcony, the shouts below, the splash of oars, the tinkle of bells, the prolonged boom of the cannon at midday, and the feeling of perfect, perfect freedom, did wonders with me; I felt as though I were growing strong, broad wings which were bearing me God knows whither. And what charm, what joy at times at the thought that another life was so close to mine! that I was the servant, the guardian, the friend, the indispensable fellow-traveller of a creature, young, beautiful, wealthy, but weak, lonely, and insulted! It is pleasant even to be ill when you know that there are people who are looking forward to your convalescence as to a holiday. One day I heard her whispering behind the door with my doctor, and then she came in to me with tear-stained eyes. It was a bad sign, but I was touched, and there was a wonderful lightness in my heart.

But at last they allowed me to go out on the balcony. The sunshine and the breeze from the sea caressed and fondled my sick body. I looked down at the familiar gondolas, which glide with feminine grace smoothly and majestically as though they were alive, and felt all the luxury of this original, fascinating civilisation. There was a smell of the sea. Some one was playing a stringed instrument and two voices were singing. How delightful it was! How unlike it was to that Petersburg night when the wet snow was falling and beating so rudely on our faces. If one looks straight across the canal, one sees the sea, and on the wide expanse towards the horizon the sun glittered on the water so dazzlingly that it hurt one's eyes to look at it. My soul yearned towards that lovely sea, which was so akin to me and to which I had given up my youth. I longed to live—to live—and nothing more.

A fortnight later I began walking freely. I loved to sit in the sun, and to listen to the gondoliers without understanding them, and for hours together to gaze at the little house where, they said, Desdemona lived—a naïve, mournful little house with a demure expression, as light as lace, so light that it looked as though one could lift it from its place with one hand. I stood for a long time by the tomb of Canova, and could not take my eyes off the melancholy lion. And in the Palace of the Doges I was always drawn to the corner where the portrait of the unhappy Marino Faliero was painted over with black. "It is fine to be an artist, a poet, a dramatist," I thought, "but since that is not vouchsafed to me, if only I could go in for mysticism!

If only I had a grain of some faith to add to the unruffled peace and serenity that fills the soul!"

In the evening we ate oysters, drank wine, and went out in a gondola. I remember our black gondola swayed softly in the same place while the water faintly gurgled under it. Here and there the reflection of the stars and the lights on the bank quivered and trembled. Not far from us in a gondola, hung with coloured lanterns which were reflected in the water, there were people singing. The sounds of guitars, of violins, of mandolins, of men's and women's voices, were audible in the dark. Zinaida Fyodorovna, pale, with a grave, almost stern face, was sitting beside me, compressing her lips and clenching her hands. She was thinking about something; she did not stir an eyelash, nor hear me. Her face, her attitude, and her fixed, expressionless gaze, and her incredibly miserable, dreadful, and icy-cold memories, and around her the gondolas, the lights, the music, the song with its vigorous passionate cry of *"Jam-mo! Jam-mo!"*—what contrasts in life! When she sat like that, with tightly clasped hands, stony, mournful, I used to feel as though we were both characters in some novel in the old-fashioned style called "The Ill-fated," "The Abandoned," or something of the sort. Both of us: she—the ill-fated, the abandoned; and I—the faithful, devoted friend, the dreamer, and, if you like it, a superfluous man, a failure capable of nothing but coughing and dreaming, and perhaps sacrificing myself. . . . But who and what needed my sacrifices now? And what had I to sacrifice, indeed?

When we came in in the evening we always drank tea in her room and talked. We did not shrink from touching on old, unhealed wounds—on the contrary, for some reason I felt a positive pleasure in telling her about my life at Orlov's, or referring openly to relations which I knew and which could not have been concealed from me.

"At moments I hated you," I said to her. "When he was capricious, condescending, told you lies, I marvelled how it was you did not see, did not understand, when it was all so clear! You kissed his hands, you knelt to him, you flattered him. . . ."

"When I . . . kissed his hands and knelt to him, I loved him . . ." she said, blushing crimson.

"Can it have been so difficult to see through him? A fine sphinx! A sphinx indeed—a *kammer-junker*! I reproach you for nothing, God forbid," I went on, feeling I was coarse, that I had not the tact, the delicacy which are so essential when you have to do with a fellow-creature's soul; in early days before I knew her I had not noticed this defect in myself. "But how could you fail to see what he was," I went on, speaking more softly and more diffidently, however.

"You mean to say you despise my past, and you are right," she said, deeply stirred. "You belong to a special class of men who cannot be judged by ordinary standards; your moral requirements are exceptionally rigorous, and I understand you can't forgive things. I understand you, and if sometimes I say the opposite, it doesn't mean that I look at things differently from you; I speak the same old nonsense simply because I haven't had time yet to wear out my old clothes and prejudices. I, too, hate and despise my past, and Orlov and my love. . . . What was that love? It's positively absurd now," she said, going to the window and looking down the canal. "All this love only clouds the conscience and confuses the mind. The meaning of life is to be found only in one thing—fighting. To get one's heel on the vile head of the serpent and to crush it! That's the meaning of life. In that alone or in nothing."

I told her long stories of my past, and described my really astounding adventures. But of the change that had taken place in me I did not say one word. She always listened to me with great attention, and at interesting places she rubbed her hands as though vexed that it had not yet been her lot to experience such adventures, such joys and terrors. Then she would suddenly fall to musing and retreat into herself, and I could see from her face that she was not attending to me.

I closed the windows that looked out on the canal and asked whether we should not have the fire lighted.

"No, never mind. I am not cold," she said, smiling listlessly. "I only feel weak. Do you know, I fancy I have grown much wiser lately. I have extraordinary, original ideas now. When I think of my past, of my life then . . . people in general, in fact, it is all summed up for me in the image of my stepmother. Coarse, insolent, soulless, false, depraved, and a morphia maniac too. My father, who was feeble and weak-willed, married my mother for her money and drove her into consumption; but his second wife, my stepmother, he loved passionately, insanely. . . . What I had to put up with! But what is the use of talking! And so, as I say, it is all summed up in her image. . . . And it vexes me that my stepmother is dead. I should like to meet her now!"

"Why?"

"I don't know," she answered with a laugh and a graceful move-ment of her head. "Good-night. You must get well. As soon as you are well, we'll take up our work. . . . It's time to begin."

After I had said good-night and had my hand on the door-handle, she said:

"What do you think? Is Polya still living there?"

"Probably."

And I went off to my room. So we spent a whole month. One grey morning when we both stood at my window, looking at the clouds which were moving up from the sea, and at the darkening canal, expecting every minute that it would pour with rain, and when a thick, narrow streak of rain covered the sea as though with a muslin veil, we both felt suddenly dreary. The same day we both set off for Florence.

XVI

It was autumn, at Nice. One morning when I went into her room she was sitting on a low chair, bent together and huddled up, with her legs crossed and her face hidden in her hands. She was weeping bit-terly, with sobs, and her long, unbrushed hair fell on her knees. The impression of the exquisite marvellous sea which I had only just seen and of which I wanted to tell her, left me all at once, and my heart ached.

"What is it?" I asked; she took one hand from her face and motioned me to go away. "What is it?" I repeated, and for the first time during our acquaintance I kissed her hand.

"No, it's nothing, nothing," she said quickly. "Oh, it's nothing, nothing. . . . Go away. . . . You see, I am not dressed."

I went out overwhelmed. The calm and serene mood in which I had been for so long was poisoned by compassion. I had a passionate longing to fall at her feet, to entreat her not to weep in solitude, but to share her grief with me, and the monotonous murmur of the sea already sounded a gloomy prophecy in my ears, and I foresaw fresh tears, fresh troubles, and fresh losses in the future. "What is she crying about? What is it?" I wondered, recalling her face and her agonised look. I remembered she was with child. She tried to conceal her condition from other people, and also from herself. At home she went about in a loose wrapper or in a blouse with extremely full folds over the bosom, and when she went out anywhere she laced herself in so tightly that on two occasions she fainted when we were out. She never spoke to me of her condition, and when I hinted that it might be as well to see a doctor, she flushed crimson and said not a word.

When I went to see her next time she was already dressed and had her hair done.

"There, there," I said, seeing that she was ready to cry again. "We had better go to the sea and have a talk."

"I can't talk. Forgive me, I am in the mood now when one wants to be alone. And, if you please, Vladimir Ivanitch, another time you want to come into my room, be so good as to give a knock at the door."

That "be so good" had a peculiar, unfeminine sound. I went away. My accursed Petersburg mood came back, and all my dreams were crushed and crumpled up like leaves by the heat. I felt I was alone again and there was no nearness between us. I was no more to her than that cobweb to that palm-tree, which hangs on it by chance and which will be torn off and carried away by the wind. I walked about the square where the band was playing, went into the Casino; there I looked at overdressed and heavily perfumed women, and every one of them glanced at me as though she would say: "You are alone; that's all right." Then I went out on the terrace and looked for a long time at the sea. There was not one sail on the horizon. On the left bank, in the lilac-coloured mist, there were mountains, gardens, towers, and houses, the sun was sparkling over it all, but it was all alien, indifferent, an incomprehensible tangle.

XVII

She used as before to come into my room in the morning to coffee, but we no longer dined together, as she said she was not hungry; and she lived only on coffee, tea, and various trifles such as oranges and caramels.

And we no longer had conversations in the evening. I don't know why it was like this. Ever since the day when I had found her in tears she had treated me somehow lightly, at times casually, even ironically, and for some reason called me "My good sir." What had before seemed to her terrible, heroic, marvellous, and had stirred her envy and enthusiasm, did not touch her now at all, and usually after listening to me, she stretched and said:

"Yes, 'great things were done in days of yore,' my good sir."

It sometimes happened even that I did not see her for days together. I would knock timidly and guiltily at her door and get no answer; I would knock again—still silence. . . . I would stand near the door and listen; then the chambermaid would pass and say coldly, *"Madame est partie."* Then I would walk about the passages of the hotel, walk and walk. . . . English people, full-bosomed ladies, waiters in swallow-tails. . . . And as I keep gazing at the long striped rug that stretches the whole length of the corridor, the idea occurs to me that I am playing in the life of this woman a strange, probably false part, and that it is beyond my power to alter that part. I run to my room and fall on my bed, and think and think, and can come to no conclusion; and all that is clear to me is that I want to live, and that the plainer and the colder and the harder her face grows, the nearer she is to me, and the more intensely and painfully I feel our kinship. Never mind "My good sir," never mind her light careless tone, never mind anything you like, only don't leave me, my treasure. I am afraid to be alone.

Then I go out into the corridor again, listen in a tremor. . . . I have no dinner; I don't notice the approach of evening. At last about eleven I hear the familiar footstep, and at the turn near the stairs Zinaida Fyodorovna comes into sight.

"Are you taking a walk?" she would ask as she passes me. "You had better go out into the air. . . . Good-night!"

"But shall we not meet again to-day?"

"I think it's late. But as you like."

"Tell me, where have you been?" I would ask, following her into the room.

"Where? To Monte Carlo." She took ten gold coins out of her pocket and said: "Look, my good sir; I have won. That's at roulette."

"Nonsense! As though you would gamble."

"Why not? I am going again to-morrow."

I imagined her with a sick and morbid face, in her condition, tightly laced, standing near the gaming-table in a crowd of cocottes, of old women in their dotage who swarm round the gold like flies round the honey. I remembered she had gone off to Monte Carlo for some reason in secret from me.

"I don't believe you," I said one day. "You wouldn't go there."

"Don't agitate yourself. I can't lose much."

"It's not the question of what you lose," I said with annoyance. "Has it never occurred to you while you were playing there that the glitter of gold, all these women, young and old, the croupiers, all the surroundings—that it is all a vile, loathsome mockery at the toiler's labour, at his bloody sweat?"

"If one doesn't play, what is one to do here?" she asked. "The toiler's labour and his bloody sweat—all that eloquence you can put off till another time; but now, since you have begun, let me go on. Let me ask you bluntly, what is there for me to do here, and what am I to do?"

"What are you to do?" I said, shrugging my shoulders. "That's a question that can't be answered straight off."

"I beg you to answer me honestly, Vladimir Ivanitch," she said, and her face looked angry. "Once I have brought myself to ask you this question, I am not going to listen to stock phrases. I am asking you," she went on, beating her hand on the table, as though marking time, "what ought I to do here? And not only here at Nice, but in general?"

I did not speak, but looked out of window to the sea. My heart was beating terribly.

"Vladimir Ivanitch," she said softly and breathlessly; it was hard for her to speak—"Vladimir Ivanitch, if you do not believe in the cause yourself, if you no longer think of going back to it, why . . . why did you drag me out of Petersburg? Why did you make me promises, why did you rouse mad hopes? Your convictions have changed; you have become a different man, and nobody blames you for it—our convictions are not always in our power. But . . . but, Vladimir Ivanitch, for God's sake, why are you not sincere?" she went on softly, coming up to me. "All these months when I have been dreaming aloud, raving, going into raptures over my plans, remodelling my life on a new pattern, why didn't you tell me the truth? Why were you silent or encouraged me by your stories, and behaved as though you were in complete sympathy with me? Why was it? Why was it necessary?"

"It's difficult to acknowledge one's bankruptcy," I said, turning round, but not looking at her. "Yes, I have no faith; I am worn out. I have lost heart. . . . It is difficult to be truthful—very difficult, and I held my tongue. God forbid that any one should have to go through what I have been through."

I felt that I was on the point of tears, and ceased speaking.

"Vladimir Ivanitch," she said, and took me by both hands, "you have been through so much and seen so much of life, you know more than I do; think seriously, and tell me, what am I to do? Teach me! If you haven't the strength to go forward yourself and take others with you, at least show me where to go. After all, I am a living, feeling, thinking being. To sink into a false position . . . to play an absurd part . . . is painful to me. I don't reproach you, I don't blame you; I only ask you."

Tea was brought in.

"Well?" said Zinaida Fyodorovna, giving me a glass. "What do you say to me?"

"There is more light in the world than you see through your window," I answered. "And there are other people besides me, Zinaida Fyodorovna."

"Then tell me who they are," she said eagerly. "That's all I ask of you."

"And I want to say, too," I went on, "one can serve an idea in more than one calling. If one has made a mistake and lost faith in one, one may find another. The world of ideas is large and cannot be exhausted."

"The world of ideas!" she said, and she looked into my face sarcastically. "Then we had better leave off talking. What's the use? . . ."

She flushed.

"The world of ideas!" she repeated. She threw her dinner-napkin aside, and an expression of indignation and contempt came into her face. "All your fine ideas, I see, lead up to one inevitable, essential step: I ought to become your mistress. That's what's wanted. To be taken up with ideas without being the mistress of an honourable, progressive man, is as good as not understanding the ideas. One has to begin with that . . . that is, with being your mistress, and the rest will come of itself."

"You are irritated, Zinaida Fyodorovna," I said.

"No, I am sincere!" she cried, breathing hard. "I am sincere!"

"You are sincere, perhaps, but you are in error, and it hurts me to hear you."

"I am in error?" she laughed. "Any one else might say that, but not you, my dear sir! I may seem to you indelicate, cruel, but I don't care: you love me? You love me, don't you?"

I shrugged my shoulders.

"Yes, shrug your shoulders!" she went on sarcastically. "When you were ill I heard you in your delirium, and ever since these adoring eyes, these sighs, and edifying conversations about friendship, about spiritual kinship. . . . But the point is, why haven't you been sincere? Why have you concealed what is and talked about what isn't? Had you said from the beginning what ideas exactly led you to drag me from Petersburg, I should have known. I should have poisoned myself then as I meant to, and there would have been none of this tedious farce. . . . But what's the use of talking!"

With a wave of the hand she sat down.

"You speak to me as though you suspected me of dishonourable intentions," I said, offended.

"Oh, very well. What's the use of talking! I don't suspect you of intentions, but of having no intentions. If you had any, I should have known them by now. You had nothing but ideas and love. For the present—ideas and love, and in prospect—me as your mistress. That's in the order of things both in life and in novels. . . . Here you abused him," she said, and she slapped the table with her hand, "but one can't help agreeing with him. He has good reasons for despising these ideas."

"He does not despise ideas; he is afraid of them," I cried. "He is a coward and a liar."

"Oh, very well. He is a coward and a liar, and deceived me. And you? Excuse my frankness; what are you? He deceived me and left me to take my chance in Petersburg, and you have deceived me and abandoned me here. But he did not mix up ideas with his deceit, and you . . ."

"For goodness' sake, why are you saying this?" I cried in horror, wringing my hands and going up to her quickly. "No, Zinaida Fyodorovna, this is cynicism. You must not be so despairing; listen to me," I went on, catching at a thought which flashed dimly upon me, and which seemed to me might still save us both. "Listen. I have passed through so many experiences in my time that my head goes round at the thought of them, and I have realised with my mind, with my racked soul, that man finds his true destiny in nothing if not in self-sacrificing love for his neighbour. It is towards that we must strive, and that is our destination! That is my faith!"

I wanted to go on to speak of mercy, of forgiveness, but there was an insincere note in my voice, and I was embarrassed.

"I want to live!" I said genuinely. "To live, to live! I want peace, tranquillity; I want warmth—this sea here—to have you near. Oh, how I wish I could rouse in you the same thirst for life! You spoke just now of love, but it would be enough for me to have you near, to hear your voice, to watch the look in your face . . . !"

She flushed crimson, and to hinder my speaking, said quickly:

"You love life, and I hate it. So our ways lie apart."

She poured herself out some tea, but did not touch it, went into the bedroom, and lay down.

"I imagine it is better to cut short this conversation," she said to me from within. "Everything is over for me, and I want nothing. . . . What more is there to say?"

"No, it's not all over!"

"Oh, very well! . . . I know! I am sick of it. . . . That's enough."

I got up, took a turn from one end of the room to the other, and went out into the corridor. When late at night I went to her door and listened, I distinctly heard her crying.

Next morning the waiter, handing me my clothes, informed me, with a smile, that the lady in number thirteen was confined. I dressed somehow, and almost fainting with terror ran to Zinaida Fyodorovna. In her room I found a doctor, a midwife, and an elderly Russian lady from Harkov, called Darya Milhailovna. There was a smell of ether. I had scarcely crossed the threshold when from the room where she was lying I heard a low, plaintive moan, and, as though it had been wafted me by the wind from Russia, I thought of Orlov, his irony, Polya, the Neva, the drifting snow, then the cab without an apron, the prediction I had read in the cold morning sky, and the despairing cry "Nina! Nina!"

"Go in to her," said the lady.

I went in to see Zinaida Fyodorovna, feeling as though I were the father of the child. She was lying with her eyes closed, looking thin and pale, wearing a white cap edged with lace. I remember there were two expressions on her face: one—cold, indifferent, apathetic; the other—a look of childish helplessness given her by the white cap. She did not hear me come in, or heard, perhaps, but did not pay attention. I stood, looked at her, and waited.

But her face was contorted with pain; she opened her eyes and gazed at the ceiling, as though wondering what was happening to her. . . . There was a look of loathing on her face.

"It's horrible . . ." she whispered.

"Zinaida Fyodorovna." I spoke her name softly. She looked at me indifferently, listlessly, and closed her eyes. I stood there a little while, then went away.

At night, Darya Mihailovna informed me that the child, a girl, was born, but that the mother was in a dangerous condition. Then I heard noise and bustle in the passage. Darya Mihailovna came to me again and with a face of despair, wringing her hands, said:

"Oh, this is awful! The doctor suspects that she has taken poison! Oh, how badly Russians do behave here!"

And at twelve o'clock the next day Zinaida Fyodorovna died.

XVIII

Two years had passed. Circumstances had changed; I had come to Petersburg again and could live here openly. I was no longer afraid of being and seeming sentimental, and gave myself up entirely to the fatherly, or rather idolatrous feeling roused in me by Sonya, Zinaida Fyodorovna's child. I fed her with my own hands, gave her her bath, put her to bed, never took my eyes off her for nights together, and screamed when it seemed to me that the nurse was just going to drop her. My thirst for normal ordinary life became stronger and more acute as time went on, but wider visions stopped short at Sonya, as though I had found in her at last just what I needed. I loved the child madly. In her I saw the continuation of my life, and it was not exactly that I fancied, but I felt, I almost believed, that when I had cast off at last my long, bony, bearded frame, I should go on living in those little blue eyes, that silky flaxen hair, those dimpled pink hands which stroked my face so lovingly and were clasped round my neck.

Sonya's future made me anxious. Orlov was her father; in her birth certificate she was called Krasnovsky, and the only person who knew of her existence, and took interest in her—that is, I—was at death's door. I had to think about her seriously.

The day after I arrived in Petersburg I went to see Orlov. The door was opened to me by a stout old fellow with red whiskers and no moustache, who looked like a German. Polya, who was tidying the drawing-room, did not recognise me, but Orlov knew me at once.

"Ah, Mr. Revolutionist!" he said, looking at me with curiosity, and laughing. "What fate has brought you?"

He was not changed in the least: the same well-groomed, unpleasant face, the same irony. And a new book was lying on the table just as of old, with an ivory paper-knife thrust in it. He had evidently been reading before I came in. He made me sit down, offered me a cigar, and with a delicacy only found in well-bred people, concealing the unpleasant feeling aroused by my face and my wasted figure, observed casually that I was not in the least changed, and that he would have known me anywhere in spite of my having grown a beard. We talked of the weather, of Paris. To dispose as quickly as possible of the oppressive, inevitable question, which weighed upon him and me, he asked:

"Zinaida Fyodorovna is dead?"

"Yes," I answered.

"In childbirth?"

"Yes, in childbirth. The doctor suspected another cause of death, but . . . it is more comforting for you and for me to think that she died in childbirth."

He sighed decorously and was silent. The angel of silence passed over us, as they say.

"Yes. And here everything is as it used to be—no changes," he said briskly, seeing that I was looking about the room. "My father, as you know, has left the service and is living in retirement; I am still in the same department. Do you remember Pekarsky? He is just the same as ever. Gruzin died of diphtheria a year ago. . . . Kukushkin is alive, and often speaks of you. By the way," said Orlov, dropping his eyes with an air of reserve, "when Kukushkin heard who you were, he began telling every one you had attacked him and tried to murder him . . . and that he only just escaped with his life."

I did not speak.

"Old servants do not forget their masters. . . . It's very nice of you," said Orlov jocosely. "Will you have some wine and some coffee, though? I will tell them to make some."

"No, thank you. I have come to see you about a very important matter, Georgy Ivanitch."

"I am not very fond of important matters, but I shall be glad to be of service to you. What do you want?"

"You see," I began, growing agitated, "I have here with me Zinaida Fyodorovna's daughter. . . . Hitherto I have brought her up, but, as you see, before many days I shall be an empty sound. I should like to die with the thought that she is provided for."

Orlov coloured a little, frowned a little, and took a cursory and sullen glance at me. He was unpleasantly affected, not so much by the "important matter" as by my words about death, about becoming an empty sound.

"Yes, it must be thought about," he said, screening his eyes as though from the sun. "Thank you. You say it's a girl?"

"Yes, a girl. A wonderful child!"

"Yes. Of course, it's not a lap-dog, but a human being. I understand we must consider it seriously. I am prepared to do my part, and am very grateful to you."

He got up, walked about, biting his nails, and stopped before a picture.

"We must think about it," he said in a hollow voice, standing with his back to me. "I shall go to Pekarsky's to-day and will ask him to go to Krasnovsky's. I don't think he will make much ado about consenting to take the child."

"But, excuse me, I don't see what Krasnovsky has got to do with it," I said, also getting up and walking to a picture at the other end of the room.

"But she bears his name, of course!" said Orlov.

"Yes, he may be legally obliged to accept the child—I don't know; but I came to you, Georgy Ivanitch, not to discuss the legal aspect."

"Yes, yes, you are right," he agreed briskly. "I believe I am talking nonsense. But don't excite yourself. We will decide the matter to our mutual satisfaction. If one thing won't do, we'll try another; and if that won't do, we'll try a third—one way or another this delicate question shall be settled. Pekarsky will arrange it all. Be so good as to leave me your address and I will let you know at once what we decide. Where are you living?"

Orlov wrote down my address, sighed, and said with a smile:

"Oh, Lord, what job it is to be the father of a little daughter! But Pekarsky will arrange it all. He is a sensible man. Did you stay long in Paris?"

"Two months."

We were silent. Orlov was evidently afraid I should begin talking of the child again, and to turn my attention in another direction, said:

"You have probably forgotten your letter by now. But I have kept it. I understand your mood at the time, and, I must own, I respect that letter. 'Damnable cold blood,' 'Asiatic,' 'coarse laugh'—that was charming and characteristic," he went on with an ironical smile. "And the fundamental thought is perhaps near the truth, though one might dispute the question endlessly. That is," he hesitated, "not dispute the thought itself, but your attitude to the question—your temperament, so to say. Yes, my life is abnormal, corrupted, of no use to any one, and what prevents me from beginning a new life is cowardice—there you are quite right. But that you take it so much to heart, are troubled, and reduced to despair by it—that's irrational; there you are quite wrong."

"A living man cannot help being troubled and reduced to despair when he sees that he himself is going to ruin and others are going to ruin round him."

"Who doubts it! I am not advocating indifference; all I ask for is an objective attitude to life. The more objective, the less danger of falling into error. One must look into the root of things, and try to see in every phenomenon a cause of all the other causes. We have grown feeble, slack—degraded, in fact. Our generation is entirely composed of neurasthenics and whimperers; we do nothing but talk of fatigue and exhaustion. But the fault is neither yours nor mine; we are of too little consequence to affect the destiny of a whole generation. We must suppose for that larger, more general causes with a solid *raison d'être* from the biological point of view. We are neurasthenics, flabby, renegades, but perhaps it's necessary and of service for generations that will come after us. Not one hair falls from the head without the will of the Heavenly Father—in other words, nothing happens by chance in Nature and in human environment. Everything has its cause and is inevitable. And if so, why should we worry and write despairing letters?"

"That's all very well," I said, thinking a little. "I believe it will be easier and clearer for the generations to come; our experience will be at their service. But one wants to live apart from future generations and not only for their sake. Life is only given us once, and one wants to live it boldly, with full consciousness and beauty. One wants to play a striking, independent, noble part; one wants to make history so that those generations may not have the right to say of each of us that we were nonentities or worse. . . . I believe what is going on about us is inevitable and not without a purpose, but what have I to do with that inevitability? Why should my *ego* be lost?"

"Well, there's no help for it," sighed Orlov, getting up and, as it were, giving me to understand that our conversation was over.

I took my hat.

"We've only been sitting her half an hour, and how many questions we have settled, when you come to think of it!" said Orlov, seeing me into the hall. "So I will see to that matter. . . . I will see Pekarsky to-day. . . . Don't be uneasy."

He stood waiting while I put on my coat, and was obviously relieved at the feeling that I was going away.

"Georgy Ivanitch, give me back my letter," I said.

"Certainly."

He went to his study, and a minute later returned with the letter. I thanked him and went away.

The next day I got a letter from him. He congratulated me on the satisfactory settlement of the question. Pekarsky knew a lady, he wrote, who kept a school, something like a kindergarten, where she took quite little children. The lady could be entirely depended upon, but before concluding anything with her it would be as well to discuss the matter with Krasnovsky—it was a matter of form. He advised me to see Pekarsky at once and to take the birth certificate with me, if I had it. "Rest assured of the sincere respect and devotion of your humble servant. . . ."

I read this letter, and Sonya sat on the table and gazed at me attentively without blinking, as though she knew her fate was being decided.

1893

Peasants

Nikolay Tchikildyeev, a waiter in the Moscow hotel, Slavyanksy Bazaar, was taken ill. His legs went numb and his gait was affected, so that on one occasion, as he was going along the corridor, he tumbled and fell down with a tray full of ham and peas. He had to leave his job. All his own savings and his wife's were spent on doctors and medicines; they had nothing left to live upon. He felt dull with no work to do, and he made up his mind he must go home to the village. It is better to be ill at home, and living there is cheaper; and it is a true saying that the walls of home are a help.

He reached Zhukovo towards evening. In his memories of childhood he had pictured his home as bright, snug, comfortable. Now, going into the hut, he was positively frightened; it was so dark, so crowded, so unclean. His wife Olga and his daughter Sasha, who had come with him, kept looking in bewilderment at the big untidy stove, which filled up almost half the hut and was black with soot and flies. What lots of flies! The stove was on one side, the beams lay slanting on the walls, and it looked as though the hut were just going to fall to pieces. In the corner, facing the door, under the holy images, bottle labels and newspaper cuttings were stuck on the walls instead of pictures. The poverty, the poverty! Of the grown-up people there were none at home; all were at work at the harvest. On the stove was sitting a white-headed girl of eight, unwashed and apathetic; she did not even glance at them as they came in. On the floor a white cat was rubbing itself against the oven fork.

"Puss, puss!" Sasha called to her. "Puss!"

"She can't hear," said the little girl; "she has gone deaf."

"How is that?"

"Oh, she was beaten."

Nikolay and Olga realized from the first glance what life was like here, but said nothing to one another; in silence they put down their bundles, and went out into the village street. Their hut was the third from the end, and seemed the very poorest and oldest-looking; the second was not much better; but the last one had an iron roof, and curtains in the windows. That hut stood apart, not enclosed; it was a tavern. The huts were in a single row, and the whole of the little village—quiet and dreamy, with willows, elders, and mountain-ash trees peeping out from the yards—had an attractive look.

Beyond the peasants' homesteads there was a slope down to the river, so steep and precipitous that huge stones jutted out bare here and there through the clay. Down the slope, among the stones and holes dug by the potters, ran winding paths; bits of broken pottery, some brown, some red, lay piled up in heaps, and below there stretched a broad, level, bright green meadow, from which the hay had been already carried, and in which the peasants' cattle were wandering. The river three-quarters of a mile from the village, ran twisting and turning, with beautiful leafy banks; beyond it was again a broad meadow, a herd of cattle, long strings of white geese; then, just as on the near side, a steep ascent uphill, and on the top of the hill a hamlet, and a church with five domes, and at a little distance the manor-house.

"It's lovely here in your parts!" said Olga, crossing herself at the sight of the church. "What space, oh Lord!"

Just at that moment the bell began ringing for service (it was Saturday evening). Two little girls, down below, who were dragging up a pail of water, looked round at the church to listen to the bell.

"At this time they are serving the dinners at the Slavyansky Bazaar," said Nikolay dreamily.

Sitting on the edge of the slope, Nikolay and Olga watched the sun setting, watched the gold and crimson sky reflected in the river, in the church windows, and in the whole air—which was soft and still and unutterably pure as it never was in Moscow. And when the sun had set the flocks and herds passed, bleating and lowing; geese flew across from the further side of the river, and all sank into silence; the soft light died away in the air, and the dusk of evening began quickly moving down upon them.

Meanwhile Nikolay's father and mother, two gaunt, bent, toothless old people, just of the same height, came back. The women—the sisters-in-law Marya and Fyokla—who had been working on the landowner's estate beyond the river, arrived home, too. Marya, the wife of Nikolay's brother Kiryak, had six children, and Fyokla, the wife of Nikolay's brother Denis—who had gone for a soldier—had two; and when Nikolay, going into the hut, saw all the family, all those bodies big and little moving about on the lockers, in the hanging cradles and in all the corners, and when he saw the greed with which the old father and the women ate the black bread, dipping it in water, he realized he had made a mistake in coming here, sick, penniless, and with a family, too—a great mistake!

"And where is Kiryak?" he asked after they had exchanged greetings.

"He is in service at the merchant's," answered his father; "a keeper in the woods. He is not a bad peasant; but too fond of his glass."

"He is no great help!" said the old woman tearfully. "Our men are a grievous lot; they bring nothing into the house, but take plenty out. Kiryak drinks, and so does the old man; it is no use hiding a sin; he knows his way to the tavern. The Heavenly Mother is wroth."

In honour of the visitors they brought out the samovar. The tea smelt of fish; the sugar was grey and looked as though it had been nibbled; cockroaches ran to and fro over the bread and among the crockery. It was disgusting to drink, and the conversation was disgusting, too—about nothing but poverty and illnesses. But before they had time to empty their first cups there came a loud, prolonged, drunken shout from the yard:

"Ma-arya!"

"It looks as though Kiryak were coming," said the old man. "Speak of the devil."

All were hushed. And again, soon afterwards, the same shout, coarse and drawn-out as though it came out of the earth:

"Ma-arya!"

Marya, the elder sister-in-law, turned pale and huddled against the stove, and it was strange to see the look of terror on the face of the strong, broad-shouldered, ugly woman. Her daughter, the child who had been sitting on the stove and looked so apathetic, suddenly broke into loud weeping.

"What are you howling for, you plague?" Fyokla, a handsome woman, also strong and broad-shouldered, shouted to her. "He won't kill you, no fear!"

From his old father Nikolay learned that Marya was afraid to live in the forest with Kiryak, and that when he was drunk, he always came for her, made a row, and beat her mercilessly.

"Ma-arya!" the shout sounded close to the door.

"Protect me, for Christ's sake, good people!" faltered Marya, breathing as though she had been plunged into very cold water. "Protect me, kind people. . . ."

All the children in the hut began crying, and looking at them, Sasha, too, began to cry. They heard a drunken cough, and a tall, black-bearded peasant wearing a winter cap came into the hut, and was the more terrible because his face could not be seen in the dim light of the little lamp. It was Kiryak. Going up to his wife, he swung his arm and punched her in the face with his fist. Stunned by the blow, she did not utter a sound, but sat down, and her nose instantly began bleeding.

"What a disgrace! What a disgrace!" muttered the old man, clambering up on to the stove. "Before visitors, too! It's a sin!"

The old mother sat silent, bowed, lost in thought; Fyokla rocked the cradle.

Evidently conscious of inspiring fear, and pleased at doing so, Kiryak seized Marya by the arm, dragged her towards the door, and bellowed like an animal in order to seem still more terrible; but at that moment he suddenly caught sight of the visitors and stopped.

"Oh, they have come, . . ." he said, letting his wife go; "my own brother and his family. . . ."

Staggering and opening wide his red, drunken eyes, he said his prayer before the image and went on:

"My brother and his family have come to the parental home . . . from Moscow, I suppose. The great capital Moscow, to be sure, the mother of cities. . . . Excuse me."

He sank down on the bench near the samovar and began drinking tea, sipping it loudly from the saucer in the midst of general silence. . . . He drank off a dozen cups, then reclined on the bench and began snoring.

They began going to bed. Nikolay, as an invalid, was put on the stove with his old father; Sasha lay down on the floor, while Olga went with the other women into the barn.

"Aye, aye, dearie," she said, lying down on the hay beside Marya; "you won't mend your trouble with tears. Bear it in patience, that is all. It is written in the Scriptures: 'If anyone smite thee on the right cheek, offer him the left one also.' . . . Aye, aye, dearie."

Then in a low singsong murmur she told them about Moscow, about her own life, how she had been a servant in furnished lodgings.

"And in Moscow the houses are big, built of brick," she said; "and there are ever so many churches, forty times forty, dearie; and they are all gentry in the houses, so handsome and so proper!"

Marya told her that she had not only never been in Moscow, but had not even been in their own district town; she could not read or write, and knew no prayers, not even "Our Father." Both she and Fyokla, the other sister-in-law, who was sitting a little way off listening, were extremely ignorant and could understand nothing. They both disliked their husbands; Marya was afraid of Kiryak, and whenever he stayed with her she was shaking with fear, and always got a headache from the fumes of vodka and tobacco with which he reeked. And in answer to the question whether she did not miss her husband, Fyokla answered with vexation:

"Miss him!"

They talked a little and sank into silence.

It was cool, and a cock crowed at the top of his voice near the barn, preventing them from sleeping. When the bluish morning light was already peeping through all the crevices, Fyokla got up stealthily and went out, and then they heard the sound of her bare feet running off somewhere.

II

Olga went to church, and took Marya with her. As they went down the path towards the meadow both were in good spirits. Olga liked the wide view, and Marya felt that in her sister-in-law she had someone near and akin to her. The sun was rising. Low down over the meadow floated a drowsy hawk. The river looked gloomy; there was a haze hovering over it here and there, but on the further bank a streak of light already stretched across the hill. The church was gleaming, and in the manor garden the rooks were cawing furiously.

"The old man is all right," Marya told her, "but Granny is strict; she is continually nagging. Our own grain lasted till Carnival. We buy flour now at the tavern. She is angry about it; she says we eat too much."

"Aye, aye, dearie! Bear it in patience, that is all. It is written: 'Come unto Me, all ye that labour and are heavy laden.' "

Olga spoke sedately, rhythmically, and she walked like a pilgrim woman, with a rapid, anxious step. Every day she read the gospel, read it aloud like a deacon; a great deal of it she did not understand, but the words of the gospel moved her to tears, and words like "forasmuch as" and "verily" she pronounced with a sweet flutter at her heart. She believed in God, in the Holy Mother, in the Saints; she believed one must not offend anyone in the world—not simple folks, nor Germans, nor gypsies, nor Jews—and woe even to those who have no compassion on the beasts. She believed this was written in the Holy Scriptures; and so, when she pronounced phrases from Holy Writ, even though she did not understand them, her face grew softened, compassionate, and radiant.

"What part do you come from?" Marya asked her.

"I am from Vladimir. Only I was taken to Moscow long ago, when I was eight years old."

They reached the river. On the further side a woman was standing at the water's edge, undressing.

"It's our Fyokla," said Marya, recognizing her. "She has been over the river to the manor yard. To the stewards. She is a shameless hussy and foulmouthed—fearfully!"

Fyokla, young and vigorous as a girl, with her black eyebrows and her loose hair, jumped off the bank and began splashing the water with her feet, and waves ran in all directions from her.

"Shameless—dreadfully!" repeated Marya.

The river was crossed by a rickety little bridge of logs, and exactly below it in the clear, limpid water was a shoal of broad-headed mullets. The dew was glistening on the green bushes that looked into the water. There was a feeling of warmth; it was comforting! What a lovely morning! And how lovely life would have been in this world, in all likelihood, if it were not for poverty, horrible, hopeless poverty, from which one can find no refuge! One had only to look round at the village to remember vividly all that had happened the day before, and the illusion of happiness which seemed to surround them vanished instantly.

They reached the church. Marya stood at the entrance, and did not dare to go farther. She did not dare to sit down either. Though they only began ringing for mass between eight and nine, she remained standing the whole time.

While the gospel was being read the crowd suddenly parted to make way for the family from the great house. Two young girls in white frocks and wide-brimmed hats walked in; with them a chubby, rosy boy in a sailor suit. Their appearance touched Olga; she made up her mind from the first glance that they were refined, well-educated, handsome people. Marya looked at them from under her brows, sullenly, dejectedly, as though they were not human beings coming in, but monsters who might crush her if she did not make way for them.

And every time the deacon boomed out something in his bass voice she fancied she heard "Ma-arya!" and she shuddered.

III

The arrival of the visitors was already known in the village, and directly after mass a number of people gathered together in the hut. The Leonytchevs and Matvyeitchevs and the Ilyitchovs came to inquire about their relations who were in service in Moscow. All the lads of Zhukovo who could read and write were packed off to Moscow and hired out as butlers and waiters (while from the village on the other side of the river the boys all became bakers), and that had been the custom from the days of serfdom long ago when a certain Luka Ivanitch, a peasant from Zhukovo, now a legendary figure, who had been a waiter in one of the Moscow clubs, would take none but his fellow-villagers into his service, and found jobs for them in taverns and restaurants; and from that time the village of Zhukovo was always called among the inhabitants of the surrounding districts Slaveytown. Nikolay had been taken to Moscow when he was eleven, and Ivan Makaritch, one of the Matvyeitchevs, at that time a head-waiter in the "Hermitage" garden, had put him into a situation. And now, addressing the Matvyeitchevs, Nikolay said emphatically:

"Ivan Makaritch was my benefactor, and I am bound to pray for him day and night, as it is owing to him I have become a good man."

"My good soul!" a tall old woman, the sister of Ivan Makaritch, said tearfully, "and not a word have we heard about him, poor dear."

"In the winter he was in service at Omon's, and this season there was a rumour he was somewhere out of town, in gardens. . . . He has aged! In old days he would bring home as much as ten roubles a day in the summer-time, but now things are very quiet everywhere. The old man frets."

The women looked at Nikolay's feet, shod in felt boots, and at his pale face, and said mournfully:

"You are not one to get on, Nikolay Osipitch; you are not one to get on! No, indeed!"

And they all made much of Sasha. She was ten years old, but she was little and very thin, and might have been taken for no more than seven. Among the other little girls, with their sunburnt faces and roughly cropped hair, dressed in long faded smocks, she with her white little face, with her big dark eyes, with a red ribbon in her hair, looked funny, as though she were some little wild creature that had been caught and brought into the hut.

"She can read, too," Olga said in her praise, looking tenderly at her daughter. "Read a little, child!" she said, taking the gospel from the corner. "You read, and the good Christian people will listen."

The testament was an old and heavy one in leather binding, with dog's-eared edges, and it exhaled a smell as though monks had come into the hut. Sasha raised her eyebrows and began in a loud rhythmic chant:

" 'And the angel of the Lord . . . appeared unto Joseph, saying unto him: Rise up, and take the Babe and His mother.' "

"The Babe and His mother," Olga repeated, and flushed all over with emotion.

" 'And flee into Egypt, . . . and tarry there until such time as . . .' "

At the word "tarry" Olga could not refrain from tears. Looking at her, Marya began to whimper, and after her Ivan Makaritch's sister. The old father cleared his throat, and bustled about to find something to give his granddaughter, but, finding nothing, gave it up with a wave of his hand. And when the reading was over the neighbors dispersed to their homes, feeling touched and very much pleased with Olga and Sasha.

As it was a holiday, the family spent the whole day at home. The old woman, whom her husband, her daughters-in-law, her grandchildren all alike called Granny, tried to do everything herself; she heated the stove and set the samovar with her own hands, even waited at the midday meal, and then complained that she was worn out with work. And all the time she was uneasy for fear someone should eat a piece too much, or that her husband and daughters-in-law would sit idle. At one time she would hear the tavern-keeper's geese going at the back of the huts to her kitchen-garden, and she would run out of the hut with a long stick and spend half an hour screaming shrilly by her cabbages, which were as gaunt and scraggy as herself; at another time she fancied that a crow had designs on her chickens, and she rushed to attack it with loud words of abuse. She was cross and grumbling from morning till night. And often she raised such an outcry that passers-by stopped in the street.

She was not affectionate towards the old man, reviling him as a lazy-bones and a plague. He was not a responsible, reliable peasant, and perhaps if she had not been continually nagging at him he would not have worked at all, but would have simply sat on the stove and talked. He talked to his son at great length about certain enemies of his, complained of the insults he said he had to put up with every day from the neighbours, and it was tedious to listen to him.

"Yes," he would say, standing with his arms akimbo, "yes. . . . A week after the Exaltation of the Cross I sold my hay willingly at thirty kopecks a pood. . . . Well and good. . . . So you see I was taking the hay in the morning with a good will; I was interfering with no one. In an unlucky hour I see the village elder, Antip Syedelnikov, coming out of the tavern. 'Where are you taking it, you ruffian?' says he, and takes me by the ear."

Kiryak had a fearful headache after his drinking bout, and was ashamed to face his brother.

"What vodka does! Ah, my God!" he muttered, shaking his aching head. "For Christ's sake, forgive me, brother and sister; I'm not happy myself."

As it was a holiday, they bought a herring at the tavern and made a soup of the herring's head. At midday they all sat down to drink tea, and went on drinking it for a long time, till they were all perspiring; they looked positively swollen from the tea-drinking, and after it began sipping the broth from the herring's head, all helping themselves out of one bowl. But the herring itself Granny had hidden.

In the evening a potter began firing pots on the ravine. In the meadow below the girls got up a choral dance and sang songs. They played the concertina. And on the other side of the river a kiln for baking pots was lighted, too, and the girls sang songs, and in the distance the singing sounded soft and musical. The peasants were noisy in and about the tavern. They were singing with drunken voices, each on his own account, and swearing at one another, so that Olga could only shudder and say:

"Oh, holy Saints!"

She was amazed that the abuse was incessant, and those who were loudest and most persistent in this foul language were the old men who were so near their end. And the girls and children heard the swearing, and were not in the least disturbed by it, and it was evident that they were used to it from their cradles.

It was past midnight, the kilns on both sides of the river were put out, but in the meadow below and in the tavern the merrymaking still went on. The old father and Kiryak, both drunk, walking arm-in-arm and jostling against each other's shoulders, went to the barn where Olga and Marya were lying.

"Let her alone," the old man persuaded him; "let her alone. . . . She is a harmless woman. . . . It's a sin. . . ."

"Ma-arya!" shouted Kiryak.

"Let her be. . . . It's a sin. . . . She is not a bad woman."

Both stopped by the barn and went on.

"I lo-ove the flowers of the fi-ield," the old man began singing suddenly in a high, piercing tenor. "I lo-ove to gather them in the meadows!"

Then he spat, and with a filthy oath went into the hut.

IV

Granny put Sasha by her kitchen-garden and told her to keep watch that the geese did not go in. It was a hot August day. The tavernkeeper's geese could make their way into the kitchen-garden by the backs of the huts, but now they were busily engaged picking up oats by the tavern, peacefully conversing together, and only the gander craned his head high as though trying to see whether the old woman were coming with her stick. The other geese might come up from below, but they were now grazing far away the other side of the river, stretched out in a long white garland about the meadow. Sasha stood about a little, grew weary, and, seeing that the geese were not coming, went away to the ravine.

There she saw Marya's eldest daughter Motka, who was standing motionless on a big stone, staring at the church. Marya had given birth to thirteen children, but she only had six living, all girls, not one boy, and the eldest was eight. Motka in a long smock was standing barefooted in the full sunshine; the sun was blazing down right on her head, but she did not notice that, and seemed as though turned to stone. Sasha stood beside her and said, looking at the church:

"God lives in the church. Men have lamps and candles, but God has little green and red and blue lamps like little eyes. At night God walks about the church, and with Him the Holy Mother of God and Saint Nikolay, thud, thud, thud! . . . And the watchman is terrified, terrified! Aye, aye, dearie," she added, imitating her mother. "And when the end of the world comes all the churches will be carried up to heaven."

"With the-ir be-ells?" Motka asked in her deep voice, drawling every syllable.

"With their bells. And when the end of the world comes the good will go to Paradise, but the angry will burn in fire eternal and unquenchable, dearie. To my mother as well as to Marya God will say: 'You never offended anyone, and for that go to the right to Paradise'; but to Kiryak and Granny He will say: 'You go to the left into the fire.' And anyone who has eaten meat in Lent will go into the fire, too."

She looked upwards at the sky, opening wide her eyes, and said:

"Look at the sky without winking, you will see angels."

Motka began looking at the sky, too, and a minute passed in silence.

"Do you see them?" asked Sasha.

"I don't," said Motka in her deep voice.

"But I do. Little angels are flying about the sky and flap, flap with their little wings as though they were gnats."

Motka thought for a little, with her eyes on the ground, and asked:

"Will Granny burn?"

"She will, dearie."

From the stone an even gentle slope ran down to the bottom, covered with soft green grass, which one longed to lie down on or to touch with one's hands. . . . Sasha lay down and rolled to the bottom. Motka with a grave, severe face, taking a deep breath, lay down, too, and rolled to the bottom, and in doing so tore her smock from the hem to the shoulder.

"What fun it is!" said Sasha, delighted.

They walked up to the top to roll down again, but at that moment they heard a shrill, familiar voice. Oh, how awful it was! Granny, a toothless, bony, hunchbacked figure, with short grey hair which was fluttering in the wind, was driving the geese out of the kitchen-garden with a long stick, shouting.

"They have trampled all the cabbages, the damned brutes! I'd cut your throats, thrice accursed plagues! Bad luck to you!"

She saw the little girls, flung down the stick and picked up a switch, and, seizing Sasha by the neck with her fingers, thin and hard as the gnarled branches of a tree, began whipping her. Sasha cried with pain and terror, while the gander, waddling and stretching his neck, went up to the old woman and hissed at her, and when he went back to his flock all the geese greeted him approvingly with "Ga-ga-ga!" Then Granny proceeded to whip Motka, and in this Motka's smock was torn again. Feeling in despair, and crying loudly, Sasha went to the hut to complain. Motka followed her; she, too, was crying on a deeper note, without wiping her tears, and her face was as wet as though it had been dipped in water.

"Holy Saints!" cried Olga, aghast, as the two came into the hut. "Queen of Heaven!"

Sasha began telling her story, while at the same time Granny walked in with a storm of shrill cries and abuse; then Fyokla flew into a rage, and there was an uproar in the hut.

"Never mind, never mind!" Olga, pale and upset, tried to comfort them, stroking Sasha's head. "She is your grandmother; it's a sin to be angry with her. Never mind, my child."

Nikolay, who was worn out already by the everlasting hubbub, hunger, stifling fumes, filth, who hated and despised the poverty, who was ashamed for his wife and daughter to see his father and mother, swung his legs off the stove and said in an irritable, tearful voice, addressing his mother:

"You must not beat her! You have no right to beat her!"

"You lie rotting on the stove, you wretched creature!" Fyokla shouted at him spitefully. "The devil brought you all on us, eating us out of house and home."

Sasha and Motka and all the little girls in the hut huddled on the stove in the corner behind Nikolay's back, and from that refuge listened in silent terror, and the beating of their little hearts could be distinctly heard. Whenever there is someone in a family who has long been ill, and hopelessly ill, there come painful moments when all timidly, secretly, at the bottom of their hearts long for his death; and only the children fear the death of someone near them, and always feel horrified at the thought of it. And now the children, with bated breath, with a mournful look on their faces, gazed at Nikolay and thought that he was soon to die; and they wanted to cry and to say something friendly and compassionate to him.

He pressed close to Olga, as though seeking protection, and said to her softly in a quavering voice:

"Olga darling, I can't stay here longer. It's more than I can bear. For God's sake, for Christ's sake, write to your sister Klavdia Abramovna. Let her sell and pawn everything she has; let her send us the money. We will go away from here. Oh, Lord," he went on miserably, "to have one peep at Moscow! If I could see it in my dreams, the dear place!"

And when the evening came on, and it was dark in the hut, it was so dismal that it was hard to utter a word. Granny, very ill-tempered, soaked some crusts of rye bread in a cup, and was a long time, a whole hour, sucking at them. Marya, after milking the cow, brought in a pail of milk and set it on a bench; then Granny poured it from the pail into a jug just as slowly and deliberately, evidently pleased that it was now the Fast of the Assumption, so that no one would drink milk and it would be left untouched. And she only poured out a very little in a saucer for Fyokla's baby. When Marya and she carried the jug down to the cellar Motka suddenly stirred, clambered down from the stove, and going to the bench where stood the wooden cup full of crusts, sprinkled into it some milk from the saucer.

Granny, coming back into the hut, sat down to her soaked crusts again, while Sasha and Motka, sitting on the stove, gazed at her, and they were glad that she had broken her fast and now would go to hell. They were comforted and lay down to sleep, and Sasha as she dozed off to sleep imagined the Day of Judgment: a huge fire was burning, somewhat like a potter's kiln, and the Evil One, with horns like a cow's, and black all over, was driving Granny into the fire with a long stick, just as Granny herself had been driving the geese.

V

On the day of the Feast of the Assumption, between ten and eleven in the evening, the girls and lads who were merrymaking in the meadow suddenly raised a clamour and outcry, and ran in the direction of the village; and those who were above on the edge of the ravine could not for the first moment make out what was the matter.

"Fire! Fire!" they heard desperate shouts from below. "The village is on fire!"

Those who were sitting above looked round, and a terrible and extraordinary spectacle met their eyes. On the thatched roof of one of the end cottages stood a column of flame, seven feet high, which curled round and scattered sparks in all directions as though it were a fountain. And all at once the whole roof burst into bright flame, and the crackling of the fire was audible.

The light of the moon was dimmed, and the whole village was by now bathed in a red quivering glow: black shadows moved over the ground, there was a smell of burning, and those who ran up from below were all gasping and could not speak for trembling; they jostled against each other, fell down, and they could hardly see in the unaccustomed light, and did not recognize each other. It was terrible. What seemed particularly dreadful was that doves were flying over the fire in the smoke; and in the tavern, where they did not yet know of the fire, they were still singing and playing the concertina as though there were nothing the matter.

"Uncle Semyon's on fire," shouted a loud, coarse voice.

Marya was fussing about round her hut, weeping and wringing her hands, while her teeth chattered, though the fire was a long way off at the other end of the village. Nikolay came out in high felt boots, the children ran out in their little smocks. Near the village constable's hut an iron sheet was struck. Boom, boom, boom! . . . floated through the air, and this repeated, persistent sound sent a pang to the heart and turned one cold. The old women stood with the holy ikons. Sheep, calves, cows were driven out of the back-yards into the street; boxes, sheepskins, tubs were carried out. A black stallion, who was kept apart from the drove of horses because he kicked and injured them, on being set free ran once or twice up and down the village, neighing and pawing the ground; then suddenly stopped short near a cart and began kicking it with his hind-legs.

They began ringing the bells in the church on the other side of the river.

Near the burning hut it was hot and so light that one could distinctly see every blade of grass. Semyon, a red-haired peasant with a long nose, wearing a reefer-jacket and a cap pulled down right over his ears, sat on one of the boxes which they had succeeded in bringing out: his wife was lying on her face, moaning and unconscious. A little old man of eighty, with a big beard, who looked like a gnome— not one of the villagers, though obviously connected in some way with the fire—walked about bareheaded, with a white bundle in his arms. The glare was reflected on his bald head. The village elder, Antip Syedelnikov, as swarthy and black-haired as a gypsy, went up to the hut with an axe, and hacked out the windows one after another—no one knew why—then began chopping up the roof.

"Women, water!" he shouted. "Bring the engine! Look sharp!"

The peasants, who had been drinking in the tavern just before, dragged the engine up. They were all drunk; they kept stumbling and falling down, and all had a helpless expression and tears in their eyes.

"Wenches, water!" shouted the elder, who was drunk, too. "Look sharp, wenches!"

The women and the girls ran downhill to where there was a spring, and kept hauling pails and buckets of water up the hill, and, pouring it into the engine, ran down again. Olga and Marya and Sasha and Motka all brought water. The women and the boys pumped the water; the pipe hissed, and the elder, directing it now at the door, now at the windows, held back the stream with his finger, which made it hiss more sharply still.

"Bravo, Antip!" voices shouted approvingly. "Do your best."

Antip went inside the hut into the fire and shouted from within.

"Pump! Bestir yourselves, good Christian folk, in such a terrible mischance!"

The peasants stood round in a crowd, doing nothing but staring at the fire. No one knew what to do, no one had the sense to do anything, though there were stacks of wheat, hay, barns, and piles of faggots standing all round. Kiryak and old Osip, his father, both tipsy, were standing there, too. And as though to justify his doing nothing, old Osip said, addressing the woman who lay on the ground:

"What is there to trouble about, old girl! The hut is insured—why are you taking on?"

Semyon, addressing himself first to one person and then to another, kept describing how the fire had started.

"That old man, the one with the bundle, a house-serf of General Zhukov's. . . . He was cook at our general's, God rest his soul! He came over this evening: 'Let me stay the night,' says he. . . . Well, we had a glass, to be sure. . . . The wife got the samovar—she was going to give the old fellow a cup of tea, and in an unlucky hour she set the samovar in the entrance. The sparks from the chimney must have blown straight up to the thatch; that's how it was. We were almost burnt ourselves. And the old fellow's cap has been burnt; what a shame!"

And the sheet of iron was struck indefatigably, and the bells kept ringing in the church the other side of the river. In the glow of the fire Olga, breathless, looking with horror at the red sheep and the pink doves flying in the smoke, kept running down the hill and up again. It seemed to her that the ringing went to her heart with a sharp stab, that the fire would never be over, that Sasha was lost. . . . And when the ceiling of the hut fell in with a crash, the thought that now the whole village would be burnt made her weak and faint, and she could not go on fetching water, but sat down on the ravine, setting the pail down near her; beside her and below her, the peasant women sat wailing as though at a funeral.

Then the stewards and watchmen from the estate the other side of the river arrived in two carts, bringing with them a fire-engine. A very young student in an unbuttoned white tunic rode up on horse-back. There was the thud of axes. They put a ladder to the burning framework of the house, and five men ran up it at once. Foremost of them all was the student, who was red in the face and shouting in a harsh hoarse voice, and in a tone as though putting out fires was a thing he was used to. They pulled the house to pieces, a beam at a time; they dragged away the corn, the hurdles, and the stacks that were near.

"Don't let them break it up!" cried stern voices in the crowd. "Don't let them."

Kiryak made his way up to the hut, with a resolute air, as though he meant to prevent the newcomers from breaking up the hut, but one of the workmen turned him back with a blow in his neck. There was the sound of laughter, the workman dealt him another blow, Kiryak fell down, and crawled back into the crowd on his hands and knees.

Two handsome girls in hats, probably the student's sisters, came from the other side of the river. They stood a little way off, looking at the fire. The beams that had been dragged apart were no longer

burning, but were smoking vigorously; the student, who was working the hose, turned the water, first on the beams, then on the
peasants, then on the women who were bringing the water.

"George!" the girls called to him reproachfully in anxiety,
"George!"

The fire was over. And only when they began to disperse they
noticed that the day was breaking, that everyone was pale and rather
dark in the face, as it always seems in the early morning when the last
stars are going out. As they separated, the peasants laughed and made
jokes about General Zhukov's cook and his cap which had been
burnt; they already wanted to turn the fire into a joke, and even
seemed sorry that it had so soon been put out.

"How well you extinguished the fire, sir!" said Olga to the student. "You ought to come to us in Moscow: there we have a fire
every day."

"Why, do you come from Moscow?" asked one of the young
ladies.

"Yes, miss. My husband was a waiter at the Slavyansky Bazaar.
And this is my daughter," she said, indicating Sasha, who was cold
and huddling up to her. "She is a Moscow girl, too."

The two young ladies said something in French to the student, and
he gave Sasha a twenty-kopeck piece.

Old Father Osip saw this, and there was a gleam of hope in his
face.

"We must thank God, your honour, there was no wind," he said,
addressing the student, "or else we should have been all burnt up
together. Your honour, kind gentlefolks," he added in embarrassment
in a lower tone, "the morning's chilly . . . something to warm one . . .
half a bottle to your honour's health."

Nothing was given him, and clearing his throat he slouched home.
Olga stood afterwards at the end of the street and watched the two
carts crossing the river by the ford and the gentlefolks walking across
the meadow; a carriage was waiting for them the other side of the
river. Going into the hut, she described to her husband with enthusiasm:

"Such good people! And so beautiful! The young ladies were like
cherubim."

"Plague take them!" Fyokla, sleepy, said spitefully.

VI

Marya thought herself unhappy, and said that she would be very glad to die; Fyokla, on the other hand, found all this life to her taste: the poverty, the uncleanliness, and the incessant quarrelling. She ate what was given her without discrimination; slept anywhere, on whatever came to hand. She would empty the slops just at the porch, would splash them out from the doorway, and then walk barefoot through the puddle. And from the very first day she took a dislike to Olga and Nikolay just because they did not like this life.

"We shall see what you'll find to eat here, you Moscow gentry!" she said malignantly. "We shall see!"

One morning, it was at the beginning of September, Fyokla, vigorous, good-looking, and rosy from the cold, brought up two pails of water; Marya and Olga were sitting meanwhile at the table drinking tea.

"Tea and sugar," said Fyokla sarcastically. "The fine ladies!" she added, setting down the pails. "You have taken to the fashion of tea every day. You better look out that you don't burst with your tea-drinking," she went on, looking with hatred at Olga. "That's how you have come by your fat mug, having a good time in Moscow, you lump of flesh!" She swung the yoke and hit Olga such a blow on the shoulder that the two sisters-in-law could only clasp their hands and say:

"Oh, holy Saints!"

Then Fyokla went down to the river to wash the clothes, swearing all the time so loudly that she could be heard in the hut.

The day passed and was followed by the long autumn evening. They wound silk in the hut; everyone did it except Fyokla; she had gone over the river. They got the silk from a factory close by, and the whole family working together earned next to nothing, twenty kopecks a week.

"Things were better in the old days under the gentry," said the old father as he wound silk. "You worked and ate and slept, everything in its turn. At dinner you had cabbage-soup and boiled grain, and at supper the same again. Cucumbers and cabbage in plenty: you could eat to your heart's content, as much as you wanted. And there was more strictness. Everyone minded what he was about."

The hut was lighted by a single little lamp, which burned dimly and smoked. When someone screened the lamp and a big shadow fell across the window, the bright moonlight could be seen. Old Osip, speaking slowly, told them how they used to live before the emancipation; how in those very parts, where life was now so poor and so dreary, they used to hunt with harriers, greyhounds, retrievers, and when they went out as beaters the peasants were given vodka; how whole waggonloads of game used to be sent to Moscow for the young masters; how the bad were beaten with rods or sent away to the Tver estate, while the good were rewarded. And Granny told them something, too. She remembered everything, positively everything. She described her mistress, a kind, God-fearing woman, whose husband was a profligate and a rake, and all of whose daughters made unlucky marriages: one married a drunkard, another married a workman, the other eloped secretly (Granny herself, at that time a young girl, helped in the elopement), and they had all three as well as their mother died early from grief. And remembering all this, Granny positively began to shed tears.

All at once someone knocked at the door, and they all started.

"Uncle Osip, give me a night's lodging."

The little bald old man, General Zhukov's cook, the one whose cap had been burnt, walked in. He sat down and listened, then he, too, began telling stories of all sorts. Nikolay, sitting on the stove with his legs hanging down, listened and asked questions about the dishes that were prepared in the old days for the gentry. They talked of rissoles, cutlets, various soups and sauces, and the cook, who remembered everything very well, mentioned dishes that are no longer served. There was one, for instance—a dish made of bulls' eyes, which was called "waking up in the morning."

"And used you to do cutlets *à la maréchal*?" asked Nikolay.

"No."

Nikolay shook his head reproachfully and said:

"Tut, tut! You were not much of a cook!"

The little girl sitting and lying on the stove stared down without blinking; it seemed as though there were a great many of them, like cherubim in the clouds. They liked the stories: they were breathless; they shuddered and turned pale with alternate rapture and terror, and they listened breathlessly, afraid to stir, to Granny, whose stories were the most interesting of all.

They lay down to sleep in silence; and the old people, troubled and excited by their reminiscences, thought how precious was youth, of which, whatever it might have been like, nothing was left in the memory but what was living, joyful, touching, and how terribly cold was death, which was not far off, better not think of it! The lamp died down. And the dusk, and the two little windows sharply defined by the moonlight, and the stillness and the creak of the cradle, reminded them for some reason that life was over, that nothing one could do would bring it back. . . . You doze off, you forget yourself, and suddenly someone touches your shoulder or breathes on your cheek—and sleep is gone; your body feels cramped, and thoughts of death keep creeping into your mind. You turn on the other side: death is forgotten, but old dreary, sickening thoughts of poverty, of food, of how dear flour is getting, stray through the mind, and a little later again you remember that life is over and you cannot bring it back. . . .

"Oh, Lord!" sighed the cook.

Someone gave a soft, soft tap at the window. It must be Fyokla come back. Olga got up, and yawning and whispering a prayer, opened the door, then drew the bolt in the outer room, but no one came in; only from the street came a cold draught and a sudden brightness from the moonlight. The street, still and deserted, and the moon itself floating across the sky, could be seen at the open door.

"Who is there?" called Olga.

"I," she heard the answer—"it is I."

Near the door, crouching against the wall, stood Fyokla, absolutely naked. She was shivering with cold, her teeth were chattering, and in the bright moonlight she looked very pale, strange, and beautiful. The shadows on her, and the bright moonlight on her skin, stood out vividly, and her dark eyebrows and firm, youthful bosom were defined with peculiar distinctness.

"The ruffians over there undressed me and turned me out like this," she said. "I've come home without my clothes . . . naked as my mother bore me. Bring me something to put on."

"But go inside!" Olga said softly, beginning to shiver, too.

"I don't want the old folks to see." Granny was, in fact, already stirring and muttering, and the old father asked: "Who is there?" Olga brought her own smock and skirt, dressed Fyokla and then both went softly into the inner room, trying not to make a noise with the door.

"Is that you, you sleek one?" Granny grumbled angrily, guessing who it was. "Fie upon you, nightwalker! . . . Bad luck to you!"

"It's all right, it's all right," whispered Olga, wrapping Fyokla up; "it's all right, dearie."

All was stillness again. They always slept badly; everyone was kept awake by something worrying and persistent: the old man by the pain in his back, Granny by anxiety and anger, Marya by terror, the children by itch and hunger. Now, too, their sleep was troubled; they kept turning over from one side to the other, talking in their sleep, getting up for a drink.

Fyokla suddenly broke into a loud, coarse howl, but immediately checked herself, and only uttered sobs from time to time, growing softer and on a lower note, until she relapsed into silence. From time to time from the other side of the river there floated the sound of the beating of the hours; but the time seemed somehow strange—five was struck and then three.

"Oh Lord!" sighed the cook.

Looking at the windows, it was difficult to tell whether it was still moonlight or whether the dawn had begun. Marya got up and went out, and she could be heard milking the cows and saying, "Stea-dy!" Granny went out, too. It was still dark in the hut, but all the objects in it could be discerned.

Nikolay, who had not slept all night, got down from the stove. He took his dress-coat out of a green box, put it on, and going to the window, stroked the sleeves and took hold of the coat-tails—and smiled. Then he carefully took off the coat, put it away in his box, and lay down again.

Marya came in again and began lighting the stove. She was evidently hardly awake, and seemed dropping asleep as she walked. Probably she had had some dream, or the stories of the night before came into her mind as, stretching luxuriously before the stove, she said:

"No, freedom is better."

VII

The master arrived—that was what they called the police inspector. When he would come and what he was coming for had been known for the last week. There were only forty households in

Zhukovo, but more than two thousand roubles of arrears of rates and taxes had accumulated.

The police inspector stopped at the tavern. He drank there two glasses of tea, and then went on foot to the village elder's hut, near which a crowd of those who were in debt stood waiting. The elder, Antip Syedelnikov, was, in spite of his youth—he was only a little over thirty—strict and always on the side of the authorities, though he himself was poor and did not pay his taxes regularly. Evidently he enjoyed being elder, and liked the sense of authority, which he could only display by strictness. In the village council the peasants were afraid of him and obeyed him. It would sometimes happen that he would pounce on a drunken man in the street or near the tavern, tie his hands behind him, and put him in the lock-up. On one occasion he even put Granny in the lock-up because she went to the village council instead of Osip, and began swearing, and he kept her there for a whole day and night. He had never lived in a town or read a book, but somewhere or other had picked up various learned expressions, and loved to make use of them in conversation, and he was respected for this though he was not always understood.

When Osip came into the village elder's hut with his tax book, the police inspector, a lean old man with a long grey beard, in a grey tunic, was sitting at a table in the passage, writing something. It was clean in the hut; all the walls were dotted with pictures cut out of the illustrated papers, and in the most conspicuous place near the ikon there was a portrait of the Battenburg who was the Prince of Bulgaria. By the table stood Antip Syedelnikov with his arms folded.

"There is one hundred and nineteen roubles standing against him," he said when it came to Osip's turn. "Before Easter he paid a rouble, and he has not paid a kopeck since."

The police inspector raised his eyes to Osip and asked:

"Why is this, brother?"

"Show Divine mercy, your honour," Osip began, growing agitated. "Allow me to say last year the gentleman at Lutorydsky said to me, 'Osip,' he said, 'sell your hay . . . you sell it,' he said. Well, I had a hundred poods for sale; the women mowed it on the watermeadow. Well, we struck a bargain all right, willingly. . . ."

He complained of the elder, and kept turning round to the peasants as though inviting them to bear witness; his face flushed red and perspired, and his eyes grew sharp and angry.

"I don't know why you are saying all this," said the police inspector. "I am asking you . . . I am asking you why you don't pay your arrears. You don't pay, any of you, and am I to be responsible for you?"

"I can't do it."

"His words have no sequel, your honour," said the elder. "The Tchikildyeevs certainly are of a defective class, but if you will just ask the others, the root of it all is vodka, and they are a very bad lot. With no sort of understanding."

The police inspector wrote something down, and said to Osip quietly, in an even tone, as though he were asking him for water:

"Be off."

Soon he went away; and when he got into his cheap chaise and cleared his throat, it could be seen from the very expression of his long thin back that he was no longer thinking of Osip or of the village elder, nor of the Zhukovo arrears, but was thinking of his own affairs. Before he had gone three-quarters of a mile Antip was already carrying off the samovar from the Tchikildyeevs' cottage, followed by Granny, screaming shrilly and straining her throat:

"I won't let you have it, I won't let you have it, damn you!"

He walked rapidly with long steps, and she pursued him panting, almost falling over, a bent, ferocious figure; her kerchief slipped on to her shoulders, her grey hair with greenish lights on it was blown about in the wind. She suddenly stopped short, and like a genuine rebel, fell to beating her breast with her fists and shouting louder than ever in a sing-song voice, as though she were sobbing:

"Good Christians and believers in God! Neighbours, they have ill-treated me! Kind friends, they have oppressed me! Oh, oh! dear people, take my part."

"Granny, Granny!" said the village elder sternly, "have some sense in your head!"

It was hopelessly dreary in the Tchikildyeevs' hut without the samovar; there was something humiliating in this loss, insulting, as though the honour of the hut had been outraged. Better if the elder had carried off the table, all the benches, all the pots—it would not have seemed so empty. Granny screamed, Marya cried, and the little girls, looking at her, cried, too. The old father, feeling guilty, sat in the corner with bowed head and said nothing. And Nikolay, too, was silent. Granny loved him and was sorry for him, but now, forgetting her pity, she fell upon him with abuse, with reproaches, shaking her fist right in his face. She shouted that it was all his fault; why had he sent them so little when he boasted in his letters that he was getting fifty roubles a month at the Slavyansky Bazaar? Why had he come, and with his family, too? If he died, where was the money to come from for his funeral . . . ? And it was pitiful to look at Nikolay, Olga, and Sasha.

The old father cleared his throat, took his cap, and went off to the village elder. Antip was soldering something by the stove, puffing out his cheeks; there was a smell of burning. His children, emaciated and unwashed, no better than the Tchikildyeevs, were scrambling about the floor; his wife, an ugly, freckled woman with a prominent stomach, was winding silk. They were a poor, unlucky family, and Antip was the only one who looked vigorous and handsome. On a bench there were five samovars standing in a row. The old man said his prayer to Battenburg and said:

"Antip, show the Divine mercy. Give me back the samovar, for Christ's sake!"

"Bring three roubles, then you shall have it."

"I can't do it!"

Antip puffed out his cheeks, the fire roared and hissed, and the glow was reflected in the samovar. The old man crumpled up his cap and said after a moment's thought:

"You give it me back."

The swarthy elder looked quite black, and was like a magician; he turned round to Osip and said sternly and rapidly:

"It all depends on the rural captain. On the twenty-sixth instant you can state the grounds for your dissatisfaction before the administrative session, verbally or in writing."

Osip did not understand a word, but he was satisfied with that and went home.

Ten days later the police inspector came again, stayed an hour and went away. During those days the weather had changed to cold and windy; the river had been frozen for some time past, but still there was no snow, and people found it difficult to get about. On the eve of a holiday some of the neighbours came in to Osip's t sit and have a talk. They did not light the lamp, as it would have been a sin to work, but talked in the darkness. There were some items of news, all rather unpleasant. In two or three households hens had been taken for the arrears, and had been sent to the district police station, and there they had died because no one had fed them; they had taken sheep, and while they were being driven away tied to one another, shifted into another cart at each village, one of them had died. And now they were discussing the question, who was to blame?

"The Zemstvo," said Osip. "Who else?"

"Of course it is the Zemstvo."

The Zemstvo was blamed for everything—for the arrears, and for the oppressions, and for the failure of the crops, though no one of them knew what was meant by the Zemstvo. And this dated from the time when well-to-do peasants who had factories, shops, and inns of their own were members of the Zemstvos, were dissatisfied with them, and took to swearing at the Zemstvos in their factories and inns.

They talked of God's not sending the snow; they had to bring in wood for fuel, and there was no driving nor walking in the frozen ruts. In old days fifteen to twenty years ago conversation was much more interesting in Zhukovo. In those days every old man looked as though he were treasuring some secret; as though he knew something and was expecting something. They used to talk about an edict in golden letters, about the division of lands, about new land, about treasures; they hinted at something. Now the people of Zhukovo had no mystery at all; their whole life was bare and open in the sight of all, and they could talk of nothing but poverty, food, there being no snow yet. . . .

There was a pause. Then they thought again of the hens, of the sheep, and began discussing whose fault it was.

"The Zemstvo," said Osip wearily. "Who else?"

VIII

The parish church was nearly five miles away at Kosogorovo, and the peasants only attended it when they had to do so for baptisms, weddings, or funerals; they went to the services at the church across the river. On holidays in fine weather the girls dressed up in their best and went in a crowd together to church, and it was a cheering sight to see them in their red, yellow, and green dresses cross the meadow; in bad weather they all stayed at home. They went for the sacrament to the parish church. From each of those who did not manage in Lent to go to confession in readiness for the sacrament the parish priest, going the round of the huts with the cross at Easter, took fifteen kopecks.

The old father did not believe in God, for he hardly ever thought about Him; he recognized the supernatural, but considered it was entirely the women's concern, and when religion or miracles were discussed before him, or a question were put to him, he would say reluctantly, scratching himself:

"Who can tell!"

Granny believed, but her faith was somewhat hazy; everything was mixed up in her memory, and she could scarcely begin to think of sins, of death, of the salvation of the soul, before poverty and her daily cares took possession of her mind, and she instantly forgot what she was thinking about. She did not remember the prayers, and usually in the evenings, before lying down to sleep, she would stand before the ikons and whisper:

"Holy Mother of Kazan, Holy Mother of Smolensk, Holy Mother of Troerutchitsy. . . ."

Marya and Fyokla crossed themselves, fasted, and took the sacrament every year, but understood nothing. The children were not taught their prayers, nothing was told them about God, and no moral principles were instilled into them; they were only forbidden to eat meat or milk in Lent. In the other families it was much the same: there were few who believed, few who understood. At the same time everyone loved the Holy Scripture, loved it with a tender, reverent love; but they had no Bible, there was no one to read it and explain it, and because Olga sometimes read them the gospel, they respected her, and they all addressed her and Sasha as though they were superior to themselves.

For church holidays and services Olga often went to neighbouring villages, and to the district town, in which there were two monasteries and twenty-seven churches. She was dreamy, and when she was on these pilgrimages she quite forgot her family, and only when she got home again suddenly made the joyful discovery that she had a husband and daughter, and then would say, smiling and radiant:

"God has sent me blessings!"

What went on in the village worried her and seemed to her revolting. On Elijah's Day they drank, at the Assumption they drank, at the Ascension they drank. The Feast of the Intercession was the parish holiday for Zhukovo, and the peasants used to drink then for three days; they squandered on drink fifty roubles of money belonging to the Mir, and then collected more for vodka from all the households. On the first day of the feast the Tchikildyeevs killed a sheep and ate of it in the morning, at dinner-time, and in the evening; they ate it ravenously, and the children got up at night to eat more. Kiryak was fearfully drunk for three whole days; he drank up everything, even his boots and cap, and beat Marya so terribly that they had to pour water over her. And then they were all ashamed and sick.

However, even in Zhukovo, in this "Slaveytown," there was once an outburst of genuine religious enthusiasm. It was in August, when throughout the district they carried from village to village the Holy Mother, the giver of life. It was still and overcast on the day when they expected *Her* at Zhukovo. The girls set off in the morning to meet the ikon, in their bright holiday dresses, and brought Her towards the evening, in procession with the cross and with singing, while the bells pealed in the church across the river. An immense crowd of villagers and strangers flooded the street; there was noise, dust, a great crush. . . . And the old father and Granny and Kiryak— all stretched out their hands to the ikon, looked eagerly at it and said, weeping:

"Defender! Mother! Defender!"

All seemed suddenly to realize that there was not an empty void between earth and heaven, that the rich and the powerful had not taken possession of everything, that there was still a refuge from injury, from slavish bondage, from crushing, unendurable poverty, from the terrible vodka.

"Defender! Mother!" sobbed Marya. "Mother!"

But the thanksgiving service ended and the ikon was carried away, and everything went on as before; and again there was a sound of coarse drunken oaths from the tavern.

Only the well-to-do peasants were afraid of death; the richer they were the less they believed in God, and in the salvation of souls, and only through fear of the end of the world put up the candles and had services said for them, to be on the safe side. The peasants who were rather poorer were not afraid of death. The old father and Granny were told to their faces that they have lived too long, that it was time they were dead, and they did not mind. They did not hinder Fyokla from saying in Nikolay's presence that when Nikolay died her husband Denis would get exemption—to return home from the army. And Marya, far from fearing death, regretted that it was so slow in coming, and was glad when her children died.

Death they did not fear, but of every disease they had an exaggerated terror. The merest trifle was enough—a stomach upset, a slight chill, and Granny would be wrapped up on the stove, and would begin moaning loudly and incessantly:

"I am dy-ing!"

The old father hurried off for the priest, and Granny received the sacrament and extreme unction. They often talked of colds, of worms, of tumours which move in the stomach and coil round to the heart. Above all, they were afraid of catching cold, and so put on thick clothes even in the summer and warmed themselves at the stove. Granny was fond of being doctored, and often went to the hospital, where she used to say she was not seventy, but fifty-eight; she supposed that if the doctor knew her real age he would not treat her, but would say it was time she died instead of taking medicine. She usually went to the hospital early in the morning, taking with her two or three of the little girls, and came back in the evening, hungry and ill-tempered—with drops for herself and ointments for the little girls. Once she took Nikolay, who swallowed drops for a fortnight afterwards, and said he felt better.

Granny knew all the doctors and their assistants and the wise men for twenty miles round, and not one of them she liked. At the Intercession, when the priest made the round of the huts with the cross, the deacon told her that in the town near the prison lived an old man who had been a medical orderly in the army, and who made wonderful cures, and advised her to try him. Granny took his advice. When the first snow fell she drove to the town and fetched an old man with a big beard, a converted Jew, in a long gown, whose face was covered with blue veins. There were outsiders at work in the hut at the time: an old tailor, in terrible spectacles, was cutting a waistcoat out of some rags, and two young men were making felt boots out of wool; Kiryak, who had been dismissed from his place for drunkenness, and now lived at home, was sitting beside the tailor mending a bridle. And it was crowded, stifling, and noisome in the hut. The converted Jew examined Nikolay and said that it was necessary to try cupping.

He put on the cups, and the old tailor, Kiryak, and the little girls stood round and looked on, and it seemed to them that they saw the disease being drawn out of Nikolay; and Nikolay, too, watched how the cups suckling at his breast gradually filled with dark blood, and felt as though there really were something coming out of him, and smiled with pleasure.

"It's a good thing," said the tailor. "Please God, it will do you good."

The Jew put on twelve cups and then another twelve, drank some tea, and went away. Nikolay began shivering; his face looked drawn, and, as the women expressed it, shrank up like a fist; his fingers turned blue. He wrapped himself up in a quilt and in a sheepskin, but got colder and colder. Towards the evening he began to be in great distress; asked to be laid on the ground, asked the tailor not to smoke; then he subsided under the sheepskin and towards morning he died.

IX

Oh, what a grim, what a long winter!

Their own grain did not last beyond Christmas, and they had to buy flour. Kiryak, who lived at home now, was noisy in the evenings, inspiring terror in everyone, and in the mornings he suffered from headache and was ashamed; and he was a pitiful sight. In the stall the starved cows bellowed day and night—a heart-rending sound to Granny and Marya. And as ill-luck would have it, there was a sharp frost all the winter, the snow drifted in high heaps, and the winter dragged on. At Annunciation there was a regular blizzard, and there was a fall of snow at Easter.

But in spite of it all the winter did end. At the beginning of April there came warm days and frosty nights. Winter would not give way, but one warm day overpowered it at last, and the streams began to flow and the birds began to sing. The whole meadow and the bushes near the river were drowned in the spring floods, and all the space between Zhukovo and the further side was filled up with a vast sheet of water, from which wild ducks rose up in flocks here and there. The spring sunset, flaming among gorgeous clouds, gave every evening something new, extraordinary, incredible—just what one does not believe in afterwards, when one sees those very colours and those very clouds in a picture.

The cranes flew swiftly, swiftly, with mournful cries, as though they were calling themselves. Standing on the edge of the ravine, Olga looked a long time at the flooded meadow, at the sunshine, at the bright church, that looked as though it had grown younger; and her tears flowed and her breath came in gasps from her passionate longing to go away, to go far away to the end of the world. It was already settled that she should go back to Moscow to be a servant, and that Kiryak should set off with her to get a job as a porter or something. Oh, to get away quickly!

As soon as it dried up and grew warm they got ready to set off. Olga and Sasha, with wallets on their backs and shoes of plaited bark on their feet, came out before daybreak: Marya came out, too, to see them on their way. Kiryak was not well, and was kept at home for another week. For the last time Olga prayed at the church and thought of her husband, and though she did not shed tears, her face puckered up and looked ugly like an old woman's. During the winter she had grown thinner and plainer, and her hair had gone a little grey, and instead of the old look of sweetness and the pleasant smile on her face, she had the resigned, mournful expression left by the sorrows she had been through, and there was something blank and irresponsive in her eyes, as though she did not hear what was said. She was sorry to part from the village and the peasants. She remembered how they had carried out Nikolay, and how a requiem had been ordered for him at almost every hut, and all had shed tears in sympathy with her grief. In the course of the summer and the winter there had been hours and days when it seemed as though these people lived worse than the beasts, and to live with them was terrible; they were coarse, dishonest, filthy, and drunken; they did not live in harmony, but quarrelled continually, because they distrusted and feared and did not respect one another. Who keeps the tavern and makes the people drunken? A peasant. Who wastes and spends on drink the funds of the commune, of the schools, of the church? A peasant. Who stole from his neighbours, set fire to their property, gave false witness at the court for a bottle of vodka? At the meetings of the Zemstvo and other local bodies, who was the first to fall foul of the peasants? A peasant. Yes, to live with them was terrible; but yet, they were human beings, they suffered and wept like human beings, and there was nothing in their lives for which one could not find excuse. Hard labour that made the whole body ache at night, the cruel winters, the scanty harvests, the overcrowding; and they had no help and none to whom they could look for help. Those of them who were a little stronger and better off could be no help, as they were themselves coarse, dishonest, drunken, and abused one another just as revoltingly; the paltriest little clerk or official treated the peasants as though they were tramps, and addressed even the village elders and church wardens as inferiors, and considered they had a right to do so. And, indeed, can any sort of help or good example be given by mercenary, greedy, depraved, and idle persons who only visit the village in order to insult, to despoil, and to terrorize? Olga remembered the pitiful, humiliated look of the old people when in the winter Kiryak had been taken to be flogged. . . . And now she felt sorry for all these people, painfully so, and as she walked on she kept looking back at the huts.

After walking two miles with them Marya said good-bye, then kneeling, and falling forward with her face on the earth, she began wailing:

"Again I am left alone. Alas, for poor me! poor, unhappy! . . ."

And she wailed like this for a long time, and for a long way Olga and Sasha could still see her on her knees, bowing down to someone at the side and clutching her head in her hands, while the rooks flew over her head.

The sun rose high; it began to get hot. Zhukovo was left far behind. Walking was pleasant. Olga and Sasha soon forgot both the village and Marya; they were gay and everything entertained them. Now they came upon an ancient barrow, now upon a row of telegraph posts running one after another into the distance and disappearing into the horizon, and the wires hummed msyteriously. Then they saw a homestead, all wreathed in green foliage; there came a scent from it of dampness, of hemp, and it seemed for some reason that happy people lived there. Then they came upon a horse's skeleton whitening in solitude in the open fields. And the larks trilled unceasingly, the corncrakes called to one another, and the landrail cried as though someone were really scraping at an old iron rail.

At midday Olga and Sasha reached a big village. There in the broad street they met the little old man who was General Zhukov's cook. He was hot, and his red, perspiring bald head shone in the sunshine. Olga and he did not recognize each other, then looked round at the same moment, recognized each other, and went their separate ways without saying a word. Stopping near the hut which looked newest and most prosperous, Olga bowed down before the open windows, and said in a loud, thin, chanting voice:

"Good Christian folk, give alms, for Christ's sake, that God's blessing may be upon you, and that your parents may be in the Kingdom of Heaven in peace eternal."

"Good Christian folk," Sasha began chanting, "give, for Christ's sake, that God's blessing, the Heavenly Kingdom . . ."

1897

Gooseberries

The whole sky had been overcast with rain-clouds from early morning; it was a still day, not hot, but heavy, as it is in grey dull weather when the clouds have been hanging over the country for a long while, when one expects rain and it does not come. Ivan Ivanovitch, the veterinary surgeon, and Burkin, the high-school teacher, were already tired from walking, and the fields seemed to them endless. Far ahead of them they could just see the windmills of the village of Mironositskoe; on the right stretched a row of hillocks which disappeared in the distance behind the village, and they both knew that this was the bank of the river, that there were meadows, green willows, homesteads there, and that if one stood on one of the hillocks one could see from it the same vast plain, telegraph-wires, and a train which in the distance looked like a crawling caterpillar, and that in clear weather one could even see the town. Now, in still weather, when all nature seemed mild and dreamy, Ivan Ivanovitch and Burkin were filled with love of that countryside, and both thought how great, how beautiful a land it was.

"Last time we were in Prokofy's barn," said Burkin, "you were about to tell me a story."

"Yes; I meant to tell you about my brother."

Ivan Ivanovitch heaved a deep sigh and lighted a pipe to begin to tell his story, but just at that moment the rain began. And five minutes later heavy rain came down, covering the sky, and it was hard to tell when it would be over. Ivan Ivanovitch and Burkin stopped in hesitation; the dogs, already drenched, stood with their tails between their legs gazing at them feelingly.

"We must take shelter somewhere," said Burkin. "Let us go to Alehin's; it's close by."

"Come along."

They turned aside and walked through mown fields, sometimes going straight forward, sometimes turning to the right, till they came out on the road. Soon they saw poplars, a garden, then the red roofs of barns; there was a gleam of the river, and the view opened on to a broad expanse of water with a windmill and a white bath-house: this was Sofino, where Alehin lived.

The watermill was at work, drowning the sound of the rain; the dam was shaking. Here wet horses with drooping heads were standing near their carts, and men were walking about covered with sacks. It was damp, muddy, and desolate; the water looked cold and malignant. Ivan Ivanovitch and Burkin were already conscious of a feeling of wetness, messiness, and discomfort all over; their feet were heavy with mud, and when, crossing the dam, they went up to the barns, they were silent, as though they were angry with one another.

In one of the barns there was the sound of a winnowing machine, the door was open, and clouds of dust were coming from it. In the doorway was standing Alehin himself, a man of forty, tall and stout, with long hair, more like a professor or an artist than a landowner. He had on a white shirt that badly needed washing, a rope for a belt, drawers instead of trousers, and his boots, too, were plastered up with mud and straw. His eyes and nose were black with dust. He recognized Ivan Ivanovitch and Burkin, and was apparently much delighted to see them.

"Go into the house, gentlemen," he said, smiling; "I'll come directly, this minute."

It was a big two-storeyed house. Alehin lived in the lower storey, with arched ceilings and little windows, where the bailiffs had once lived; here everything was plain, and there was a smell of rye bread, cheap vodka, and harness. He went upstairs into the best rooms only on rare occasions, when visitors came. Ivan Ivanovitch and Burkin were met in the house by a maid-servant, a young woman so beautiful that they both stood still and looked at one another.

"You can't imagine how delighted I am to see you, my friends," said Alehin, going into the hall with them. "It is a surprise! Pelagea," he said, addressing the girl, "give our visitors something to change into. And, by the way, I will change too. Only I must first go and wash, for I almost think I have not washed since spring. Wouldn't you like to come into the bath-house? and meanwhile they will get things ready here."

Beautiful Pelagea, looking so refined and soft, brought them towels and soap, and Alehin went to the bath-house with his guests.

"It's a long time since I had a wash," he said, undressing. "I have got a nice bath-house, as you see——my father built it——but I somehow never have time to wash."

He sat down on the steps and soaped his long hair and his neck, and the water round him turned brown.

"Yes, I must say," said Ivan Ivanovitch meaningly, looking at his head.

"It's a long time since I washed . . ." said Alehin with embarrassment, giving himself a second soaping, and the water near him turned dark blue, like ink.

Ivan Ivanovitch went outside, plunged into the water with a loud splash, and swam in the rain, flinging his arms out wide. He stirred the water into waves which set the white lilies bobbing up and down; he swam to the very middle of the millpond and dived, and came up a minute later in another place, and swam on, and kept on diving, trying to touch the bottom.

"Oh, my goodness!" he repeated continually, enjoying himself thoroughly. "Oh, my goodness!" He swam to the mill, talked to the peasants there, then returned and lay on his back in the middle of the pond, turning his face to the rain. Burkin and Alehin were dressed and ready to go, but he still went on swimming and diving. "Oh, my goodness! . . ." he said. "Oh, Lord, have mercy on me! . . ."

"That's enough!" Burkin shouted to him.

They went back to the house. And only when the lamp was lighted in the big drawing-room upstairs, and Burkin and Ivan Ivanovitch, attired in silk dressing-gowns and warm slippers, were sitting in arm-chairs; and Alehin, washed and combed, in a new coat, was walking about the drawing-room, evidently enjoying the feeling of warmth, cleanliness, dry clothes, and light shoes; and when lovely Pelagea, stepped noiselessly on the carpet and smiling softly, handed tea and jam on a tray——only then Ivan Ivanovitch began on his story, and it seemed as though not only Burkin and Alehin were listening, but also the ladies, young and old, and the officers who looked down upon them sternly and calmly from their gold frames.

"There are two of us brothers," he began——"I, Ivan Ivanovitch, and my brother, Nikolay Ivanovitch, two years younger. I went in for a learned profession and became a veterinary surgeon, while Nikolay sat in a government office from the time he was nineteen. Our father, Tchimsha-Himalaisky, was a kantonist, but he rose to be an officer and left us a little estate and the rank of nobility. After his death the little estate went in debts and legal expenses; but, anyway, we had spent our childhood running wild in the country. Like peasant children, we passed our days and nights in the fields and the woods, looked after horses, stripped the bark off the trees, fished, and so on. . . . And, you know, whoever has once in his life caught perch or has seen the migrating of the thrushes in autumn, watched how they float in flocks over the village on bright, cool days, he will never be a real townsman, and will have a yearning for freedom to the day of his death. My brother was miserable in the government office. Years passed by, and he went on sitting in the same place, went on writing the same papers and thinking of one and the same thing—how to get into the country. And this yearning by degrees passed into a definite desire, into a dream of buying himself a little farm somewhere on the banks of a river or a lake.

"He was a gentle, good-natured fellow, and I was fond of him, but I never sympathized with this desire to shut himself up for the rest of his life in a little farm of his own. It's the correct thing to say that a man needs no more than six feet of earth. But six feet is what a corpse needs, not a man. And they say, too, now, that if our intellectual classes are attracted to the land and yearn for a farm, it's a good thing. But these farms are just the same as six feet of earth. To retreat from town, from the struggle, from the bustle of life, to retreat and bury oneself in one's farm—it's not life, it's egoism, laziness, it's monasticism of a sort, but monasticism without good works. A man does not need six feet of earth or a farm, but the whole globe, all nature, where he can have room to display all the qualities and peculiarities of his free spirit.

"My brother Nikolay, sitting in his government office, dreamed of how he would eat his own cabbages, which would fill the whole yard with such a savoury smell, take his meals on the green grass, sleep in the sun, sit for whole hours on the seat by the gate gazing at the fields and the forest. Gardening books and the agricultural hints in calendars were his delight, his favourite spiritual sustenance; he enjoyed reading newspapers, too, but the only things he read in them were the advertisements of so many acres of arable land and a grass meadow with farm-houses and buildings, a river, a garden, a mill and millponds, for sale. And his imagination pictured the garden-paths, flowers and fruit, starling cotes, the carp in the pond, and all that sort of thing, you know. These imaginary pictures were of different kinds according to the advertisements which he came across, but for some reason in every one of them he had always to have gooseberries. He could not imagine a homestead, he could not picture an idyllic nook, without gooseberries.

" 'Country life has its conveniences,' he would sometimes say. 'You sit on the verandah and you drink tea, while your ducks swim on the pond, there is a delicious smell everywhere, and . . . and the gooseberries are growing.'

"He used to draw a map of his property, and in every map there were the same things—(*a*) house for the family, (*b*) servants' quarters, (*c*) kitchen-garden, (*d*) gooseberry-bushes. He lived parsimoniously, was frugal in food and drink, his clothes were beyond description; he looked like a beggar, but kept on saving and putting money in the bank. He grew fearfully avaricious. I did not like to look at him, and I used to give him something and send him presents for Christmas and Easter, but he used to save that too. Once a man is absorbed by an idea there is no doing anything with him.

"Years passed: he was transferred to another province. He was over forty, and he was still reading the advertisements in the papers and saving up. Then I heard he was married. Still with the same object of buying a farm and having gooseberries, he married an elderly and ugly widow without a trace of feeling for her, simply because she had filthy lucre. He went on living frugally after marrying her, and kept her short of food, while he put her money in the bank in his name.

"Her first husband had been a postmaster, and with him she was accustomed to pies and home-made wines, while with her second husband she did not get enough black bread; she began to pine away with this sort of life, and three years later she gave up her soul to God. And I need hardly say that my brother never for one moment imagined that he was responsible for her death. Money, like vodka, makes a man queer. In our town there was a merchant who, before he died, ordered a plateful of honey and ate up all his money and lottery tickets with the honey, so that no one might get the benefit of it. While I was inspecting cattle at a railway-station, a cattle-dealer fell under an engine and had his leg cut off. We carried him into the waiting-room, the blood was flowing—it was a horrible thing—and he kept asking them to look for his leg and was very much worried about it; there were twenty roubles in the boot on the leg that had been cut off, and he was afraid they would be lost."

"That's a story from a different opera," said Burkin.

"After his wife's death," Ivan Ivanovitch went on, after thinking for half a minute, "my brother began looking out for an estate for himself. Of course, you may look about for five years and yet end by making a mistake, and buying something quite different from what you have dreamed of. My brother Nikolay bought through an agent a mortgaged estate of three hundred and thirty acres, with a house for the family, with servants' quarters, with a park, but with no orchard, no gooseberry-bushes, and no duck-pond; there was a river, but the water in it was the colour of coffee, because on one side of the estate there was a brickyard and on the other a factory for burning bones. But Nikolay Ivanovitch did not grieve much; he ordered twenty gooseberry-bushes, planted them, and began living as a country gentleman.

"Last year I went to pay him a visit. I thought I would go and see what it was like. In his letters my brother called his estate 'Tchumbaroklov Waste, alias Himalaiskoe.' I reached 'alias Himalaiskoe' in the afternoon. It was hot. Everywhere there were ditches, fences, hedges, fir-trees planted in rows, and there was no knowing how to get to the yard, where to put one's horse. I went up to the house, and was met by a fat red dog that looked like a pig. It wanted to bark, but it was too lazy. The cook, a fat, barefooted woman, came out of the kitchen, and she, too, looked like a pig, and said that her master was resting after dinner. I went in to see my brother. He was sitting up in bed with a quilt over his legs; he had grown older, fatter, wrinkled; his cheeks, his nose, and his mouth all stuck out—he looked as though he might begin grunting into the quilt at any moment.

"We embraced each other, and shed tears of joy and of sadness at the thought that we had once been young and now were both greyheaded and near the grave. He dressed, and led me out to show me the estate.

" 'Well, how are you getting on here?' I asked.

" 'Oh, all right, thank God; I am getting on very well.'

"He was no more a poor timid clerk, but a real landowner, a gentleman. He was already accustomed to it, had grown used to it, and liked it. He ate a great deal, went to the bath-house, was growing stout, was already at law with the village commune and both factories, and was very much offended when the peasants did not call him 'Your Honour.' And he concerned himself with the salvation of his soul in a substantial, gentlemanly manner, and performed deeds of charity, not simply, but with an air of consequence. And what deeds of charity! He treated the peasants for every sort of disease with soda and castor oil, and on his name-day had a thanksgiving service in the middle of the village, and then treated the peasants to a gallon of vodka—he thought that was the thing to do. Oh, those horrible gallons of vodka! One day the fat landowner hauls the peasants up before the district captain for trespass, and next day, in honour of a holiday, treats them to a gallon of vodka, and they drink and shout 'Hurrah!' and when they are drunk bow down to his feet. A change of life for the better, and being well-fed and idle develop in a Russian the most insolent self-conceit. Nikolay Ivanovitch, who at one time in the government office was afraid to have any views of his own, now could say nothing that was not gospel truth, and uttered such truths in the tone of a prime minister. 'Education is essential, but for the peasants it is premature.' 'Corporal punishment is harmful as a rule, but in some cases it is necessary and there is nothing to take its place.'

" 'I know the peasants and understand how to treat them,' he would say. 'The peasants like me. I need only to hold up my little finger and the peasants will do anything I like.'

"And all this, observe, was uttered with a wise, benevolent smile. He repeated twenty times over 'We noblemen,' 'I as a noble'; obviously he did not remember that our grandfather was a peasant, and our father a soldier. Even our surname Tchimsha-Himalaisky, in reality so incongruous, seemed to him now melodious, distinguished, and very agreeable.

"But the point just now is not he, but myself. I want to tell you about the change that took place in me during the brief hours I spent at his country place. In the evening, when we were drinking tea, the cook put on the table a plateful of gooseberries. They were not bought, but his own gooseberries, gathered for the first time since the bushes were planted. Nikolay Ivanovitch laughed and looked for a minute in silence at the gooseberries, with tears in his eyes; he could not speak for excitement. Then he put one gooseberry in his mouth, looked at me with the triumph of a child who has at last received his favourite toy, and said:

" 'How delicious!'

"And he ate them greedily, continually repeating, 'Ah, how delicious! Do taste them!'

"They were sour and unripe, but, as Pushkin says:

" 'Dearer to us the falsehood that exalts
Than hosts of baser truths.'

"I saw a happy man whose cherished dream was so obviously fulfilled, who had attained this object in life, who had gained what he wanted, who was satisfied with his fate and himself. There is always, for some reason, an element of sadness mingled with my thoughts of human happiness, and, on this occasion, at the sight of a happy man I was overcome by an oppressive feeling that was close upon despair. It was particularly oppressive at night. A bed was made up for me in the room next to my brother's bedroom, and I could hear that he was awake, and that he kept getting up and going to the plate of gooseberries and taking one. I reflected how many satisfied, happy people there really are! What a suffocating force it is! You look at life: the insolence and idleness of the strong, the ignorance and brutishness of the weak, incredible poverty all about us, overcrowding, degeneration, drunkenness, hypocrisy, lying. . . . Yet all is calm and stillness in the houses and in the streets; of the fifty thousand living in a town, there is not one who would cry out, who would give vent to his indignation aloud. We see the people going to market for provisions, eating by day, sleeping by night, talking their silly nonsense, getting married, growing old, serenely escorting their dead to the cemetery; but we do not see and we do not hear those who suffer, and what is terrible in life goes on somewhere behind the scenes. . . . Everything is quiet and peaceful, and nothing protests but mute statistics: so many people gone out of their minds, so many gallons of vodka drunk, so many children dead from malnutrition. . . . And this order of things is evidently necessary; evidently the happy man only feels at ease because the unhappy bear their burdens in silence, and without that silence happiness would be impossible. It's a case of general hypnotism. There ought to be behind the door of every happy, contented man some one standing with a hammer continually reminding him with a tap that there are unhappy people; that however happy he may be, life will show him her laws sooner or later, trouble will come for him—disease, poverty, losses, and no one will see or hear, just as now he neither sees nor hears others. But there is no man with a hammer; the happy man lives at his ease, and trivial daily cares faintly agitate him like the wind in the aspen-tree—and all goes well.

"That night I realized that I, too, was happy and contented," Ivan Ivanovitch went on, getting up. "I too, at dinner and at the hunt liked to lay down the law on life and religion, and the way to manage the peasantry. I, too, used to say that science was light, that culture was essential, but for the simple people reading and writing was enough for the time. Freedom is a blessing, I used to say; we can no more do without it than without air, but we must wait a little. Yes, I used to talk like that, and now I ask, 'For what reason are we to wait?' " asked Ivan Ivanovitch, looking angrily at Burkin. "Why wait, I ask you? What grounds have we for waiting? I shall be told, it can't be done all at once; every idea takes shape in life gradually, in its due time. But who is it says that? Where is the proof that it's right? You will fall back upon the natural order of things, the uniformity of phenomena; but is there order and uniformity in the fact that I, a living, thinking man, stand over a chasm and wait for it to close of itself, or to fill up with mud at the very time when perhaps I might leap over it or build a bridge across it? And again, wait for the sake of what? Wait till there's no strength to live? And meanwhile one must live, and one wants to live!

"I went away from my brother's early in the morning, and ever since then it has been unbearable for me to be in town. I am oppressed by its peace and quiet; I am afraid to look at the windows, for there is no spectacle more painful to me now than the sight of a happy family sitting round the table drinking tea. I am old and am not fit for the struggle; I am not even capable of hatred; I can only grieve inwardly, feel irritated and vexed, but at night my head is hot from the rush of ideas, and I cannot sleep. . . . Ah, if I were young!"

Ivan Ivanovitch walked backwards and forwards in excitement, and repeated: "If I were young!"

He suddenly went up to Alehin and began pressing first one of his hands and then the other.

"Pavel Konstantinovitch," he said in an imploring voice, "don't be calm and contented, don't let yourself be put to sleep! While you are young, strong, confident, be not weary in well-doing! There is no happiness, and there ought not to be; but if there is a meaning and an object in life, that meaning and object is not our happiness, but something greater and more rational. Do good!"

And all this Ivan Ivanovitch said with a pitiful, imploring smile, as though he were asking him a personal favour.

Then all three sat in arm-chairs at different ends of the drawing-room and were silent. Ivan Ivanovitch's story had not satisfied either Burkin or Alehin. When the generals and ladies gazed down from their gilt frames, looking in the dusk as though they were alive, it was dreary to listen to the story of the poor clerk who ate gooseberries. They felt inclined, for some reason, to talk about elegant people, about women. And their sitting in the drawing-room where every-thing—the chandeliers in their covers, the arm-chairs, and the carpet under their feet—reminded them that those very people who were now looking down from their frames had once moved about, sat, drunk tea in this room, and the fact that lovely Pelagea was moving noiselessly about was better than any story.

Alehin was fearfully sleepy; he had got up early, before three o'clock in the morning, to look after his work, and now his eyes were closing; but he was afraid his visitors might tell some interest-ing story after he had gone, and he lingered on. He did not go into the question whether what Ivan Ivanovitch had just said was right and true. His visitors did not talk of groats, nor of hay, nor of tar, but of something that had no direct bearing on his life, and he was glad and wanted them to go on.

"It's bed-time, though," said Burkin, getting up. "Allow me to wish you good-night."

Alehin said good-night and went downstairs to his own domain, while the visitors remained upstairs. They were both taken for the night to a big room where there stood two old wooden beds deco-rated with carvings, and in the corner was an ivory crucifix. The big cool beds, which had been made by the lovely Pelagea, smelt agree-ably of clean linen.

Ivan Ivanovitch undressed in silence and got into bed.

"Lord forgive us sinners!" he said, and put his head under the quilt.

His pipe lying on the table smelt strongly of stale tobacco, and Burkin could not sleep for a long while, and kept wondering where the oppressive smell came from.

The rain was pattering on the window-panes all night.

1898

About Love

At lunch next day there were very nice pies, crayfish, and mutton cutlets; and while we were eating, Nikanor, the cook, came up to ask
what the visitors would like for dinner. He was a man of medium
height, with a puffy face and little eyes; he was close-shaven, and it
looked as though his moustaches had not been shaved, but had been
pulled out by the roots. Alehin told us that the beautiful Pelagea was
in love with this cook. As he drank and was of a violent character, she
did not want to marry him, but was willing to live with him without.
He was very devout, and his religious convictions would not allow
him to "live in sin"; he insisted on her marrying him, and would
consent to nothing else, and when he was drunk he used to abuse her
and even beat her. Whenever he got drunk she used to hide upstairs
and sob, and on such occasions Alehin and the servants stayed in the
house to be ready to defend her in case of necessity.

We began talking about love.

"How love is born," said Alehin, "why Pelagea does not love
somebody more like herself in her spiritual and external qualities, and
why she fell in love with Nikanor, that ugly snout—we all call him
'The Snout'—how far questions of personal happiness are of consequence in love—all that is unknown; one can take what view ones
likes of it. So far only one incontestable truth has been uttered about
love: 'This is a great mystery.' Everything else that has been written
or said about love is not a conclusion, but only a statement of questions which have remained unanswered. The explanation which
would seem to fit one case does not apply in a dozen others, and the
very best thing, to my mind, would be to explain every case individ-
ually without attempting to generalize. We ought, as the doctors say,
to individualize each case."

"Perfectly true," Burkin assented.

"We Russians of the educated class have a partiality for these
questions that remain unanswered. Love is usually poeticized, deco-
rated with roses, nightingales; we Russians decorate our loves with

these momentous questions, and select the most uninteresting of them, too. In Moscow, when I was a student, I had a friend who shared my life, a charming lady, and every time I took her in my arms she was thinking what I would allow her a month for housekeeping and what was the price of beef a pound. In the same way, when we are in love we are never tired of asking ourselves questions: whether it is honourable or dishonourable, sensible or stupid, what this love is leading up to, and so on. Whether it is a good thing or not I don't know, but that it is in the way, unsatisfactory, and irritating, I do know."

It looked as though he wanted to tell some story. People who lead a solitary existence always have something in their hearts which they are eager to talk about. In town bachelors visit the baths and the restaurants on purpose to talk, and sometimes tell the most interesting things to bath attendants and waiters; in the country, as a rule, they unbosom themselves to their guests. Now from the window we could see a grey sky, trees drenched in the rain; in such weather we could go nowhere, and there was nothing for us to do but to tell stories and to listen.

"I have lived at Sofino and been farming for a long time," Alehin began, "ever since I left the University. I am an idle gentleman by education, a studious person by disposition; but there was a big debt owing on the estate when I came here, and as my father was in debt partly because he had spent so much on my education, I resolved not to go away, but to work till I paid off the debt. I made up my mind to this and set to work, not, I must confess, without some repugnance. The land here does not yield much, and if one is not to farm at a loss one must employ serf labour or hired labourers, which is almost the same thing, or put it on a peasant footing—that is, work the fields oneself and with one's family. There is no middle path. But in those days I did not go into such subtleties. I did not leave a clod of earth unturned; I gathered together all the peasants, men and women, from the neighbouring villages; the work went on at a tremendous pace. I myself ploughed and sowed and reaped, and was bored doing it, and frowned with disgust, like a village cat driven by hunger to eat cucumbers in the kitchen-garden. My body ached, and I slept as I walked. At first it seemed to me that I could easily reconcile this life of toil with my cultured habits; to do so, I thought, all that is necessary is to maintain a certain external order in life. I established myself upstairs here in the best rooms, and ordered them to bring me there coffee and liquor after lunch and dinner, and when I went to bed I read every night the *Vyestnik Evropi*. But one day our priest, Father Ivan, came and drank up all my liquor at one sitting; and the *Vyestnik Evropi* went to the priest's daughters; as in the summer, especially at the haymaking, I did not succeed in getting to my bed at all, and slept in the sledge in the barn, or somewhere in the forester's lodge, what chance was there of reading? Little by little I moved downstairs, began dining in the servants' kitchen, and of my former luxury nothing is left but the servants who were in my father's service, and whom it would be painful to turn away.

"In the first years I was elected here an honourary justice of the peace. I used to have to go to the town and take part in the sessions of the congress and of the circuit court, and this was a pleasant change for me. When you live here for two or three months without a break, especially in the winter, you begin at last to pine for a black coat. And in the circuit court there were frock-coats, and uniforms, and dress-coats, too, all lawyers, men who have received a general education; I had some one to talk to. After sleeping in the sledge and dining in the kitchen, to sit in an arm-chair in clean linen, in thin boots, with a chain on one's waistcoat, is such luxury!

"I received a warm welcome in the town. I made friends eagerly. And of all my acquaintanceships the most intimate and, to tell the truth, the most agreeable to me was my acquaintance with Luganovitch, the vice-president of the circuit court. You both know him: a most charming personality. It all happened just after a celebrated case of incendiarism; the preliminary investigation lasted two days; we were exhausted. Luganovitch looked at me and said:

" 'Look here, come round to dinner with me.'

"This was unexpected, as I knew Luganovitch very little, only officially, and I had never been to his house. I only just went to my hotel room to change and went off to dinner. And here it was my lot to meet Anna Alexyevna, Luganovitch's wife. At that time she was still very young, not more than twenty-two, and her first baby had been born just six months before. It is all a thing of the past; and now I should find it difficult to define what there was so exceptional in her, what it was in her attracted me so much; at the time, at dinner, it was all perfectly clear to me. I saw a lovely young, good, intelligent, fascinating woman, such as I had never met before; and I felt her at once some one close and already familiar, as though that face, those cordial, intelligent eyes, I had seen somewhere in my childhood, in the album which lay on my mother's chest of drawers.

"Four Jews were charged with being incendiaries, were regarded as a gang of robbers, and, to my mind, quite groundlessly. At dinner I was very much excited, I was uncomfortable, and I don't know what I said, but Anna Alexyevna kept shaking her head and saying to her husband:

" 'Dmitry, how is this?'

"Luganovitch is a good-natured man, one of those simple-hearted people who firmly maintain the opinion that once a man is charged before a court he is guilty, and to express doubt of the correctness of a sentence cannot be done except in legal form on paper, and not at dinner and in private conversation.

" 'You and I did not set fire to the place,' he said softly, 'and you see we are not condemned, and not in prison.'

"And both husband and wife tried to make me eat and drink as much as possible. From some trifling details, from the way they made the coffee together, for instance, and from the way they understood each other at half a word, I could gather that they lived in harmony and comfort, and that they were glad of a visitor. After dinner they played a duet on the piano; then it got dark, and I went home. That was at the beginning of spring.

"After that I spent the whole summer at Sofino without a break, and I had no time to think of the town, either, but the memory of the graceful fair-haired woman remained in my mind all those days; I did not think of her, but it was as though her light shadow were lying on my heart.

"In the late autumn there was a theatrical performance for some charitable object in the town. I went into the governor's box (I was invited to go there in the interval); I looked, and there was Anna Alexyevna sitting beside the governor's wife; and again the same irresistible, thrilling impression of beauty and sweet, caressing eyes, and again the same feeling of nearness. We sat side by side, then went to the foyer.

" 'You've grown thinner,' she said; 'have you been ill?'

" 'Yes, I've had rheumatism in my shoulder, and in rainy weather I can't sleep.'

" 'You look dispirited. In the spring, when you came to dinner, you were younger, more confident. You were full of eagerness, and talked a great deal then; you were very interesting, and I really must confess I was a little carried away by you. For some reason you often came back to my memory during the summer, and when I was getting ready for the theatre today I thought I should see you.'

"And she laughed.

" 'But you look dispirited today,' she repeated; 'it makes you seem older.'

"The next day I lunched at the Luganovitchs'. After lunch they drove out to their summer villa, in order to make arrangements there for the winter, and I went with them. I returned with them to the town, and at midnight drank tea with them in quiet domestic surroundings, while the fire glowed, and the young mother kept going to see if her baby girl was asleep. And after that, every time I went to town I never failed to visit the Luganovitchs. They grew used to me, and I grew used to them. As a rule I went in unannounced, as though I were one of the family.

" 'Who is there?' I would hear from a faraway room, in the drawling voice that seemed to me so lovely.

" 'It is Pavel Konstantinovitch,' answered the maid or the nurse.

"Anna Alexyevna would come out to me with an anxious face, and would ask every time:

" 'Why is it so long since you have been? Has anything happened?'

"Her eyes, the elegant refined hand she gave me, her indoor dress, the way she did her hair, her voice, her step, always produced the same impression on me of something new and extraordinary in my life, and very important. We talked together for hours, were silent, thinking each our own thoughts, or she played for hours to me on the piano. If there were no one at home I stayed and waited, talked to the nurse, played with the child, or lay on the sofa in the study and read; and when Anna Alexyevna came back I met her in the hall, took all her parcels from her, and for some reason I carried those parcels every time with as much love, with as much solemnity, as a boy.

"There is a proverb that if a peasant woman has no troubles she will buy a pig. The Luganovitchs had no troubles, so they made friends with me. If I did not come to the town I must be ill or something must have happened to me, and both of them were extremely anxious. They were worried that I, an educated man with a knowledge of languages, should, instead of devoting myself to science or literary work, live in the country, rush round like a squirrel in a rage, work hard with never a penny to show for it. They fancied that I was unhappy, and that I only talked, laughed, and ate to conceal my sufferings, and even at cheerful moments when I felt happy I was aware of their searching eyes fixed upon me. They were particularly touching when I really was depressed, when I was being worried by some creditor or had not money enough to pay interest on the proper day. The two of them, husband and wife, would whisper together at the window; then he would come to me and say with a grave face:

" 'If you really are in need of money at the moment, Pavel Konstantinovitch, my wife and I beg you not to hesitate to borrow from us.'

"And he would blush to his ears with emotion. And it would happen that, after whispering in the same way at the window, he would come up to me, with red ears, and say:

" 'My wife and I earnestly beg you to accept this present.'

"And he would give me studs, a cigar-case, or a lamp, and I would send them game, butter, and flowers from the country. They both, by the way, had considerable means of their own. In early days I often borrowed money, and was not very particular about it—borrowed wherever I could—but nothing in the world would have induced me to borrow from the Luganovitchs. But why talk of it?

"I was unhappy. At home, in the fields, in the barn, I thought of her; I tried to understand the mystery of a beautiful, intelligent young woman's marrying some one so uninteresting, almost an old man (her husband was over forty), and having children by him; to understand the mystery of this uninteresting, good, simple-hearted man, who argued with such wearisome good sense, at balls and evening parties kept near the more solid people, looking listless and superfluous, with a submissive, uninterested expression, as though he had been brought there for sale, who yet believed in his right to be happy, to have children by her; and I kept trying to understand why she had met him first and not me, and why such a terrible mistake in our lives need have happened.

"And when I went to the town I saw every time from her eyes that she was expecting me, and she would confess to me herself that she had had a peculiar feeling all that day and had guessed that I should come. We talked a long time, and were silent, yet we did not confess our love to each other, but timidly and jealously concealed it. We were afraid of everything that might reveal our secret to ourselves. I loved her tenderly, deeply, but I reflected and kept asking myself what our love could lead to if we had not the strength to fight against it. It seemed to be incredible that my gentle, sad love could all at once coarsely break up the even tenor of the life of her husband, her children, and all the household in which I was so loved and trusted. Would it be honourable? She would go away with me, but where? Where could I take her? It would have been a different matter if I had had a beautiful, interesting life—if, for instance, I had been struggling for the emancipation of my country, or had been a celebrated man of science, an artist or a painter; but as it was it would mean taking her from one everyday humdrum life to another as humdrum or perhaps more so. And how long would our happiness last? What would happen to her in case I was ill, in case I died, or if we simply grew cold to one another?

"And she apparently reasoned in the same way. She thought of her husband, her children, and of her mother, who loved the husband like a son. If she abandoned herself to her feelings she would have to lie, or else to tell the truth, and in her position either would have been equally terrible and inconvenient. And she was tormented by the question whether her love would bring me happiness—would she not complicate my life, which, as it was, was hard enough and full of all sorts of trouble? She fancied she was not young enough for me, that she was not industrious nor energetic enough to begin a new life, and she often talked to her husband of the importance of my marrying a girl of intelligence and merit who would be a capable housewife and a help to me—and she would immediately add that it would be difficult to find such a girl in the whole town.

"Meanwhile the years were passing. Anna Alexyevna already had two children. When I arrived at the Luganovitchs' the servants smiled cordially, the children shouted that Uncle Pavel Konstantinovitch had come, and hung on my neck; every one was overjoyed. They did not understand what was passing in my soul, and thought that I, too, was happy. Every one looked on me as a noble being. And grown-ups and children alike felt that a noble being was walking about their rooms, and that gave a peculiar charm to their manner towards me, as though in my presence their life, too, was purer and more beautiful. Anna Alexyevna and I used to go to the theatre together, always walking there; we used to sit side by side in the stalls, our shoulders touching. I would take the opera-glass from her hands without a word, and feel at that minute that she was near me, that she was mine, that we could not live without each other; but by some strange misunderstanding, when we came out of the theatre we always said good-bye and parted as though we were strangers. Goodness knows what people were saying about us in the town already, but there was not a word of truth in it all!

"In the latter years Anna Alexyevna took to going away for frequent visits to her mother or to her sister; she began to suffer from low spirits, she began to recognize that her life was spoilt and unsatisfied, and at times she did not care to see her husband nor her children. She was already being treated for neurasthenia.

"We were silent and still silent, and in the presence of outsiders she displayed a strange irritation in regard to me; whatever I talked about, she disagreed with me, and if I had an argument she sided with my opponent. If I dropped anything, she would say coldly:

" 'I congratulate you.'

"If I forgot to take the opera-glass when we were going to the theatre, she would say afterwards:

" 'I knew you would forget it.'

"Luckily or unluckily, there is nothing in our lives that does not end sooner or later. The time of parting came, as Luganovitch was appointed president in one of the western provinces. They had to sell their furniture, their horses, their summer villa. When they drove out to the villa, and afterwards looked back as they were going away, to look for the last time at the garden, at the green roof, every one was sad, and I realized that I had to say good-bye not only to the villa. It was arranged that at the end of August we should see Anna Alexyevna off to the Crimea, where the doctors were sending her, and that a little later Luganovitch and the children would set off for the western province.

"We were a great crowd to see Anna Alexyevna off. When she had said good-bye to her husband and her children and there was only a minute left before the third bell, I ran into her compartment to put a basket, which she had almost forgotten, on the rack, and I had to say good-bye. When our eyes met in the compartment our spiritual fortitude deserted us both; I took her in my arms, she pressed her face to my breast, and tears flowed from her eyes. Kissing her face, her shoulders, her hands wet with tears—oh, how unhappy we were!— I confessed my love for her, and with a burning pain in my heart I realized how unnecessary, how petty, and how deceptive all that had hindered us from loving was. I understood that when you love you must either, in your reasonings about that love, start from what is highest, from what is more important than happiness or unhappiness, sin or virtue in their accepted meaning, or you must not reason at all.

"I kissed her for the last time, pressed her hand, and parted for ever. The train had already started. I went into the next compartment—it was empty—and until I reached the next station I sat there crying. Then I walked home to Sofino. . . ."

While Alehin was telling his story, the rain left off and the sun came out. Burkin and Ivan Ivanovitch went out on the balcony, from which there was a beautiful view over the garden and the mill-pond, which was shining now in the sunshine like a mirror. They admired it, and at the same time they were sorry that this man with the kind, clever eyes, who had told them this story with such genuine feeling, should be rushing round and round this huge estate like a squirrel on a wheel instead of devoting himself to science or something else which would have made his life more pleasant; and they thought what a sorrowful face Anna Alexyevna must have had when he said good-bye to her in the railway-carriage and kissed her face and shoulders. Both of them had met her in the town, and Burkin knew her and thought her beautiful.

1898

The Darling

Olenka, the daughter of the retired collegiate assessor, Plemyanniakov, was sitting in her back porch, lost in thought. It was hot, the flies were persistent and teasing, and it was pleasant to reflect that it would soon be evening. Dark rainclouds were gathering from the east, and bringing from time to time a breath of moisture in the air.

Kukin, who was the manager of an open-air theatre called the Tivoli, and who lived in the lodge, was standing in the middle of the garden looking at the sky.

"Again!" he observed despairingly. "It's going to rain again! Rain every day, as though to spite me. I might as well hang myself! It's ruin! Fearful losses every day."

He flung up his hands, and went on, addressing Olenka:

"There! that's the life we lead, Olga Semyonovna. It's enough to make one cry. One works and does one's utmost; one wears oneself out, getting no sleep at night, and racks one's brain what to do for the best. And then what happens? To begin with, one's public is ignorant, boorish. I give them the very best operetta, a dainty masque, first rate music-hall artists. But do you suppose that's what they want! They don't understand anything of that sort. They want a clown; what they ask for is vulgarity. And then look at the weather! Almost every evening it rains. It started on the tenth of May, and it's kept it up all May and June. It's simply awful! The public doesn't come, but I've to pay the rent just the same, and pay the artists."

The next evening the clouds would gather again, and Kukin would say with an hysterical laugh:

"Well, rain away, then! Flood the garden, drown me! Damn my luck in this world and the next! Let the artists have me up! Send me to prison!—to Siberia!—the scaffold! Ha, ha, ha!"

And next day the same thing.

Olenka listened to Kukin with silent gravity, and sometimes tears came into her eyes. In the end his misfortunes touched her; she grew to love him. He was a small thin man, with a yellow face, and curls combed forward on his forehead. He spoke in a thin tenor; as he talked his mouth worked on one side, and there was always an expression of despair on his face; yet he aroused a deep and genuine affection in her. She was always fond of some one, and could not exist without loving. In earlier days she had loved her papa, who now sat in a darkened room, breathing with difficulty; she had loved her aunt who used to come every other year from Bryansk; and before that, when she was at school, she had loved her French master. She was a gentle, soft-hearted, compassionate girl, with mild, tender eyes and very good health. At the sight of her full rosy cheeks, her soft white neck with a little dark mole on it, and the kind, naïve smile, which came into her face when she listened to anything pleasant, men thought, "Yes, not half bad," and smiled too, while lady visitors could not refrain from seizing her hand in the middle of a converstion, exclaiming in a gush of delight, "You darling!"

The house in which she had lived from her birth upwards, and which was left her in her father's will, was at the extreme end of the town, not far from the Tivoli. In the evenings and at night she could hear the band playing, and the crackling and banging of fireworks, and it seemed to her that it was Kukin struggling with his destiny, storming the entrenchments of his chief foe, the indifferent public; there was a sweet thrill at her heart, she had no desire to sleep, and when he returned home at daybreak, she tapped softly at her bedroom window, and showing him only her face and one shoulder through the curtain, she gave him a friendly smile. . . .

He proposed to her, and they were married. And when he had a closer view of her neck and her plump, fine shoulders, he threw up his hands, and said:

"You darling!"

He was happy, but as it rained on the day and night of his wedding, his face still retained an expression of despair.

They got on very well together. She used to sit in his office, to look after things in the Tivoli, to put down the accounts and pay the wages. And her rosy cheeks, her sweet, naïve, radiant smile, were to be seen now at the office window, now in the refreshment bar or behind the scenes of the theatre. And already she used to say to her acquaintances that the theatre was the chief and most important thing in life, and that it was only through the drama that one could derive true enjoyment and become cultivated and humane.

"But do you suppose the public understands that?" she used to say. "What they want is a clown. Yesterday we gave 'Faust Inside Out,' and almost all the boxes were empty; but if Vanitchka and I had been producing some vulgar thing, I assure you the theatre would have been packed. Tomorrow Vanitchka and I are doing 'Orpheus in Hell.' Do come."

And what Kukin said about the theatre and the actors she repeated. Like him she despised the public for their ignorance and their indifference to art; she took part in the rehearsals, she corrected the actors, she kept an eye on the behaviour of the musicians, and when there was an unfavourable notice in the local paper, she shed tears, and then went to the editor's office to set things right.

The actors were fond of her and used to call her "Vanitchka and I," and "the darling"; she was sorry for them and used to lend them small sums of money, and if they deceived her, she used to shed a few tears in private, but did not complain to her husband.

They got on well in the winter too. They took the theatre in the town for the whole winter, and let it for short terms to a Little Russian company, or to a conjurer, or to a local dramatic society. Olenka grew stouter, and was always beaming with satisfaction, while Kukin grew thinner and yellower, and continually complained of their terrible losses, although he had not done badly all the winter. He used to cough at night, and she used to give him hot raspberry tea or lime-flower water, to rub him with eau-de-Cologne and to wrap him in her warm shawls.

"You're such a sweet pet!" she used to say with perfect sincerity, stroking his hair. "You're such a pretty dear!"

Towards Lent he went to Moscow to collect a new troupe, and without him she could not sleep, but sat all night at her window, looking at the stars, and she compared herself with the hens, who are awake all night and uneasy when the cock is not in the hen-house. Kukin was detained in Moscow, and wrote that he would be back at Easter, adding some instructions about the Tivoli. But on the Sunday before Easter, late in the evening, came a sudden ominous knock at the gate; some one was hammering on the gate as though on a barrel—boom, boom, boom! The drowsy cook went flopping with her bare feet through the puddles, as she ran to open the gate.

"Please open," said some one outside in a thick bass. "There is a telegram for you."

Olenka had received telegrams from her husband before, but this time for some reason she felt numb with terror. With shaking hands she opened the telegram and read as follows:

"Ivan Petrovitch died suddenly to-day. Awaiting immate instructions fufuneral Tuesday."

That was how it was written in the telegram—"fufuneral," and the utterly incomprehensible word "immate." It was signed by the stage manager of the operatic company.

"My darling!" sobbed Olenka. "Vanitchka, my precious, my darling! Why did I ever meet you! Why did I know you and love you! Your poor heart-broken Olenka is all alone without you!"

Kukin's funeral took place on Tuesday in Moscow, Olenka returned home on Wednesday, and as soon as she got indoors she threw herself on her bed and sobbed so loudly that it could be heard next door, and in the street.

"Poor darling!" the neighbours said, as they crossed themselves. "Olga Semyonovna, poor darling! How she does take on!"

Three months later Olenka was coming home from mass, melancholy and in deep mourning. It happened that one of her neighbours, Vassily Andreitch Pustovalov, returning home from church, walked back beside her. He was the manager at Babakayev's, the timber merchant's. He wore a straw hat, a white waistcoat, and a gold watch-chain, and looked more like a country gentleman than a man in trade.

"Everything happens as it is ordained, Olga Semyonovna," he said gravely, with a sympathetic note in his voice; "and if any of our dear ones die, it must be because it is the will of God, so we ought to have fortitude and bear it submissively."

After seeing Olenka to her gate, he said good-bye and went on. All day afterwards she heard his sedately dignified voice, and whenever she shut her eyes she saw his dark beard. She liked him very much. And apparently she had made an impression on him too, for not long afterwards an elderly lady, with whom she was only slightly acquainted, came to drink coffee with her, and as soon as she was seated at table began to talk about Pustovalov, saying that he was an excellent man whom one could thoroughly depend upon, and that any girl would be glad to marry him. Three days later Pustovalov came himself. He did not stay long, only about ten minutes, and he did not say much, but when he left, Olenka loved him—loved him so much that she lay awake all night in a perfect fever, and in the morning she sent for the elderly lady. The match was quickly arranged, and then came the wedding.

Pustovalov and Olenka got on very well together when they were married.

Usually he sat in the office till dinner-time, then he went out on business, while Olenka took his place, and sat in the office till evening, making up accounts and booking orders.

"Timber gets dearer every year; the price rises twenty per cent," she would say to her customers and friends. "Only fancy we used to sell local timber, and now Vassitchka always has to go for wood to the Mogilev district. And the freight!" she would add, covering her cheeks with her hands in horror. "The freight!"

It seemed to her that she had been in the timber trade for ages and ages, and that the most important and necessary thing in life was timber; and there was something intimate and touching to her in the very sound of words such as "baulk," "post," "beam," "pole," "scantling," "batten," "lath," "plank," etc.

At night when she was asleep she dreamed of perfect mountains of planks and boards, and long strings of wagons, carting timber somewhere far away. She dreamed that a whole regiment of six-inch beams forty feet high, standing on end, was marching upon the timber-yard; that logs, beams, and boards knocked together with the resounding crash of dry wood, kept falling and getting up again, piling themselves on each other. Olenka cried out in her sleep, and Pustovalov said to her tenderly: "Olenka, what's the matter, darling? Cross yourself!"

Her husband's ideas were hers. If he thought the room was too hot, or that business was slack, she thought the same. Her husband did not care for entertainments, and on holidays he stayed at home. She did likewise.

"You are always at home or in the office," her friends said to her. "You should go to the theatre, darling, or to the circus."

"Vassitchka and I have no time to go to theatres," she would answer sedately. "We have no time for nonsense. What's the use of these theatres?"

On Saturdays Pustovalov and she used to go to the evening service; on holidays to early mass, and they walked side by side with softened faces as they came home from church. There was a pleasant fragrance about them both, and her silk dress rustled agreeably. At home they drank tea, with fancy bread and jams of various kinds, and afterwards they ate pie. Every day at twelve o'clock there was a savoury smell of beet-root soup and of mutton or duck in their yard, and on fast-days of fish, and no one could pass the gate without feeling hungry. In the office the samovar was always boiling, and customers were regaled with tea and cracknels. Once a week the couple went to the baths and returned side by side, both red in the face.

"Yes, we have nothing to complain of, thank God," Olenka used to say to her acquaintances. "I wish every one were as well off as Vassitchka and I."

When Pustovalov went away to buy wood in the Mogilev district, she missed him dreadfully, lay awake and cried. A young veterinary surgeon in the army, called Smirnin, to whom they had let their lodge, used sometimes to come in the evening. He used to talk to her and play cards with her, and this entertained her in her husband's absence. She was particularly interested in what he told her of his home life. He was married and had a little boy, but was separated from his wife because she had been unfaithful to him, and now he hated her and used to send her forty roubles a month for the maintenance of their son. And hearing of all this, Olenka sighed and shook her head. She was sorry for him.

"Well, God keep you," she used to say to him at parting, as she lighted him down the stairs with a candle. "Thank you for coming to cheer me up, and may the Mother of God give you health."

And she always expressed herself with the same sedateness and dignity, the same reasonableness, in imitation of her husband. As the veterinary surgeon was disappearing behind the door below, she would say:

"You know, Vladimir Platonitch, you'd better make it up with your wife. You should forgive her for the sake of your son. You may be sure the little fellow understands."

And when Pustovalov came back, she told him in a low voice about the veterinary surgeon and his unhappy home life, and both sighed and shook their heads and talked about the boy, who, no doubt, missed his father, and by some strange connection of ideas, they went up to the holy ikons, bowed to the ground before them and prayed that God would give them children.

And so the Pustovalovs lived for six years quietly and peaceably in love and complete harmony.

But behold! one winter day after drinking hot tea in the office, Vassily Andreitch went out into the yard without his cap on to see about sending off some timber, caught cold and was taken ill. He had the best doctors, but he grew worse and died after four months' illness. And Olenka was a widow once more.

"I've nobody, now you've left me, my darling," she sobbed, after her husband's funeral. "How can I live without you, in wretchedness and misery! Pity me, good people, all alone in the world!"

She went about dressed in black with long "weepers," and gave up wearing hat and gloves for good. She hardly ever went out, except to church, or to her husband's grave, and led the life of a nun. It was not till six months later that she took off the weepers and opened the shutters of the windows. She was sometimes seen in the mornings, going with her cook to market for provisions, but what went on in her house and how she lived now could only be surmised. People guessed, from seeing her drinking tea in her garden with the veterinary surgeon, who read the newspaper aloud to her, and from the fact that, meeting a lady she knew at the post-office, she said to her:

"There is no proper veterinary inspection in our town, and that's the cause of all sorts of epidemics. One is always hearing of people's getting infection from the milk supply, or catching diseases from horses and cows. The health of domestic animals ought to be as well cared for as the health of human beings."

She repeated the veterinary surgeon's words, and was of the same opinion as he about everything. It was evident that she could not live a year without some attachment, and had found new happiness in the lodge. In any one else this would have been censured, but no one could think ill of Olenka; everything she did was so natural. Neither she nor the veterinary surgeon said anything to other people of the change in their relations, and tried, indeed, to conceal it, but without success, for Olenka could not keep a secret. When he had visitors, men serving in his regiment, and she poured out tea or served the supper, she would begin talking of the cattle plague, of the foot and mouth disease, and of the municipal slaughter-houses. He was dreadfully embarrassed, and when the guests had gone, he would seize her by the hand and hiss angrily:

"I've asked you before not to talk about what you don't understand. When we veterinary surgeons are talking among ourselves, please don't put your word in. It's really annoying."

And she would look at him with astonishment and dismay, and ask him in alarm: "But, Voloditchka, what *am* I to talk about?"

And with tears in her eyes she would embrace him, begging him not to be angry, and they were both happy.

But this happiness did not last long. The veterinary surgeon departed, departed for ever with his regiment, when it was transferred to a distant place—to Siberia, it may be. And Olenka was left alone.

Now she was absolutely alone. Her father had long been dead, and his armchair lay in the attic, covered with dust and lame of one leg. She got thinner and plainer, and when people met her in the street they did not look at her as they used to, and did not smile to her; evidently her best years were over and left behind, and now a new sort of life had begun for her, which did not bear thinking about. In the evening Olenka sat in the porch, and heard the band playing and the fireworks popping in the Tivoli, but now the sound stirred no response. She looked into her yard without interest, thought of nothing, wished for nothing, and afterwards, when night came on she went to bed and dreamed of her empty yard. She ate and drank as it were unwillingly.

And what was worst of all, she had no opinions of any sort. She saw the objects about her and understood what she saw, but could not form any opinion about them, and did not know what to talk about. And how awful it is not to have any opinions! One sees a bottle, for instance, or the rain, or a peasant driving in his cart, but what the bottle is for, or the rain, or the peasant, and what the meaning of it, one can't say, and could not even for a thousand roubles. When she had Kukin, or Pustovalov, or the veterinary surgeon, Olenka could explain everything, and give her opinion about anything you like, but now there was the same emptiness in her brain and in her heart as there was in her yard outside. And it was as harsh and as bitter as wormwood in the mouth.

Little by little the town grew in all directions. The road became a street, and where the Tivoli and the timber-yard had been, there were new turnings and houses. How rapidly time passes! Olenka's house grew dingy, the roof got rusty, the shed sank on one side, and the whole yard was overgrown with docks and stinging-nettles. Olenka herself had grown plain and elderly; in summer she sat in the porch, and her soul, as before, was empty and dreary and full of bitterness. In winter she sat at her window and looked at the snow. When she caught the scent of spring, or heard the chime of the church bells, a sudden rush of memories from the past came over her, there was a tender ache in her heart, and her eyes brimmed over with tears; but this was only for a minute, and then came emptiness again and the sense of the futility of life. The black kitten, Briska, rubbed against her and purred softly, but Olenka was not touched by these feline caresses. That was not what she needed. She wanted a love that would absorb her whole being, her whole soul and reason—that would give her ideas and an object in life, and would warm her old blood. And she would shake the kitten off her skirt and say with vexation:

"Get along; I don't want you!"

And so it was, day after day and year after year, and no joy, and no opinions. Whatever Mavra, the cook, said she accepted.

One hot July day, towards evening, just as the cattle were being driven away, and the whole yard was full of dust, some one suddenly knocked at the gate. Olenka went to open it herself and was dumbfounded when she looked out: she saw Smirnin, the veterinary surgeon, grey-headed, and dressed as a civilian. She suddenly remembered everything. She could not help crying and letting her head fall on his breast without uttering a word, and in the violence of her feeling she did not notice how they both walked into the house and sat down to tea.

"My dear Vladimir Platonitch! What fate has brought you?" she muttered, trembling with joy.

"I want to settle here for good, Olga Semyonovna," he told her. "I have resigned my post, and have come to settle down and try my luck on my own account. Besides, it's time for my boy to go to school. He's a big boy. I am reconciled with my wife, you know."

"Where is she?" asked Olenka.

"She's at the hotel with the boy, and I'm looking for lodgings."

"Good gracious, my dear soul! Lodgings? Why not have my house? Why shouldn't that suit you? Why, my goodness, I wouldn't take any rent!" cried Olenka in a flutter, beginning to cry again. "You live here, and the lodge will do nicely for me. Oh dear! how glad I am!"

Next day the roof was painted and the walls were whitewashed, and Olenka, with her arms akimbo, walked about the yard giving directions. Her face was beaming with her old smile, and she was brisk and alert as though she had waked from a long sleep. The veterinary's wife arrived—a thin, plain lady, with short hair and a peevish expression. With her was her little Sasha, a boy of ten, small for his age, blue-eyed, chubby, with dimples in his cheeks. And scarcely had the boy walked into the yard when he ran after the cat, and at once there was the sound of his gay, joyous laugh.

"Is that your puss, auntie?" he asked Olenka. "When she has little ones, do give us a kitten. Mamma is awfully afraid of mice."

Olenka talked to him, and gave him tea. Her heart warmed and there was a sweet ache in her bosom, as though the boy had been her own child. And when he sat at the table in the evening, going over his lessons, she looked at him with deep tenderness and pity as she murmured to herself:

"You pretty pet! . . . my precious! . . . Such a fair little thing, and so clever."

" 'An island is a piece of land which is entirely surrounded by water,' " he read aloud.

"An island is a piece of land," she repeated, and this was the first opinion to which she gave utterance with positive conviction after so many years of silence and dearth of ideas.

Now she had opinions of her own, and at supper she talked to Sasha's parents, saying how difficult the lessons were at the high schools, but that yet the high-school was better than a commercial one, since with a high-school education all careers were open to one, such as being a doctor or an engineer.

Sasha began going to the high school. His mother departed to Harkov to her sister's and did not return; his father used to go off every day to inspect cattle, and would often be away from home for three days together, and it seemed to Olenka as though Sasha was entirely abandoned, that he was not wanted at home, that he was being starved, and she carried him off to her lodge and gave him a little room there.

And for six months Sasha had lived in the lodge with her. Every morning Olenka came into his bedroom and found him fast asleep, sleeping noiselessly with his hand under his cheek. She was sorry to wake him.

"Sashenka," she would say mournfully, "get up, darling. It's time for school."

He would get up, dress and say his prayers, and then sit down to breakfast, drink three glasses of tea, and eat two large cracknels and half a buttered roll. All this time he was hardly awake and a little ill-humoured in consequence.

"You don't quite know your fable, Sashenka," Olenka would say, looking at him as though he were about to set off on a long journey. "What a lot of trouble I have with you! You must work and do your best, darling, and obey your teachers."

"Oh, do leave me alone!" Sasha would say.

Then he would go down the street to school, a little figure, wearing a big cap and carrying a satchel on his shoulder. Olenka would follow him noiselessly.

"Sashenka!" she would call after him, and she would pop into his hand a date or a caramel. When he reached the street where the school was, he would feel ashamed of being followed by a tall, stout woman; he would turn round and say:

"You'd better go home, auntie. I can go the rest of the way alone."

She would stand still and look after him fixedly till he had disappeared at the school-gate.

Ah, how she loved him! Of her former attachments not one had been so deep; never had her soul surrendered to any feeling so spontaneously, so disinterestedly, and so joyously as now that her maternal instincts were aroused. For this little boy with the dimple in his cheek and the big school cap, she would have given her whole life, she would have given it with joy and tears of tenderness. Why? Who can tell why?

When she had seen the last of Sasha, she returned home, contented and serene, brimming over with love; her face, which had grown younger during the last six months, smiled and beamed; people meeting her looked at her with pleasure.

"Good-morning, Olga Semyonovna, darling. How are you, darling?"

"The lessons at the high school are very difficult now," she would relate at the market. "It's too much; in the first class yesterday they gave him a fable to learn by heart, and a Latin translation and a problem. You know it's too much for a little chap."

And she would begin talking about the teachers, the lessons, and the school books, saying just what Sasha said.

At three o'clock they had dinner together: in the evening they learned their lessons together and cried. When she put him to bed, she would stay a long time making the Cross over him and murmuring a prayer; then she would go to bed and dream of that far-away misty future when Sasha would finish his studies and become a doctor or an engineer, would have a big house of his own with horses and a carriage, would get married and have children. . . . She would fall asleep still thinking of the same thing, and tears would run down her cheeks from her closed eyes, while the black cat lay purring beside her: "Mrr, mrr, mrr."

Suddenly there would come a loud knock at the gate.

Olenka would wake up breathless with alarm, her heart throbbing. Half a minute later would come another knock.

"It must be a telegram from Harkov," she would think, beginning to tremble from head to foot. "Sasha's mother is sending for him from Harkov. . . . Oh, mercy on us!"

She was in despair. Her head, her hands, and her feet would turn chill, and she would feel that she was the most unhappy woman in the world. But another minute would pass, voices would be heard: it would turn out to be the veterinary surgeon coming home from the club.

"Well, thank God!" she would think.

And gradually the load in her heart would pass off, and she would feel at ease. She would go back to bed thinking of Sasha, who lay sound asleep in the next room, sometimes crying out in his sleep:

"I'll give it you! Get away! Shut up!"

1899

The New Villa

I

Two miles from the village of Obrutchanovo a huge bridge was being built. From the village, which stood up high on the steep river-bank, its trellis-like skeleton could be seen, and in foggy weather and on still winter days, when its delicate iron girders and all the scaffolding around was covered with hoar frost, it presented a picturesque and even fantastic spectacle. Kutcherov, the engineer who was building the bridge, a stout, broad-shouldered, bearded man in a soft crumpled cap drove through the village in his racing droshky or his open carriage. Now and then on holidays navvies working on the bridge would come to the village; they begged for alms, laughed at the women, and sometimes carried off something. But that was rare; as a rule the days passed quietly and peacefully as though no bridge-building were going on, and only in the evening, when camp fires gleamed near the bridge, the wind faintly wafted the songs of the navvies. And by day there was sometimes the mournful clang of metal, don-don-don.

It happened that the engineer's wife came to see him. She was pleased with the river-banks and the gorgeous view over the green valley with trees, churches, flocks, and she began begging her husband to buy a small piece of ground and to build them a cottage on it. Her husband agreed. They bought sixty acres of land, and on the high bank in a field, where in earlier days the cows of Obrutchanovo used to wander, they built a pretty house of two storeys with a terrace and a verandah, with a tower and a flagstaff on which a flag fluttered on Sundays—they built it in about three months, and then all the winter they were planting big trees, and when spring came and everything began to be green there were already avenues to the new house, a gardener and two labourers in white aprons were digging near it, there was a little fountain, and a globe of looking-glass flashed so brilliantly that it was painful to look at. The house had already been named the New Villa.

On a bright, warm morning at the end of May two horses were brought to Obrutchanovo to the village blacksmith, Rodion Petrov. They came from the New Villa. The horses were sleek, graceful beasts, as white as snow, and strikingly alike.

"Perfect swans!" said Rodion, gazing at them with reverent admiration.

His wife Stepanida, his children and grandchildren came out into the street to look at them. By degrees a crowd collected. The Lytchkovs, father and son, both men with swollen faces and entirely beardless, came up bareheaded. Kozov, a tall, thin old man with a long, narrow beard, came up leaning on a stick with a crook handle: he kept winking with his crafty eyes and smiling ironically as though he knew something.

· "It's only that they are white; what is there in them?" he said. "Put mine on oats, and they will be just as sleek. They ought to be in a plough and with a whip, too. . . ."

The coachman simply looked at him with disdain, but did not utter a word. And afterwards, while they were blowing up the fire at the forge, the coachman talked while he smoked cigarettes. The peasants learned from him various details: his employers were wealthy people; his mistress, Elena Ivanovna, had till her marriage lived in Moscow in a poor way as a governess; she was kind-hearted, compassionate, and fond of helping the poor. On the new estate, he told them, they were not going to plough or to sow, but simply to live for their pleasure, live only to breathe the fresh air. When he had finished and led the horses back a crowd of boys followed him, the dogs barked, and Kozov, looking after him, winked sarcastically.

"Landowners, too-oo!" he said. "They have built a house and set up horses, but I bet they are nobodies—landowners, too-oo."

Kozov for some reason took a dislike from the first to the new house, to the white horses, and to the handsome, well-fed coachman. Kozov was a solitary man, a widower; he had a dreary life (he was prevented from working by a disease which he sometimes called a rupture and sometimes worms); he was maintained by his son, who worked at a confectioner's in Harkov and sent him money; and from early morning till evening he sauntered at leisure about the river or about the village; if he saw, for instance, a peasant carting a log, or fishing, he would say: "That log's dry wood—it is rotten," or, "They won't bite in weather like this." In times of drought he would declare that there would not be a drop of rain till the frost came; and when the rains came he would say that everything would rot in the fields, that everything was ruined. And as he said these things he would wink as though he knew something.

At the New Villa they burned Bengal lights and sent up fireworks in the evenings, and a sailing-boat with red lanterns floated by Obrutchanovo. One morning the engineer's wife, Elena Ivanovna, and her little daughter drove to the village in a carriage with yellow wheels and a pair of dark bay ponies; both mother and daughter were wearing broad-brimmed straw hats, bent down over their ears.

This was exactly at the time when they were carting manure, and the blacksmith Rodion, a tall, gaunt old man, bareheaded and barefooted, was standing near his dirty and repulsive-looking cart and, flustered, looked at the ponies, and it was evident by his face that he had never seen such little horses before.

"The Kutcherov lady has come!" was whispered around. "Look, the Kutcherov lady has come!"

Elena Ivanovna looked at the huts as though she were selecting one, and then stopped at the very poorest, at the windows of which there were so many children's heads—flaxen, red, and dark. Stepanida, Rodion's wife, a stout woman, came running out of the hut; her kerchief slipped off her grey head; she looked at the carriage facing the sun, and her face smiled and wrinkled up as though she were blind.

"This is for your children," said Elena Ivanovna, and she gave her three roubles.

Stepanida suddenly burst into tears and bowed down to the ground. Rodion, too, flopped to the ground, displaying his brownish bald head, and as he did so he almost caught his wife in the ribs with the fork. Elena Ivanovna was overcome with confusion and drove back.

II

The Lytchkovs, father and son, caught in their meadows two carthorses, a pony, and a broad-faced Aalhaus bull-calf, and with the help of red-headed Volodka, son of the blacksmith Rodion, drove them to the village. They called the village elder, collected witnesses, and went to look at the damage.

"All right, let 'em!" said Kozov, winking, "le-et 'em! Let them get out of it if they can, the engineers! Do you think there is no such thing as law? All right! Send for the police inspector, draw up a statement! . . ."

"Draw up a statement," repeated Volodka.

"I don't want to let this pass!" shouted the younger Lytchkov. He shouted louder and louder, and his beardless face seemed to be more and more swollen. "They've set up a nice fashion! Leave them free, and they will ruin all the meadows! You've no sort of right to ill-treat people! We are not serfs now!"

"We are not serfs now!" repeated Volodka.

"We got on all right without a bridge," said the elder Lytchkov gloomily; "we did not ask for it. What do we want a bridge for? We don't want it!"

"Brothers, good Christians, we cannot leave it like this!"

"All right, let 'em!" said Kozov, winking. "Let them get out of it if they can! Landowners, indeed!"

They went back to the village, and as they walked the younger Lytchkov beat himself on the breast with his fist and shouted all the way, and Volodka shouted, too, repeating his words. And meanwhile quite a crowd had gathered in the village round the thoroughbred bull-calf and the horses. The bull-calf was embarrassed and looked up from under his brows, but suddenly lowered his muzzle to the ground and took to his heels, kicking up his hind legs; Kozov was frightened and waved his stick at him, and they all burst out laughing. Then they locked up the beasts and waited.

In the evening the engineer sent five roubles for the damage, and the two horses, the pony and the bull-calf, without being fed or given water, returned home, their heads hanging with a guilty air as though they were convicted criminals.

On getting the five roubles the Lytchkovs, father and son, the village elder and Volodka, punted over the river in a boat and went to a hamlet on the other side where there was a tavern, and there had a long carousal. Their singing and the shouting of the younger Lytchkov could be heard from the village. Their women were uneasy and did not sleep all night. Rodion did not sleep either.

"It's a bad business," he said, sighing and turning from side to side. "The gentleman will be angry, and then there will be trouble. . . . They have insulted the gentleman. . . . Oh, they've insulted him. It's a bad business. . . ."

It happened that the peasants, Rodion amongst them, went into their forest to divide the clearings for mowing, and as they were returning home they were met by the engineer. He was wearing a red cotton shirt and high boots; a setter dog with its long tongue hanging out, followed behind him.

"Good-day, brothers," he said.

The peasants stopped and took off their hats.

"I have long wanted to have a talk with you, friends," he went on. "This is what it is. Ever since the early spring your cattle have been in my copse and garden every day. Everything is trampled down; the pigs have rooted up the meadow, are ruining everything in the kitchen garden, and all the undergrowth in the copse is destroyed. There is no getting on with your herdsmen; one asks them civilly, and they are rude. Damage is done on my estate every day and I do nothing—I don't fine you or make a complaint; meanwhile you impounded my horses and my bull-calf and exacted five roubles. Was that right? Is that neighbourly?" he went on, and his face was so soft and persuasive, and his expression was not forbidding. "Is that the way decent people behave? A week ago one of your people cut down two oak saplings in my copse. You have dug up the road to Eresnevo, and now I have to go two miles round. Why do you injure me at every step? What harm have I done you? For God's sake, tell me! My wife and I do our utmost to live with you in peace and harmony; we help the peasants as we can. My wife is a kind, warm-hearted woman; she never refuses you help. That is her dream—to be of use to you and your children. You reward us with evil for our good. You are unjust, my friends. Think of that. I ask you earnestly to think it over. We treat you humanely; repay us in the same coin."

He turned and went away. The peasants stood a little longer, put on their caps and walked away. Rodion, who always understood everything that was said to him in some peculiar way of his own, heaved a sigh and said:

"We must pay. 'Repay in coin, my friends' . . . he said."

They walked to the village in silence. On reaching home Rodion said his prayer, took off his boots, and sat down on the bench beside his wife. Stepanida and he always sat side by side when they were at home, and always walked side by side in the street; they ate and they drank and they slept always together, and the older they grew the more they loved one another. It was hot and crowded in their hut, and there were children everywhere—on the floors, in the windows, on the stove. . . . In spite of her advanced years Stepanida was still bearing children, and now, looking at the crowd of children, it was hard to distinguish which were Rodion's and which were Volodka's. Volodka's wife, Lukerya, a plain young woman with prominent eyes and a nose like the beak of a bird, was kneading dough in a tub; Volodka was sitting on the stove with his legs hanging.

"On the road near Nikita's buckwheat . . . the engineer with his dog . . ." Rodion began, after a rest, scratching his ribs and his elbow. " 'You must pay,' says he . . . 'coin,' says he. . . . Coin or no coin, we shall have to collect ten kopecks from every hut. We've offended the gentleman very much. I am sorry for him. . . ."

"We've lived without a bridge," said Volodka, not looking at anyone, "and we don't want one."

"What next; the bridge is a government business."

"We don't want it."

"Your opinion is not asked. What is it to you?"

" 'Your opinion is not asked,' " Volodka mimicked him. "We don't want to drive anywhere; what do we want with a bridge? If we have to, we can cross by the boat."

Someone from the yard outside knocked at the window so violently that it seemed to shake the whole hut.

"Is Volodka at home?" he heard the voice of the younger Lytchkov. "Volodka, come out, come along."

Volodka jumped down off the stove and began looking for his cap.

"Don't go, Volodka," said Rodion diffidently. "Don't go with them, son. You are foolish, like a little child; they will teach you no good; don't go!"

"Don't go, son," said Stepanida, and she blinked as though about to shed tars. "I bet they are calling you to the tavern."

" 'To the tavern,' " Volodka mimicked.

"You'll come back drunk again, you currish Herod," said Lukerya, looking at him angrily. "Go along, go along, and may you burn up with vodka, you tailless Satan!"

"You hold your tongue," shouted Volodka.

"They've married me to a fool, they've ruined me, a luckless orphan, you red-headed drunkard . . ." wailed Lukerya, wiping her face with a hand covered with dough. "I wish I had never set eyes on you."

Volodka gave her a blow on the ear and went off.

III

Elena Ivanovna and her little daughter visited the village on foot. They were out for a walk. It was a Sunday, and the peasant women and girls were walking up and down the street in their brightly-coloured dresses. Rodion and Stepanida, sitting side by side at their door, bowed and smiled to Elena Ivanovna and her little daughter as to acquaintances. From the windows more than a dozen children stared at them; their faces expressed amazement and curiosity, and they could be heard whispering:

"The Kutcherov lady has come! The Kutcherov lady!"

"Good-morning," said Elena Ivanovna, and she stopped; she paused, and then asked: "Well, how are you getting on?"

"We get along all right, thank God," answered Rodion, speaking rapidly. "To be sure we get along."

"The life we lead!" smiled Stepanida. "You can see our poverty yourself, dear lady! The family is fourteen souls in all, and only two bread-winners. We are supposed to be blacksmiths, but when they bring us a horse to shoe we have no coal, nothing to buy it with. We are worried to death, lady," she went on, and laughed. "Oh, oh, we are worried to death."

Elena Ivanovna sat down at the entrance and, putting her arm round her little girl, pondered something, and judging from the little girl's expression, melancholy thoughts were straying through her mind, too; as she brooded she played with the sumptuous lace on the parasol she had taken out of her mother's hands.

"Poverty," said Rodion, "a great deal of anxiety—you see no end to it. Here, God sends no rain . . . our life is not easy, there is no denying it."

"You have a hard time in this life," said Elena Ivanovna, "but in the other world you will be happy."

Rodion did not understand her, and simply coughed into his clenched hand by way of reply. Stepanida said:

"Dear lady, the rich men will be all right in the next world, too. The rich put up candles, pay for services; the rich give to beggars, but what can the poor man do? He has no time to make the sign of the cross. He is the beggar of beggars himself; how can he think of his soul? And many sins come from poverty; from trouble we snarl at one another like dogs, we haven't a good word to say to one another, and all sorts of things happen, dear lady—God forbid! It seems we have no luck in this world nor the next. All the luck has fallen to the rich."

She spoke gaily; she was evidently used to talking of her hard life. And Rodion smiled, too; he was pleased that his old woman was so clever, so ready of speech.

"It is only on the surface that the rich seem to be happy," said Elena Ivanovna. "Every man has his sorrow. Here my husband and I do not live poorly, we have means, but are we happy? I am young, but I have had four children; my children are always being ill. I am ill, too, and constantly being doctored."

"And what is your illness?" asked Rodion.

"A woman's complaint. I get no sleep; a continual headache gives me no peace. Here I am sitting and talking, but my head is bad, I am weak all over, and I should prefer the hardest labour to such a condition. My soul, too, is troubled; I am in continual fear for my children, my husband. Every family has its own trouble of some sort; we have ours. I am not of noble birth. My grandfather was a simple peasant, my father was a tradesman in Moscow; he was a plain, uneducated man, too, while my husband's parents were wealthy and distinguished. They did not want him to marry me, but he disobeyed them, quarrelled with them, and they have not forgiven us to this day. That worries my husband; it troubles him and keeps him in constant agitation; he loves his mother, loves her dearly. So I am uneasy, too, my soul is in pain."

Peasants, men and women, were by now standing round Rodion's hut and listening. Kozov came up, too, and stood twitching his long, narrow beard. The Lytchkovs, father and son, drew near.

"And say what you like, one cannot be happy and satisfied if one does not feel in one's proper place." Elena Ivanovna went on. "Each of you has his strip of land, each of you works and knows what he is working for; my husband builds bridges—in short, everyone has his place, while I, I simply walk about. I have not my bit to work. I don't work, and feel as though I were an outsider. I am saying all this that you may not judge from outward appearances; if a man is

expensively dressed and has means it does not prove that he is satisfied with his life."

She got up to go away and took her daughter by the hand.

"I like your place here very much," she said, and smiled, and from
that faint, diffident smile one could tell how unwell she really was,
how young and how pretty; she had a pale, thinnish face with dark
eyebrows and fair hair. And the little girl was just such another as her
mother: thin, fair, and slender. There was a fragrance of scent about
them.

"I like the river and the forest and the village," Elena Ivanovna
went on; "I could live here all my life, and I feel as though here I
should get strong and find my place. I want to help you—I want to
dreadfully—to be of use, to be a real friend to you. I know your
need, and what I don't know I feel, my heart guesses. I am sick,
feeble, and for me perhaps it is not possible to change my life as I
would. But I have children. I will try to bring them up that they may
be of use to you, may love you. I shall impress upon them continually
that their life does not belong to them, but to you. Only I beg you
earnestly, I beseech you, trust us, live in friendship with us. My husband is a kind, good man. Don't worry him, don't irritate him. He is
sensitive to every trifle, and yesterday, for instance, your cattle were
in our vegetable garden, and one of your people broke down the
fence to the bee-hives, and such an attitude to us drives my husband
to despair. I beg you," she went on in an imploring voice, and she
clasped her hands on her bosom—"I beg you to treat us as good
neighbours; let us live in peace! There is a saying, you know, that
even a bad peace is better than a good quarrel, and, 'Don't buy property, but buy neighbours.' I repeat my husband is a kind man and
good; if all goes well we promise to do everything in our power for
you; we will mend the roads, we will build a school for your children.
I promise you."

"Of course we thank you humbly, lady," said Lytchkov the father,
looking at the ground; "you are educated people; it is for you to
know best. Only, you see, Voronov, a rich peasant at Eresnevo, promised to build a school; he, too, said, 'I will do this for you,' 'I will do
that for you,' and he only put up the framework and refused to go on.
And then they made the peasants put the roof on and finish it; it cost
them a thousand roubles. Voronov did not care; he only stroked his
beard, but the peasants felt it a bit hard."

"That was a crow, but now there's a rook, too," said Kozov, and he winked.

There was the sound of laughter.

"We don't want a school," said Volodka sullenly. "Our children go to Petrovskoe, and they can go on going there; we don't want it."

Elena Ivanovna seemed suddenly intimidated; her face looked paler and thinner, she shrank into herself as though she had been touched with something coarse, and walked away without uttering another word. And she walked more and more quickly, without looking round.

"Lady," said Rodion, walking after her, "lady, wait a bit; hear what I would say to you."

He followed her without his cap, and spoke softly as though begging.

"Lady, wait and hear what I will say to you."

They had walked out of the village, and Elena Ivanovna stopped beside a cart in the shade of an old mountain ash.

"Don't be offended, lady," said Rodion. "What does it mean? Have patience. Have patience for a couple of years. You will live here, you will have patience, and it will all come round. Our folks are good and peaceable; there's no harm in them; it's God's truth I'm telling you. Don't mind Kozov and the Lytchkovs, and don't mind Volodka. He's a fool; he listens to the first that speaks. The others are quite folks; they are silent. Some would be glad, you know, to say a word from the heart and to stand up for themselves, but cannot. They have a heart and a conscience, but no tongue. Don't be offended . . . have patience. . . . What does it matter?"

Elena Ivanovna looked at the broad, tranquil river, pondering, and tears flowed down her cheeks. And Rodion was troubled by those tears; he almost cried himself.

"Never mind . . ." he muttered. "Have patience for a couple of years. You can have the school, you can have the roads, only not all at once. If you went, let us say, to sow corn on that mound you would first have to weed it out, to pick out all the stones, and then to plough, and work and work . . . and with the people, you see, it is the same . . . you must work and work until you overcome them."

The crowd had moved away from Rodion's hut, and was coming along the street towards the mountain ash. They began singing songs and playing the concertina, and they kept coming closer and closer. . . .

"Mamma, let us go away from here," said the little girl, huddling up to her mother, pale and shaking all over; "let us go away, mamma!"

"Where?"

"To Moscow. . . . Let us go, mamma."

The child began crying.

Rodion was utterly overcome; his face broke into profuse perspiration; he took out of his pocket a little crooked cucumber, like a half-moon, covered with crumbs of rye bread, and began thrusting it into the little girl's hands.

"Come, come," he muttered, scowling severely; "take the little cucumber, eat it up. . . . You mustn't cry. Mamma will whip you. . . . She'll tell your father of you when you get home. Come, come. . . ."

They walked on, and he still followed behind them, wanting to say something friendly and persuasive to them. And seeing that they were both absorbed in their own thoughts and their own griefs, and not noticing him, he stopped and, shading his eyes from the sun, looked after them for a long time till they disappeared into their copse.

IV

The engineer seemed to grow irritable and petty, and in every trivial incident saw an act of robbery or outrage. His gate was kept bolted even by day, and at night two watchmen walked up and down the garden beating a board; and they gave up employing anyone from Obrutchanovo as a labourer. As ill-luck would have it someone (either a peasant or one of the workmen) took the new wheels off the cart and replaced them by old ones, then soon afterwards two bridles and a pair of pincers were carried off, and murmurs arose even in the village. People began to say that a search should be made at the Lytchkovs' and at Volodka's, and then the bridles and the pincers were found under the hedge in the engineer's garden; someone had thrown them down there.

It happened that the peasants were coming in a crowd out of the forest, and again they met the engineer on the road. He stopped, and without wishing them good-day he began, looking angrily first at one, then at another:

"I have begged you not to gather mushrooms in the park and near the yard, but to leave them for my wife and children, but your girls come before daybreak and there is not a mushroom left. . . . Whether one asks you or not it makes no difference. Entreaties, and friendliness, and persuasion I see are all useless."

He fixed his indignant eyes on Rodion and went on:

"My wife and I behaved to you as human beings, as to our equals, and you? But what's the use of talking! It will end by our looking down upon you. There is nothing left!"

And making an effort to restrain his anger, not to say too much, he turned and went on.

On getting home Rodion said his prayer, took off his boots, and sat down beside his wife.

"Yes . . ." he began with a sigh. "We were walking along just now, and Mr. Kutcherov met us. . . . Yes. . . . He saw the girls at daybreak. . . . 'Why don't they bring mushrooms,' he said . . . 'to my wife and children?' he said. . . . And then he looked at me and he said: 'I and my wife will look after you,' he said. I wanted to fall down at his feet, but I hadn't the courage. . . . God give him health. . . . God bless him! . . ."

Stephania crossed herself and sighed.

"They are kind, simple-hearted people," Rodion went on. " 'We shall look after you.' . . . He promised me that before everyone. In our old age . . . it wouldn't be a bad thing. . . . I should always pray for the them. . . . Holy Mother, bless them. . . ."

The Feast of the Exaltation of the Cross, the fourteenth of September, was the festival of the village church. The Lytchkovs, father and son, went across the river early in the morning and returned to dinner drunk; they spent a long time going about the village, alternately singing and swearing; then they had a fight and went to the New Villa to complain. First Lytchkov the father went into the yard with a long ashen stick in his hands. He stopped irresolutely and took off his hat. Just at that moment the engineer and his family were sitting on the verandah, drinking tea.

"What do you want?" shouted the engineer.

"Your honour . . ." Lytchkov began, and burst into tears. "Show the Divine mercy, protect me . . . my son makes my life a misery . . . your honour. . . ."

Lytchkov the son walked up, too; he, too, was bareheaded and had a stick in his hand; he stopped and fixed his drunken senseless eyes on the verandah.

"It is not my business to settle your affairs," said the engineer. "Go to the rural captain or the police officer."

"I have been everywhere. . . . I have lodged a petition . . ." said Lytchkov the father, and he sobbed. "Where can I go now? He can kill me now, it seems. He can do anything. Is that the way to treat a father? A father?"

He raised his stick and hit his son on the head; the son raised his stick and struck his father just on his bald patch such a blow that the stick bounced back. The father did not even flinch, but hit his son again and again on the head. And so they stood and kept hitting one another on the head, and it looked not so much like a fight as some sort of a game. And peasants, men and women, stood in a crowd at the gate and looked into the garden, and the faces of all were grave. They were the peasants who had come to greet them for the holiday, but seeing the Lytchkovs, they were ashamed and did not go in.

The next morning Elena Ivanovna went with the children to Moscow. And there was a rumour that the engineer was selling his house. . . .

V

The peasants had long ago grown used to the sight of the bridge, and it was difficult to imagine the river at that place without a bridge. The heap of rubble left from the building of it had long been over-grown with grass, the navvies were forgotten, and instead of the strains of the "Dubinushka" that they used to sing, the peasants heard almost every hour the sounds of a passing train.

The New Villa has long ago been sold; now it belongs to a government clerk who comes here from the town for the holidays with his family, drinks tea on the terrace, and then goes back to the town again. He wears a cockade on his cap; he talks and clears his throat as though he were a very important official, though he is only of the rank of a collegiate secretary, and when the peasants bow he makes no response.

In Obrutchanovo everyone has grown older; Kozov is dead. In Rodion's hut there are even more children. Volodka has grown a long red beard. They are still as poor as ever.

In the early spring the Obrutchanovo peasants were sawing wood near the station. And after work they were going home; they walked without haste one after the other. Broad saws curved over their shoulders; the sun was reflected in them. The nightingales were singing in the bushes on the bank, larks were trilling in the heavens. It was quiet at the New Villa; there was not a soul there, and only golden pigeons—golden because the sunlight was streaming upon them—were flying over the house. All of them—Rodion, the two Lytchkovs, and Volodka—thought of the white horses, the little ponies, the fireworks, the boat with the lanterns; they remembered how the engineer's wife, so beautiful and so grandly dressed, had come into the village and talked to them in such a friendly way. And it seemed as though all that had never been; it was like a dream or a fairy-tale.

They trudged along, tired out, and mused as they went. . . . In their village, they mused, the people were good, quiet, sensible, fearing God, and Elena Ivanovna, too, was quiet, kind, and gentle; it made one sad to look at her, but why had they not got on together? Why had they parted like enemies? How was it that some mist had shrouded from their eyes what mattered most, and had let them see nothing but damage done by cattle, bridles, pincers, and all those trivial things which now, as they remembered them, seemed so nonsensical? How was it that with the new owner they lived in peace, and yet had been on bad terms with the engineer?

And not knowing what answer to make to these questions they were all silent except Volodka, who muttered something.

"What is it?" Rodion asked.

"We lived without a bridge . . ." said Volodka gloomily. "We lived without a bridge, and did not ask for one . . . and we don't want it. . . ."

No one answered him and they walked on in silence with drooping heads.

1899

On Official Duty

The deputy examining magistrate and the district doctor were going to an inquest in the village of Syrnya. On the road they were overtaken by a snowstorm; they spent a long time going round and round, and arrived, not at midday, as they had intended, but in the evening when it was dark. They put up for the night at the Zemstvo hut. It so happened that it was in this hut that the dead body was lying—the corpse of the Zemstvo insurance agent, Lesnitsky, who had arrived in Syrnya three days before and, ordering the samovar in the hut, had shot himself, to the great surprise of everyone; and the fact that he had ended his life so strangely, after unpacking his eatables and laying them out on the table, and with the samovar before him, led many people to suspect that it was a case of murder; an inquest was necessary.

In the outer room the doctor and the examining magistrate shook the snow off themselves and knocked it off their boots. And meanwhile the old village constable, Ilya Loshadin, stood by, holding a little tin lamp. There was a strong smell of paraffin.

"Who are you?" asked the doctor.

"Conshtable, . . ." answered the constable.

He used to spell it "conshtable" when he signed the receipts at the post office.

"And where are the witnesses?"

"They must have gone to tea, your honour."

On the right was the parlour, the travellers' or gentry's room; on the left the kitchen, with a big stove and sleeping shelves under the rafters. The doctor and the examining magistrate, followed by the constable, holding the lamp high above his head, went into the parlour. Here a still, long body covered with white linen was lying on the floor close to the table-legs. In the dim light of the lamp they could clearly see, besides the white covering, new rubber goloshes, and everything about it was uncanny and sinister: the dark walls, and the silence, and the goloshes, and the stillness of the dead body. On the table stood a samovar, cold long ago; and round it parcels, probably the eatables.

"To shoot oneself in the Zemstvo hut, how tactless!" said the doctor. "If one does want to put a bullet through one's brains, one ought to do it at home in some outhouse."

He sank on to a bench, just as he was, in his cap, his fur coat, and his felt overboots; his fellow-traveller, the examining magistrate, sat down opposite.

"These hysterical, neurasthenic people are great egoists," the doctor went on hotly. "If a neurasthenic sleeps in the same room with you, he rustles his newspaper; when he dines with you, he gets up a scene with his wife without troubling about your presence; and when he feels inclined to shoot himself, he shoots himself in a village in a Zemstvo hut, so as to give the maximum of trouble to everybody. These gentlemen in every circumstance of life think of no one but themselves! That's why the elderly so dislike our 'nervous age.'"

"The elderly dislike so many things," said the examining magistrate, yawning. "You should point out to the elder generation what the difference is between the suicides of the past and the suicides of to-day. In the old days the so-called gentleman shot himself because he had made away with Government money, but nowadays it is because he is sick of life, depressed. . . . Which is better?"

"Sick of life, depressed; but you must admit that he might have shot himself somewhere else."

"Such trouble!" said the constable, "such trouble! It's a real affliction. The people are very much upset, your honour; they haven't slept these three nights. The children are crying. The cows ought to be milked, but the women won't go to the stall—they are afraid . . . for fear the gentleman should appear to them in the darkness. Of course they are silly women, but some of the men are frightened too. As soon as it is dark they won't go by the hut one by one, but only in a flock together. And the witnesses too. . . ."

Dr. Startchenko, a middle-aged man in spectacles with a dark beard, and the examining magistrate Lyzhin, a fair man, still young, who had only taken his degree two years before and looked more like a student than an official, sat in silence, musing. They were vexed that they were late. Now they had to wait till morning, and to stay here for the night, though it was not yet six o'clock; and they had before them a long evening, a dark night, boredom, uncomfortable beds, beetles, and cold in the morning; and listening to the blizzard that howled in the chimney and in the loft, they both thought how unlike all this was the life which they would have chosen for themselves and of which they had once dreamed, and how far away they both were from their contemporaries, who were at that moment walking about the lighted streets in town without noticing the weather, or were getting ready for the theatre, or sitting in their studies over a book. Oh, how much they would have given now only to stroll along the Nevsky Prospect, or along Petrovka in Moscow, to listen to decent singing, to sit for an hour or so in a restaurant!

"Oo-oo-oo-oo!" sang the storm in the loft, and something outside slammed viciously, probably the signboard on the hut. "Oo-oo-oo-oo!"

"You can do as you please, but I have no desire to stay here," said Startchenko, getting up. "It's not six yet, it's too early to go to bed; I am off. Von Taunitz lives not far from here, only a couple of miles from Syrnya. I shall go to see him and spend the evening there. Constable, run and tell my coachman not to take the horses out. And what are you going to do?" he asked Lyzhin.

"I don't know; I expect I shall go to sleep."

The doctor wrapped himself in his fur coat and went out. Lyzhin could hear him talking to the coachman and the bells beginning to quiver on the frozen horses. He drove off.

"It is not nice for you, sir, to spend the night in here," said the constable; "come into the other room. It's dirty, but for one night it won't matter. I'll get a samovar from a peasant and heat it directly. I'll heap up some hay for you, and then you go to sleep, and God bless you, your honour."

A little later the examining magistrate was sitting in the kitchen drinking tea, while Loshadin, the constable, was standing at the door talking. He was an old man about sixty, short and very thin, bent and white, with a naïve smile on his face and watery eyes; and he kept smacking with his lips as though he were sucking a sweetmeat. He was wearing a short sheepskin coat and high felt boots, and held his stick in his hand all the time. The youth of the examining magistrate aroused his compassion, and that was probably why he addressed him familiarly.

"The elder gave orders that he was to be informed when the police superintendent or the examining magistrate came," he said, "so I suppose I must go now. . . . It's nearly three miles to the *volost*, and the storm, the snowdrifts, are something terrible—maybe one won't get there before midnight. Ough! how the wind roars!"

"I don't need the elder," said Lyzhin. "There is nothing for him to do here."

He looked at the old man with curiosity, and asked:

"Tell me, grandfather, how many years have you been constable?"

"How many? Why, thirty years. Five years after the Freedom I began going as constable, that's how I reckon it. And from that time I have been going every day since. Other people have holidays, but I am always going. When it's Easter and the church bells are ringing and Christ has risen, I still go about with my bag—to the treasury, to the post, to the police superintendent's lodgings, to the rural captain, to the tax inspector, to the municipal office, to the gentry, to the peasants, to all orthodox Christians. I carry parcels, notices, tax papers, letters, forms of different sorts, circulars, and to be sure, kind gentleman, there are all sorts of forms nowadays, so as to note down the numbers—yellow, white, and red—and every gentleman or priest or well-to-do peasant must write down a dozen times in the year how much he has sown and harvested, how many quarters or poods he has of rye, how many of oats, how many of hay, and what the weather's like, you know, and insects, too, of all sorts. To be sure you can write what you like, it's only a regulation, but one must go and give out the notices and then go again and collect them. Here, for instance, there's no need to cut open the gentleman; you know yourself it's a silly thing, it's only dirtying your hands, and here you have been put to trouble, your honour; you have come because it's the regulation; you can't help it. For thirty years I have been going round according to regulation. In the summer it is all right, it is warm and dry; but in the winter and autumn it's uncomfortable. At times I have been almost drowned and almost frozen; all sorts of things have happened—wicked people set on me in the forest and took away my bag; I have been beaten, and I have been before a court of law."

"What were you accused of?"

"Of fraud."

"How do you mean?"

"Why, you see, Hrisanf Grigoryev, the clerk, sold the contractor some boards belonging to someone else—cheated him, in fact. I was mixed up in it. They sent me to the tavern for vodka; well, the clerk did not share with me—did not even offer me a glass; but as through my poverty I was—in appearance, I mean—not a man to be relied upon, not a man of any worth, we were both brought to trial; he was sent to prison, but, praise God! I was acquitted on all points. They read a notice, you know, in the court. And they were all in uniforms—in the court, I mean. I can tell you, your honour, my duties for anyone not used to them are terrible, absolutely killing; but to me it is nothing. In fact, my feet ache when I am not walking. And at home it is worse for me. At home one has to heat the stove for the clerk in the *volost* office, to fetch water for him, to clean his boots."

"And what wages do you get?" Lyzhin asked.

"Eighty-four roubles a year."

"I'll bet you get other little sums coming in. You do, don't you?"

"Other little sums? No, indeed! Gentlemen nowadays don't often give tips. Gentlemen nowadays are strict, they take offense at anything. If you bring them a notice they are offended, if you take off your cap before them they are offended. 'You have come to the wrong entrance,' they say. 'You are a drunkard,' they say. 'You smell of onion; you are a blockhead; you are the son of a bitch.' There are kind-hearted ones, of course; but what does one get from them? They only laugh and call one all sorts of names. Mr. Altuhin, for instance, he is a good-natured gentleman; and if you look at him he seems sober and in his right mind, but so soon as he sees me he shouts and does not know what he means himself. He gave me such a name. 'You,' said he, . . ." The constable uttered some word, but in such a low voice that it was impossible to make out what he said.

"What?" Lyzhin asked. "Say it again."

" 'Administration,' " the constable repeated aloud. "He has been calling me that for a long while, for the last six years. 'Hullo, Administration!' But I don't mind; let him, God bless him! Sometimes a lady will send one a glass of vodka and a bit of pie, and one drinks to her health. But peasants give more; peasants are more kind-hearted, they have the fear of God in their hearts: one will give a bit of bread, another a drop of cabbage soup, another will stand one a glass. The village elders treat one to tea in the tavern. Here the witnesses have gone to their tea. 'Loshadin,' they said, 'you stay here and keep watch for us,' and they gave me a kopeck each. You see, they are frightened, not being used to it, and yesterday they gave me fifteen kopecks and offered me a glass."

"And you, aren't you frightened?"

"I am, sir; but of course it is my duty, there is no getting away from it. In the summer I was taking a convict to the town, and he set upon me and gave me such a drubbing! And all around were fields, forest—how could I get away from him? It's just the same here. I remember the gentleman, Mr. Lesnitsky, when he was so high, and I knew his father and mother. I am from the village of Nedoshtcho-tova, and they, the Lesnitsky family, were not more than three-quarters of a mile from us and less than that, their ground next to ours, and Mr. Lesnitsky had a sister, a God-fearing and tender-hearted lady. Lord keep the soul of Thy servant Yulya, eternal memory to her! She was never married, and when she was dying she divided all her property; she left three hundred acres to the monastery, and six hundred to the commune of peasants of Nedoshtchotova to commemorate her soul; but her brother hid the will, they do say burnt it in the stove, and took all this land for himself. He thought, to be sure, it was for his benefit; but—nay, wait a bit, you won't get on in the world through injustice, brother. The gentleman did not go to confession for twenty years after. He kept away from the church, to be sure, and died impenitent. He burst. He was a very fat man, so he burst lengthways. Then everything was taken from the young master, from Seryozha, to pay the debts—everything there was. Well, he had not gone very far in his studies, he couldn't do anything, and the president of the Rural Board, his uncle—'I'll take him'—Seryozha, I mean—thinks he, 'for an agent; let him collect the insurance, that's not a difficult job,' and the gentleman was young and proud, he wanted to be living on a bigger scale and in better style and with more freedom. To be sure it was a come-down for him to be jolting about the district in a wretched cart and talking to the peasants; he would walk and keep looking on the ground, looking on the ground and saying nothing; if you called his name right in his ear, 'Sergey Sergeyitch!' he would look round like this, 'Eh?' and look down on the ground again, and now you see he has laid hands on himself. There's no sense in it, your honour, it's not right, and there's not making out what's the meaning of it, merciful Lord! Say your father was rich and you are poor; it is mortifying, there's no doubt about it, but there, you must make up your mind to it. I used to live in good style, too; I had two horses, your honour, three cows, I used to keep twenty head of sheep; but the time has come, and I am left with nothing but a wretched bag, and even that is not mine but Government property. And now in our Nedoshtchotova, if the truth is to be told, my house is the worst of the lot. Makey had four footmen, and now Makey is a footman himself. Petrak had four labourers, and now Petrak is a labourer himself."

"How was it you became poor?" asked the examining magistrate.

"My sons drink terribly. I could not tell you how they drink, you wouldn't believe it."

Lyzhin listened and thought how he, Lyzhin, would go back sooner or later to Moscow, while this old man would stay here for ever, and would always be walking and walking. And how many times in his life he would come across such battered, unkempt old men, not "men of any worth," in whose souls fifteen kopecks, glasses of vodka, and a profound belief that you can't get on in this life by dishonesty, were equally firmly rooted.

Then he grew tired of listening, and told the old man to bring him some hay for his bed. There was an iron bedstead with a pillow and a quilt in the traveller's room, and it could be fetched in; but the dead man had been lying by it for nearly three days (and perhaps sitting on it just before his death), and it would be disagreeable to sleep upon it now. . . .

"It's only half-past seven," thought Lyzhin, glancing at his watch. "How awful it is!"

He was not sleepy, but having nothing to do to pass away the time, he lay down and covered himself with a rug. Loshadin went in and out several times, clearing away the tea-things; smacking his lips and sighing, he kept tramping round the table; at last he took his little lamp and went out, and, looking at his long, grey-headed, bent figure from behind, Lyzhin thought:

"Just like a magician in an opera."

It was dark. The moon must have been behind the clouds, as the windows and the snow on the window-frames could be seen distinctly.

"Oo-oo-oo-oo!" sang the storm, "Oo-oo-oo-oo!"

"Ho-ho-ly sa-aints!" wailed a woman in the loft, or it sounded like it. "Ho-ho-ly sa-aints!"

"B-booh!" something outside banged against the wall. "Trah!"

The examining magistrate listened: there was no woman up there, it was the wind howling. It was rather cold, and he put his fur coat over his rug. As he got warm he thought how remote all this—the storm, and the hut, and the old man, and the dead body lying in the next room—how remote it all was from the life he desired for himself, and how alien it all was to him, how petty, how uninteresting. If this man had killed himself in Moscow or somewhere in the neighbourhood, and he had had to hold an inquest on him there, it would have been interesting, important, and perhaps he might even have been afraid to sleep in the next room to the corpse. Here, nearly a thousand miles from Moscow, all this was seen somehow in a different light; it was not life, they were not human beings, but something only existing "according to the regulation," as Loshadin said; it would leave not the faintest trace in the memory, and would be forgotten as soon as he, Lyzhin, drove away from Syrnya. The fatherland, the real Russia, was Moscow, Petersburg; but here he was in the provinces, the colonies. When one dreamed of playing a leading part, of becoming a popular figure, of being, for instance, examining magistrate in particularly important cases or prosecutor in a circuit court, of being a society lion, one always thought of Moscow. To live, one must be in Moscow; here one cared for nothing, one grew easily resigned to one's insignificant position, and only expected one thing of life—to get away quickly, quickly. And Lyzhin mentally moved about the Moscow streets, went into the familiar houses, met his kindred, his comrades, and there was a sweet pang at his heart at the thought that he was only twenty-six, and that if in five or ten years he could break away from here and get to Moscow, even then it would not be too late and he would still have a whole life before him. And as he sank into unconsciousness, as his thoughts began to be confused, he imagined the long corridor of the court at Moscow, himself delivering a speech, his sisters, the orchestra which for some reason kept droning: "Oo-oo-oo-oo! Oo-oo-oo-oo!"

"Booh! Trah!" sounded again. "Booh!"

And he suddenly recalled how one day, when he was talking to the bookkeeper in the little office of the Rural Board, a thin, pale gentleman with black hair and dark eyes walked in; he had a disagreeable look in his eyes such as one sees in people who have slept too long after dinner, and it spoilt his delicate, intelligent profile; and the high boots he was wearing did not suit him, but looked clumsy. The book-keeper had introduced him: "This is our insurance agent."

"So that was Lesnitsky, . . . this same man," . . . Lyzhin reflected now.

He recalled Lesnitsky's soft voice, imagined his gait, and it seemed to him that someone was walking beside him now with a step like Lesnitsky's.

All at once he felt frightened, his head turned cold.

"Who's there?" he asked in alarm.

"The conshtable!"

"What do you want here?"

"I have come to ask, your honour—you said this evening that you did not want the elder, but I am afraid he may be angry. He told me to go to him. Shouldn't I go?"

"That's enough, you bother me," said Lyzhin with vexation, and he covered himself up again.

"He may be angry. . . . I'll go, your honour. I hope you will be comfortable," and Loshadin went out.

In the passage there was coughing and subdued voices. The witnesses must have returned.

"We'll let those poor beggars get away early to-morrow, . . ." thought the examining magistrate; "we'll begin the inquest as soon as it is daylight."

He began sinking into forgetfulness when suddenly there were steps again, not timid this time but rapid and noisy. There was the slam of a door, voices, the scratching of a match. . . .

"Are you asleep? Are you asleep?" Dr. Startchenko was asking him hurriedly and angrily as he struck one match after another; he was covered with snow, and brought a chill air in with him. "Are you asleep? Get up! Let us go to Von Taunitz's. He has sent his own horses for you. Come along. There, at any rate, you will have supper, and sleep like a human being. You see I have come for you myself. The horses are splendid, we shall get there in twenty minutes."

"And what time is it now?"

"A quarter past ten."

Lyzhin, sleepy and discontented, put on his felt overboots, his fur-lined coat, his cap and hood, and went out with the doctor. There was not a very sharp frost, but a violent and piercing wind was blowing and driving along the street the clouds of snow which seemed to be racing away in terror: high drifts were heaped up already under the fences and at the doorways. The doctor and the examining magistrate got into the sledge, and the white coachman bent over them to button up the cover. They were both hot.

"Ready!"

They drove through the village. "Cutting a feathery furrow," thought the examining magistrate, listlessly watching the action of the trace horse's legs. There were lights in all the huts, as though it were the eve of a great holiday: the peasants had not gone to bed because they were afraid of the dead body. The coachman preserved a sullen silence, probably he had felt dreary while he was waiting by the Zemstvo hut, and now he, too, was thinking of the dead man.

"At the Von Taunitz's," said Startchenko, "they all set upon me when they heard that you were left to spend the night in the hut, and asked me why I did not bring you with me."

As they drove out of the village, at the turning the coachman suddenly shouted at the top of his voice: "Out of the way!"

They caught a glimpse of a man: he was standing up to his knees in the snow, moving off the road and staring at the horses. The examining magistrate saw a stick with a crook, and a beard and a bag, and he fancied that it was Loshadin, and even fancied that he was smiling. He flashed by and disappeared.

The road ran at first along the edge of the forest, then along a broad forest clearing; they caught glimpses of old pines and a young birch copse, and tall, gnarled young oak trees standing singly in the clearings where the wood had lately been cut; but soon it was all merged in the clouds of snow. The coachman said he could see the forest; the examining magistrate could see nothing but the trace horse. The wind blew on their backs.

All at once the horses stopped.

"Well, what is it now?" asked Startchenko crossly.

The coachman got down from the box without a word and began running round the sledge, treading on his heels; he made larger and larger circles, getting further and further away from the sledge, and it looked as though he were dancing; at last he come back and began to turn off to the right.

"You've got off the road, eh?" asked Startchenko.

"It's all ri-ight. . . ."

Then there was a little village and not a single light in it. Again the forest and the fields. Again they lost the road, and again the coach-man got down from the box and danced round the sledge. The sledge flew along a dark avenue, flew swiftly on. And the heated trace horse's hoofs knocked against the sledge. Here there was a fearful roaring sound from the trees, and nothing could be seen, as though they were flying on into space; and all at once the glaring light at the entrance and the windows flashed upon their eyes, and they heard the good-natured, drawn-out barking of dogs. They had arrived.

While they were taking off their fur coats and their felt boots below, "Un Petit Verre de Clicquot" was being played upon the piano overhead, and they could hear the children beating time with their feet. Immediately on going in they were aware of the snug warmth and special smell of the old apartments of a mansion where, whatever the weather outside, life is so warm and clean and comfortable.

"That's capital!" said Von Taunitz, a fat man with an incredibly thick neck and with whiskers, as he shook the examining magistrate's hand. "That's capital! You are very welcome, delighted to make your acquaintance. We are colleagues to some extent, you know. At one time I was deputy prosecutor; but not for long, only two years. I came here to look after the estate, and here I have grown old—an old fogey, in fact. You are very welcome," he went on, evidently restrain-ing his voice so as not to speak too loud; he was going upstairs with his guests. "I have no wife; she's dead. But here, I will introduce my daughters," and turning round, he shouted down the stairs in a voice of thunder: "Tell Ignat to have the sledge ready at eight o'clock to-morrow morning."

His four daughters, young and pretty girls, all wearing grey dresses and with their hair done up in the same style, and their cousin, also young and attractive, with her children, were in the drawing-room. Startchenko, who knew them already, began at once begging them to sing something, and two of the young ladies spent a long time declaring they could not sing and that they had no music; then the cousin sat down to the piano, and with trembling voices, they sang a duet from "The Queen of Spades." Again "Un Petit Verre de Clicquot" was played, and the children skipped about, beating time with their feet. And Startchenko pranced about too. Everybody laughed.

Then the children said good-night and went off to bed. The exam-ining magistrate laughed, danced a quadrille, flirted, and kept wondering whether it was not all a dream? The kitchen of the Zemstvo hut, the heap of hay in the corner, the rustle of the beetles, the revolting poverty-stricken surroundings, the voices of the witnesses, the wind, the snow storm, the danger of being lost; and then all at once this splendid, brightly lighted room, the sounds of the piano, the lovely girls, the curly-headed children, the gay, happy laughter—such a transformation seemed to him like a fairy tale, and it seemed incredible that such transitions were possible at the distance of some two miles in the course of one hour. And dreary thoughts prevented him from enjoying himself, and he kept thinking this was not life here, but bits of life, fragments, that everything here was accidental, that one could draw no conclusions from it; and he even felt sorry for these girls, who were living and would end their lives in the wilds, in a province far away from the center of culture, where nothing is accidental, but everything is in accordance with reason and law, and where, for instance, every suicide is intelligible, so that one can explain why it has happened and what is its significance in the general scheme of things. He imagined that if the life surrounding him here in the wilds were not intelligible to him, and if he did not see it, it meant that it did not exist at all.

At supper the conversation turned on Lesnitsky.

"He left a wife and child," said Startchenko. "I would forbid neurasthenics and all people whose nervous system is out of order to marry, I would deprive them of the right and possibility of multiplying their kind. To bring into the world nervous, invalid children is a crime."

"He was an unfortunate young man," said Von Taunitz, sighing gently and shaking his head. "What a lot one must suffer and think about before one brings oneself to take one's own life, . . . a young life! Such a misfortune may happen in any family, and that is awful. It is hard to bear such a thing, insufferable. . . ."

And all the girls listened in silence with grave faces, looking at their father. Lyzhin felt that he, too, must say something, but he couldn't think of anything, and merely said:

"Yes, suicide is an undesirable phenomenon."

He slept in a warm room, in a soft bed covered with a quilt under which there were fine clean sheets, but for some reason did not feel comfortable: perhaps because the doctor and Von Taunitz were, for a long time, talking in the adjoining room, and overhead he heard, through the ceiling and in the stove, the wind roaring just as in the Zemstvo hut, and as plaintively howling: "Oo-oo-oo-oo!"

Van Taunitz's wife had died two years before, and he was still unable to resign himself to his loss and, whatever he was talking about, always mentioned his wife; and there was no trace of a prosecutor left about him now.

"Is it possible that I may some day come to such a condition?" thought Lyzhin, as he fell asleep, still hearing through the wall his host's subdued, as it were bereaved, voice.

The examining magistrate did not sleep soundly. He felt hot and uncomfortable, and it seemed to him in his sleep that he was not at Von Taunitz's, and not in a soft clean bed, but still in the hay at the Zemstvo hut, hearing the subdued voices of the witnesses; he fancied that Lesnitsky was close by, not fifteen paces away. In his dreams he remembered how the insurance agent, black-haired and pale, wearing dusty high boots, had come into the bookkeeper's office. "This is our insurance agent. . . ."

Then he dreamed that Lesnitsky and Loshadin the constable were walking through the open country in the snow, side by side, supporting each other; the snow was whirling about their heads, the wind was blowing on their backs, but they walked on, singing: "We go on, and on, and on. . . ."

The old man was like a magician in an opera, and both of them were singing as though they were on the stage:

"We go on, and on, and on! . . . You are in the warmth, in the light and snugness, but we are walking in the frost and the storm, through the deep snow. . . . We know nothing of ease, we know nothing of joy. . . . We bear all the burden of this life, yours and ours. . . . Oo-oo-oo-oo! We go on, and on, and on. . . ."

Lyzhin woke and sat up in bed. What a confused, bad dream! And why did he dream of the constable and the agent together? What nonsense! And now while Lyzhin's heart was throbbing violently and he was sitting on his bed, holding his head in his hands, it seemed to him that there really was something in common between the lives of the insurance agent and the constable. Don't they really go side by side holding each other up? Some tie unseen, but significant and essential, existed between them, and even between them and Von Taunitz and between all men—all men; in this life, even in the remotest desert, nothing is accidental, everything is full of one common idea, everything has one soul, one aim, and to understand it it is not enough to think, it is not enough to reason, one must have also, it seems, the gift of insight into life, a gift which is evidently not bestowed on all. And the unhappy man who had broken down, who had killed himself—the "neurasthenic," as the doctor called him— and the old peasant who spent every day of his life going from one man to another, were only accidental, were only fragments of life for one who thought of his own life as accidental, but were parts of one organism—marvellous and rational—for one who thought of his own life as part of that universal whole and understood it. So thought Lyzhin, and it was a thought that had long lain hidden in his soul, and only now it was unfolded broadly and clearly to his consciousness.

He lay down and began to drop asleep; and again they were going along together, singing: "We go on, and on, and on. . . . We take from life what is hardest and bitterest in it, and we leave you what is easy and joyful; and sitting at supper, you can coldly and sensibly discuss why we suffer and perish, and why we are not as sound and as satisfied as you."

What they were singing had occurred to his mind before, but the thought was somewhere in the background behind his other thoughts, and flickered timidly like a far-away light in foggy weather. And he felt that this suicide and the peasant's sufferings lay upon his conscience, too; to resign himself to the fact that these people, submissive to their fate, should take up the burden of what was hardest and gloomiest in life—how awful it was! To accept this, and to desire for himself a life full of light and movement among happy and contented people, and to be continually dreaming of such, means dreaming of fresh suicides of men crushed by toil and anxiety, or of men weak and outcast whom people only talk of sometimes at supper with annoyance or mockery, without going to their help. . . . And again:

"We go on, and on, and on . . ." as though someone were beating with a hammer on his temples.

He woke early in the morning with a headache, roused by a noise; in the next room Von Taunitz was saying loudly to the doctor:

"It's impossible for you to go now. Look what's going on outside. Don't argue, you had better ask the coachman; he won't take you in such weather for a million."

"But it's only two miles," said the doctor in an imploring voice.

"Well, if it were only half a mile. If you can't, then you can't. Directly you drive out of the gates it is perfect hell, you would be off the road in a minute. Nothing will induce me to let you go, you can say what you like."

"It's bound to be quieter towards evening," said the peasant who was heating the stove.

And in the next room the doctor began talking of the rigorous climate and its influence on the character of the Russian, of the long winters which, by preventing movement from place to place, hinder the intellectual development of the people; and Lyzhin listened with vexation to these observations and looked out of window at the snow drifts which were piled on the fence. He gazed at the white dust which covered the whole visible expanse, at the trees which bowed their heads despairingly to right and then to left, listened to the howling and the banging, and thought gloomily:

"Well, what moral can be drawn from it? It's a blizzard and that is all about it. . . ."

At midday they had lunch, then wandered aimlessly about the house; they went to the windows.

"And Lesnitsky is lying there," thought Lyzhin, watching the whirling snow, which raced furiously round and round upon the drifts. "Lesnitsky is lying there, the witnesses are waiting. . . ."

They talked of the weather, saying that the snowstorm usually lasted two days and nights, rarely longer. At six o'clock they had dinner, then they played cards, sang, danced; at last they had supper. The day was over, they went to bed.

In the night, towards morning, it all subsided. When they got up and looked out of window, the bare willows with their weakly drooping branches were standing perfectly motionless; it was dull and still, as though nature now were ashamed of its orgy, of its mad nights, and the license it had given to its passions. The horses, harnessed tandem, had been waiting at the front door since five o'clock in the morning. When it was fully daylight the doctor and the examining magistrate put on their fur coats and felt boots, and, saying good-bye to their host, went out.

At the steps beside the coachman stood the familiar figure of the constable, Ilya Loshadin, with an old leather bag across his shoulder and no cap on his head, covered with snow all over, and his face was red and wet with perspiration. The footman who had come out to help the gentleman and cover their legs looked at him sternly and said:

"What are you standing here for, you old devil? Get away!"

"Your honour, the people are anxious," said Loshadin, smiling naïvely all over his face, and evidently pleased at seeing at last the people he had waited for so long. "The people are very uneasy, the children are crying. . . . They thought, your honour, that you had gone back to the town again. Show us the heavenly mercy, our benefactors! . . ."

The doctor and the examining magistrate said nothing, got into the sledge, and drove to Syrnya.

1899

The Lady with the Dog

I

It was said that a new person had appeared on the sea-front: a lady with a little dog. Dmitri Dmitritch Gurov, who had by then been a fortnight at Yalta, and so was fairly at home there, had begun to take an interest in new arrivals. Sitting in Verney's pavilion, he saw, walking on the sea-front, a fair-haired young lady of medium height, wearing a *béret*; a white Pomeranian dog was running behind her.

And afterwards he met her in the public gardens and in the square several times a day. She was walking alone, always wearing the same *béret*, and always with the same white dog; no one knew who she was, and every one called her simply "the lady with the dog."

"If she is here alone without a husband or friends, it wouldn't be amiss to make her acquaintance," Gurov reflected.

He was under forty, but he had a daughter already twelve years old, and two sons at school. He had been married young, when he was a student in his second year, and by now his wife seemed half as old again as he. She was a tall, erect woman with dark eyebrows, staid and dignified, and, as she said of herself, intellectual. She read a great deal, used phonetic spelling, called her husband, not Dmitri, but Dimitri, and he secretly considered her unintelligent, narrow, inelegant, was afraid of her, and did not like to be at home. He had begun being unfaithful to her long ago—had been unfaithful to her often, and, probably on that account, almost always spoke ill of women, and when they were talked about in his presence, used to call them "the lower race."

It seemed to him that he had been so schooled by bitter experience that he might call them what he liked, and yet he could not get on for two days together without "the lower race." In the society of men he was bored and not himself, with them he was cold and uncommunicative; but when he was in the company of women he felt free, and knew what to say to them and how to behave; and he was at ease with them even when he was silent. In his appearance, in his character, in his whole nature, there was something attractive and elusive which allured women and disposed them in his favour; he knew that, and some force seemed to draw him, too, to them.

Experience often repeated, truly bitter experience, had taught him long ago that with decent people, especially Moscow people—always slow to move and irresolute—every intimacy, which at first so agreeably diversifies life and appears a light and charming adventure, inevitably grows into a regular problem of extreme intricacy, and in the long run the situation becomes unbearable. But at every fresh meeting with an interesting woman this experience seemed to slip out of his memory, and he was eager for life, and everything seemed simple and amusing.

One evening he was dining in the gardens, and the lady in the *béret* came up slowly to take the next table. Her expression, her gait, her dress, and the way she did her hair told him that she was a lady, that she was married, that she was in Yalta for the first time and alone, and that she was dull there. . . . The stories told of the immorality in such places as Yalta are to a great extent untrue; he despised them, and knew that such stories were for the most part made up by persons who would themselves have been glad to sin if they had been able; but when the lady sat down at the next table three paces from him, he remembered these tales of easy conquests, of trips to the mountains, and the tempting thought of a swift, fleeting love affair, a romance with an unknown woman, whose name he did not know, suddenly took possession of him.

He beckoned coaxingly to the Pomeranian, and when the dog came up to him he shook his finger at it. The Pomeranian growled: Gurov shook his finger at it again.

The lady looked at him and at once dropped her eyes.

"He doesn't bite," she said, and blushed.

"May I give him a bone?" he asked; and when she nodded he asked courteously, "Have you been long in Yalta?"

"Five days."

"And I have already dragged out a fortnight here."

There was a brief silence.

"Time goes fast, and yet it is so dull here!" she said, not looking at him.

"That's only the fashion to say it is dull here. A provincial will live in Belyov or Zhidra and not be dull, and when he comes here it's 'Oh, the dulness! Oh, the dust!' One would think he came from Grenada."

She laughed. Then both continued eating in silence, like strangers, but after dinner they walked side by side; and there sprang up between them the light jesting conversation of people who are free and satisfied, to whom it does not matter where they go or what they talk about. They walked and talked of the strange light on the sea: the water was of a soft warm lilac hue, and there was a golden streak from the moon upon it. They talked of how sultry it was after a hot day. Gurov told her that he came from Moscow, that he had taken his degree in Arts, but had a post in a bank; that he had trained as an opera-singer, but had given it up, that he owned two houses in Moscow. . . . And from her he learnt that she had grown up in Petersburg, but had lived in S—— since her marriage two years before, that she was staying another month in Yalta, and that her husband, who needed a holiday too, might perhaps come and fetch her. She was not sure whether her husband had a post in a Crown Department or under the Provincial Council—and was amused by her own ignorance. And Gurov learnt, too, that she was called Anna Sergeyevna.

Afterwards he thought about her in his room at the hotel— thought she would certainly meet him next day; it would be sure to happen. As he got into bed he thought how lately she had been a girl at school, doing lessons like his own daughter; he recalled the diffidence, the angularity, that was still manifest in her laugh and her manner of talking with a stranger. This must have been the first time in her life she had been alone in surroundings in which she was followed, looked at, and spoken to merely from a secret motive which she could hardly fail to guess. He recalled her slender, delicate neck, her lovely grey eyes.

"There's something pathetic about her, anyway," he thought, and fell asleep.

II

A week had passed since they had made acquaintance. It was a holiday. It was sultry indoors, while in the street the wind whirled the dust round and round, and blew people's hats off. It was a thirsty day, and Gurov often went into the pavilion, and pressed Anna

Sergeyevna to have syrup and water or an ice. One did not know what to do with oneself.

In the evening when the wind had dropped a little, they went out on the groyne to see the steamer come in. There were a great many people walking about the harbour; they had gathered to welcome some one, bringing bouquets. And two peculiarities of a well-dressed Yalta crowd were very conspicuous: the elderly ladies were dressed like young ones, and there were great numbers of generals.

Owing to the roughness of the sea, the steamer arrived late, after the sun had set, and it was a long time turning about before it reached the groyne. Anna Sergeyevna looked through her lorgnette at the steamer and the passengers as though looking for acquaintances, and when she turned to Gurov her eyes were shining. She talked a great deal and asked disconnected questions, forgetting next moment what she had asked; then she dropped her lorgnette in the crush.

The festive crowd began to disperse; it was too dark to see people's faces. The wind had completely dropped, but Gurov and Anna Sergeyevna still stood as though waiting to see some one else come from the steamer. Anna Sergeyevna was silent now, and sniffed the flowers without looking at Gurov.

"The weather is better this evening," he said. "Where shall we go now? Shall we drive somewhere?"

She made no answer.

Then he looked at her intently, and all at once put his arm round her and kissed her on the lips, and breathed in the moisture and the fragrance of the flowers; and he immediately looked round him, anxiously wondering whether any one had seen them.

"Let us go to your hotel," he said softly. And both walked quickly.

The room was close and smelt of the scent she had bought at the Japanese shop. Gurov looked at her and thought: "What different people one meets in the world!" From the past he preserved memories of careless, good-natured women, who loved cheerfully and were grateful to him for the happiness he gave them, however brief it might be; and of women like his wife who loved without any genuine feeling, with superfluous phrases, affectedly, hysterically, with an expression that suggested that it as not love nor passion, but something more significant; and of two or three others, very beautiful, cold women, on whose faces he had caught a glimpse of a rapacious expression—an obstinate desire to snatch from life more than it could give, and these were capricious, unreflecting, domineering, unintelligent women not in their first youth, and when Gurov grew cold to them their beauty excited his hatred, and the lace on their linen seemed to him like scales.

But in this case there was still the diffidence, the angularity of inexperienced youth, an awkward feeling; and there was a sense of consternation as though some one had suddenly knocked at the door. The attitude of Anna Sergeyevna—"the lady with the dog"—to what had happened was somehow peculiar, very grave, as though it were her fall—so it seemed, and it was strange and inappropriate. Her face dropped and faded, and on both sides of it her long hair hung down mournfully; she mused in a dejected attitude like "the woman who was a sinner" in an old-fashioned picture.

"It's wrong," she said. "You will be the first to despise me now."

There was a water-melon on the table. Gurov cut himself a slice and began eating it without haste. There followed at least half an hour of silence.

Anna Sergeyevna was touching; there was about her the purity of a good, simple woman who had seen little of life. The solitary candle burning on the table threw a faint light on her face, yet it was clear that she was very unhappy.

"How could I despise you?" asked Gurov. "You don't know what you are saying."

"God forgive me," she said, and her eyes filled with tears. "It's awful."

"You seem to feel you need to be forgiven."

"Forgiven? No. I am a bad, low woman; I despise myself and don't attempt to justify myself. It's not my husband but myself I have deceived. And not only just now; I have been deceiving myself for a long time. My husband may be a good, honest man, but he is a flunkey! I don't know what he does there, what his work is, but I know he is a flunkey! I was twenty when I was married to him. I have been tormented by curiosity; I wanted something better. 'There must be a different sort of life,' I said to myself. I wanted to live! To live, to live! . . . I was fired by curiosity . . . you don't understand it, but, I swear to God, I could not control myself; something happened to me: I could not be restrained. I told my husband I was ill, and came here. . . . And here I have been walking about as though I were dazed, like a mad creature; . . . and now I have become a vulgar, contemptible woman whom any one may despise."

Gurov felt bored already, listening to her. He was irritated by the naïve tone, by this remorse, so unexpected and inopportune; but for the tears in her eyes, he might have thought she was jesting or playing a part.

"I don't understand," he said softly. "What is it you want?"

She hid her face on his breast and pressed close to him.

"Believe me, believe me, I beseech you . . ." she said. "I love a pure, honest life, and sin is loathsome to me. I don't know what I am doing. Simple people say: 'The Evil One has beguiled me.' And I may say of myself now that the Evil One has beguiled me."

"Hush, hush! . . . he muttered.

He looked at her fixed, scared eyes, kissed her, talked softly and affectionately, and by degrees she was comforted, and her gaiety returned; they both began laughing.

Afterwards when they went out there was not a soul on the seafront. The town with its cypresses had quite a deathlike air, but the sea still broke noisily on the shore; a single barge was rocking on the waves, and a lantern was blinking sleepily on it.

They found a cab and drove to Oreanda.

"I found out your surname in the hall just now: it was written on the board—Von Diderits," said Gurov. "Is your husband a German?"

"No; I believe his grandfather was a German, but he is an Orthodox Russian himself."

At Oreanda they sat on a seat not far from the church, looked down at the sea, and were silent. Yalta was hardly visible through the morning mist; white clouds stood motionless on the mountain-tops. The leaves did not stir on the trees, grasshoppers chirruped, and the monotonous hollow sound of the sea rising up from below, spoke of the peace, of the eternal sleep awaiting us. So it must have sounded when there was no Yalta, no Oreanda here; so it sounds now, and it will sound as indifferently and monotonously when we are all no more. And in this constancy, in this complete indifference to the life and death of each of us, there lies hid, perhaps, a pledge of our eternal salvation, of the unceasing movement of life upon earth, of unceasing progress towards perfection. Sitting beside a young woman who in the dawn seemed so lovely, soothed and spellbound in these magical surroundings—the sea, mountains, clouds, the open sky—Gurov thought how in reality everything is beautiful in this world when one reflects: everything except what we think or do ourselves when we forget our human dignity and the higher aims of our existence.

A man walked up to them—probably a keeper—looked at them and walked away. And this detail seemed mysterious and beautiful, too. They saw a steamer come from Theodosia, with its lights out in the glow of dawn.

"There is dew on the grass," said Anna Sergeyevna, after a silence.

"Yes. It's time to go home."

They went back to the town.

Then they met every day at twelve o'clock on the sea-front, lunched and dined together, went for walks, admired the sea. She complained that she slept badly, that her heart throbbed violently; asked the same questions, troubled now by jealousy and now by the fear that he did not respect her sufficiently. And often in the square or gardens, when there was no one near them, he suddenly drew her to him and kissed her passionately. Complete idleness, these kisses in broad daylight while he looked round in dread of some one's seeing them, the heat, the smell of the sea, and the continual passing to and fro before him of idle, well-dressed, well-fed people, made a new man of him; he told Anna Sergeyevna how beautiful she was, how fascinating. He was impatiently passionate, he would not move a step away from her, while she was often pensive and continually urged him to confess that he did not respect her, did not love her in the least, and thought of her as nothing but a common woman. Rather late almost every evening they drove somewhere out of town, to Oreanda or to the waterfall; and the expedition was always a success, the scenery invariably impressed them as grand and beautiful.

They were expecting her husband to come, but a letter came from him, saying that there was something wrong with his eyes, and he entreated his wife to come home as quickly as possible. Anna Sergeyevna made haste to go.

"It's a good thing I am going away," she said to Gurov. "It's the finger of destiny!"

She went by coach and he went with her. They were driving the whole day. When she had got into a compartment of the express, and when the second bell had rung, she said:

"Let me look at you once more . . . look at you once again. That's right."

She did not shed tears, but was so sad that she seemed ill, and her face was quivering.

"I shall remember you . . . think of you," she said. "God be with you; be happy. Don't remember evil against me. We are parting forever—it must be so, for we ought never to have met. Well, God be with you."

The train moved off rapidly, its lights soon vanished from sight, and a minute later there was no sound of it, as though everything had conspired together to end as quickly as possible that sweet delirium, that madness. Left alone on the platform, and gazing into the dark distance, Gurov listened to the chirrup of the grasshoppers and the hum of the telegraph wires, feeling as though he had only just waked up. And he thought, musing, that there had been another episode or adventure in his life, and it, too, was at an end, and nothing was left of it but a memory. . . . He was moved, sad, and conscious of a slight remorse. This young woman whom he would never meet again had not been happy with him; he was genuinely warm and affectionate with her, but yet in his manner, his tone, and his caresses there had been a shade of light irony, the coarse condescension of a happy man who was, besides, almost twice her age. All the time she had called him kind, exceptional, lofty; obviously he had seemed to her different from what he really was, so he had unintentionally deceived her. . . .

Here at the station was already a scent of autumn; it was a cold evening.

"It's time for me to go north," thought Gurov as he left the platform. "High time!"

III

At home in Moscow everything was in its winter routine; the stoves were heated, and in the morning it was still dark when the children were having breakfast and getting ready for school, and the nurse would light the lamp for a short time. The frosts had begun already. When the first snow has fallen, on the first day of sledge-driving it is pleasant to see the white earth, the white roofs, to draw soft, delicious breath, and the season brings back the days of one's youth. The old limes and birches, white with hoar-frost, have a good-natured expression; they are nearer to one's heart than cypresses and palms, and near them one doesn't want to be thinking of the sea and the mountains.

Gurov was Moscow born; he arrived in Moscow on a fine frosty day, and when he put on his fur coat and warm gloves, and walked along Petrovka, and when on Saturday evening he heard the ringing of the bells, his recent trip and the places he had seen lost all charm for him. Little by little he became absorbed in Moscow life, greedily read three newspapers a day, and declared he did not read the Moscow papers on principle! He already felt a longing to go to restaurants, clubs, dinner-parties, anniversary celebrations, and he felt flattered at entertaining distinguished lawyers and artists, and at playing cards with a professor at the doctors' club. He could already eat a whole plateful of salt fish and cabbage. . . .

In another month, he fancied, the image of Anna Sergeyevna would be shrouded in a mist in his memory, and only from time to time would visit him in his dreams with a touching smile as others did. But more than a month passed, real winter had come, and everything was still clear in his memory as though he had parted with Anna Sergeyevna only the day before. And his memories glowed more and more vividly. When in the evening stillness he heard from his study the voices of his children, preparing their lessons, or when he listened to a song or the organ at the restaurant, or the storm howled in the chimney, suddenly everything would rise up in his memory: what had happened on the groyne, and the early morning with the mist on the mountains, and the steamer coming from Theodosia, and the kisses. He would pace a long time about his room, remembering it all and smiling; then his memories passed into dreams, and in his fancy the past was mingled with what was to come. Anna Sergeyevna did not visit him in dreams, but followed him about everywhere like a shadow and haunted him. When he shut his eyes he saw her as though she were living before him, and she seemed to him lovelier, younger, tenderer than she was; and he imagined himself finer than he had been in Yalta. In the evenings she peeped out at him from the bookcase, from the fireplace, from the corner—he heard her breathing, the caressing rustle of her dress. In the street he watched the women, looking for some one like her.

He was tormented by an intense desire to confide his memories to some one. But in his home it was impossible to talk of his love, and he had no one outside; he could not talk to his tenants nor to any one at the bank. And what had he to talk of? Had he been in love, then? Had there been anything beautiful, poetical, or edifying or simply interesting in his relations with Anna Sergeyevna? And there was nothing for him but to talk vaguely of love, of woman, and no one guessed what it meant; only his wife twitched her black eyebrows, and said: "The part of a lady-killer does not suit you at all, Dimitri."

One evening, coming out of the doctors' club with an official with whom he had been playing cards, he could not resist saying:

"If only you knew what a fascinating woman I made the acquaintance of in Yalta!"

The official got into his sledge and was driving away, but turned suddenly and shouted:

"Dmitri Dmitritch!"

"What?"

"You were right this evening: the sturgeon was a bit too strong!"

These words, so ordinary, for some reason moved Gurov to indignation, and struck him as degrading and unclean. What savage manners, what people! What senseless nights, what uninteresting, uneventful days! The rage for card-playing, the gluttony, the drunkenness, the continual talk always about the same thing. Useless pursuits and conversations always about the same things absorb the better part of one's time, the better part of one's strength, and in the end there is left a life grovelling and curtailed, worthless and trivial, and there is no escaping or getting away from it—just as though one were in a madhouse or a prison.

Gurov did not sleep all night, and was filled with indignation. And he had a headache all next day. And the next night he slept badly; he sat up in bed, thinking, or paced up and down his room. He was sick of his children, sick of the bank; he had no desire to go anywhere or to talk of anything.

In the holidays in December he prepared for a journey, and told his wife he was going to Petersburg to do something in the interests of a young friend—and he set off for S———. What for? He did not very well know himself. He wanted to see Anna Sergeyevna and to talk with her—to arrange a meeting, if possible.

He reached S——— in the morning, and took the best room at the hotel, in which the floor was covered with grey army cloth, and on the table was an inkstand, grey with dust and adorned with a figure on horseback, with its hat in its hand and its head broken off. The hotel porter gave him the necessary information; Von Diderits lived in a house of his own in Old Gontcharny Street—it was not far from the hotel: he was rich and lived in good style, and had his own horses; every one in the town knew him. The porter pronounced the name "Dridirits."

Gurov went without haste to Old Gontcharny Street and found the house. Just opposite the house stretched a long grey fence adorned with nails.

"One would run away from a fence like that," thought Gurov, looking from the fence to the windows of the house and back again.

He considered: to-day was a holiday, and the husband would probably be at home. And in any case it would be tactless to go into the house and upset her. If he were to send her a note it might fall into her husband's hands, and then it might ruin everything. The best thing was to trust to chance. And he kept walking up and down the street by the fence, waiting for the chance. He saw a beggar go in at the gate and dogs fly at him; then an hour later he heard a piano, and the sounds were faint and indistinct. Probably it was Anna Sergeyevna playing. The front door suddenly opened, and an old woman came out, followed by the familiar white Pomeranian. Gurov was on the point of calling to the dog, but his heart began beating violently, and in his excitement he could not remember the dog's name.

He walked up and down, and loathed the grey fence more and more, and by now he thought irritably that Anna Sergeyevna had forgotten him, and was perhaps already amusing herself with some one else, and that that was very natural in a young woman who had nothing to look at from morning till night but that confounded fence. He went back to his hotel room and sat for a long while on the sofa, not knowing what to do, then he had dinner and a long nap.

"How stupid and worrying it is!" he thought when he woke and looked at the dark windows: it was already evening. "Here I've had a good sleep for some reason. What shall I do in the night?"

He sat on the bed, which was covered by a cheap grey blanket, such as one sees in hospitals, and he taunted himself in his vexation:

"So much for the lady with the dog . . . so much for the adventure. . . . You're in a nice fix. . . ."

That morning at the station a poster in large letters had caught his eye. "The Geisha" was to be performed for the first time. He thought of this and went to the theatre.

"It's quite possible she may go to the first performance," he thought.

The theatre was full. As in all provincial theatres, there was a fog above the chandelier, the gallery was noisy and restless; in the front row the local dandies were standing up before the beginning of the performance, with their hands behind them; in the Governor's box the Governor's daughter, wearing a boa, was sitting in the front seat, while the Governor himself lurked modestly behind the curtain with only his hands visible; the orchestra was a long time tuning up; the stage curtain swayed. All the time the audience were coming in and taking their seats Gurov looked at them eagerly.

Anna Sergeyevna, too, came in. She sat down in the third row, and when Gurov looked at her his heart contracted, and he understood clearly that for him there was in the whole world no creature so near, so precious, and so important to him; she, this little woman, in no way remarkable, lost in a provincial crowd, with a vulgar lorgnette in her hand, filled his whole life now, was his sorrow and his joy, the one happiness that he now desired for himself, and to the sounds of the inferior orchestra, of the wretched provincial violins, he thought how lovely she was. He thought and dreamed.

A young man with small side-whiskers, tall and stooping, came in with Anna Sergeyevna and sat down beside her; he bent his head at every step and seemed to be continually bowing. Most likely this was the husband whom at Yalta, in a rush of bitter feeling, she had called a flunkey. And there really was in his long figure, his side-whiskers, and the small bald patch on his head, something of the flunkey's obsequiousness; his smile was sugary, and in his buttonhole there was some badge of distinction like the number on a waiter.

During the first interval the husband went away to smoke; she remained alone in her stall. Gurov, who was sitting in the stalls, too, went up to her and said in a trembling voice, with a forced smile:

"Good-evening."

She glanced at him and turned pale, then glanced again with horror, unable to believe her eyes, and tightly gripped the fan and the lorgnette in her hands, evidently struggling with herself not to faint. Both were silent. She was sitting, he was standing, frightened by her confusion and not venturing to sit down beside her. The violins and the flute began tuning up. He felt suddenly frightened; it seemed as though all the people in the boxes were looking at them. She got up and went quickly to the door; he followed her, and both walked senselessly along passages, and up and down stairs, and figures in legal, scholastic, and civil service uniforms, all wearing badges, flitted before their eyes. They caught glimpses of ladies, of fur coats hanging on pegs; the draughts blew on them, bringing a smell of stale tobacco. And Gurov, whose heart was beating violently, thought:

"Oh, heavens! Why are these people here and this orchestra! . . ."

And at that instant he recalled how when he had seen Anna Sergeyevna off at the station he had thought that everything was over and they would never meet again. But how far they were still from the end!

On the narrow, gloomy staircase over which was written, "To the Amphitheatre," she stopped.

"How you have frightened me!" she said, breathing hard, still pale and overwhelmed. "Oh, how you have frightened me! I am half dead. Why have you come? Why?"

"But do understand, Anna, do understand . . ." he said hastily in a low voice. "I entreat you to understand. . . ."

She looked at him with dread, with entreaty, with love; she looked at him intently, to keep his features more distinctly in her memory.

"I am so unhappy," she went on, not heeding him. "I have thought of nothing but you all the time; I live only in the thought of you. And I wanted to forget, to forget you; but why, oh, why, have you come?"

On the landing above them two schoolboys were smoking and looking down, but that was nothing to Gurov; he drew Anna Sergeyevna to him, and began kissing her face, her cheeks, and her hands.

"What are you doing, what are you doing!" she cried in horror, pushing him away. "We are mad. Go away to-day; go away at once. . . . I beseech you by all that is sacred, I implore you. . . . There are people coming this way!"

Some one was coming up the stairs.

"You must go away," Anna Sergeyevna went on in a whisper. "Do you hear, Dmitri Dmitritch? I will come and see you in Moscow. I have never been happy; I am miserable now, and I never, never shall be happy, never! Don't make me suffer still more! I swear I'll come to Moscow. But now let us part. My precious, good, dear one, we must part!"

She pressed his hand and began rapidly going downstairs, looking round at him, and from her eyes he could see that she really was unhappy. Gurov stood for a little while, listened, then, when all sound had died away, he found his coat and left the theatre.

IV

And Anna Sergeyevna began coming to see him in Moscow. Once in two or three months she left S——, telling her husband that she was going to consult a doctor about an internal complaint—and her husband believed her, and did not believe her. In Moscow she stayed at the Slaviansky Bazaar hotel, and at once sent a man in a red cap to Gurov. Gurov went to see her, and no one in Moscow knew of it.

Once he was going to see her in this way on a winter morning (the messenger had come the evening before when he was out). With him walked his daughter, whom he wanted to take to school: it was on the way. Snow was falling in big wet flakes.

"It's three degrees above freezing-point, and yet it is snowing," said Gurov to his daughter. "The thaw is only on the surface of the earth; there is quite a different temperature at a greater height in the atmosphere."

"And why are there no thunderstorms in the winter, father?"

He explained that, too. He talked, thinking all the while that he was going to see *her*, and no living soul knew of it, and probably never would know. He had two lives: one, open, seen and known by all who cared to know, full of relative truth and of relative falsehood, exactly like the lives of his friends and acquaintances; and another life running its course in secret. And through some strange, perhaps accidental, conjunction of circumstances, everything that was essential, of interest and of value to him, everything in which he was sincere and did not deceive himself, everything that made the kernel of his life, was hidden from other people; and all that was false in him, the sheath in which he hid himself to conceal the truth—such, for instance, as his work in the bank, his discussions at the club, his "lower race," his presence with his wife at anniversary festivities—all that was open. And he judged of others by himself, not believing in what he saw, and always believing that every man had his real, most interesting life under the cover of secrecy and under the cover of night. All personal life rested on secrecy, and possibly it was partly on that account that civilised man was so nervously anxious that personal privacy should be respected.

After leaving his daughter at school, Gurov went on to the Slaviansky Bazaar. He took off his fur coat below, went upstairs, and softly knocked at the door. Anna Sergeyevna, wearing his favourite grey dress, exhausted by the journey and the suspense, had been expecting him since the evening before. She was pale; she looked at him, and did not smile, and he had hardly come in when she fell on his breast. Their kiss was slow and prolonged, as though they had not met for two years.

"Well, how are you getting on there?" he asked. "What news?"

"Wait; I'll tell you directly. . . . I can't talk."

She could not speak; she was crying. She turned away from him, and pressed her handkerchief to her eyes.

"Let her have her cry out. I'll sit down and wait," he thought, and he sat down in an arm-chair.

Then he rang and asked for tea to be brought him, and while he drank his tea she remained standing at the window with her back to him. She was crying from emotion, from the miserable consciousness that their life was so hard for them; they could only meet in secret, hiding themselves from people, like thieves! Was not their life shattered?

"Come, do stop!" he said.

It was evident to him that this love of theirs would not soon be over, that he could not see the end of it. Anna Sergeyevna grew more and more attached to him. She adored him, and it was unthinkable to say to her that it was bound to have an end some day; besides, she would not have believed it!

He went up to her and took her by the shoulders to say something affectionate and cheering, and at that moment he saw himself in the looking-glass.

His hair was already beginning to turn grey. And it seemed strange to him that he had grown so much older, so much plainer during the last few years. The shoulders on which his hands rested were warm and quivering. He felt compassion for this life, still so warm and lovely, but probably already not far from beginning to fade and wither like his own. Why did she love him so much? He always seemed to women different from what he was, and they loved in him not himself, but the man created by their imagination, whom they had been eagerly seeking all their lives; and afterwards, when they noticed their mistake, they loved him all the same. And not one of them had been happy with him. Time passed, he had made their acquaintance, got on with them, parted, but he had never once loved; it was anything you like, but not love.

And only now when his head was grey he had fallen properly, really in love—for the first time in his life.

Anna Sergeyevna and he loved each other like people very close and akin, like husband and wife, like tender friends; it seemed to them that fate itself had meant them for one another, and they could not understand why he had a wife and she a husband; and it was as though they were a pair of birds of passage, caught and forced to live in different cages. They forgave each other for what they were ashamed of in their past, they forgave everything in the present, and felt that this love of theirs had changed them both.

In moments of depression in the past he had comforted himself with any arguments that came into his mind, but now he no longer cared for arguments; he felt profound compassion, he wanted to be sincere and tender. . . .

"Don't cry, my darling," he said. "You've had your cry; that's enough. . . . Let us talk now, let us think of some plan."

Then they spent a long while taking counsel together, talked of how to avoid the necessity for secrecy, for deception, for living in different towns and not seeing each other for long at a time. How could they be free from this intolerable bondage?

"How? How?" he asked, clutching his head. "How?"

And it seemed as though in a little while the solution would be found, and then a new and splendid life would begin; and it was clear to both of them that they had still a long, long road before them, and that the most complicated and difficult part of it was only just beginning.

1899